A TIME TRAVEL SCI-FI ADVENTURE

ALIEN SON

G. S. KENNEY

Alien Son

Cover art: Deranged Doctor, derangeddoctordesign.com

More about the author: *https://www.gskenney.com/*

Praise for Saving Aran, Book 1 of the Sons of Aran series

"A city boy named Cort uncovers his intimate connection to nature in G.S. Kenney's *Saving Aran: Redemption for a Ravaged Planet (Sons of Aran Book 1)*, an eloquent science fiction adventure novel with an essential environmental message. Filled with lyrical writing and intriguing, magnetic characters, Kenney's novel is an empowering work about fighting for love and home."
 - **Self-Publishing Review**

"An incredible amount of world-building sets the stage for a story that will grip the reader and not let go. . . . There are many aspects that make this book incredible. It is a powerful coming-of-age tale. This book is brilliantly presented as an environmental thriller. The mystic aspects are captivating and keep the story exciting. The action scenes are edge-of-the-seat exciting. There is drama, there is danger, there are tears and there is joy. This book simply has it all."
 - **N. N. Light**

To sign up for G. S. Kenney's newsletter and get a free copy of a future history of Eden's world, please visit *https://www.gskenney.com*.

Chapter One

EARTH, YEAR 3222

R everend Guide Salvatore advanced the hologram frame by frame. His long, manicured forefinger stabbed the control button as if to keep it in its place. There was silence in the darkened conference room as the members of Aiana Kim's thesis committee leaned forward, studying each frame, barely breathing.

Between one frame and the next, a young red-haired woman appeared in the holo.

Aiana caught her breath. Her hand went to her mouth and then subconsciously pushed a loose strand of her own red hair behind her ear. She placed the hand back into her lap and held it there with the other, more obedient one.

Aiana had seen this holo a dozen times, and the moment never failed to astonish her. To terrify her.

She was looking at herself—true to every detail, red hair gleaming and wild in the lamplit evening. This crystal-clear image of herself stood, in the holo, at the base of a statue that made the place easily identifiable, and the era. Aiana had never been there. Of course not. In all of history, this was one place and time no historian could travel to, not even in theory. But there she was in the holo, true to life, even the way she tucked her hair behind her ear. She was gathering a group of people tightly around her, apparently instructing them to keep close and hold hands.

"Incredible," Salvatore muttered, bending over and squinting at the meter-high figures in the air where the conference table normally stood. A teacher and a scholar, he was the world's leading expert on Taerlin's life and the literature and folklore surrounding it. Except for the stole he wore, Salvatore looked more like a professor than an ordained Guide, his posture slightly hunched like a man who'd spent too much time poring over ancient texts, his dark hair thinning and going to grey. He walked around the miniature scene. Deep vertical lines folded the space between his eyebrows into clefts of concentration.

Only the occasional scraping of a chair as Salvatore stalked in front of someone marred the silence., Shaking his head slowly, Salvatore turned to look at Aiana. His eyes asked the question Aiana had been wondering about since the first time she saw this holo. *Why her?*

Salvatore turned back to the holo, and then looked at her again. He walked slowly around her as if she were one more media projection. Then he sighed, putting aside the unanswerable question.

He advanced the media.

The woman in the holo looked up, and the viewpoint shifted to include a young man who ran toward the gathered group. He was slender, but with the solid muscles and broad chest that seemed, like a gazelle, to be built for running. His red-and-white beaded vest flapped open; the breeze tousled his brown hair and riffled the downy white feathers tied to the ends of the thong that bound it. He held the hand of a boy who ran by his side. The boy's eyes focused on the face of the man he ran with. The man met the eyes of the woman, and his expectant smile widened into wholehearted joy. His face shone like the sun after a late afternoon thunderstorm, turning the entire world to gold.

Salvatore froze the frame. He stared open-mouthed at the man. His breathing quickened, and he clasped his hand to his heart.

Aiana wondered whether the guide might be about to have an unfortunate cardiac event. Yes, that holo might do that to a religious person. The scene was captured so clearly that everyone in this room might have been present at the moment the hologram was made

There was no mistaking the man. Without question, he was Taerlin.

She looked at the people around her, their faces lit in the glow of the holo images. Raj Smithjon, her advisor, stared as intently as the guide, his grey hair in its usual disarray as he ran his long fingers through it again and again. Maria Zhou, head of the History Department and of Aiana's thesis committee, her black hair pulled severely into a bun that seemed to tighten the corners of her eyes into an expression of perpetual disapproval, frowned but did not look away. The two other members of Aiana's committee crowded close by Zhou, Professors Hossen and Vikram, both of them with eyes large and mouths agape.

Aiana knew what she was going to have to ask these people, and her heart pounded in fear that they might deny her—and even more so, that they might say yes.

Aiana turned back to the holo images. She was no longer astonished at seeing *him*, not anymore, not after all the times she'd watched this holo. But the look that passed between the two of them still amazed her. Without a doubt, it was a look of complicity. And perhaps more.

If he had not been who he was, Aiana would have wanted to know the man who had looked at her like she was the most important person in his world.

But being who he was—meeting him would put her in a spotlight she'd do anything to avoid. Then again, it would make her career. A historian with first-hand experience of Taerlin! And she had to consider the likelihood that, since it had already happened, it was inevitable.

As the Guide advanced the media frame by slow frame, the man in the holo reached out to Aiana's image, then paused. He looked off to his left. His mouth framed an "O" of—what? Surprise? Anger? Was he shouting something? And then he was bowled over in a blur of unexpected action. A few frames later, the blur resolved itself into a second man, crew-cut and long-jowled, scowling. Words were exchanged.

Aiana knew Old Standard pretty well—anyone studying this era had to—but she couldn't lip-read it. The two men said something, all in slow motion as the Guide shakily single-stepped the frames. The people in the holo joined hands in a jagged line, with the red-haired woman at one end and the two men at the other. Within a few frames, the entire line of people stepped forward and—disappeared.

Oneiroportation. It must be. Discounting a miracle, there was no other explanation.

"It's a miracle!" breathed the Guide. "The actual Blessed Ascension." He made the sign of obeisance, fingertips to lips to heart.

The Blessed Ascension, arguably the most significant event of the millennium. For believers, the most significant event of all time. Aiana stood and, with a still trembling hand, turned up the lights in the room. It was a university conference room of indeterminate age, richly paneled in actual wood that had darkened over the centuries to a lustrous brown.

She turned to Zhou, who sat as straight as a soldier, a forbidding person despite her small size. Aiana cleared her throat, which seemed suddenly full of raw cotton. She took a deep breath, then said, "As you know, my current thesis proposal does not include oneiromorphic travel to the era."

"Indeed. We wouldn't have approved it if it had. Travel to this era has already been attempted one hundred seventy-two times—"

"—but never successfully," Smithjon finished, his flat voice suggesting how many times he'd heard this line. "My candidate and I are aware of that."

"The university no longer considers thesis proposals involving such travel." Zhou said, with a nod to the guide. She turned to Smithjon, her smile frosty, her eyes subarctic. "It's a waste of time and resources."

The other two members of the committee nodded solemnly.

Did they not understand what they'd just been looking at? With her family connections, Aiana might have influenced who was on her committee. She might have arranged for people who would approve her thesis even before it was written. But she wanted to succeed on her own, fairly, without anyone's help. Besides, she had been pleased about Zhou, the toughest critic on the faculty. Aiana didn't want any favors. She wanted them to be tough.

But not dense.

She took a deep breath and let it out. Perhaps they were simply slow in grasping the unexpected. She glanced at Smithjon, who had steepled his fingers in front of his mouth. Reluctant to oppose Zhou? Well, Aiana had no such scruples. Facts were—undeniably—facts. "Seeing myself in a holo from that era should be impossible, too—even in theory. But there I am, and here we all sit, watching."

No one said anything to that, not even the guide, who stood apparently lost in thought, stroking the media control as if it were a holy object.

Smithjon cleared his throat and ran his fingers through his hair. "My candidate and I believe we must change the scope of this thesis. Perhaps we must make a one hundred seventy-third attempt at travel to the era."

There. It was on the table. Her breath caught as fear threatened to overtake her. She fought it down, forcing a deep breath in, then out. "This completely changes the direction of my thesis, but given the evidence..." She swept her arm across the center of the room, where the holo scene had played out. "... I believe I must do it."

There was a moment of silence marked by the fluttering of papers as the academics glanced furtively around, trying to read one another's intentions.

Zhou sighed. "Does anyone disagree?"

No one did.

"One oneiroport, one month," Zhou said.

Aiana stiffened. "That might not be enough!"

"Either you will be able to enter the era, or you will not."

"Yes," said Smithjon, "it shouldn't take a month just to know about that. But clearly a time loop is involved, and it could be a large one. My candidate will have to find the time and place of her entry, and we cannot know how long *that* might take."

"How much time are you asking for, then? As you know, the equipment is expensive; energy costs are nearly prohibitive; and demand for the 'port within the department is high."

Smithjon nodded. "Of course. Perhaps, Aiana, you could indicate what you might do if you cannot go there directly?"

She had already discussed this with her advisor at length. "You saw how he was dressed. The vest is clearly Richmundian. Although the academic community dismisses the New Richmund connection, a considerable body of folklore persists about it. If I can't reach this location on Earth, I'll look for him on New Richmund."

"An entire planet sparsely inhabited for thousands of years is a large place to try to discover one man. If he was ever there. The clothing might have come from . . ." Zhou shrugged, letting the sentence drop.

Aiana's fists and jaw tightened. She forced herself to relax both. She met Zhou's gaze and held it. "It will be far easier than Earth, with its billions of people. But in either case I may need the 'port for more than just one month."

"It's a large project," Smithjon said, prompting her.

"If it works, it's the thesis of the century." A brash assertion, but not an exaggeration. Initially, she had greatly preferred her original thesis proposal with its innovative number crunching and no time travel required. No contact with actual historical figures. But the prospect of an actual meeting with Taerlin was too big an opportunity to turn away from. She looked at the guide, hoping for his support. "We would finally have records of Taerlin's life. Direct, verifiable records that meet current research standards."

Salvatore nodded slowly. "Yes, that would be worth a great deal. But such a search might take years."

"Reverend Guide, if I am given permission to proceed, I promise I will see it through. Today you have seen tangible evidence that I will succeed."

The words were bold, but a quaver in her voice betrayed the knot in her stomach. Her aunt and uncle had always given her everything, but it was time she started making her own way. Putting aside her old, safe thesis topic, the one Uncle Mark had encouraged, for this new, risky one was a step in that direction. And though it seemed she must succeed—did not the holo before them prove it?—no one could say how difficult or dangerous the project would be.

And if—when—she succeeded, she could name her position. Professor Aiana Kim, PhD, Chair, History Department. She lifted her chin and stared at them until all of them but Zhou, her lips pressed tight, looked away.

"You will need," said Zhou, "a grant to pay for it."

Zhou knew very well what resources Aiana's Uncle Mark commanded as executive director of the rich and powerful One Galaxy Foundation. The demand was genteel blackmail.

"I'll apply to the OGF for a grant, but I'm not going to ask for any special favors." Aiana's hand had once more knotted itself into a fist, and again she forced it to relax. "The project will stand on its own merit."

"Or it won't," Zhou warned.

Aiana narrowed her eyes, suspecting that the university would be happy to accept all the money it could wheedle out of the OGF through her. Well, this would be the end of it. She needed to succeed on her own. Unable to think of a moderate response, she nodded curtly, then turned toward Salvatore. "Reverend Guide? Will the Temple permit an attempt to contact *him*?"

Salvatore stroked his chin, considering. "Given the evidence we have seen today—and the Foundation's authentication of the original—how could we not?"

A rustling of papers revealed that Vikram and Hossen had not prepared beforehand. The authentication was in the documentation that Aiana had provided. The holo here today was a copy of a copy. The original, verifiably over six hundred years old, lay deeply buried on a back shelf in the executive vault of the OGF, exactly where she had found it. Her Uncle Mark, one of only two or three people in the privately held organization who had access to the vault, had allowed her admittance for her research. The foundation's experts had authenticated the original, which was unique among all the known recordings of the Blessed Ascension in its clarity and freshness, its complete lack of artistic rendering.

"But of course the Temple will demand continued oversight of the project since it involves the Blessed Ascension. And—" Salvatore cleared his throat while tilting his head so that the meaning of what he was about to say would not be lost. "—of course it will also require this holo." The single copy Aiana had made was stored securely in her own files, and she would surrender it to no one. But this copy of her copy? She had assumed someone would want to take it from her.

"I will apply to the Foundation for a grant to cover as much as three years of research," Aiana said. "And knowing that I will need significant 'port time, I will also ask that they provide a dedicated oneiroport."

Zhou looked at her but said nothing.

Aiana wasn't sure exactly what else Zhou wanted, unless she was angling to get the department an additional oneiroport—the breathtakingly expensive device that enabled time travel through amplified lucid dreaming. "I will ask that the 'port remain with the department after the research is complete?"

"A donation of one oneiroport," Zhou said, "and an appropriate supplement to the department's energy budget to cover the cost of one year of research. *One* year, Miss Kim, not three. Enough is enough."

Aiana hated the thought that she might have to return in a year to wheedle more time from the committee on a 'port she herself would provide. But she could see that Zhou would not be moved further. She turned to Salvatore. "Reverend Guide, I would be thrilled if you would join my committee. You probably know more about the life of Taerlin than any scholar alive today. As for the holo, you know that the Foundation owns the original, but I would be happy to give you this copy—now, if you wish."

Salvatore murmured his thanks and removed the media from the player.

Aiana looked around the table. Every one of them wanted something. Then she thought of the man in the recording, of that look on his face when their eyes met, the electricity she felt just watching the holo. She *would* find him.

Not for personal reasons, she reminded herself, feeling like she might be lying. No, purely for professional reasons. She would find him and come back and write a thesis that would catapult her into the front ranks of all historians.

When all was said and done, she wanted as much as the rest of them. More.

Chapter Two

ARAN, YEAR 2466

MIKEL'S RECORDING

I loved Aiana from the moment I first set eyes on her. Loved her and eventually lost her, as was perhaps inevitable. "History," she often said, "has already been written." But a person cannot love so immediately and so deeply without such a loss cutting scars across his soul. With time, the loss may stop hurting and help to build character and strength instead, but never again would there be such a love as that one.

But enough of self-pity. I have a story to tell, and I will tell it, though Aiana has told me that it will do no good. Still, I can hope. Perhaps, from her perspective, history has already been written, but history will continue to be written after her time, and even she cannot see into the future. I hope that someday someone will find this recording and use it to set the record straight. I hope, even, that someday Aiana will return to me.

My name is Mikel Pelerin. My story starts the day the starship *Falcon* prepared to return from New Richmund to Earth. I was planning to be on that ship.

I'd recently graduated from university with a double major in astrophysical engineering and xenology. I would like to say that there wasn't much difference between me and any other new grads—except perhaps for my obsessive work habits and grades to match, good enough to win the junior berth on Earth's first faster-than-light starship.

But that would be a lie. I was, and am, different from every other person on Earth. I am Earth's only interstellar half-breed. I was raised by a single mother, and she did not reveal my father's identity on my birth certificate. He is officially recorded as "Unknown." There were lots of single mothers in my day, and this wasn't unusual. But my mother and I did know who my father was; we simply chose to avoid the notoriety that would have come if everyone else knew, too. He was the New Richmund native Cort-Naran, who stowed away on a starship to plead with the government of United Earth in order to save his world, which he called Aran in his language. He died a martyr and a hero, slowly poisoned by Earth's atmosphere, before I was born.

The truth is that I'd dreamed all my life of visiting my father's world, the world he'd loved so much he'd been willing to die for it. Even though it had seemed an impossibility, I'd dreamed of this visit. More than dreamed, I'd prepared for it by the choice of my majors and the energy with which I threw myself into my studies. I was glad to return to Earth, my home planet, but after only a week on New Richmund, and most of that just in the clearing by the ship, it felt too soon to be leaving.

As we prepared the ship for takeoff, Efrim, the ship's captain, stood on the top of the ramp surveying the small clearing that was his domain. Beyond, ancient khena trees towered over our ship, trees maybe three or four times the girth and twice the height of Earth's redwoods. The smooth bark glinted in rainbows where the sunlight touched it, a forest of straight columns rising fifty meters or more before they leafed out. The lacy canopy of leaves shifting in the breeze rose another hundred meters, playing patterns of light and shadow on the forest floor. Birdsong floated on a breeze that carried the fresh pungency of the earth and a hint of a fragrance like rosemary, maybe, or mint.

I doubted that Efrim noticed any of this. With close-cropped iron-gray hair and a jaw so stiff that it might have lacked the muscles necessary for smiling, Efrim had the discipline of a career military man. He watched us and frowned. Occasionally he consulted his comm, probably measuring our progress against his timetable. "We'll leave this afternoon," he said. "Charl, run the checklist on the near-planet propulsion system. Mikel can handle the storage."

Charl grunted assent. He left the pile of rover components I'd disassembled and gave me the self-satisfied smile of a person who'd successfully unloaded a particularly boring task onto someone else. He headed for the hatchway.

Time was getting short. The thought tightened the knot that had been growing in my stomach. I glanced at our prisoner, a native named Corodh-an-Aran.

Two days ago, the native had slipped past the sensors of our defensive perimeter as effortlessly as the breeze from the forest, bringing with him fresh meat and an offer of companionship. He spoke Standard as well as we did, and seeing how we stumbled over his foreign name, he shook his head and smiled as if he'd expected no better, and allowed us to call him Cort.

Efrim had responded by arresting him, in compliance with an old directive to bring in a number of natives for questioning. One of the names on the list was Cort's. Chained to a tree to prevent his escape, Cort conversed quietly in his own language with his friend Lennard, the xenologist on whose account we were here. They ignored Efrim's announcement just as they'd ignored our preparations all morning.

Efrim intended to bring Cort back to Earth. Our planetary base here had been abandoned some sixteen standard years prior, destroyed by a volcano, and unable to be rebuilt because of the anti-exploitation sentiment my father had stirred up. Our trip had been authorized only as a one-time mercy mission to return Lennard's ailing Richmundian wife Lela to her home planet, but Efrim knew—we all did—that the government still hoped to reestablish a presence here. Earth's economy had been in the doldrums for more than a decade, unemployment was rampant, and increasing discontent had led to demonstrations and occasional violence in some parts of the world. Many economists and pundits believed that it would take access to a massive source of wealth such as the khena wood on New Richmund to jumpstart a recovery cycle. Efrim's theory was that the government would be glad for the excuse to authorize another trip to bring Cort back when the questioning was complete.

My theory was that we would likely be bringing Cort to his death on Earth—just like my father. I'd always wished I could visit New Richmond, yes, but I certainly didn't want to be a party to the ongoing oppression of the native people. Despite my orders, I felt I owed it to my father and to my conscience to find a way to free Cort and save his life. But Charl had been the last one on sentry duty the previous night, and he still had the key to the handcuffs. I couldn't figure out a way to get it from him.

Cort's eyes met mine, his unreadable golden eyes with no whites. I looked away, feeling guilty. I touched the ring of precious khena wood hidden in my pocket, which Cort had given me yesterday for safekeeping so that it wouldn't fall into my shipmates' hands.

When Efrim and Charl had gone off in the rover the day before, they left me guarding Cort. They figured that as a xenology major, I'd like the chance to talk with him. This was true, but they had no idea how deeply that interest was rooted in my parentage; they had no inkling of my father's identity. Lennard had taken Lela back to her village and was still somewhere behind Cort on the trail. Cort and I were alone.

"How are you doing?" I asked him, feeling uncomfortable about his situation. "You need anything?"

He raised an eyebrow and smiled a one-sided ironic smile that reminded me of my father, and said, "The key?"

I looked away, my face hot. I could feel his assessing gaze on me.

"I know you can't," he said. "Bad joke." He reached a hand toward me, and the chain clinked softly. It didn't reach.

"I'm sorry."

He was looking at me in an intense way, like he was measuring me against some standard. I wondered what it was and whether I'd be found wanting.

"It's not your fault. Don't worry about it." A pause. An almost too-casual change of subject. "How old are you, Mikel?"

"Twenty, standard. Almost twenty-one, New Richmund."

"Hmm." He looked at me so carefully I felt a chill, though the air was warm. "I'm thirty-six, New Richmund. I don't know what it is in Earth years."

"Why . . . why do you ask?"

He squinted another long, assessing look at me and said, "I never knew my father. He left Aran when I was a baby. My mother said that he stowed away on one of your starships and went to Earth."

The world went dizzy around me for a moment as its pieces rearranged themselves to include the probability I had a brother on Aran.

I took in a deep breath, and I let it out along with the secret I'd been holding in for so long. I sat down beside him. I looked at my hands, turning them over and back as if I'd suddenly see a difference. But they were the same hands I'd always had, long-fingered, nails chipped, a little dirty from the work I'd been doing. If I looked in a mirror, would I see my father's face? "What . . . what are you saying?"

He smiled his crooked smile that so reminded me of my father and shook his head slightly. "Mikel, I never knew what my father looked like, but I've seen a great many starmen—people from Earth who lived on the base. You don't look quite like the rest of them. Starmen are spindly, with narrow chests and shallow lungs. They may vary in complexion or in how much fat they carry, but they're all built like that. But you . . . you have a strong build, and you aren't fatigued or short of breath like your shipmates. And besides . . . you know how we change?"

"Yes, Lennard wrote about it in his book. Your people who lived near the base tended to have lighter eyes, but the eyes of those who left the city for the forest grew more golden, like those of the forest dwellers."

"That's right. And *you* are already changing like that. Two days ago, your eyes were clear blue, but today when I look close I can see gold specks in them. If you stay here a few weeks, I'd bet you'll lose the blue altogether, and you'll look a lot more like me. There's no mistaking my people's blood in you. My father's blood."

I couldn't deny it, but there were limits to what I could do for this brother I'd only just met. "Look, I'm sorry, Cort, but I can't—"

He made a dismissive gesture. "These chains? It's not your problem. I'll handle it myself. But tell me. Are you planning to go back with the others?" He asked the question in a neutral voice, and his expression said nothing.

What did he want me to say? No, Cort, I just found out you're my brother about two minutes ago, and now I plan to stay here on Aran with you forever? I had a life on Earth, a career. My mother. I was raised on Earth; it was my home. It would be one thing to stay on Aran for a longer visit than this brief one, but to choose to live here for the rest of my life—I'd have to have a lot more experience of the planet before I made *that* kind of decision! "I have to. It's my job."

"And you're content with this?"

Not when he asked it that way, but the issue was complicated. Besides, what choice did I have? "It's the agreement I made when I signed up."

"Well, it would be better if you were staying here, but take this anyway." He twisted off the ring of khena wood he wore on his fourth finger. The ring flashed in a rainbow of living colors where the sunlight hit it, an object of exotic beauty, as valuable as it was rare.

I held up my hands, palms out, refusing the gift. "Oh, no, I couldn't. It's . . . beautiful. But it's yours. Keep it."

"It's the ring that attached a sapling to its parent tree. I planted it for our father. If something happens to me tomorrow or the next day, I don't want it to fall into the hands of those greedy shipmates of yours. Besides, you may be closer to our father's spirit than I am. This feels right to me. I want you to have it."

"Do you think he might . . ." You'd think I'd have gotten over my father's death years ago, but there was a familiar lump in my throat. Some people say you never get over the death of a parent.

"Be reborn?" Cort asked.

I nodded.

"Who can know this? But we can hope, you and I. Maybe the tree I planted will help. Here, take it."

I took the ring. It fit perfectly, flashing on my middle finger. I managed to squeeze a hoarse "Thank you" past the lump in my throat.

We sat together silently for a few minutes. I stole furtive glances at him, still trying to put him into place as my long-lost brother, while Cort pretended that he didn't notice, that he was busy with something or another on one of his handcuffs.

"Why do you think he . . . our father . . . went to Earth?"

Cort thought for a moment. "I'd guess he decided that before he set out for the city, and that was probably why he came to the city in the first place. That means the whynywir probably told him to go."

"The whynywir told him?" I echoed. "You think so?" This idea put a different shading on my father's mission, though I couldn't fathom what it might signify.

"Like I said, I'm just speculating. But it seems probable to me."

"Why would they—"

Cort shushed me with an upraised hand and a shake of his head. "Enough. I don't know. The whynywir don't tell us why."

A few minutes later, Efrim and Charl had showed up on the rover, exhausted from an excursion far shorter than they'd planned. Not long after that, Lennard, too, arrived.

Lennard drifted close to where I was working, making an elaborate show of casualness. Tall and thin, gangly as a teenager who hadn't yet grown into his size, Lennard was a well-respected senior professor, and his book on Richmundian culture had made it onto the bestseller list. He was something of a celebrity, and when his Richmundian wife Lela started to grow sick from Earth's air, our ship had been ordered to help Lennard bring her home.

The xenologist looked toward the ship's hatchway, where Charl had disappeared a moment before, then to the base of the ramp where Efrim had settled down to calculate the takeoff sequence on his remote. Then he shifted his gaze to Cort, who was staring at his handcuffs as if he might open them by force of will.

"Can we talk?" Lennard asked.

"I want to help," I blurted out, "but I can't figure out how." Efrim wasn't far away, so I spoke quietly despite my feeling of urgency.

"Thank you for the thought," Lennard said in a voice that managed to convey at the same time grandfatherly kindness and unusual stress. "But you shouldn't take any risks. Don't jeopardize your position."

"My position! If we don't do something, they're going to kill him!"

"No, they're not. He's going to handle it himself."

"But how? How can he--?"

Lennard shrugged. "I'm sure he's figured something out. He has his ways. Can we talk about something else for a moment, while we have a chance?"

I tried to push my concern for Cort far enough out of my thoughts to make room for whatever Lennard had in mind. "All right."

"The whynywir. You've heard of them?"

Twice now in as many days. I put down my socket wrench and turned to face him. "I read your book."

The whynywir were the true aliens of New Richmund, as elusive as they were intriguing. None of the natives Lennard talked with had actually seen them, but there was general agreement that the whynywir were avian in nature, large, fierce. That's how they were depicted in the few drawings the natives made. Some of the natives said that they were guardians of the well-being of the great forest. Or of the whole world. A few people claimed to communicate with the whynywir telepathically. A consummate xenologist, Lennard had not attempted to judge the truth of these claims. It was sufficient as a scientist simply to report what the natives believed and to show how all their beliefs fit together into a complete system.

"Oh. Yes, of course," he said. "Are you interested in them?"

Was I ever! When I wasn't thinking about how to get the keys from Charl, I'd thought about them a lot since my conversation with Cort yesterday. If the whynywir had sent my father to Earth as Cort believed, I wanted to understand what *they* thought they had done and why. Of all people, why had they picked him? I felt for the wooden ring in my pocket. "Yes, I am. Very much so."

"Even if it means staying here when the rest of us leave?"

That took me aback, particularly since Cort had mentioned the same thing the day before. "What are you thinking?"

Lennard half turned away from me, looking down. I wondered if he felt guilty about something. "Nothing," he said, "I was just exploring possibilities. In the abstract."

"I've thought about staying here," I admitted, keeping my voice low. "But it's only a fantasy. I'm an Earthman. I can't desert my position, my career."

"Well, I've thought about it, too." Lennard clapped me on the shoulder as if he'd just discovered we were both rooting for the same team, instant old pals. "No one knows very much about the whynywir. Um—except maybe Cort there. Everything I wrote about them in my book was based on hearsay and folktales, the stories of the humans. I've never seen the whynywir myself. No one from Earth has. But if the chance should arise . . . I would do a great deal to make sure we don't pass it by. This would be the most important piece of new work in xenology since the discovery of New Berkeley. But here I am rambling again. You should get back to work before your captain catches you slacking off."

I watched Lennard amble away. The xenologist seemed to have something on his mind, and I wondered whether it had anything to do with me. But perhaps it was nothing. I finished stacking the last of the rover assembly components onto the gravlev to load in the ship, still trying to figure out how to get the key from Charl's pocket. Maybe I just wasn't desperate enough yet.

In any event, I never got the chance.

Lennard drifted over to where Cort sat and touched him sympathetically on the shoulder. In an instant Cort twisted Lennard's arm, toppling him off balance. Lennard cried out and fell, his arm bent behind him in Cort's tight grip. Cort held near Lennard's neck the point of a sharp white object that could have been a sliver of bone.

Cort spoke quietly in the startled silence. "The needle is poisoned, Efrim. One scratch will kill him. If you wish this man to live, you will release me now."

I forgot to breathe. My heart pounded. I couldn't believe that Cort was threatening anyone like this, least of all his friend. Was the needle really poisoned? Or was this some kind of ruse the two of them had concocted? In that one instant, I realized that my previous view of New Richmund was overly influenced by what had happened to my father. The idea that the "good" Richmundians were being exploited by the "bad" Earthmen was entirely too simplistic. How much did any of us—even Lennard—really know of the dark side of Richmundian culture?

Cort's expression was deadly serious, perhaps even hostile, and as for Lennard . . . He'd told me Cort was planning something—so had Cort, come to that. But Lennard couldn't have been expecting this. The blood had drained from his face, and his wide eyes watching Efrim pleaded for his life. It wasn't a look he could have faked.

For a moment, no one moved. Then Efrim frowned and folded his arms over his chest. "What kind of bluff is this?"

"It's no bluff," Cort said. "Tell him, Lennard."

But Leonard said nothing, his eyes pleading, until Cort eased the needle slightly farther from the pulse that now throbbed in his neck. Lennard swallowed. "He's a hunter. In my book I list eighteen different weapons hunters are known to use. Poison darts are on the list. I've no doubt . . ." His voice was hoarse. He swallowed again and licked dry lips.

Efrim took a deep breath and glared at Lennard as if Lennard were somehow at fault for this breach of orderly procedure. Then he said, "Charl, release the prisoner."

Charl descended the ramp and stepped toward Cort. I let out the breath I hadn't realized I was holding. But Cort said, "No. Let him do it." He gestured with his head toward me.

Efrim clenched and unclenched a fist. He didn't take orders, he gave them. He spoke through teeth tighter than one of the rover's lug nuts. "Fine."

Charl raised an amused eyebrow and handed the key to me.

I walked toward Cort.

"Slowly," Cort said. "Make no sudden moves." His eyes, whites showing, flashed danger.

My heart pounded and my hands shook, but I managed to comply. Carefully, I released first one handcuff and then the other. I took the cable and backed away as Cort stood, pulling Lennard up with him. Then he let go of the xenologist, who stumbled forward a few steps.

Cort quickly put several trees between himself and us, but from my vantage point near the edge of the clearing I could still see him in the shadows. I expected him to slip into the forest as quietly as he'd arrived, but that's not what happened. Lennard said, "Wait, Cort. You have a promise to keep."

Cort stopped.

Efrim drew his laser and aimed near the tree where he had last seen the native. Lasers sold to citizens were usually set to nonlethal force limits, but as an officer in the Space Force, Efrim had one that could use the full electromagnetic spectrum, and it could kill in a number of unpleasant ways. "You're still under arrest," he said.

Cort ignored Efrim as if the laser were a child's toy. He shook his head and said to Lennard, "Don't insist on this."

While they were talking, I could see Charl at the edge of my vision, shifting from one foot to the other. If the situation got out of hand again, Cort would be the one who would get hurt. I moved closer to Charl so that I stood between him and Cort. At least I might block a potential threat from that direction.

"But I do insist," Lennard said. In his fluent Arantu he added, "You owe this to me, Corodh-an-Aran. You gave your word."

The native broke eye contact, then spoke quietly in his own tongue. "As you say."

Lennard turned to Efrim. "Before all this happened . . ." With a sweeping gesture, he included the entire campsite, and presumably Cort's imprisonment and his own recent peril. ". . . he agreed to take me to see the whynywir."

"Whynywir!" Charl interjected over my shoulder. "That's some kind of myth, right? Giant flying vampires or something?" We all turned toward him, and he looked down, scuffing the ground with his foot. "Read about it in your book."

"Not in *my* book, surely!" Lennard objected.

"SNI Study Notes. Abridged version."

"I'll talk with the abridgers when I get back. But for now, since Cort is still willing to take me, I intend to go with him. The Richmundians are alien in their way, but they're still human." Lennard gave me a sideways look. Perhaps, like Cort, he had seen in my telltale turning-gold eyes the signs of my mixed parentage. "The whynywir are the true aliens on this planet. I want to make contact with them."

Efrim shook his head, his lips a thin, tight line that barred all argument. "No. My orders are to bring you back to Earth, and to Earth you will come, even if I have to put you in chains to get you there. Lennard, you must be crazy even to think about going with this . . . this *savage*, after he has just threatened your life. A savage who, I might add, is still under arrest."

But Cort had slipped farther back among the trees, clearly no longer a prisoner. And without active provocation, Efrim lacked authority to pull the trigger.

If anything, however, the agony on Lennard's face deepened. His hands moved with agitation. "Cort is my friend. He would never have threatened me if we hadn't driven him to it." His voice broke, the great man pleading like a child. "Do you realize what this means for the science of xenology? It's momentous! I have to do it, Efrim."

"My orders, Lennard," Efrim said, unmoved. "And yours."

Our orders. Lennard had reached the barrier of law that bounded our lives. He looked around desperately, and his eyes alighted on me, as if seeing me for the first time. "What about Mikel, then? He majored in xenology. Let him go instead of me."

My breath caught in my throat. I opened my mouth to say something, I have no idea what, but before I could utter a word, Efrim answered quickly. "That's ridiculous! He's my crew."

"It's not ridiculous at all," Lennard said. "This is an opportunity unparalleled in the history of xenology. I can't let it pass by. I can't, Efrim. And . . ." He slowed his voice down, imbuing each word with as much significance as he could muster. "Neither . . . can . . . you." He paused, head tilted, looking at Efrim from under his brows, allowing his words to sink in. "Mikel's your junior crewman. You use him mostly as unskilled labor. You and Charl know everything you need to guide the ship back to Earth. I will take on whatever routine tasks you would use Mikel for. I understand that your orders are explicit concerning me, given my . . . celebrity . . . but do they say you must bring Mikel home, too? Let him stay here, Efrim."

"I am responsible for the safety of my crew." But Efrim looked right, left, at the ground. He was wavering.

"You know the government is not uninterested in returning here." Lennard smiled like an archer who'd hit a bulls-eye. "What better reason than picking up a scientist with a breakthrough discovery?"

Of course, I wasn't technically a scientist, professionally speaking—not yet. I'd need to complete my graduate studies for that, but I understood that Lennard was trying to make a point to Efrim. And a breakthrough discovery! It was what I'd dreamed of—my chance to achieve something notable. Not as great an act as my father's, true. Who could match his noble cause and his ultimate sacrifice? But if I succeeded, this would be something that would have made him proud of me.

It wasn't cold, but when a breeze lifted the hair along the back of my neck, I shivered.

Efrim nodded slowly as he grasped the political implications. The whole forest seemed to hold its breath as he thought it over. "Yes," he said, "they might respond positively to that reason." He turned to me. "Mikel, it's your choice. Stay if you wish, or come back with us. If you decide to stay, I can't promise we'll be allowed to return for you. And if we don't return . . ." He shrugged and shook his head. He didn't have to complete the sentence.

Lennard looked at me, intense with missionary zeal, as if he were trying to force his will on me telepathically: *Stay here. You must do it.* Efrim watched me too, open to either outcome. Charl surveyed the rover components I'd been packing, probably wondering how much of this work he'd be stuck with if I decided to stay on planet.

Ten minutes ago, I would have wanted this chance like I wanted to breathe, but now I hesitated. My heart was working double time. I tried to swallow, but my mouth was too dry. There were two problems. The first was that a return trip home was not guaranteed. I didn't want to be marooned here, but I felt that the opportunity was worth the risk. The bigger problem was Cort. I no longer knew what to make of him. He had just threatened his friend's life. Had that been as real a threat as it looked, or was it just an act? If Efrim had said no to his release, would Cort have killed his friend? Were there circumstances under which he might kill . . . me?

I no longer knew if I wanted to be left alone with him.

But I forced myself to look at this from Cort's point of view. We'd responded to his overtures of friendship by imprisoning him. We had threatened his life and what he saw as his immortal spirit by planning to take him back to Earth. We had given him no choice but this desperate act.

Clearly, Lennard continued to trust him, and Cort had been kind to me. He was my brother—well, my half-brother, but still . . . Surely he wouldn't kill me.

Despite this morning's events, I wanted him to want me to stay. Did he? I couldn't tell. I needed a sign.

Deep in the shadows of the great khena, Cort inclined his head once, deliberately.

I had to do it. I had to know Aran better, had to understand my father, had to make something of myself.

"I'll stay."

Chapter Three

EARTH, YEAR 3222

Aiana Kim checked the time on her comm. Raj Smithjon was late for their meeting, and she'd promised Uncle Mark and Aunt Jen she'd be home for dinner. The coffee shop was already beginning to clear as the resident students made their way to the dining hall.

She wished this meeting weren't necessary. She wished it were already finished. She took a careful sip of her too-hot tea to ease the tightness in her stomach. She had been allowed only a year to do her research, and the clock was running. Only a year to find the most famous person in the last millennium, a man who had changed civilization as they knew it. A man whose very existence created barriers through which no historian could pass.

It was no surprise that the research wasn't going well.

And yet . . . and yet there was the holographic recording. The incontrovertible evidence that she must succeed—if only she could figure out *how*.

Raj Smithjon hurried into the coffee shop, chill air clinging to his jacket, his grey hair in its usual disarray. He rubbed his hands together and blew on them to warm them. "Freezing out there," he said. "I seem to have misplaced my gloves." He slipped off the jacket and hung it on the back of the chair next to hers. "I see you already have some tea. Mind if I get some? Am I late?"

"No, go ahead. And yes, a little. But it's fine. Don't change." She meant it, too—there was not a student in the History Department who didn't adore Professor Smithjon, with his self-effacing manner and his brilliant mind. Though she wished she didn't have this current problem, he was the best person in the world to help deal with it. When he returned to the table after fetching his tea, she was smiling.

"So, give me an update," he said, sitting down. "Any news?"

Aiana shook her head. "No. I've tried every day for the last three weeks, but I can't seem to get back to, well, any time in the entire twenty-fifth century. Not anywhere on Earth."

"But somewhere else . . .?"

Her cheeks grew warm, and she looked away, remembering the holo. The man's vest was indisputably Richmundian, though whether he himself had come from New Richmund could be debated. Had been debated inconclusively by historians for generations.

"I tried New Richmund, too," she said. "Some of the earlier attempts by other people got a lot closer to the actual time frame than I have." She watched him, gauging his reaction, and her stomach knotted up again. All of her childhood shyness rose up in her, the paralyzing fear of failure and rejection, of not being worthy of all the advantages that her aunt and uncle had given her.

She drank some tea to calm her anxiety, hoping Smithjon hadn't noticed. Hoping he didn't see her failure as an indication of greater inadequacy.

He interlaced his fingers and rested his chin on them, thinking. "Doesn't mean anything," he said at last. "Could be lots of reasons. In your case, we have to consider the likelihood of a time loop, one that could be quite large or complex. Possibly you've traveled there already, perhaps more than once. Or . . . will have. If you've already gone there, you wouldn't be able to get anywhere near the time again."

"But this is the first time I'm going!"

Smithjon emptied two sugar packets into his tea and stirred. Then he wrapped his hands around the steaming cup. "I believe, young lady, that subjective physics is a required course in second-year history studies." A mischievous smile crinkled the corners of his eyes. "So *you* tell me. What does 'first' mean in this context?"

Aiana let out an exaggerated sigh, the longsuffering student. "Yes, of course you're right. It has no meaning in this context. If a time loop exists, then it is always, and immutably without beginning or end, exactly the way it is."

"And history . . .?"

". . . has already been written." The guiding principle of the History Department.

He took a swallow of his tea and then another, and let out a long "Ah!" of contentment. "Well, so if a time loop exists and you're in it, then the laws of subjective physics would demand . . . what?"

Always the professor.

"That I cannot approach the loop from the outside," she answered dutifully, "except at the one spot where I enter it."

"And you will not succeed simply by continuing to try to force your way into the time loop at the wrong entry place."

"Yes, Professor." Her voice sounded thin to her, like a child's. She wished she could disappear. She again fought away the anxiety and sat up straighter, pushing back her hair.

"How many attempts have you made?"

She felt her face grow hot again and brought the steaming cup of tea to her lips to mask it. "Eighteen on Earth. Seven on New Richmond."

"So then, wouldn't you agree that the twenty-fifth century does not appear to be the time when you enter the time loop?"

"Unfortunately, yes."

"Oh, it's not so unfortunate." His eyes glinted with good humor. "You've ruled out the obvious entry point. That's real progress! Now, don't be upset, Aiana, but I'm sure Professor Zhou would not want you to continue with this approach. And I must say, given your results so far, I'd have to agree with her."

Aiana's fear of failure flooded back. Uncle Mark had persuaded the foundation to donate an oneiroport to the university because of her. She owed it to him to succeed, but instead she'd reached a dead end. Her eyes wide, she drew in a sharp breath. "She can't take away the 'port. That's mine."

"It's the university's, dedicated to your use at the moment. But remember—your time on the machine is limited. Professor Zhou is not being unreasonable in wanting to see you finish your work as quickly as practicable." Smithjon leaned toward her, his hand outstretched in a placating gesture.

Aiana had known it might come to this, but she had hoped for some way out. Now she must face her failure and move past it. She straightened her spine, soldierlike. She would do whatever was necessary. "Very well. Enough is enough. Time to go to Plan B."

"New Richmund."

"Yes."

Smithjon leaned back in his chair. "So you have come to the problem of the needle in the haystack."

"I'm afraid so."

"And your strategy is . . .?"

She sighed. "I'm not sure. I'd welcome your ideas. At first I thought I'd search there contemporaneously with Taerlin's own time, but I can't get there, either. I did a little research on it, and while only a few people have tried traveling to New Richmund during Taerlin's time, no one has succeeded. And the problem is worse on New Richmund because we don't even know for sure what 'contemporaneous' means regarding Taerlin."

He tilted his head, puzzled. "Why not?"

"The problem is that the faster-than-light drive was just coming into use. If he traveled from New Richmund to Earth, he might have taken twelve years to do it, or twenty, or he might have done it in less than a year. We don't know which. Also, we don't know how soon before the Blessed Ascension he came over. So I'm looking at, let's say, thirty years—perhaps more—and an entire planet, hundreds of thousands of people, to try to find him in. It's a smaller haystack than Earth with its billions of people, but still a haystack."

Smithjon drank more tea, frowned, and then looked at his cup as if seeing it for the first time. "It's already getting cold." He put the cup down. "I see your point. The search wouldn't be easy. Might take years."

"But I don't have years!" Aiana's frustration frayed the edges of her voice. "I only have one year, and I've already determined I can't get to his era on New Richmund either."

"Yet we all saw that holo. We know you found him, or you will."

Aiana watched a group of students leave the coffee shop, laughing and joking, their voices loud in the nearly empty room. A whiff of cold air penetrated the coffee shop as the door slammed.

"When my first thesis proposal was accepted, I never dreamed I might meet Taerlin in person," she said. "The idea of going back in time and meeting historical people never appealed to me." Appealed! It terrified her, even now. "I didn't even use the 'port much in my undergrad classes. All I wanted was just to catch a glimpse of his influence in the shadows behind the financial transactions that created the One World Foundation. Data analysis. I'm good at that. And, of course, my uncle was happy to encourage my interest in history by opening the foundation's records to me. You understand, I have an advantage that other students don't have, but that just means I have to set the bar higher than the others and make sure I succeed. Now that I'm committed to this new direction, I want to complete the project as quickly and as well as I can."

"So . . . what's your alternative?"

Aiana looked around. The coffee shop was almost empty. A couple of students sat together at a table along the far wall, heads down over a book, talking quietly. A group gathered around a large table argued so animatedly she thought the conversation must be about sports. She leaned toward Smithjon and lowered her voice. "I'm not a religious person. Are you?"

He tilted his head, rubbing thoughtfully at his chin. He drew a breath, seemingly about to ask the obvious question, *Does it matter?* But he let the breath and the question go. "No."

Aiana leaned closer to him. "That holo might show the Blessed Ascension as the guide says, but to me it looks like oneiroportation."

"All right. For the sake of argument, let's say that it was."

"If it was oneiroportation, then Taerlin must have been taking all those people *somewhere*. Somewhere more specific than Paradise."

"And you think it may have been New Richmund."

"Because of how he was dressed, yes."

"But in that case, Aiana, you've just widened your haystack from a window of maybe thirty years to . . ." He wiggled a hand along an imaginary line in the air. ". . . three thousand years. Thirty thousand. Who knows how many?"

"Not," she said, pausing deliberately to drink her tepid tea, "necessarily."

He raised an eyebrow. "Go on."

"There has long been a theory among the anthropologists that, given the genomic similarities, the people of New Richmund and those of Earth must share a common background."

"Yes, yes. Never proven."

"But never disproven."

"True enough. Before oneiroportation, it would have been difficult to prove. Now, it would be easy enough, but for centuries New Richmund has been on the list of inhabited planets that we aren't allowed to contact, much less visit. No one is interested in spending the time and money to do the research. There's no practical benefit." He lifted his cup to his lips.

"But if, as I suspect, oneiroportation is involved, maybe, just maybe, Taerlin is taking those people back to the beginning of the human population of New Richmund."

Smithjon half-choked on his tea. He coughed and cleared his throat. "That's quite a leap of faith for a person who claims not to be religious." He coughed again. "Sorry."

She handed him a paper napkin. "But with oneiroportation it would be so easy to do! Anyone with a 'port can carry anything, or bring anyone they're in physical contact with. Even lots of people holding hands, and the energy involved isn't that much more than the energy needed just to sustain the oneiromorph. It shouldn't be that hard to ascertain. I can survey the planet remotely to determine when the first humans appeared. I can start by tracing the existing settlements back in time. By programming the 'port, I should be able to do that very quickly. And if a first human settlement does show up, then the odds would be high that he's involved in it. And that would narrow my haystack considerably. What do you think?"

"Interesting hypothesis." Smithjon tilted his chair back and nodded contemplatively, seemingly oblivious to the chair's complaining groan. A silence stretched out.

Aiana could feel her heart racing again. The few other conversations in the room seemed unnaturally loud. She took a deep breath and told herself to wait calmly, to give the man a chance to think.

"It makes a certain amount of sense," he said at last. He scanned the room cautiously and then leaned closer to her. He lowered his voice. "Perhaps it isn't a Blessed Ascension at all. Humans disappear suddenly from Earth; humans appear suddenly on New Richmund. Humans who are genetically quite similar. Oneiroportation would explain it." He nodded, slowly at first and then with increasing enthusiasm. "All right, Aiana, search for the first humans on New Richmund. If they appear suddenly, as you suspect, then it's a good guess that Taerlin is involved somehow. It's worth a try."

"Thanks, Professor."

"Be sure to keep me informed. When's your next outing?"

"Tomorrow morning." Aiana looked at her comm and gasped. "Oh, no; I'm late! Uncle Mark's coming home for dinner; I have to run." She pushed her chair back and stood.

Smithjon stood as well, smiling. "Yes, by all means. We don't want your Uncle Mark angry at us; he's been a great benefactor to the university."

Aiana returned the smile. "To me, too. He and Aunt Jen took me in and raised me after my parents died. I was only five." She remembered her parents, but in a distant, shining kind of way, like a dream of angels. "And they've given me so much."

"They've given a lot to the university, too," Smithjon said.

"Yes." Aiana felt a wave of sadness. "I'm . . . I'm glad they are so generous, but I also feel terribly responsible to them. I'd have only myself to blame if I fail at this."

"Aiana." Smithjon put his hand on hers. "You're a dedicated student and a hard worker. The university didn't admit you because you are your uncle's niece. You were admitted on your own merits, and you won't fail. Remember, we've already seen the proof of that."

Aiana tried to be unobtrusive as she wiped a tear from her eye. "Thanks, Raj. But now I really do have to go. Uncle Mark travels so much, it's a rare treat when he's in town, and I don't want to miss a minute. Thanks for the advice."

"Advice, yes. That's what we advisors are for. Good luck tomorrow."

"Thanks. I can hardly wait. I'll keep you posted." She grabbed her coat from a hook and flew out the door.

Chapter Four

ARAN, YEAR 2466

MIKEL'S RECORDING, continued

"**L**ook!" Cort stopped and turned, pointing to the sky. I followed his finger, and saw a flash of light streaking through the mid-afternoon daylight: the starship lifting toward Earth. My lifeline, severed.

The flare of light vanished as the ship left the atmosphere.

I would be out of communication with Earth for two Standard years—if the government sent a ship back for me. Otherwise, abandoned here, with everything I'd worked to achieve lost forever.

I made myself take a few slow breaths. It wouldn't be a bad life. Physically, New Richmund was as close to paradise as planets come. With an axial tilt of only fourteen degrees, its seasonal changes were small, and the thick atmosphere minimized them further. Away from the mountains and the poles, the weather was perfect, with lots of sunshine interspersed with pleasant, warm rains.

And I wouldn't be alone, either. I refused to think about it that way. I was on my father's world, among his people, with my brother. My childhood daydreams, come true.

But I had never dreamed of this particular brother, one who might be a calculating killer. True, we had provoked Cort by holding him prisoner. But Cort's coldness, his cunning had been real. And so had Lennard's fear. Even if he and Cort were in collusion, had Lennard actually offered to give up his life to save his friend? And was Cort the kind of man who would have taken him up on that offer?

I studied Cort, trying not to be too obvious about it. He certainly looked the savage, much more so than my father ever did in the news holos. My father had worn his hair neatly trimmed as we do on Earth, his clothes pressed and new-looking, with only one Richmundian garment—a suede vest elaborately decorated with red and white beads.

But Cort! Like an animal's, Cort's golden eyes showed no whites. He wore a sleeveless vest and short pants roughly sewn of leather and decorated in asymmetrical patterns with bits of bone, small stones, pieces of colored fabric, and bright feathers. This self-decoration carried into the odd scraps and feathers he had woven into his long, dark hair, which glinted with reddish highlights in the afternoon sunshine. Two gems, one red and one pale blue, shone from the skin near his hairline about five centimeters above his right ear.

After this morning, I realized how little I knew any of them—my father, his people, or most especially Cort. I took another deep breath.

Cort was watching me intently. What was that about? Did he have some other nasty trick up his sleeve?

I needed time to think, and distance. I stepped back, keeping an eye on him while trying hard not to look directly at him.

"Do you want to talk about this morning, Mikel?" he asked.

Of course I wanted to talk about it, but it was still too recent and too raw. I couldn't. I took another step back and shook my head. "No. I'm okay."

He looked at me as if he were assessing the probability that I might pass out right there on the trail. "You starmen sure have a funny way of expressing yourselves. Look at you. You're not okay. You have questions. I want to answer them."

I shook my head.

"Please."

I forced my breathing into a regular pattern. We'd have to deal with this sometime; maybe sooner would be better than later. Maybe we could just start with the facts. Even so, the question was hard to ask, catching on some roughness in my throat. "Was the needle really poisoned?"

He didn't avoid my accusing eyes. "Yes," he said. "It's a snake tooth filled with venom. Very deadly. Even a small scratch would kill."

My heart was pounding.

"Go ahead. Ask." He spoke as matter-of-factly as a professor reviewing a lesson with his student, but his eyes begged me.

"You . . . have it with you?"

"Yes."

"Still?"

"Of course."

"But why?"

He shrugged slightly. "It could be useful." Almost as an afterthought, he added, "That snake was my kiri." A kiri—the animal companion of the hunters on this world. I glanced at the red crystal near Cort's hairline, the crystal he would use to communicate with his kiri.

I hadn't thought snakes might be kiris. I pictured a slimy snake slithering around Cort's chest and arms, and I shivered. I preferred to think of the kiri as furry animals like wolves or bobcats, something a human could relate to. Not snakes.

"It seems . . . dangerous."

"The world is dangerous. Do you think otherwise?"

I couldn't reply, barely managing to shake my head. I rubbed my hands together, icy fingertips over icy fingertips, cold to the bone.

"Go on." Cort's eyes seemed to bore into me. "Ask. You need to ask."

"How . . ." The words surfaced through my fear as if from deep under Arctic waters. I could still see Lennard's eyes, wide, the whites showing all around the irises. The vein in his neck throbbing, just millimeters from the poisoned needle. "How can I know . . . you won't . . . do that to me . . . some day?"

A slight smile tugged at Cort's lips and warmed his eyes. He let out a breath. "Because I don't have your permission."

I blinked. I don't know what answer I might have been expecting, but it wasn't this. "And you had Lennard's?"

"I did. We discussed this last night. In fact, it was his idea."

Lennard's idea? I hissed in a breath and then forgot to let it out for so long that the world swayed dizzily. I had seen the two of them talking quietly, heads together in the deepening twilight. I'd even tried to eavesdrop, telling myself that I needed the practice in Arantu, but I'd been unable to follow their quiet, rapid conversation. "Why? I don't get it."

"Don't you?" The smile was broader now. "Lennard knew—as you do not—that the poison was not intended for him. I would have used it on myself if Efrim failed to free me."

"You would have killed yourself?"

"Rather than be taken from Aran? Yes, of course. But Lennard hated this idea and hoped to prevent it. And he thought we had a good shot at it."

"But Lennard was afraid! I saw him!"

"Lennard is not accustomed to taking risks. He was afraid of a situation that could have gone wrong in a hundred ways, some worse than you imagine. He was afraid for me, for all of us. And most of all, he was afraid of the needle of deadly poison so close to his neck. Wouldn't you be? He and I discussed this. His fear had to be convincing enough to sway your captain."

Yes, I would have been afraid, too. I didn't like even the thought of it. "What if you had slipped?"

He lifted a shoulder in a slight shrug of dismissal. "I would not have slipped."

"But you *could* have."

"That's why I didn't want to take the chance. For me, dying here, on Aran . . . I'll be reborn. Death is not such a big event. But for Lennard . . . he's a Starman. If he died here, who knows whether he would be reborn or not? But he's like all of you starmen, to him death is a big deal, whether his or mine, and he insisted we had to try his idea. Finally, I agreed. I told him that if we both lived I'd do something for him, whatever he might feel would even the debt. And that seemed to satisfy him. I should have guessed that he would have in mind the one thing I would have never done otherwise."

I began to see how everything fit together. "To see the whynywir!"

"Yes," Cort said. "I didn't expect he'd ask for that, or I wouldn't have made such an offer. It's a mistake." He emphasized the word with the kind of distaste a religious person might save for the word 'perversion.' "People stay away from the whynywir, and with good reason. No sane person would seek them out unless he had to."

"But Lennard *did* have to. This is one of the greatest opportunities in the history of xenology—meeting a truly alien species! It's what we all hope for, and Lennard is a xenologist to his bones. But then after running that risk, he didn't get to go after all."

"No." The word came out like a sigh. Cort looked off into the forest. The call of a distant bird punctuated the silence. "I think he knew he wouldn't."

"What?" My mind was whirling. The pieces of Lennard's and Cort's elaborate game were not going to fit together after all. "Why would he ask for this if he knew he wouldn't be able to go?"

"If I know Lennard, he'll find a way to get something out of it. He'll probably be on the ship that comes back to pick you up. But in any case, he wanted the chance to advance this science of his, to be sure that at least one of you two could go—if not him, then you."

"Me? But I never—"

"Very sensible of you." Cort turned and started back down the trail. "We'll do something else with the time we have."

"Wait a minute, Cort! Just wait a minute." I took off my pack and put it down and stood solidly beside it, as if by sheer inertia I could stop him from moving so quickly. When he turned again, I started with the one firm thing we had just established. "Lennard wanted me to go and study the whynywir."

"If he couldn't go himself, yes, because you're trained in his science. But this idea of visiting the whynywir is crazy, as I tried to explain to him. A bad mistake. People don't go there unless invited. Unless *required*."

"But Lennard risked his life!"

"Yes, you could say that. But it was a small risk, and this is a big mistake."

Cort seemed to take the threat to Lennard's life lightly, but I couldn't. A small risk, yes—but one with big consequences. What measure of risk is acceptable against the loss of one's life? For Lennard's sake and for my own sense of justice, I had to do the right thing; I had given Lennard my word. He would be counting on me to do some first-rate research—research worthy of the opportunity he'd given me. And Cort had incurred a debt that must be repaid.

On top of this, there were the whynywir themselves. Even had I owed Lennard nothing, I'd want to go. How could I not? The true aliens of New Richmund, and in the hundred fifty years since we arrived here, no one from Earth had ever met them. Making contact with the whynywir would be the career opportunity of a lifetime for any xenologist. Establishing communication with them would be an accomplishment worthy of my father.

I had an added incentive: I might learn more from these aliens about my father and what induced him to risk his life by traveling to Earth.

There was no way I was going to give all this up.

"It's not a mistake. We have to go. We owe it to Lennard. We both gave our word."

Cort's shoulders slumped. "Mikel, it's not necessary. We don't have to do this if you don't want to."

Ignoring his discomfort, I said. "But I do want to." And I meant it.

Cort let a moment of silence grow between us, as if hoping that I would, on my own, miraculously come to my senses. Then he shrugged and said, "Well, let's go, then. No sense wasting any more time. How do you starmen say? 'It's your funeral.'"

We walked in silence through the khenaran for an hour or more. Sunlight filtered through the high, lacy leaves of the great khena trees, tracing breeze-chased patterns on the forest floor. Our footsteps fell silently on delicate, decaying leaves that covered the humus-rich earth like a light layer of down. The forest breathed a verdant aroma that made me think of mint and sage and rosemary.

It wasn't like the forests on Earth, with their mixture of species and their undergrowth of bushes and scrub. Here there were only the giant khena spaced across an almost parklike and resilient ground. I'd seen holos of the khenaran, of course, and I knew the khena of New Richmund were larger across and taller than any trees on our planet, even the redwoods. At one time I could have parroted back statistics of height and diameter, tensile and compressive strength,

estimated acreage. But to actually walk among these trees . . .
It was like being in a cathedral constructed by ancient giants
in worship of an unknowable but magnificent god.

Shortly before sunset we came to a rocky area where the
majestic khena hadn't gained a foothold. The area was shady
with densely packed lesser trees that had grown scraggly as
they vied for the sunlight. The ground was uneven. The trail
we followed was narrow, even nonexistent in spots.

Cort broke the silence so suddenly that I started. "Mikel,
we need to talk a little more about the whynywir. I won't keep
bringing them up, I promise, but I want to make sure you know
what you're getting into."

That seemed fair enough. "All right."

Cort ducked under a branch. We had come to a small
stream, and he stopped at its edge until I caught up with
him. "I don't think you appreciate the danger. People say the
whynywir *eat* humans sometimes."

"Oh." My mouth was suddenly dry. "I thought they were
supposed to be ethical."

He crossed the stream from rock to rock so nimbly he
might have been walking on solid ground. I followed more
awkwardly. I tried to step where he had, but my ankles were
shaking under the effort to stay balanced on the uneven,
slippery surfaces while bearing the weight of my pack. Cort
gave me a hand as I stepped off the last rock. "Their ethics
aren't the same as ours. Certainly not like the ethics *you've*
grown up with. Maybe we're not at the top of the food chain
the whynywir see. Maybe *they* are. But the food chain is a part
of Aran, and the whynywir are committed to Aran's welfare."

I paused, trying to comprehend this scheme of things. Did
the whynywir see humans the way humans back on Earth see
dogs or cattle? Domesticated animals? "And so humans here
let the whynywir advise them, even though the whynywir
might also eat them?"

"Those of us who wear the blue crystal." Cort touched his
own blue gem. "There are certain questions on which only
the whynywir can guide us. For they are very wise, and they
remember their other lives, and they talk with the khena, and
through the khena the whynywir know Aran as we cannot."

"They remember their other lives?" It was one thing to
believe you would live again and again, but quite another

to remember doing it. "Do people, I mean humans, also remember?"

"Sometimes you ask very odd questions, Mikel. No, we don't. Our memories only go one lifetime deep, and that's one of the reasons the whynywir are so much wiser than we are."

"Do you know this about the whynywir for a fact, or is it just what you've been told?"

Cort stopped, considering.

I waited.

"I know for a fact that they're wise, and their advice is valued and obeyed. *I* obey them. As for the rest, that's what I've heard, and I believe it."

"Do you need a blue crystal to talk with the whynywir?"

"To the best of my knowledge, yes. Certainly *I* do. Even so, they talk with me only when they feel like it. Not often."

"So, if I need a blue crystal to talk with them, how would I get one?"

Cort sighed. He opened his mouth, and then closed it, sighed again, and shook his head. "You're not going to get one. The whynywir assign the crystals as they see fit."

"Might I borrow yours, then?"

He touched the gem with one finger, caressing it lightly. "This is not an ornament. It's attached to the bone. It takes another crystal wearer to put it in, and I've never heard of anyone taking one out. Until after they're dead, of course; then the crystals go back to the whynywir to be given to someone else."

"They don't work unless they're attached?"

He shook his head. "No. And only when the whynywir choose after that."

"How will I talk with them, then?"

"Mikel, I don't know." He sounded exasperated. "Maybe they'll talk with you directly somehow. If it's possible at all, it will be when you're right there in the valley with them. Or maybe they'll allow me to translate. Probably not, though. I've been trying to get them to agree to your visit all afternoon, and they're ignoring me. Without an invitation . . ." He shook his head and made a clicking sound with his tongue. "I don't know what they'll do, but it isn't going to be pleasant. Better if we went somewhere else."

"We are *not*—" Weariness gave my voice a sharper edge than I intended.

Cort held up a hand. "Yes, I know." He took in a long breath and let it out. "You're intent on going, and I'm going with you. But without permission, we'll have to go as pilgrims, wearing white. We'll throw ourselves on their mercy, if they have any. One of us is going to have to find and kill a white-furred animal. Probably you, since you're the real pilgrim here."

He paused, considering. "I guess you'd better start practicing using that knife. It's a good idea anyway. In fact, I'll teach you what I can about hunting while we're on our way. You might need to get your own food in case something happens to me."

I wasn't worried about anything happening to Cort, but I did want to learn how to hunt. I eagerly agreed.

Between us we had two knives: Cort's, plus one that Lennard had lent me with apologies that he couldn't give it outright since it had been a gift to him. Cort called these "bone knives." The blades were indeed the yellow-brown color of old bone, but they seemed to be some kind of dense rock that had been flaked or sheared to a razor edge, and they were as tough as steel. Cort's blade was a good twenty-five centimeters long; mine, a bit shorter. The handle of each one had been wrapped in rawhide to protect the hunter's hands, and the entire weapon was balanced to perfection. We also had an assortment of other weapons that Cort seemed to pull out of thin air, such as the poisoned snake tooth and a leather sling with which he was deadly accurate.

In addition, we had one laser, but that was my secret. Despite Cort's instruction to take nothing from Earth that wasn't essential, Efrim had thrust the laser into my hand, and I had accepted it. In the aftermath of that unsettling morning, I hadn't known what kind of protection I might need. I kept the laser wrapped in a spare shirt at the bottom of my pack, and I wasn't ready to tell Cort I had brought it.

"Since we're going to be together for a while, do you think we might speak Arantu?" I asked Cort the next day. I spoke in Arantu, the unfamiliar consonants and syllables catching on my tongue. "I'd like to get better at it."

Cort stopped and looked at me in surprise as I drew abreast of him, a slow smile spreading first to his eyes and then to his mouth. "I didn't know you spoke it at all," he answered in his own language, a good sign.

"Not very well. You'll have to talk slowly and carefully."

He nodded slowly, as if he were assessing me all over again from scratch, and what he found pleased him. "I can do that." He did indeed speak slowly and clearly. "Let's start with my name, shall we? Mine, and our father's. You know we have the same name, don't you?"

I followed him as we started again down the trail. Our footfalls were nearly silent on the soft loam beneath the trees. The air was as humid as it could be, short of raining, and a light mist shortened softened the view ahead.

"We pronounced it differently on Earth, but yes, I suspected as much. Let's see. 'Aran' means forest, right? The forest of khena, and also the name you call the planet, right? So 'an-Aran' would be the possessive form, 'of forest' or 'for forest'. But what does 'Corodh' mean?"

"Ah, that's the hard part," he said. "There's no word for it in Standard. It has to do with caring about the rightness of things being as they should be, or of being restored to balance. The best word I know in your language is 'justice', but that's too abstract. This name comes with a responsibility to Aran. To preserve and protect and restore her, always, life after life."

"Life after life," I repeated.

"You starmen don't believe our spirits are reborn, sometimes as people, sometimes as other creatures, sometimes even as trees. You don't believe any of that, do you?"

"I believe that *you* believe it. I like the idea."

"It might not be true for you starmen, anyway. You're not of Aran like we are." He paused. "The other ones, anyway. But you're different. You're going to have to choose. You know that, don't you?"

"Choose?"

"Between Aran and Earth. You cannot belong to both."

I laughed, a sound that had a ragged don't-let-it-be-true edge to it. "If that ship doesn't come back for me in two years, the choice will be made for me." How ironic it would be, after my father was stranded on Earth, for me to be stranded on Aran. "I wish . . . our father could have returned here."

"I, too."

I touched the khena-wood ring I wore. "Would you like your ring back? It's probably safe from my, what did you call them? My greedy shipmates."

He looked back over his shoulder at me. "No. You keep it. That seems right to me. You knew him better than I did."

"Only from the holos and from what my mother told me. You must have heard stories or something, too. I'd like to hear whatever you know about him."

"It's not much. I know he didn't grow up in the city like my mother. He came from the forest. A lot of people did in those days because large areas of khenaran were demolished by the harvesting machines and without the khenaran, people couldn't live in the villages. The starmen offered housing in the city as compensation, and where else were the people going to go?"

"Do you know where in the forest?"

Cort squinted at me in a way that seemed to ask, "Now why would you ask me that?" But he said, "A village, like any other. Not one of the destroyed ones. I don't think he'd ever had contact with the starmen before. My mother said he was pretty naïve. She said she felt sorry for him, and one thing led to another, and then that led to . . . me."

"But if he didn't live in one of the destroyed villages, why did he go to the city?"

"I would guess he probably already knew he wanted to go to Earth. He was Corodh-an-Aran, you know. He was probably desperate to save the khenaran your people were destroying."

"You said the whynywir told him to go."

Cort stopped walking and crossed his arms over his chest, frowning. "I did *not* say that. I said that I believed it was possible the whynywir told him. I have no first-hand knowledge."

"Oh. I'm sorry."

Cort started walking again.

"You know he succeeded," I said after a while. "Not right away. There was too much money in harvesting the khena wood, and people found his beliefs, well, primitive. Amusing. But he pleaded for the trees till the very end, and after he died people began seeing him in a different light: a man of dignity who was willing to die for what he believed in. After the volcano destroyed the planetary base, it was our father's martyrdom that made it politically impossible for us to return and rebuild the base. He was a truly great man." A man who had accomplished so much for an entire planet that I would probably never prove worthy of him.

One night, when Cort and I were camped in a rocky area clear of the forest, we lay on our backs, blankets cushioning the hard ground, and we looked up at the night sky. Both moons were down, and stars glittered in the sky in unfathomable multitudes. On Earth, with our light pollution, the skies were never as dark as this, never as brilliant.

I realized I had no idea which star was my home star. "Cort, do you know which star is Sol?"

"You're a Starman, and you don't know?"

I could feel the heat of blood rushing to my face, and I was grateful it was dark. "Well, we normally don't get to look at it from this perspective."

He shifted on his blanket. "That was one of the first things they taught us in that school you starmen ran," he said. "But I don't think it's up now."

"You went to our school?"

"I grew up in the city, remember? All those displaced people around your base. When I was a child, I went to that school. Most of us city children did. It was mandatory for at least one child in every family—educating the poor savages, you know, and the only way we could get ahead. You starmen have a real attitude." He shifted his weight to his elbow, and I could feel him glaring at me.

"Hey, not me!" I held up a calming hand. "At least I try not to. I just want to know what it was like for you. Tell me about the school."

Cort sighed and shook his head as if to clear it. "Sorry." He lay back again. "We studied mathematics and physics, and we learned to speak Standard. We studied the history of Earth and its literature. They told us that the very best students might hope for a position in the base or on a starship and maybe even travel to Earth. It was all I ever wanted when I was a child."

He gave a sad little laugh that hinted of childhood innocence long ago lost. "Back then we didn't know Earth's atmosphere would kill us. But your captain Efrim thought he was going to take me to Earth against my will, and he knew full well that I would die. He knew I would die too far from Aran for my spirit to be reborn here, and he didn't care. Typical Starman. Just like your people let our father die. What's one primitive savage, more or less?"

"Now, that's not fair!" I answered heatedly. "They didn't know about the air back when our father died! And they didn't know what death away from here means to your people!" I was taken aback by my own defensiveness.

"Didn't they? Do you mean that he took ill and died all of a sudden and there was no time to get him on a ship? In all the time he lived there, he never mentioned that if he dies away from this place—our forest—he wouldn't be reborn?"

He must have already figured out the answers to those questions, and in a rush, so did I. As much as they loved him after his death, my people had murdered my father by their indifference.

"I guess I can't blame you for how you feel about us."

Cort shifted, his blanket rustling slightly, and he raised himself to look at me, a dark presence against the black sky. I wondered what he could see of my features by starlight. "Oh, I like some of you well enough. Lennard, for example. He hardly seems like a Starman at all."

"But not most of us."

"No." There was a rigid certainty in his voice, a dam holding back a flood of accusations, the death of our father just the beginning. Maybe he had other personal grievances, too, injustices done to himself or his family or friends. To the planet. We starmen were *dh'corodh*, Cort's opposite: we were unjust; we lacked balance; we had no concern for the rightness of things as they should be. We were murderers of trees, despoilers of the environment, displacers of people from their homes.

I fell silent, afraid to ask the obvious question.

But Cort seemed to know what was on my mind. "I like *you* pretty well," he said. "Most of the time. But you're going to have to decide how much of a Starman you want to be."

Despite myself, I laughed. "I like you pretty well, too. Most of the time. You're very well educated for a primitive savage."

Cort let out a snort of derision and muttered, "Starman." But he said it with affection.

I returned to studying the sky and wondered aloud, "Do you have constellations?"

"Oh, yes. All the old stories end up with someone or something that you can see up in the sky today." He pointed to an irregular hexagon of bright stars almost overhead. "Look, there's Anarani's Children. And just next to them, the Wolf with his bright red eye. Can you see it?"

"Is there a Whynywir up there somewhere?"

Cort's blanket rustled again as he turned to look at me once more. "No. The whynywir are from here. It's people who are from the sky."

The world seemed to shift slightly sideways at this. From Earth? All I could make out was a darker-than-black sense of his bulk less than a meter away. "People are from the sky?"

"That's what the old stories say. The First People were born from the womb of the Sky Mother. When they came to Aran, they found the whynywir already here. The whynywir and the khena and most of the animals, too. The whole world was already made but empty of people. And the people came with wolves and ferrets and . . . well, animals of their own."

The old stories. Not a people on our world or any other that doesn't have its own creation myth, or didn't, sometime in their early history. "You see the sky as a womb?"

"Some part of it somewhere, I guess. It's dark enough. A mother has to have a womb, don't you think, even a Sky Mother?"

I tried to picture the sky as a womb, but I couldn't. To me, it was infinitely open. I smiled, though Cort couldn't see me. "Yes, of course," I said.

Sometimes I just love xenology.

The weeks on the trail lengthened to months. Cort and I were speaking Arantu all the time now, and I had become fairly proficient in the language. He taught me the rudiments of his hunting skills. I learned how to track the larger animals, how to trap the smaller ones, and how to throw a knife accurately, at least if the target was stationary.

I got lucky and killed an albino alandhal, a small creature with ears like a rabbit's and a long, tufted tail. Cort helped me tan and prepare the hide. I fashioned two headbands of sorts from the alandhal's fur, one for me and one for Cort. With this headband and my lengthening hair, I felt like . . . like I thought a native might feel. I was starting to feel at home here on my father's world. I couldn't wait till my hair was long enough to braid things into it, like Cort did. I also realized I had started to feel differently about Earth, to think of it as a distant planet, far away, part of someone else's life, not mine.

We came around the curve of a great boulder, leaving behind the few scrub trees that remained at this altitude. The path turned to our left into an up-sloping, narrow valley, rocky and barren, topped on three sides by a bare ridge of upthrust bedrock. We had been climbing into colder weather for a week, and a biting breeze blew around the rock at us, carrying the smell of damp earth and a hint of rain.

Cort stopped and pointed to a depression in the ridge ahead of us, black against the cerulean sky. "We'll cross that ridge in a couple of hours. A large band of whynywir lives in the next valley. We should be there by mid-afternoon."

My heart leapt. After four months, we were here! "Great!"

He tilted his head and raised an eyebrow. "Maybe. For you. But for me . . . The whynywir have finally answered me. They told me to leave."

I swallowed hard, remembering that Cort had said he and all crystal wearers obeyed the whynywir. "So . . . you're going to leave?"

He gave me one of his squinty looks, as if I'd just said up was down. "No. I am not going to leave. Don't even think it. I promised to take you to the whynywir, and that's what we'll do."

"But do you think they'll kill us, or eat us, or something?"

Cort drew a deep breath and let it out. He spoke almost apologetically. "Not you, no. You're starborn. No one knows whether your spirit will be born again here. As long as you do nothing to harm the whynywir, they'll probably leave you alone."

"But you?"

He shrugged and answered impatiently. "Who knows what the whynywir do, or why? I might be fine, or . . . It'll work out, one way or another. Let's go." He started up the trail.

"Wait!" I took hold of his shoulder to stop him. "If the whynywir attack, I'll fight them with you. I—" I almost told him about the laser then, but something held me back. "We'll stand the best chance in a fight if we stick together."

"Don't be ridiculous. We are not going to fight the whynywir. Just listen to me. In that valley there's a lake fed by hot springs. You can find it from the mist. There's enough small game, though no larger animals, not with the whynywir nearby. There are sheltered spots. Caves. I spent a whole winter there once, when I was younger. You'll be able to live there too."

"Cut it out! We'll both live there."

"Of course," he said. "Could be. But if not . . . you should know what to do, just in case. When you leave here, head south. Where the ship landed is only a few weeks' journey north of where the city used to be. Anyone you meet can keep you pointed in the right direction. You speak Arantu well enough. They'll give you any food you need, too. You'll be all right."

I shook my head more and more vigorously as he spoke. A roughness in my throat scraped against my voice. "Stop it! You'll be all right, too."

"Yes, of course, one way or another."

"Look, why don't you wait here? Since they won't harm me, I'll go on alone."

"Believe me, I've thought about it. I do wrong to disobey them, but I owe you and Lennard this debt. Remember—I would have died the morning your ship left, but for Lennard. The gift he gave me . . . these months with you . . ." He smiled warmly and let the sentence fade.

"Never mind that. I don't want you to get hurt."

"I promised Lennard I'd help you, and if we need the crystal to communicate, I'm the one who has it." He put a hand on my shoulder. "I've alarmed you too much. Maybe they won't do anything to me. I don't know. Anyway, even if they kill me, death here on Aran is not the catastrophe it is for your people. If I've come to the end of this lifetime, I'll have another."

He turned and started walking toward the pass.

I watched him climb up the valley, but I couldn't make my feet move. He could really sound pompous about this "end of this lifetime" thing, but I couldn't take the danger so casually. If Cort was going to get hurt, maybe I owed it to him to reconsider.

I tried to picture turning around and giving up, but I couldn't. Hardly a waking hour passed that I didn't think about them. Hardly a night went by that I didn't dream of that first historic meeting. I would fulfill Cort's and my promises to Lennard; I would discover breakthroughs for science and humanity. I would learn everything I could from the whynywir about my father. We'd come too far. We'd invested too much.

Too much was at stake to turn back now.

Besides, try as I would, I couldn't imagine an advanced, ethical civilization that would harm a person for so little cause. Cort was probably overly influenced by the old myths. His behavior was unsettling, but I didn't believe he would be so calm if either his life or mine was in real danger. It seemed more likely that entering the whynywir's valley was some Arantu rite. According to Lennard's book, rites of passage were common among the people of Aran, as indeed they are among people everywhere.

I shook my head to clear it and trotted after him, but he was already far ahead of me. He set a stiff pace, as if he were looking forward to whatever was coming—or wanted to get it over with. I tried to catch up, but I couldn't.

At the crest of the ridge, I stopped. Maybe I had something of an Arantu physiognomy as Cort said, but I wasn't as powerfully built as he was. I needed a rest from the grueling pace. And the panorama took away what little breath I had left. The valley that spread out below us was lush and green, in contrast to the barren, rocky terrain we had been hiking through. The breeze that blew from it smelled of vegetation and loam. On three sides the valley was surrounded by steep, rocky walls, but ahead of us it tilted down and away in woods and meadows as far as I could see. A mist to my right obscured the warm lake Cort had mentioned. I fumbled for the camera in the side pocket of my pack.

As I started moving again, I noticed a few specks in the sky, distantly approaching avians. The whynywir! Sheer awe held me still. I was the first person from Earth ever to see a whynywir. I clicked several pictures. They approached swiftly, circling nearer and nearer, seven beautiful white creatures, long-winged and graceful in flight.

Cort dropped his pack of food and the skins he carried. He was already two hundred meters ahead of me and moving quickly down the slope. It was almost as if he was trying to create the largest possible distance between us—and I thought with alarm that he might be trying to keep me safe from whatever he suspected might happen to him.

"Cort! Wait!"

He ignored me.

I shoved the camera into a pocket so that I could move faster, but I couldn't catch up. The slope was so steep I had to pick my way down.

As they swooped closer, I realized the whynywir were larger than I had imagined. The smallest among them sailed on wings a good three meters across; the largest, maybe even twice that wingspan. They circled Cort, seeming to ignore me.

"Stop!" I shouted, but I might as well have been shouting at the moon.

One of the creatures screeched at me, revealing a mouthful of sharp carnivore's teeth.

I pulled the pack off my back. Stumbling down the steep hill, I groped inside it for the laser. Too slow, too slow, too slow! Adrenalin set my heart pounding as if its racing could make up for the clumsiness of my feet and hands.

One of the great creatures swooped into me, knocking me off balance.

I fell.

The pack tumbled out of my hands and down the hill. I almost followed it, but managed to regain my footing. I climbed to my feet, breathing in rough gasps.

The whynywir circled so close to Cort that he could no longer escape their narrowing perimeter. He stopped and, improbably, glanced back at me. His expression was peaceful, like the ancient pictures of martyrs dying in flames.

Tooth and claw, the whynywir attacked Cort. He covered his face with his arms but otherwise did nothing to resist them. Blood poured from gashes on his neck, back, shoulders, and arms. He crumpled to the ground.

The great birds ripped and tore at him and then, as if by common agreement, they rose into the air toward the cliffs on the north side of the valley. The largest of them carried Cort's limp and battered body.

My brother's murder had taken less than two minutes.

Chapter Five

ARAN, YEAR BC 1945

Aiana's stomach was as tight as the proverbial Gordian knot. But this was not a knot a knife could cut through. Only action would do that. From the shadows of the khenaran she watched the people of a small village going about their tasks.

The houses weren't much to look at. One room, most of them, framed in wooden poles, not from the mighty khena trees of course, but from some scrub species that wouldn't be considered either straight or strong enough almost anywhere on Earth. But this wasn't Earth. The weather was mild, and all that was needed was enough support to hold up a roof of thick leaves that could keep out the rain.

Beyond the houses, the khenaran reared up skyward, a cliff-wall of forest, rainbow-lit where sunlight fell on the towering trunks, dwarfing the village nestled at its edge.

The houses ranged around a central area where small children played and about a dozen older people—adults and children alike—worked at tasks that kept the village alive and comfortable. Five women sat in a circle sewing tanned skins into garments and decorating them with beads and feathers. A boy of maybe twelve years operated a wooden loom under the watchful eyes of two older men, perhaps a father and an uncle. As Aiana watched, several people came and went from the clearing to other places, perhaps for gathering, farming, or hunting. Two women assembled the ingredients for a stew that had already started cooking over an open fire at one side of the clearing, and the aroma mingled with that of the khenaran, like an exotic dish with onions, cinnamon, and mint.

It was a lovely picture. Idyllic.

This village was the first human settlement on the planet.

She'd spent the last month mapping the period extensively through the 'port's instrumentation, a viewpoint distanced by height and data enhancement from the planet's surface. She had collected, analyzed, and organized disparate data sources into strong patterns of information that revealed the expansion of human settlement on the planet. Data manipulation was her area of expertise, safely remote from immersion in the actual period of study, safely sheltered from the expectations of other people. That this was the first village, there was no doubt.

And now it had come to this: To walk into a village in a foreign time and place, to establish her credentials with these strangers, to convince them to give her information that as a scholar and historian she might actually hope to use.

It seemed impossible.

From a computer-generated viewpoint high above, she'd seen this village appear, and then another eight villages within the next few years. But try as she might, Aiana could not get onto the surface of the planet within a standard century of the date the humans had arrived. There would be no eyewitness account of the first settlement, since no one living here now would have been alive at the time the village was first settled.

Would they have any useful information? If the original settlers had passed down any memory of Taerlin, it would prove her conjecture that he was involved in the settlement of the planet—worth a thesis in itself, perhaps, if the temple would allow it. But this was not the thesis she was hoping to write. On the other hand, if the people here now had no memory of him, it would prove or disprove nothing, but for her it would be another dead end. And five months of her year's lease on the oneiroport would have been wasted.

She would never find out if she didn't get moving.

Aiana tucked her hair back behind her ear and took a deep breath. She forced the muscles in her arms to relax, and remembered to unclench her hands. Holding them loose and open, she raised her chin and walked into the village.

"Mama!" a child called. "Look! Here comes Taera!" The little girl spoke Arantu, but Aiana had no trouble with the language. The university offered a self-paced course, and Aiana had studied it both dreaming and awake. She was fairly fluent.

But what name had the child used? Almost Taerlin, but not quite. Taera? A coincidence?

All eyes turned toward her. Aiana suddenly felt conspicuous in her white dress, which flowed from a clasp at her shoulder. She had dreamed herself perfect, eyes as green as she wished they really were, clear skin with no annoying freckles. And wearing this dress. She had walked into the village this way and couldn't change it now, not in front of all these people.

"Hello," she said. Her voice quavered a little. She tried to smile.

A woman of middle age rose from the sewing circle and approached her. She had dark hair and golden skin, and she smiled in a way that suggested she had never had occasion to use any other expression. "Come," she said. The woman looped her arm in Aiana's. "Taera. You are most welcome. My name is Kiko."

Well, the "welcome" was good; the warm gesture, even better. Aiana patted Kiko's hand and smiled at her as if their friendship had always existed. She didn't want to upset anything—or more to the point, anyone—by quarreling with the name. "Thank you. It's good to be here."

Kiko sat back down, making room beside her. Aiana sat beside Kiko, and others around the circle introduced themselves. A dozen names; of the others, Aiana managed to remember only Inez to her left, and large, dark-skinned, soft-eyed Benna across the circle.

"I brought some spices and herbs I thought you might like." When Aiana traveled in time and space, her oneiromorph could bring along whatever material objects she could carry or otherwise bring. It took more energy than the simple oneiromorphic transformation, but not much more, and the 'port had its own reactor. "Saffron. Cardamom. Oregano.

Rosemary. Cinnamon." Aiana used the words in Standard, not knowing any equivalents in Arantu. She passed around small, tightly woven silk pouches of the spices.

Inez brushed her fingers lightly over the little satchels, red and blue and green. "It's a beautiful fabric."

"Yes. Silk." Another word in Standard. The pouches were biodegradable; perhaps in time the word would disappear, too.

"My grandmother had a dress like this."

No doubt one of the few things the settlers brought with them. "From Earth?"

"Yes. It's old and worn now."

The woman's eyes lowered to assess Aiana's dress then quickly looked away. White. New. Spotless. Probably a bad choice, but done was done. "Your suede clothing is much more durable," Aiana said. "And so pretty, with the decorations you've made." She touched the fringe of Inez's sleeve. "Soft, too."

"Have you come looking for Taerlin?" Kiko asked suddenly.

Aiana's heart caught in her throat. It took a moment to start breathing again. "How did you know?"

"Before he left he said you would be here someday looking for him, and that when you came we should tell you that you know where to find him." Kiko tilted her head slightly. "Do you?"

Of course she didn't! Would she be here now, if she knew where and when to find him? How could he possibly expect her to join him anywhere, when they hadn't even met yet?

There were, as nearly as Aiana could figure out, only two possibilities, and she needed to know which one it was. "I'm . . . not sure," she said. "But I have to ask: are you sure it's *me* he left the message for? Me, and not someone . . . who might, perhaps, resemble me?"

"You are Taera, yes? Or perhaps you're calling yourself Aiana? He said it might be either. We all know what you look like; our parents told us since we were children, and we have told our children in turn." She turned to a boy of about seven, who clung to her arm, his thumb in his mouth, and watched Aiana with round, golden eyes. "Haven't we, dear?"

The boy nodded, silent. His eyes never left Aiana's face.

So . . . not a case of mistaken identity, then. Her heart raced; she was breathing hard, as if the air were in short supply. There was only one other possibility.

She had entered the time loop.

She ran her hand over her face and pushed back her hair. She was thrilled and terrified at the same time. There would be no getting out of any of it now.

"How long ago did he leave the message?" she asked. She prayed that it was only a short time, that perhaps he had ended up in this timeframe and would be coming back soon.

"Oh, long before I was born," Kiko said. "I heard it first from my grandmother, who came here with him."

Aiana thought she knew the answer to the next question she had to ask. "Is anyone still alive from that time?"

"Oh, no." Inez's words bubbled with her barely contained laughter. "And most of my generation's parents have died, as well. But we all know the story."

"The story."

"Yes. How you and Taerlin loved each other and quarreled. How you left before he came back. How he was so sad for so long afterwards. Impossible to be around, my grandfather said."

The others murmured agreement, and Benna added, "There was no comforting him."

They were looking at her as if she had the answer to a riddle, an explanation they'd waited for generations to hear. Her feeling of inadequacy overwhelmed her. "I . . ." She what? Could she tell them she didn't know anything about it? No, that would get too complicated too quickly. If she couldn't tell the whole truth, she also couldn't—wouldn't—lie to them. "I got here as soon as I could. But what happened to Taerlin?"

Inez answered. "Oh, eventually he went off with one of the groups going to other places, and he left you that message, and so we have waited for you to come back."

"And here I am," Aiana said. She felt she was sinking under a wave of sorrow so viscous and heavy that she could barely move her lungs. She'd never even met the man, and already she'd loved him and lost him.

She forced herself to breathe. "Thank you," she said. Her voice was thick under the weight of that impending loss. "You've waited generations to tell me this, and I appreciate it." Though what on Earth—or off—she might do about it, she had no idea. "And now at last you're free from all your waiting."

"Oh no!" Kiko's laughter was joined by the others, laughter so hearty that others in the clearing turned their heads and smiled. "This is the Village That Waits. Waiting is our legacy. We will be waiting with you for as long as you wait here."

"Here? He told you that?"

"No, Taera. You did. Don't you remember?"

Chapter Six

ARAN, YEAR 2466

MIKEL'S RECORDING, continued

It was a long time before I had the strength to move. I felt no anger, no grief, nothing, only a kind of numbness. In a stupor, I walked down to the site of the attack. The grass all around was spattered with my brother's blood. Nothing else was left of him.

I knelt and touched the grass. The blood, still wet, stained my fingers. I wept, and I couldn't stop.

Later, the sun descended toward the peaks behind me, and the air grew chilly. I stood again. My legs, stiff from kneeling for so long, almost buckled under me. I climbed back to pick up Cort's pack. Its worn suede still smelled of him, and a sudden surge of anger rose like bile in my throat. In that moment, I could have murdered every last one of the vile creatures—but the moment passed. I choked back my anger as I made my way down the steep slope. I picked up my own pack and reached the lake where Cort had said I would find shelter, as the late afternoon shadows lengthened into night.

I camped in a shallow cave a short walk from the lake. I felt numb, exhausted, but I couldn't sleep. I took out my tablet and recorded the events of the day as best I could remember them. At last I fell into a fitful sleep, dreaming muddled dreams of

Cort and waking, sometimes in tears and sometimes in a rage, and always to his absence. When dawn at last lightened the mouth of my cave, I could sleep no more.

What had Lennard written about the death rites of the Arantu people? Cort had planted a tree for our father, but our father had died far from home, and Cort felt he needed help. Sometimes people did plant trees for people who died here, but not always. The criteria were unclear. When I returned to the khenaran, I would find a village and seek guidance. For now, I resolved to retrieve what I could of my brother's body and provide a decent burial.

Those damned whynywir.

I was not off to a good beginning here, my thoughts all edged with anger.

I touched the ring I wore on my middle finger, feeling its cool smoothness as a benediction, and I promised our father that I'd see a completion to this. It was time to visit the cliffs at the far side of the valley.

I thought of the blue crystal. Cort had protected his face, so the crystal would still be with the body, unless the whynywir had removed it. Maybe they'd already sent it somewhere else; Cort had said there was a shortage. But maybe, just maybe the whynywir might let me have it. That at least would be something salvaged from this disaster.

As soon as I left the mist that surrounded the lake, I could see the western rim of the valley where we had come in. It was bleak and bare, with rocks jutting from the stubble of grass that clung to the thin soil. Below, to the east, the soil was richer, and plants more plentiful. The whynywir cliffs rose forbiddingly beyond the woods that covered the valley to the north of the lake; these woods were comprised not of the great khena of the forest outside, but of deciduous trees whose leaves were already burnished and dark, almost purple, with the coming autumn. I missed the familiar reds and golds of autumn leaves on Earth.

I hiked through the woods, fighting an undergrowth of vines and bushes, some of them thorny. The woods were harder to traverse than they looked; by the time I emerged on the other side it was almost noon. Trees gave way to bushes and these to grass, and the grass to rocks that became the cliffs of the valley's walls, where the whynywir had taken Cort's body.

I stood and studied those cliffs for a long time. The difficult vertical climb seemed an appropriate culmination of this whole trip so far. Nothing had gone as I'd hoped. What kind of creatures were these whynywir? How could they have killed Cort with so little cause? My throat tightened, anger threatening once again. Would I ever be able to feel the empathy I'd need to communicate properly? Could I ever convince them to care about my mission?

My mission. All my reasons for continuing were still there, and now Cort's death added an extra burden of responsibility. I owed it to Lennard, to myself, and now to Cort too, to continue. There was no room here for rage. I took a deep breath, two, three, and when I was calm once more, I started climbing the rocks.

Two whynywir took flight from a cave mouth above and swooped over me. Their faces were darkly furred or feathered, with golden eyes disconcertingly like my brother's but without his warmth and humor. Expressionless just-doing-our-job faces. Animal faces.

They closed in, baring impressive teeth. The tight circles they flew around me impeded my forward progress

I stopped climbing and tried to talk with them. "Hello, my name is . . ."

They battered me with their wings and swiped at me with their claws, ripping a gash in my left arm that screamed with pain. I hissed in a breath, refusing to cry out.

Their eyes never left me, but I could still read no expression on their faces, nothing that suggested intelligence.

I backed away, but I kept talking, my voice sharper and higher with the pain. ". . . Mikel. I'm from, ah, from Earth. That is, from the stars, and—"

A bite from one of them drew blood on my right arm.

My heart pounded, and I swiped wildly at the nearest one, but it had already flown on. I wasn't even close. I retreated to the edge of the bushes. Having driven me away from the cliff, the whynywir flew back to a cave opening near the top of the cliff.

I shouted at them. "Listen, I just want to talk with you. My father was Corodh-an-Aran, the one you sent to Earth. Remember? I want to learn about you so that . . ."

They disappeared into the cave, leaving me in mid-sentence.

I babbled at them for a long time after that, sometimes screaming, sometimes crying, sometimes talking like a rational scientist. None of it made a bit of a difference. All I could think was that the whynywir had sent my father to his death and now they had killed my brother. My enmity twisted my fists into knots and tasted like metal in my mouth.

I wanted revenge.

The strength of this feeling shocked me back into some semblance of rationality. I swallowed my urge for revenge, but the grief didn't go away. More than ever, I wanted at least to open communication that would make these deaths worthwhile, a price paid for *something*.

I'd have to try again, but for now the message was clear enough. My first communication with this alien race wasn't exactly an invitation to come over for dinner. Considering who dinner might be, this was probably a good thing. I smiled grimly. Maybe there wasn't much of a body left to retrieve. Maybe just shreds and pieces. Maybe only bones.

Who knows, with those teeth, maybe not even bones.

I don't know how long I sat leadenly among the bushes staring at the cliffs above, wanting to be dead myself. Somehow, I pulled myself together. I examined both my arms; the bleeding had already stopped. If I couldn't bury Cort's body, I'd make some other memorial.

I skirted the edge of the woods to reach the spot where Cort had fallen. The grass lay flat and dully darkened with dried blood—blood that the first rain would wash away. Like my father, my brother was gone.

I wanted some kind of permanent reminder. I needed hard work to take my mind off my grief. For the rest of the afternoon I hauled stones as large as I could carry, and I built a cairn to mark the spot of Cort's death.

If the whynywir thought to drive me away, they were in for a surprise. The longer I worked, the more my resolve hardened to stay in this valley through the winter if necessary in order to make contact with them. Cort had sacrificed his life for this, and I would do everything in my power to succeed.

Brief cold downpours occasionally punctuated the warm days, and the warm, humid breeze that blew off the lake wasn't enough to take the chill out of the air at night. I slept wrapped in both Cort's blanket and mine, but nothing could warm the coldness I felt inside, alone in this alien place, my father's world where I was a stranger.

Every morning I took my camera and tablet and walked to the cliffs of the valley's northern wall where the whynywir made their homes. They ignored me. I talked to them, but there was no sign that any of them listened. I started each day by trying to get a little closer than I had the day before; but each day, amid a flurry of flapping wings and threatening teeth and claws, the whynywir firmly shooed me away. I spent the rest of the time each morning observing from a safe spot at the edge of the woods. I learned to identify three or four of the beasts by unique markings on their pelts, but most of them looked to me like larger or smaller versions of the same creature. They seemed to all behave the same. On several occasions, I counted the arrivals and departures in an entire day. Twenty-two out, fourteen back. Seventeen out, sixteen back. Twenty out, twenty-five back. So . . . they stayed out overnight, at least some of them. Where did they go? How far? For how long? I felt more like a zoologist than a xenologist. I was studying by observation creatures that I couldn't communicate with directly.

Sometimes when they attacked me on my forays up the cliff face I screamed and beat at their heads and wings. But these rages invariably left me bitten and cut up, and the whynywir uninjured and uncaring.

There was no sign that these great avians were in the least intelligent, much less the moral conscience and dominant life form of the planet that Cort claimed. Would Lennard have seen the situation the way I did? Or would he have recognized some sign of intelligence that I had missed? I had fallen far short of what he'd hoped for me, of what I'd hoped for myself.

I wondered if, like me, Lennard would have grown close to despair.

One afternoon, I walked, lost in thought, from the lake back to my camp. I was once again considering making my way to the location where I would later rendezvous with the starship. But then I would have nothing to show for this expedition, having learned nothing about the whynywir except their cruelty and indifference. And Cort would have sacrificed himself for nothing. It had been so stupid of me not to listen to him, so stupid.

I didn't notice the pair of alandhal roasting over a fire in front of my cave's mouth until the breeze brought the smell of cooking meat to me. It smelled wonderful.

"Hungry?"

The voice from behind pierced my two-week loneliness like a knife. I whirled around and there, in a spot I had just walked by, stood Cort. I wasn't sure if I was hallucinating.

The question must have been written on my face, for Cort said, "Oh, I'm alive, all right." He started up the path toward me. Pain crossed his features as he walked, and he favored his right leg. "It was questionable for a while. The whynywir don't think I should be moving around yet."

"Nice of them to be concerned about you." The words tasted like acid in my mouth, and I spat them out. I didn't realize until I spoke just how much my hatred of the great creatures had wormed its way into my thinking.

He ignored my tone of voice. "They've taken good care of me. It was you I was worried about. You've lost weight. Have you been eating all right?"

I'd absorbed just enough hunting and trapping skills from him that I'd managed to catch the occasional alandhal and skhuri, a couple of snakes, and an amphibious frog-like creature. And I'd identified two species of edible berries and a leafy plant that grew at the edge of the lake and tasted a lot like watercress. "I get by."

"I brought a couple of alandhal. I hope you're hungry."

Then the shock of his presence wore off. "You're alive!" I threw my arms around him.

"Ow! Hey, careful!" His arms flapped for a moment, unsure of where they were wanted. I adjusted my hug, and he hugged me in return.

I held him at arms length to look at his face, and I laughed as the weight of loss lifted. "You are solid flesh-and-bones alive! I want to hear all about this."

"After dinner." He returned my smile, but the pain-etched lines on his face made him look older and sadder, an impression heightened by his halting gait. "I'll stay with you tonight, but tomorrow I have to go back. They've been using some kind of herbs on these cuts—" He turned slightly so that I could see his back. It was covered with dark, thick, irregular scabs, as were the back of his arms.

They looked pretty bad. "There'll be scars."

He shrugged.

"Look, I have antibiotics in my pack. And bandages. They have to be better than just herbs. Stay with me, Corodh-an-Aran. I'll take care of you."

With an almost unnoticeable shake of his head, Cort said, "I can't. I gave my word I'd go back. And I'm healing all right now; it's just going to take a little time."

"You gave your word to them? But they're the ones who did this to you! And what about me?" Fueled by my desperation, my voice crescendoed sharply. "I missed you. Damn it, Corodh-an-Aran, I missed you a lot. And I need your help. You gave *me* your word, too."

Cort said nothing. He busied himself with basting the meat, turning it, and stoking the fire. When he had caught up with his cooking activities, he began scraping the insides of the skins.

"I thought you were dead," I said. "I grieved for you. I built you a cairn."

He stopped scraping and looked at me. "A cairn? Really? You'll have to show me. No one's ever built me one of those."

I refused his overture. I shrugged. "It doesn't matter now. You're not dead."

"I would have been, but . . . apparently, I'm still needed."

"Needed?"

"I can't explain it. But they seem to think I might still serve some useful purpose in this lifetime. They didn't want me in their valley, but they don't want me dead, either. So here I am."

"Lucky you."

Cort nodded, taking my words at face value. "Yes. Lucky. I don't know how long I was unconscious. When I came to, I was as weak as a baby and living as a nestling among the whynywir. Almost as if I had been born again." He laughed, an odd coughing sound that spoke of pain in ribs and lungs.

Born again among the whynywir? I felt cold, but my curiosity got the better of me. I pulled out my tablet. "What was it like?"

"I could tell they communicated." His hand moved unconsciously toward his blue crystal. "But the conversations . . . were beyond me. As if they were taking place in another room where I couldn't go." He shook his head. "Still, I was too weak to leave, and so I stayed. After a while, they talked with me a bit. The young ones, anyway. Some of them remembered . . . being human."

This seemed entirely implausible, given how the whynywir had acted toward me. "They actually remembered being human?" I echoed. "They told you that?"

"Yes, well, maybe. It was implied, but seemed to have no importance. I couldn't quite tell whether one of them was human in the immediately past lifetime, or some number of lifetimes ago, or whether they were relating stories of other whynywir having been human some time or another."

"Or maybe just making up stories?"

"I suppose it could be that, though they don't seem the type to make up stories." He fell into a moment's silent reverie. "I guess I'm getting more tolerant as I get older," he said. "The whynywir don't get on my nerves like they used to."

I could feel my temperature rising. Maybe they didn't get on *his* nerves, but I was close to my limit. A tsunami of desperation, rage, humiliation, and failure flooded through me, and my words tumbled all over one another to keep ahead of it. "Corodh-an-Aran, I have to talk with the whynywir! I'm not getting anywhere studying them. I keep trying to communicate and climb up there on my own, but I haven't had any luck at all. Could I go back with you?"

He shook his head. "No. I did ask, but they've forbidden it."

"But why?"

"I don't know. I just don't think they're interested in you."

"Well, they should be! I'm the son of the man they sent off to a distant world to die a final death, remember? If not me, they owe something to *him*, don't you think?"

"Calm down, Mikel." He touched my shoulder.

I didn't want his touch, didn't want his advice, and I definitely didn't want to calm down. I took a step away, and his hand dropped.

"The whynywir do what's best for Aran. Not for me or you. Or him."

I was almost shouting. "How can this possibly be what's best for Aran?"

He shrugged, not meeting my eyes.

When Cort returned to the cliffs the next morning, I walked with him.

"I can make my own way back," he said. "It would be better if you didn't come."

"I come this way all the time. Besides, what else can I do?"

Cort didn't argue. He leaned wearily on my shoulder for support. I was hoping the whynywir would allow me to stay with him on the difficult climb up the cliff's face. Then I would be there, and maybe they would let me remain among them. Surely any half-intelligent creature would understand that the man needed help!

But apparently the whynywir did not fall into that category. As we emerged from the woods, a good half-dozen of them swept from their nests in the cliff, swooping agitatedly closer.

"Leave me now," Cort said. The words came out like a sigh, and he hoisted himself off my shoulder.

"I won't."

"No, you must." Cort stood straight, turning to face me. "They'll attack if you come any closer. I don't want you to get hurt, and I'm in no condition to help defend you."

"No way," I said, bracing my arm around his back. Anger stiffened my resolve. "Let's go. I'm not leaving you. They're going to have to deal with me, and the sooner, the better."

He shrugged off my hold, shaking his head, his lips a thin line of determination and pain. He started climbing without me, but I stayed as close as I could behind him.

The whynywir plunged from above, narrowly missing Cort as they lanced at my back and shoulders. I had to let go of a rock I'd gripped for the climb in order to protect my head. My balance weakened, and I tottered precariously.

A large whynywir flew hard against my shoulder.

I fell, toppling rock over sky over rock, grabbing for any hold, finding none. Fragments of images blinked across my sight: Cort's face, his hand over his mouth in alarm; cloudless blue sky; dirt, rocks, weeds. I grabbed for the tall stems but they pulled loose, dirt and gravel tumbling after me.

An eternity later, I lay battered among bushes at the bottom of the climb.

It was dark. A breeze cooled my torn face.

No, it wasn't dark—my eyes were closed. I opened them. Cort climbed slowly up the slope of the cliff, not much farther along than where I'd been attacked. Perhaps only a few moments had passed, but he didn't look back. No doubt the infernal creatures had told him not to.

Slowly, I sat up. I moved my arm, which felt achingly bruised but not broken. I touched my face and found blood, but not much. I probed numerous other cuts and scrapes that burned raw, but were not deep. I stood. My right leg screamed resistance, probably sprained, the ankle already swelling. Back to the lake then, if I could make it. I needed to wash and soak these wounds and break out my first-aid kit.

When I reached the line of the first trees, I turned to look at Cort, but he had already disappeared. My fists clenched so tightly that the knuckles turned white, and a cut on one of them opened up, dripping blood down my arm.

I had come to hate the whynywir.

I grew angrier at the whynywir as each day passed. They seemed completely capricious. Capricious, deciding to kill Cort. Capricious, carrying him off and saving him. Capricious, telling him when he could come and go. Had sending my father off to his death also been caprice?

I also hated the whynywir for ignoring me. If a representative of another world wanted to make contact with them, what kind of culture would be indifferent to him? Yet, if Cort was to be believed, the whynywir were so wrapped up in their provincial little planet that it was beneath them to notice me. Was I to return home a failure?

More important, *was* Cort, in fact, to be believed? I was beginning to suspect that the whynywir weren't intelligent at all. Maybe this whole thing was a delusion of Cort's, hearing voices in his head that he attributed to these giant avians in the belief that he was communicating through the crystal. If he'd spent an entire winter up here in this valley alone with the whynywir as he said, maybe the experience had given him hallucinations.

This theory explained a lot of things: Cort's ability to cohabit with the whynywir, their disinterest in me, Cort's apparent desire to keep me away from them, the utter lack of any sign of civilization among the great creatures.

My anger was exacerbated by the growling of my stomach and the multitude of my pains, especially my right leg. My hobbling clumsiness reduced whatever chance I had to catch any of the small, timid creatures that populated the woods. I lived on berries and water and the occasional small creatures, more bones than meat, caught in my makeshift snares.

I spent hours at the edge of the woods by the whynywir's cliff hoping to see Cort, to see some change in the whynywir's behavior—any sign he might have influenced them.

After a few days with no change, I would have been happy simply for any sign he was still alive. Where was he? Surely, if he had continued healing, he would have returned to me by now. I was plagued with the fear that he might need my help. I couldn't bear the thought of letting him die—again.

If I truly thought that the whynywir were just animals, I'd have to go up there and try to rescue him. And the only way I could see to do that was to climb the cliff, laser in hand, and kill as many of the creatures as necessary until they stopped opposing me. A one-man military rescue mission. The whynywir had no chance against the weapon. The carnage would be brutal.

I hated the idea of such violence against these creatures whom my brother respected, unpleasant as they were. Nevertheless, I didn't rule it out. Not yet, anyway. I needed to think this through carefully. I dug my tablet out of my pack and brought it over to the edge of the woods by the whynywir cliff, where I could watch them. I began organizing my data.

First, Cort believed them to be intelligent, even wise. I grimaced as I wrote this on my tablet. I had no objective evidence whatsoever to support this claim. The whynywir behaved in a manner consistent with a colony of predatory birds on Earth, nothing more. I marked whynywir intelligence as unproven.

Two, Cort obeyed them—and he said that our father had done so as well. No, he *conjectured* about our father. I thought about Cort's actions. He said that he received the whynywir's orders, that he respected their orders, that he followed their orders. But I had no evidence of any actual orders. Could he be hallucinating? I put a question mark here. I didn't know as a fact either whether the whynywir gave orders, or whether humans in general followed them if given.

All right, three. Humans and whynywir were antagonistic to one another. True for humans, from what Cort had said. Observed with my own eyes for the whynywir.

Four, the whynywir were the dominant civilization on the planet. I looked up at the cliffs, reddish gold in the afternoon sunlight. Was this a myth of the humans, or was there evidence of a civilization here? I had lived in the valley for four weeks and attempted interaction with the whynywir almost every morning. By now, I should be able to tell. Every beginning xenology student is required to memorize the six signs of civilization, a list distilled from our experiences on over a dozen planets, four of which had, without a doubt, civilized alien races. To count as a civilization, an alien culture should exhibit at least three of the six signs.

I wrote the list in separate rows on my tablet: arts and sciences, language and rituals, structures and adornment.

Arts. No visible signs of any art, fine or practical. The interiors of the caves might contain artwork, but Cort hadn't mentioned any. I marked this "probably not."

Sciences, theoretical and practical. I laughed at the very idea of whynywir science, but then I imagined Cort saying, "Wait a minute. If the whynywir don't have any science, then where do the crystals come from?"

"Good point. They have to come from somewhere," I answered my imaginary interlocutor.

"We get them from the whynywir," he would say.

"All right, but did they produce them? There's no evidence of laboratories, electricity, reactors, or any of the technology that would be needed to engineer crystals capable of enabling telepathy between species. If the crystals work more simply, perhaps on some kind of broadcast technology, where are the power generators, signal towers, and orbiting satellites?"

I envisioned him standing slightly behind me, out of sight, leaning against a tree, thinking. I smiled at the thought of him and didn't turn around. I didn't want to ruin the illusion. "Maybe they made them sometime in the past," he said.

"Maybe so, but not now." I shook my head, overruling him.

"They're treating my wounds with herbs," he said. I imagined an edge of desperation in his voice.

"Your wounds look terrible. You need antibiotics." Another point in my favor. I wrote "No" for science.

Language. "They're telepathic," said my imaginary Cort. "They talk with us occasionally through the crystals. Also, I'm aware of them conversing here."

"How do you know it's the whynywir talking?"

He glared at the back of my head. "I know."

"But aside from that," I persisted, "there's no objective evidence of language. Nothing like words, only screeching sounds like animals. No gestures or evocative movements, which might accompany even telepathy, if there were any."

"You don't need 'objective evidence.' I'm *telling* you."

At this point, I realized that all the evidence I had of whynywir civilization came from what Cort had told me, and none of it from the whynywir. Even Lennard's book contained no hard evidence, only the stories told by the people of Aran. If you listened to all the stories told by people on Earth, we'd be surrounded by intelligent, civilized species: dolphins, elephants, dogs, cats, birds, and who knows what-all. At best, all the so-called evidence about the whynywir was an artifact of the human culture, not of the whynywir themselves. I marked "No" for language. Then I relented and changed it to a "Maybe" that I didn't quite believe.

"It's not 'maybe,'" my imaginary Cort muttered. "It's 'yes.'"

Rituals. None were mentioned in Lennard's book. "I don't know of any," Cort said. "I'll grant you that, no rituals."

On to structures, then. The afternoon sun cast dark shadows at the cave mouths. There was no evidence that these caves were artificially made or that the openings had been enlarged. It was as pure an example of found habitat as one might ever see. "Do you agree?" I asked my imaginary brother.

I envisioned him shifting his weight uncomfortably and scanning the cliffs as if he might suddenly see something he'd never noticed before. "No structures."

Adornment. I thought about Cort with all the bits of feathers and bone and whatnot worked into his hair. I wished I could turn around and really see him there. My father, too, with his delicately patterned red and white vest. The humans on this planet understood adornment. The whynywir did not. "You're not going to argue this one, are you?"

"No."

That left the whynywir with five "No"s and one "Maybe" in my column. In Cort's column they got one "Yes," one "Maybe," and the rest "No"s. Either way, it added up to a big "No" for civilization.

I put down my tablet and began pacing back and forth, keeping close enough to the trees not to set off the alarms among the whynywir. I didn't want to be attacked again, not now. I kept staring at the cliffs, hoping that maybe some feature of the topography or some unexpected activity of the inhabitants might enlighten me. But of course nothing happened.

I went back to my tablet. All right, I thought. The whynywir are not intelligent, except at best in the way that animals like dogs or dolphins are. Dolphins have been known to save people, but that doesn't mean they're civilized. They're animals, plain and simple.

I couldn't quite believe it. Cort's words—and my father's actions—weighed too heavily with me. I had risked my career, no—to put it in the true perspective, I had risked my *life* and Cort's on the chance that the whynywir would interact with me somehow. I had gambled that they would reveal something to me that would increase my people's understanding of this planet, that would seal the success of my father's mission, and that would establish me as his worthy son.

I had failed in all these things, and now I faced a set of grim choices. I could pack what remained of my meager supplies and try to find my way back to the rendezvous point, possibly dying in the journey. I could settle in here for the winter where, if Cort didn't show up again, I would almost certainly die of starvation. Or I could make one last desperate attempt to rescue him and probably get killed by the whynywir.

Each of these options seemed likely to lead to my death and the failure of my mission. Among them, there was only one terrible, risky long shot. This, too, might lead to my death, but it also might lead to a substantial breakthrough in communication with the whynywir. It was the only path that had the possibility of a positive outcome.

A desperate and bold idea had been gaining hold in my mind since I'd dismissed the idea of a one-man commando raid on the cliffs. Like a weed with beautiful flowers and poisonous leaves, the idea was seductive and dangerous. It was seductive because if the whynywir were more than just animals, it would force a change in the situation. It was dangerous because I couldn't foresee what that change would be.

I decided to harm one of the whynywir. I had already gambled Cort's life and my own. I couldn't see why I shouldn't gamble one more life, not at this point.

If Cort was telling the truth, then the whynywir would be unable to ignore me any longer. The words he'd spoken before we entered the whynywir's valley took on a new and more promising meaning: "As long as you do nothing to harm the whynywir, they'll leave you alone." And sure enough, they had. They hadn't even talked to me. It now seemed obvious that I needed to harm them in order to get their attention. Cort had been unable to get them to acknowledge my presence, but I could do it myself.

I didn't know what the whynywir would do once they made that acknowledgment, but if Cort was right, they wouldn't kill me. They didn't know whether I had an immortal spirit. Besides, if the whynywir themselves had immortal spirits as Cort said, my crime wouldn't be that bad; if my actions caused the death of one of the creatures, it would be reborn. At least they would believe that.

On the other hand, if the scientific evidence was correct, then I would just be injuring another animal; we hunted for meat all the time. The whynywir would do nothing—but at least I would know. In this case, Cort might show up again, assuming that he was still alive. I couldn't foresee what he might do, but it couldn't be any worse than if I did nothing.

The gamble seemed worth taking; I had nothing left to lose. The next morning dawned crisp and chill, a harbinger of winter. I woke early, dug the laser out of my backpack, and went hunting.

When I looked back from the edge of the woods, the morning sunlight glowed golden in the mist above the lake. The air trembled with expectation. Except for me, nothing moved through the thick woods. The birds fell silent as I approached, then started up again behind me. At the far edge of the woods, the cliffs shone pale in morning sunlight. I crept as far as the whynywir had permitted me, and hidden in the shadows behind a tree, I waited.

Several hours passed. I had ample time to reconsider. Twice, I almost went back to my little camp, but the prospect of failure was more intolerable than the unpleasant action I now contemplated.

As day turned to evening, a flight of the great avians descended toward the mouth of one of the caves in which they made their nests. I braced my arms against the tree and aimed carefully at one of them.

My heart raced. My hands shook. I couldn't bring myself to fire. My civilized background fought against me. My scientific training rebelled. I couldn't injure a possibly intelligent creature in cold blood.

The whynywir vanished into their caves.

I cursed myself for my lack of boldness.

Another group of four appeared, flying toward the caves. This was my last chance. If I couldn't make myself act now, I never would. I braced myself again, aimed at the largest one among them, and clenched my teeth against the bile that rose to my throat.

I fired.

The whynywir managed a few unsteady beats of one of its long wings. The other wing hung limp. The whynywir plummeted to the ground. The laser blast may not have killed the great creature, but the fall probably did.

The remaining three whynywir circled twice over the spot where their companion had fallen, then continued on their way. Did they plan to leave the corpse behind?

It wasn't my concern. My work was done for now. If the whynywir didn't come for me, then Cort would. If he didn't, then I would have to contemplate attempting to rescue him. This would involve more slaughter than I wanted to think about. No. Surely they would come. I headed back to my camp to wait.

Chapter Seven

EARTH, YEAR 3223

"**W**hy didn't Professor Zhou say what the meeting was about when she scheduled it?" Aiana breathed hard, barely keeping up with Smithjon's long-legged stride. "I always put the topic in my notices to the committee, and I append the background material as well. Isn't that the standard procedure?" The day was chilly, and she wasn't dressed for it. She welcomed the brisk pace even though it reminded her that she needed more exercise.

"Yes. And if you didn't do that on your own, I would make you. But you are the student; you have more obligations and fewer privileges. Professor Zhou can do as she wishes."

Aiana sighed. She couldn't get over the feeling that this committee meeting was trouble.

"Well, what do *you* think it might be about?"

Smithjon shrugged. They had reached the building where the meeting room was located, and the door slid open as they approached it. He went to the elevator and pressed the button. Its door opened.

"What, the elevator?" Aiana laughed, stepping in behind him, still breathing hard. "This, from the man whose office is on the top floor of a six-story walkup?"

He ducked his head with an embarrassed smile and pressed the button for the third floor. "Never could find the stairway in this building. I guess we'll know soon enough what they want. I assume you've brought the current status update."

"Yes, of course, but it's not much different from before."

It was a real conference room this time, not the ad-hoc arrangement of student tables and chairs that they'd pulled into a rough circle at most of their other meetings. A heavy matte-gray table molded from some ultra-high-density material dominated the center of the room. The lighting was all indirect, and cold.

The committee was already assembled, clustered around Zhou at the far end of the table. Zhou and Hossen talked in low tones, their heads bent together over Hossen's comm, but they looked up when Smithjon entered with Aiana at his heels. Vikram closed his comm, still frowning at whatever he had been working on. Reverend Guide Salvatore, representative of the holy temple, sat alone on the other side of the table, his head in his hands, fingers splayed at his forehead.

"You're late, Miss Kim," Zhou said. She frowned, her lips in a taut line.

"My fault. Sorry." Smithjon smiled sheepishly at Zhou as he took a seat opposite the Guide and put his papers on the table. Aiana sat next to him.

Zhou's mouth twitched downward. "Never mind. We're all busy. Let's begin. It's been some time since the last status report. How about an update?"

Some time? Less than the month that normally lapsed between reports. Aiana's heart quickened. They weren't going to cancel the project, were they? "There's not much new," she said. She hesitated and looked at Smithjon, who nodded encouragingly.

Aiana cleared her throat, which seemed suddenly full of raw cotton, and took a deep breath. "As you already know, I found the place of the first human settlement on New Richmund, but I was about a standard century too late. Nevertheless, the people there remembered Taerlin and . . . and, um, me. Apparently, some time in the past, I had already asked them to keep waiting with me for Taerlin to appear, which seems to mean that he's going to appear there sometime."

"Yes, that was in the previous report, and—?"

"The problem is that we don't know exactly when. So in the three weeks since the last report, I've been appearing every so often at that village." Aiana paused, remembering the people she had come to know as children during that first trip, and then on her next trip as young adults. On the subsequent five or so trips they had children of their own, grew old, died. Whole generations had come and gone. People she had grown fond of. People whose children and whose children's children she had loved and mourned. People whom only she remembered.

She swallowed and brought herself back to the present. "I'm 'porting twice a day, and so I've been able to cover almost eight centuries, but he hasn't shown up yet. We're still waiting."

Zhou drummed impatient fingernails on the table, her lips chiseled into a hard red line. "This is an extravagant waste of the university's good resources. You're using our 'port to do nothing but wait?"

"I do believe," Aiana retorted, "that machine is dedicated to my use for another ten months yet." She tried to keep the words cool, but there was a knife edge in them.

Smithjon touched her arm lightly, a warning.

"Nine months," Zhou corrected, "and one week."

Aiana backpedaled. "I'm sorry. I know the energy cost alone is large. But clearly, this is a time loop, and a very complicated one at that. Now that I'm in it, I have to keep following it the way it unfolds. I can't just skip forward to Taerlin's time. Believe me, I tried that a few times, and I just keep ending up in this waiting pattern. Apparently, I have to keep showing up in that place so that the people will remember through the generations to help me look for him. If he comes when I'm not there, they'll ask him to wait for me. I'm trying to be frugal, both of resources and also of my time. I'm only there once every twenty years, their time, and not for long. Just enough to keep the memory of me fresh in their minds. And of course, in case there are any developments I need to know about. I suspect he won't actually show up until sometime within a few decades of when he appeared on Earth. I'll increase the frequency of my visits as the time gets closer." She attempted a smile. "I don't want to miss him."

"How do you know," Salvatore asked, spacing his words with ominous deliberation, "that this Taerlin you're waiting for on New Richmund is the same one as our Taerlin here? You know that the name means only 'messiah,' don't you? There might be . . . a different one for a different planet."

The question came like a blow. She winced and wrapped her hands around her chest. What if he wasn't the same one? "I . . . I guess I don't know for sure. But doesn't it seem likely? Someone called Taerlin removes people bodily from the Earth, and someone called Taerlin brings people bodily to New Richmund. It's not a common name;why should it be the same in both languages? Occam's Razor alone would suggest . . ."

The guide made a slight move away from her, raising a warning hand. "Be careful," he said. "You are not implying the Blessed Ascension did not occur, are you?"

Smithjon shook his head in a barely noticeable movement.

"I didn't mean to imply anything about the Blessed Ascension, Reverend Guide," Aiana said, too quickly. "Of course, Taerlin may, er, must have transported many people bodily to Paradise. But mightn't he also have brought a few of them to New Richmund's distant past?"

The guide did something with his mouth that might have been a cold smile—or a grimace. "Perhaps. But Occam's Razor . . ."

". . . only applies when it applies." She tried for a smile that might warm his up a little. "And what happened, happened. I guess we'll see soon enough whether the Taerlin on New Richmund is the same as the one we know here."

"And we may hope that he is not," Salvatore said.

She was stunned into silence for a moment. "Reverend Guide, may I ask why?"

He broke eye contact with her and studied his fingertips, steepled in front of him. "There are some in the temple hierarchy who find your research . . . upsetting. Some of those people are highly placed enough to put an end to such research. I would be sorry to see that."

"But if the Taerlin on New Richmund is a different man from the one we're seeking, then my research has failed anyway. I am aiming to produce a direct record of Taerlin's life, a verifiable record that meets current research standards. I thought you and the temple supported this project."

"I for one would be happy to have such a record. It would be . . . remarkable. But there are other, more serious considerations."

"So, you're telling me that they might not continue to support the project? That they might prefer I find some other person, not our Taerlin? That if I find our Taerlin, they might try to get the project canceled?"

Salvatore stood, pushing back his chair with a loud scrape. "I am telling you to be careful. *Very* careful." He gathered his few papers and his comm, and started for the door.

"Wait!" Aiana's words came out sharper than she intended. Smithjon started visibly, and Aiana softened her voice. "Please, Reverend Guide. Just a moment more. I . . . I wasn't going to bring this up until I got closer to the expected time, in a few months. But under the circumstances, and since Professor Zhou is keeping such close track of the time"—Aiana nodded toward the professor—"I am almost certainly going to need an extension beyond the nine months and one week remaining to me."

"How much?" Zhou demanded.

"Another month? Or, um, two?"

"Two months!" Zhou's frown deepened. "Perhaps we would do better just to cancel this project right now."

"No." Salvatore took a few steps back toward the table. "This could be a unique opportunity to lay to rest once and for all the idea that Taerlin ever went to New Richmond. The temple would be very pleased to obtain this result. Perhaps"—he glanced at Aiana—"it would even be worthy as a thesis."

Aiana opened her mouth to mention, once again, what it would be worth if the man she sought on New Richmund was Earth's Taerlin. Then she thought better of it. What she needed was the extra time; whatever they had to tell themselves so that she got it was fine with her.

Zhou drew in a deep breath and then let it out in a long sigh. "Very well. Send me your calculations, Miss Kim. Assuming they check out, you may have a one-month extension, no more. Is that understood?"

"Yes. Thank you, Professor."

"Thank him," Zhou said, nodding toward Salvatore. "We can all now hope that you fail."

Chapter Eight

ARAN, YEAR 2466

MIKEL'S RECORDING, continued

I stayed close to my cave and the lake all the next day. Remembering the sight of the wounded whynywir falling, its one wing useless, twisted my stomach. I didn't want to think of it and couldn't think of anything else. I felt somehow . . . dirty. I wanted this to be over, and the sooner the better. Why did they not come, Cort, or the whynywir, or both?

I swam; I walked; I paced; I fretted. I polished my field notes. I avoided the woods and beyond them the cliffs where the whynywir nested. I kept the laser nearby; unlike my brother, I would not just fold up ready to die if they attacked me. I didn't think it would come to that, but if they attacked, I was determined to defend myself.

That night, sleep eluded me. I tossed restlessly in my blankets and slept fitfully at best. I woke a dozen times to find that it was still dark.

When at last I saw a faint brightening of the sky, I abandoned the attempt to sleep, and I got up for a quick dip in the lake.

I almost walked right by Cort before I saw him, as still as the rock he was sitting on. He wore a vest of alandhal skins crudely sewn together, fur on the inside, but even in the dim light I could see the lines of scars on his bare arms. Braided into his hair were a number of white feathers of fluffy whynywir down, each as large as my hand and fluttering gently in the slight breeze. "Good morning," he said. He spoke gently. His eyes were sad.

"Corodh-an-Aran!" All of my worries of the last two weeks and the tension that had been building since yesterday released in an outpouring of words. "I'm glad to see you! They let you go? How are you? It looks like you're healing pretty well. I worried about you. I didn't know if you were still alive. I was beginning to think I'd have to go up there and rescue you."

"And how were you going to do that?" He smiled, just a little. His eyes were still sad.

"I . . ." Belatedly, I thought it was probably better not to say. "Well, somehow."

"How many of them would you have killed?"

I saw now that it wasn't a smile, maybe more like a grimace of pain. "They've hurt you!"

"*You've* hurt me."

"I?"

Cort watched me silently, and I fidgeted under his even gaze. "Why?" he asked at last. "And don't tell me it was a rescue mission."

Lying would have defeated my purpose. I told him.

"You think the whynywir are not intelligent?" he asked unbelievingly when I had finished. "Are just animals?"

"From the evidence I have so far, the possibility exists. The probability."

Cort sighed. "Oh, Mikel, I have failed both them and you! But you've taken the matter out of my hands. You're right in this—the whynywir have noticed you. The one you killed was an old one and wise, a respected voice in the whynywir community. He will be missed."

"But if his spirit is immortal . . ."

"He will be reborn, but it will be centuries before his voice carries the wisdom and weight that it has—had—now. I regret that this has happened. I regret that you were the one to cause it. I regret that I ever brought you here."

I looked down, no longer able to meet his sad, steady gaze. I still couldn't tell whether he told the simple truth or was fabricating an elaborate story. I felt a weight of grief in my chest, but whether for myself, or for him, or for the poor dead creature was hard to say. Maybe for all of us, but I couldn't apologize. I had wanted—needed—to effect a change, and the fact that Cort had returned was a measure of my success.

"What's going to happen to me, then? Do they want to kill me?"

Cort shook his head. "No, Mikel. No one knows whether *your* spirit is immortal or not, and if it isn't . . . The whynywir don't want such a death on their conscience. On the conscience of Aran. I believe that what they have planned for you may be exactly what you wanted."

"Which is . . .?"

"A crystal of your own," he said. "They want to communicate with you."

If he had offered me a blue crystal before we came to the valley of the whynywir, or if the events that had occurred since then had been different, I would have been thrilled. This would have been—perhaps still was—the professional achievement of a lifetime. But now . . . Death's shadow hung over us. I didn't trust Cort to make the implant gently or the whynywir to use it well. "No, thanks," I said. "I *would* like to talk with them, but through you."

"You don't have a choice." He spoke with a firmness that offered no alternative. A threat, then.

I took a step back toward the cave, where I had left both the laser and my knife.

"Is this what you're looking for, Starman?" Cort reached under his vest and pulled my laser from his belt.

The epithet stung. Did he dislike starmen enough to shoot me with my own weapon? "How did you . . .?"

"I took it from your cave last night. It didn't seem wise to leave it with you." He pointed the laser at me.

Oh. Right. Much wiser to leave it with *him*.

The sight of my own weapon aimed at me was unnerving. I stared at the wrong end of it, mesmerized. The red power light glowed like the eye of a snake. Like the eye of the poisonous snake whose fang Cort used to threaten Lennard with death. Lennard, and now me. I wondered whether Cort had ever held a laser before or had any idea how to use it, but I didn't want to find out by trial and error. I forced my eyes from the weapon and looked at his face. The mixture of sorrow and determination on it alarmed me more than if he'd been angry.

He switched the power mode to active.

"In case you're wondering whether I've ever used one of these," he said, "I have. I grew up in the city, remember." He turned the weapon from side to side. "Ah. Here it is. Intensity control and spectrum modulation are in a slightly different place. It was illegal to trade weapons to the 'savages'"—here he used a pejorative word in Standard—"but we had ways of getting them. Hold still."

He fired.

The shot tore so close to my left shoulder that it singed the fur of my vest and I could feel the heat of it, or at least I imagined I did. My heart pounded. I jumped to my right. "Hey! Watch it!"

I thought of the whynywir I'd shot yesterday, its left wing hanging useless as it plummeted to the ground.

"Sweet," Cort said. "Easy to use. Accurate. And more lightweight than the models I remember." He took a step forward, and I inched back until I stood against the boulder that formed the side of my cave. Without taking his eyes off me, he placed a small bladder of liquid onto the ground in front of me. "Drink this."

I ignored the liquid. I touched the cool smoothness of my wooden ring, but I was watching the weapon, its muzzle wide and dangerous like a snake's open mouth. "But you won't kill me. You don't want to be responsible for my death. How did you put it? 'The conscience of Aran?'"

Cort sighed. "Many things may be done with a laser short of death. I wish you had never brought this weapon here. But since you have . . . You drink that, Mikel. And quickly, for I know how to kill with this thing much better than I know how to maim." He wore the grim expression of one who wanted this unpleasant business completed as soon as possible, one way or another.

"What is it?" I asked. "Poison?"

I realized how stupid this question was the minute the words left my mouth. Cort had no shortage of options for killing me if he wanted. The list crowded my mind, starting with the snake-venom fang he'd threatened Lennard with, passing through a number of cute tricks with the laser, and ending with a simple throw of his knife.

"Pain killer," he said.

I hesitated a moment more, but I can't deny I wanted the crystal. Ached for it. I decided that my odds were better with the contents of the small bladder than with the wrong end of my laser. I drank the liquid.

It tasted awful.

I remember little of what happened next. I do remember Cort telling me to keep very still. This seemed like a silly remark, since I didn't feel at all like moving. But the silliness made me giggle, and the giggling made me shake, and Cort's expression of displeasure at my shaking sent me into gales of laughter.

Somewhere in there, I lost consciousness.

When I woke, the shadows were short; it was around noon. Was it the same day? Had Cort made the implant? I touched the area of my forehead between my right eye and ear, and discovered a soft bandage of some kind of skin wrapped around my head.

Cort lay stretched out on the ground near my cave, but as soon as I moved, he sat up, looking at me with concern. "How do you feel?"

"Thirsty." My voice scraped along my throat. "I don't hear any whynywir."

He passed me a bota made of skins that was full of water still cold from some source other than my hot-spring-fed lake. "The crystal is in place, but you won't hear anything yet. Your mind isn't attuned to it. When you heal a little better, I'll give you another drug that will allow you to begin communicating through the crystal. Maybe tomorrow."

"I can still take it out." But I knew I wouldn't. Cort was right; I wanted this communication with the whynywir. It was what I'd come here for.

He shook his head and said, "It attaches itself to the bone, Mikel. It's yours till you die."

I sighed and sat back, feeling at peace for the first time since coming to this valley. More than that: thrilled. I was about to travel farther into alien communication than any xenologist had ever gone.

"Where do you think these crystals come from?" I asked.

"We get them from the whynywir."

"Yes, I know, but where do *they* get them?"

He took a deep breath, let it out slowly, took another, and looked up into the mist. "They say that when the whynywir agreed to let the Sky Mother's children stay here, she took off her own necklace of stars and gave it to the whynywir in gratitude."

"From the sky a long time ago, when the first humans came?"

"Sounds a lot less picturesque when you say it, but could be something like that."

"It's not a technology anything like ours."

He looked sharply at me, and his voice had an edge to it. "Spoken like a Starman. Who says it has to be yours?"

"No, no one. I was just thinking about where your first humans might have come from."

"Mikel, we came here so long ago your people probably hadn't even evolved yet."

I laughed, feeling oddly lighthearted in the face of the impending unknown. "Hey, maybe we came from somewhere else too, but we just don't remember it. How else could we both be so genetically similar?"

Cort shrugged. He had lost interest. "Maybe."

I pulled out my tablet and brought my field notes up to date with the information about the crystals. I wondered if this would be the last entry I ever wrote. Perhaps I would lose interest in science, like the whynywir. Perhaps something would go wrong—a hitherto undiagnosed allergy to crystal—and I would die. None of this seemed likely, but it wouldn't hurt to be prepared.

"Cort."

He looked up from the fire he was starting.

"If I die, promise me that you'll bring my tablet back to the ship when they come."

"You're not going to die. Don't even think it."

"I'm just saying *if*."

"All right. *If* you die, I'll bring them your tablet. Anything else?"

Well . . . since he'd asked. "Would you be willing to continue making notes on it? I don't know if your observations would count the same way as mine since you're not a trained xenologist."

"Thank goodness for that!"

I ignored this. "But they would be valuable anyway. If you would write or dictate anything that happens or that occurs to you about the whynywir and the crystals. Do you know how to use this?"

"I think so. I've watched you, and the controls are pretty much the same as the ones we used in school in the city."

"Good. Thank you. At least my death won't have been in vain."

Cort left his fire and came over to where I sat. He met my eyes and held them, and spoke as sternly as a sergeant. "Stop that, Mikel! I swear to you, I will not allow you to die."

"Right. Unless the whynywir order you to."

His expression hardened, and he let a moment pass. "They won't," he said. "And neither will I."

I didn't see what he could do if I had a seizure or something, but there seemed no sense in arguing "what ifs." So I just thanked him again and went back to my notes.

After a while, I left the camp and went down to the lake, and Cort let me go. I looked across the lake at the woods and the distant cliffs beyond, where the whynywir lived.

What would be different after tomorrow? I had no idea. The crystal was silent.

"Drink this."

It was a replay of the day before. I was sure that if I resisted, my laser would reappear. But resistance was no longer on my mind. I was committed. I took this second small bladder of liquid from Cort and said only, "I hope this doesn't taste as bad as the stuff you gave me before."

Cort leaned forward and replied solemnly, "Worse." When I gasped, he laughed in a kindly got-you-didn't-I way. "No, it doesn't," he said, "but this is not for the taste. Just drink it."

In fact, the drink was thick and sweet and very good. When I handed the empty bladder back to him, he said, "I measured the dose according to the whynywirs' instructions, but I gather that it's quite a bit more than usual. I don't know what that's going to mean for you."

My vision seemed to distort at the edges. I squinted to make my eyes focus and forced my mouth to shape words. "Am I going to die?"

I waited, hanging onto a consciousness that was already trying to drift off like an unmoored boat in a current.

"No, of course not." Cort looked right, left, right, but not at me.

"Tell me. The truth." My lips were hard to work; the words slid thickly off my tongue. I tried to keep watching him, but I was also losing the battle with focusing my eyes.

"I swear, Mikel. Not if I can help it, you won't."

"I'm sorry . . . I've caused you so much trouble." I couldn't tell if I'd managed to squeeze my voice out.

"Mikel, listen to me. I don't know if you'll believe me, but I will be here for you. Whatever happens, I will be here."

I think he said more, but I couldn't focus on his words any longer. Something else was happening that demanded my attention. Someone was talking.

> *Do you hear us yet, Starman?*
> *(He is listening. Can you feel it?)*
> *((Many listen, but few hear.))*
> *Starman, do you hear us?*

The voices were beautiful, like a melody and all its harmonic overtones. Like the waves on a pebble beach. But something about them bothered me. Starman? No, I didn't want to be that. *My name is Mikel,* I told them. It was the last time that I would use that name—and the whynywir ignored it.

> *You will be one of us, human*
> *To replace the one that was lost*
> *(though none can replace him)*
> *((Certainly not this young human with his*

arrogant ways))
(but what choice do we have?)
He must learn
and learn quickly
(the human is dangerous)

No . . . I don't want to be dangerous. I just want to understand you.

Understand, you will
(only too well, perhaps)
((survival is another matter))

Beneath and behind the voices of the whynywir that talked with me was a growing volume of other voices. Soon the other voices were as loud as the ones that had been talking to me. Thousands of conversations flooded my head, and I could understand all of them clearly and simultaneously. Thousands of conversations, and yet all of them woven into one conversation, its participants looping in and out of the different threads.

Humans unconsciously focus. Anyone who has ever been in a crowded room knows this. Dozens of conversations could be taking place on all sides of us, yet we focus on the one conversation at hand. But I had lost this ability. Every one of the thousand voices in my mind made sense, and because they all made sense, I listened to them all, and the words vanished as soon as they were said. It was too much. I was adrift on a great river of thought.

I was more than human, with a greatly enhanced capacity to receive such volumes of information, and yet less than whynywir, with my limited capacity to process and respond to the information I was receiving. I no longer thought of myself as Mikel. I no longer knew or cared who—or what—I was. I no longer had the ability to act.

My head blazed with pain.

Cort was worried about me. I knew he was. I heard him talking to the whynywir.

What's wrong with him, whynywir?

Wrong, Corodh-an-aran?
Nothing is wrong.
It is no more than what he
asked for
(deserves)

But he's not responding at all. His pupils are completely contracted, like pinpoints. He's not looking at anything.

He has no need of looking.
He listens.
He hears us. (all of us)
((even you))

Mikel, do you hear me?
I heard him, but I couldn't answer. There was too much else going on all at once. Too much meaningful else. I drifted.

The whynywir talked with a dozen or more crystal-wearers. These were conversations much like the one with Cort: the human talked as humans do, and the whynywir answered, two or three or four of them in what seemed like music, like a simple kind of harmony, nursery songs. They talked about things that were clearly important to the humans—a child's illness, a young woman's visions, my own apparent absence—but of no particular interest to the whynywir. The whynywir conducted these conversations as an indulgence of a species of limited intelligence.

Beyond the crystal conversations, the whynywir talked among themselves. These conversations were much more complex and interesting. The subjects largely concerned

Aran: volcanic activity in one location; a species of insect dying out in another; how well the khena were recovering from a flood in a third place. As many as a hundred or more of the great avians participated in a conversation. And there might have been hundreds of conversations. Any one whynywir might join in several conversations at the same time, and for this reason all the conversations were at some level linked together into one large meta-conversation, the planet conversing with itself about its being.

All the whynywir participated, and all listened and heard everything and understood. I too heard everything and understood. But participation was beyond me.

Beneath the conversations of the whynywir was something else. Something that was like singing or humming.

No, not like that at all. It was like the flow of feelings in music or dreams when a person drifts into sleep.

No, that's not it, either. It was something deep and harmonic underlying everything. Mostly tones of well-being and peace, but there were variations from place to place. I came to understand that I was listening to the khena. Their song was beautiful.

I didn't want to ever stop listening.

Whynywir, it's been a week like this. He's barely breathing. He hasn't eaten. He only drinks because I pour water into his mouth.

Time is of no significance, Corodh-an-Aran.
He learns
(what he must learn)

Whynywir, please. We have to leave soon if we're going to make it out of here before the snows, but he grows weaker every day.

It is no concern of ours, Corodh-an-Aran.
(We did not invite you here.)
It is his own doing.

My doing. My doing and my fault. My brother sick with worry while I drifted. I wanted to see him. I had to tell him I was all right. I struggled to find my eyes and, finding them, to focus. It was hard, with everything going on. My head throbbed with pain.

He saw me look at him. He leaned over and touched my face. "Mikel . . ."

The touch helped, though the name meant nothing. I wanted to speak to him but didn't even manage a groan. The voices called me. The collective whynywir consciousness overwhelmed me. I couldn't keep hold of the image of his face.

"Mikel, don't leave me." His spoken words lost meaning, and I drifted again in the flood of whynywir voices.

Whynywir, if you won't put a stop to this, I'll do it myself. I have more of this drug. I'm going to take it. I have to talk with him. Tell me the dose.

> *It is beyond you, Corodh-an-Aran.*
> *Humans cannot communicate with one another*
> *through the crystal*
> *And even if you could . . .*
> *(would he answer?)*

If you won't tell me how much, I'm going to take the whole thing, as much as you gave him.

> *It's nothing to us, Corodh-an-Aran*
> *(Do as you will)*

It's something to me! I shouted silently, to my own surprise. *How much should it be?*

Half, replied the whynywir, *no more.*

> *((A third.))*
> *(Less, perhaps)*

Even so, it may not help.
None have ever tried this.

Tell him, then. The focus was difficult and painful. But I listened as the whynywir told Cort the dosage, to make sure it was right.

⁂

Mikel? Do you hear me? This was better, much better. Easier.
You, and all the voices. So many. Do you hear them?
I hear . . . something . . . when I concentrate. But it's you I need to talk with.
I hear them all. All of them. Just like I hear you. They're all important. None matter.
No, listen to me. This matters. You have to learn to focus again, or you'll die. Do you understand?
But I had drifted. *What?*
He shook me. *Listen, Mikel. The voices will always be there, but now you have to focus on me. Look at me. Use your eyes. You have to learn to control your body again, if you want to live.*
I looked at him. My head hurt. He was crying. Why? *Is living so important?* I asked. *Is anything?*
It's important to me.
But you threw your life away before. You walked down here and let them attack you.
That was different, Mikel. I will be reborn.
Whereas I . . . ?
No one can know this. You're losing focus; look at me!
It was hard, but I kept my focus. *I have no immortal spirit? I don't know.*
I was wounded. I had shared the conversation of the planet, and yet I could not share in its life? And what about my father? Had he truly and forever lost his life? If anyone knew, it would be the whynywir. I had to know. And so I asked them.

Your father
Who would know this?
(Star-fled) ((If not you))
(Starborn)

I am human, whynywir. How can I know about either him or me?

Their amusement washed over me, the tolerance of an adult for the antics of an infant.

Who
(if not you)?

Are you saying that I . . . that he . . . that I . . . I couldn't complete the thought. If there was one thing worse than being his unworthy successor, it was being his failure of a . . . Maybe it was fortunate that we humans never remembered our prior lives.

No one knows about you.
(Starborn . . .)
How can we know?
(Yet in time
((perhaps . . .))
you will know the answer to this question)
((if you stay here long enough))

You mean, until I die? That wasn't nearly good enough. *I want to stay here. I could never leave. But I have to know about him and about myself, and before I die.*

Humans are so impatient, brothers, don't you
think?
(Their lives are so short) ((sad creatures))
They remember nothing from life to life.
((One there is who might answer some of these

questions for you))
But the journey is not easy
(your brother will be unable to carry you)
((perhaps he is right)) you will have to walk.

Who? I asked.
Remember.
No! Cort spoke urgently. *I don't want to lose you again.*
I'll come back. Underlying all the conversations that took place in the collective consciousness of the whynywir mind was a collective memory—my memory now, more memory than I could possibly absorb. Memory back to the most distant time, a million years before the first humans appeared on Aran.

No, what I was searching for wasn't back that far.

I remembered when humans first appeared, a small band who were, perhaps, refugees from their home world. They came in a—I couldn't make sense of the memory. Some kind of place . . . A ship, perhaps? And on the ship was a—again, the memory seemed odd, filtered by whynywir experience. Some kind of artificial consciousness. An advanced computer, perhaps? A computer that still existed and operated in—yes, it was here on Aran! The location was not far, but still it would be a walk of many weeks—if in fact I could walk at all.

Memories swirled around me. All accessible, all interesting. All mine. Every event on the planet from thousands of perspectives since the beginning of the whynywir racial consciousness. I remembered Corodh-an-Aran since he—or I should say they, since there were more than one of them—first appeared with the humans. Yes, they were there from the first, beings committed to action, to keeping Aran safe—the central reason the whynywir decided to allow the human aliens to live on the planet.

Corodh-an-Aran! I had to go back. Reluctantly, I left the whynywir memories, from which there was so much to learn. *I kept my promise,* I told Cort, and when he saw the focus return to my eyes, he grinned like it was the best gift ever.

I was difficult for Cort. Between the weakening of my disused muscles, my inability to concentrate sufficiently to control them, and the raging pain in my head, I could hardly walk. I leaned heavily on him as he led us out of the whynywir's valley. In addition, he carried all the blankets and supplies that, coming in, we had split between us.

But walk, I did. I wanted to find the ship and the computer of the first human settlers, and I needed Cort's help. That I walk by myself was the one condition he insisted upon.

At least I walked some of the time. Sometimes, though, the whynywir conversations were so overwhelming or the pain in my head so great that I forgot to walk, and then my legs folded under me and I collapsed wherever I happened to be. And Cort, worried and upset, would shake me and call me—whatever he had to do to get my attention back. Sometimes he was successful. And sometimes he just waited.

We moved south and west from the whynywir valley and then turned north on the start of what promised to be a slow journey to the site of the ship.

The more I struggled to focus, the greater a price I paid in the pain of my ongoing headaches. Some days, they tore at my skull, my eyes, my temples so violently that I couldn't get up, could barely manage to eat. I tried to use the painkillers I'd brought—not that my meager supply would have lasted more than a week. But even that was impossible; they made me groggy; I couldn't focus; and then I couldn't walk at all. Only when I slept, or when I lost concentration, did the headaches ease—but never completely. I lived in constant pain.

Here's what I remember of that winter. Snow fell up in the mountains, blocking the passes in and out of a dozen valleys where whynywir live. Thirty-two whynywir chicks were born, as tiny as one joint of my finger, and crawled or were assisted into their fathers' pouches, where they would live and grow until the snow melted. A tectonic plate deep under the ocean shifted against its neighbor, sending a major ocean current several hundred kilometers closer to one of the poles than usual. This in turn brought unusually heavy rains during what should have been a mostly sunny season. Some kind of virus decimated a population of rodents close to the equator; their main predators suffered a hungry season and many died, solving an overpopulation of the creatures. Several hundred khena trees became aware and joined their fellows' song. A hunter and his barely functional brother made stumbling progress through hundreds of kilometers of forest.

As I got better at concentrating on the mundane aspects of life as a human, my lapses of concentration and control grew fewer. Still, I was far short of normal. Simply walking and watching where I was going required all the concentration I could muster.

Despite my social inabilities, we stopped in villages from time to time. We had to. We needed directions. And maybe too, Cort needed occasional human contact; though I regained some control over my mouth and tongue and throat and began to speak again in the normal human way, I wasn't exactly good company.

But I was there. I learned to shut out the conversations of the whynywir as if my life depended on doing so, and probably it did. No, not to shut them out, exactly. I heard and understood everything. I couldn't help it. But I learned—with difficulty, and not always successfully—to focus. I became like a man who lives beside a great waterfall. The roar of the falls was not always foremost in my consciousness, but it was always there, and unless Cort was shouting at me, as he found ways to do, I didn't hear him.

This village was like many we had seen. A dozen dwellings framed in hardwood poles and covered in overlapping leathery leaves as large as a person's armspan circled around a communal cooking and work area. Some fifty inhabitants scraped a living from a combination of vegetable gardening, trapping small game, and fishing in the river that flowed nearby. As always, we were welcomed warmly. Cort had hunted and brought with him the still-warm carcass of a dhelo, and a feast was soon in the making.

Three of the villagers set up a drumming on instruments with voices ranging from a deep bass to a heart-pounding tenor. I settled contentedly into the rhythm of the drums; into the song of the khena, which floated like a melody on the rhythm of the drums; into the movements of the people as they went about their work, as graceful as dancing to the rhythm of the drums. It all fit together the way the smell of fresh air blends with the dappled patterns of sunlight woven by the breezes in the forest.

I paid no attention to Cort's conversation, until he shook me strongly by the shoulder. "Listen to me, will you?" he shouted.

A small group of villagers stared with open curiosity at what they must have thought was the hunter and his idiot brother.

"I'm sorry. The khena . . ."

"I know. But pay attention now. I think we may have reached our destination, but I'm not sure. See what you think." Cort gestured to a small, round man, who stood by his side. "This is Almo. Almo, tell my brother what you just told me."

"Your brother asked about a ship or vessel of some kind," Almo said. "I know of nothing like that. But Corodh-an-Aran thought you might be interested in Taera, the One Who Waits."

The name meant nothing to me. I shrugged. "Go on."

"You know that we are close to the place where the Ancient Ones first came to Aran. Taera has appeared in that place from time to time since ancient days. Or maybe she's always there, but only becomes visible from time to time."

"She? A person?"

Almo hesitated, his head tilted in perplexity as if the question were complicated. "I think so. But Taera never ages; she has appeared as she is since we first settled in this place. And so . . . maybe not a person at all."

An android?

"What does she wait for?" Cort asked.

Almo shook his head. "We don't know. We know only that she waits. Our village waits with her. When she is ready, she will instruct us further."

"Maybe we should go see this Taera, Mikel," Cort said. "What do you think? Even if she's not what you're looking for, if she is as ancient as the villagers think, she may be able at least to provide direction."

Chapter Nine

ARAN, YEAR 2467

Taera was glad to be back on Aran. She liked her dream life much better than her waking one these days. And Aiana—surely she must feel the same way when conscious as when sleeping. Why else would she escape to the 'port as often as she did? She had been coming to this place twice a day as measured in Aiana's waking time, over six hundred visits in ten elapsed months of her life—and she would never grow tired of it.

Taera felt more at home among the people of the village than she did at the university. Here, people laughed a lot, as if they knew their lives were a gift. Here, everyone welcomed her without reservation. Here, she never once felt the pressure to succeed, or the crushing fear of failure.

She initiated the routine sequence that would allow her to leave the 'port and still find it here when she returned.

After granting a one-month extension, her committee hadn't been subtle in warning her that the university would not give her more time unless she succeeded in finding this New Richmund Taerlin. She yearned for him to arrive, to meet him, to move on with the project, one way or the other. But she also wished this interlude of warm interactions with her village might never end. She intended to enjoy it while it lasted.

A chime sounded in the 'port.

Taera looked at a monitor that recreated a miniature but detailed holo image of the outside surroundings. The 'port was in a pretty meadow high on a hill not far from the village, fringed with tall evergreen khenaran. A sun-sparkled clear stream flowed at its edge. Flowers bloomed in a year-round parade of color; right now, the meadow was filled with red blossoms.

Three people were coming her way, shadowed by the great trees.

Taera laughed out loud. "Good! Visitors!"

Though the shadows under the trees were too dark for her to make out the faces, Taera recognized Almo by his gait. The man's good humor and energy reverberated into his stride, which was more like skipping or dancing than walking. Taera knew most of the people in the village, but she didn't recognize the other two men. She made a mental note to adjust the brightness and contrast of the display to bring out more detail in objects among the trees.

One of the strangers moved purposefully but slowly, each step hard won. An old man, by his gait. The other drew a bit ahead and then slowed for his companion time and again, as if torn between eagerness and solicitude.

It was this man who came first out of the shadows of the khena. Taera's hand flew to her lips as she drew in a breath. Taerlin! But no, the resemblance was only slight. This man had two crystals at his hairline, the hunter's red and the seer's blue. Could he be the other one of whom the first women spoke, Taerlin's brother, the hunter Corodh-an-Aran?

If so, then . . .

The companion emerged from the shadows, and he was not an old man at all.

For a moment Taera altogether forgot to breathe.

Yes! It was him. Taerlin, here at last!

Her heart leapt into doubletime. She felt dizzy. She could remember nothing of what she'd planned to do when he arrived. She was not prepared. She needed time.

But there was no time.

Taera dreamed that one wall of the 'port was a mirror, and then it was. She gave herself a critical review, straightened her dress, and tucked the errant curls of her red hair back into the ribbon that bound it. Her hand shook slightly, but the image in the mirror reassured her. Green eyes. Good. Much better than the hazel ones she had in waking life. Clear skin, no freckles. Perfect. She smiled and reminded herself that everything would go well because it all already had. She took a deep breath and let it out slowly.

She walked through the wall of the oneiroport.

She wanted to stare at him—Taerlin, live, in person. But once she started looking at him, she might never stop. In any event, it was Almo who skipped forward in the lead. "Hello, Almo," she said. "It's good to see you. I see you've brought me visitors."

Taerlin stumbled slightly, and the hunter held out a steadying arm.

Almo bounced on the balls of his feet and gestured toward the others. "This is—"

She smiled and interrupted. "Yes, I know."

She still wasn't ready to meet Taerlin's eyes. Those eyes. How he had looked at her in that holo.

She turned instead to the hunter. "Corodh-an-Aran! This is a pleasure indeed!"

"Cort," said the hunter. "Call me Cort."

And then it could no longer be avoided.

She turned her gaze to Taerlin.

It was everything she'd feared.

It was wonderful.

He had unusual eyes, too golden for Earth, but flecked with blue like no eyes she had yet seen on Aran. And he was staring at her as if there were no other living creature on the planet. She felt a wave of lightheaded dizziness as if she were falling into his eyes, but she couldn't stop looking. Her chest tightened, too constricted for her breath. When at last she found her voice again, the words were shaky. "Taerlin, most welcome! I've been waiting for you."

He shook his head slightly and seemed confused. Corodh-an-Aran's grip on his arm tightened as if to hold him upright. Was he unwell? "My . . . my name is . . ." The sentence fell away, unfinished, as if he wasn't sure he could rely on the faculty of speech. He blushed.

And a beautiful blush it was, too. Taera laughed with the sheer delight of him, with the improbable idea that a man of Taerlin's charisma and importance might be shy like her. "I know your name, Taerlin," she said, hoping to put him at ease. "How could I not know you?"

He leaned on his brother, definitely unsteady. It wouldn't do at all for the man to die of some Aran-born disease before he went back to Earth. Perhaps, if she could get him to her instruments in the 'port, she could diagnose the problem and help him.

She wanted to help him in every way she could.

If she was going to get him into the 'port, the less time spent explaining, the better. She reached for his hand. "Come with me."

Taerlin took her hand. His touch was firm and steady, but so warm that she worried he might be feverish. Corodh-an-Aran didn't relax his grip on Taerlin's arm. It would be good to have him there too, for support. She held out her other hand. "You too, Coro—uh, Cort."

For a moment the hunter didn't move. He looked at Taerlin, and whatever nonverbal communication passed between them, the hunter seemed satisfied. He took her proffered hand.

Taera thanked Almo and then led the two brothers through the wall she could see quite clearly, but which she knew was invisible to them, and into the 'port.

And things started falling apart.

The hunter dropped her hand at once, wariness approaching panic in his eyes. He turned back to the inner wall of the 'port, visible now that he was inside, its dull metal cold like the interior of a ship. He pushed against it, but of course it resisted him solidly.

Taera started to reassure him, but on her other side, Taerlin cried out, dropped her hand, and clutched at the crystal in his forehead. He fell to his knees and then to the floor.

Taera drew in a panicky breath, and her heart's doubletime beat made everything seem to move more slowly. What if he died right here in the 'port?

But no. He wouldn't. He already hadn't.

She knelt beside him. His eyes were closed, but he was breathing. She felt his forehead. It was hot. A pulse in his neck throbbed. He moaned.

Cort ran to them. He met Taera's eyes, questioning, accusing.

She shook her head, hoping it wasn't anything she'd done.

Cort bent over his brother and smoothed the hair from his forehead.

Taerlin moaned again, and his eyes fluttered open. "What—" He blinked and looked around, at his brother, at the 'port, at her. "Where are we? Who are you?"

"I am called Taera," she said, still concerned. There was no easy way to explain where they were, not even in the best of times, certainly not while he was in this condition. "This is my place."

"Are you all right?" Cort asked.

"Yes, I'm fine," he said. Gingerly, he touched the spot on his left shoulder where he had fallen, shrugged, smiled a bit apologetically, and began to get up. Still a bit unsteady on his feet, he accepted his brother's proffered hand. He rubbed his fingers over the blue crystal embedded in his forehead as if to assure himself that it was still there. "The crystal . . . There are no voices here. No memories. Nothing. It . . . took me by surprise, that's all, like the release of a great pressure. I've struggled against it for so long."

The two men exchanged a look in which some communication seemed to take place.

Taera watched them. While she waited out their silence, she considered the possibility that the crystal was somehow to blame for Taerlin's condition.

Cort turned toward her. "Are we still on Aran?"

"Yes—and no." Seeing his sudden pallor, she added, "There is no danger here. We aren't far, but I'll take you back outside if you wish."

He swallowed and looked longingly at the wall they'd come through. Then he squared his shoulders. "I'm not leaving him."

She liked the man very much in that moment.

"I'm all right," Taerlin said. "Really." He took a step away from his brother and stood straight, chin raised.

"I never meant to cause either of you discomfort," Taera said to Cort. "I'm sorry. Let me take you back outside, and in a few moments I'll bring Taerlin out also. But I'd like to examine his crystal first. It may need an adjustment."

"Go on," Taerlin said. "I'll be out in a minute. It's all right."

"He'll be all right," she echoed. The words sounded hollow. She tried to make herself look and feel self-assured—straight posture, smiling— and reached a hand toward the hunter. "Come."

Cort looked from her to Taerlin, who gave him a feeble smile, and then back again. He took her hand, and they stepped out through the wall into the clearing.

Cort took a deep breath of Aran's air, and he said, "I am counting on you to keep him safe." He didn't add "or else," but his fierce expression and grim voice implied a threat.

"I will."

He peered into her eyes as if he might see any lie written on the inside of her pupils. Finding none, he nodded.

"This won't take long," she added, and then she walked back through the wall of the 'port.

She found Taerlin examining her computer and communications equipment on the far side of the room. She wondered how much of it he understood. Eight hundred years. Even if the functionality was similar, the interfaces had probably evolved beyond his comprehension. For all he knew, she might as well be from Alpha Centauri. And maybe, come to think of it, she should keep quiet about her origin; it would raise too many uncomfortable questions.

"Corodh-an-Aran will wait for you just outside."

"Yes, I know." He turned toward her. "What's all this . . . equipment?" he asked, gesturing toward the computer bank. His gaze was intense, as if he could see through her skin and into her soul. As if she were the most desirable woman he'd ever seen.

But of course, it couldn't mean anything; they'd just met. Maybe he looked at everyone like that, like they were the most important people on the planet. Maybe everyone was, to him. "I'll give you a tour sometime. But right now, I want to see about that crystal."

"It's permanently attached."

Did he think she was that ignorant? Surely he was joking. She laughed a bit uncertainly, and he smiled in return. Oh, what a smile he had! She could see now where his legendary charisma originated. People would probably follow him to the ends of the earth for a smile like that. But not her, not now. She had to stay on task. "Yes, I know. But it may still be adjusted."

"You won't make me stop hearing the whynywir, will you?"

"You want to hear them?"

"Oh, yes! It's a gift . . . beyond measure."

"You want to hear them all the time, or just when they talk to you?"

"All the time, yes." His eyes were soft in the memory of the whynywir, and he looked at her as if asking her to understand.

A gift beyond measure. She couldn't even imagine what this meant, much less how it must feel to him.

She was glad she'd taken the time to learn about the crystals after hearing from the early villagers that Taerlin and his brother had them. As with many things, the foundation had had a hand in inventing the technology. That had been a couple of centuries back, but the technology had never been put to use on Earth. Fortunately, the foundation kept detailed documentation, and she'd found an early cristallofactum in perfect working condition still sitting on the shelf in the foundation's vaults. "I can do that. But maybe you'd like me to make the crystal a bit quieter. It would ease the pain. Would that be all right?"

"Perfect," he said.

"Come." She took his hand to lead him to the seat by the control panel where the cristallofactum was housed. His hand was warm. He squeezed her fingers a little. With a shock of surprise, she turned to look at him to find on his face an intensity of expression that for a frozen instant she was sure was desire. Her body responded more strongly than she ever had to anyone in waking life.

Oh, the perils of conducting research in the dream state! Answering his desire with her own would be so easy.

It would be unspeakably wrong.

It was the one thing that would throw her objectivity and her research into question. It would also destroy her reputation.

"Here," she said, the word rushing out in the hurry to put the awkward moment behind them. "Sit here." She put her hands on the back of the seat and rolled it toward him.

He sat and studied the instrumentation with exaggerated interest. He smoothed his vest, which wasn't the least rumpled.

No sense in wasting any more time. Taera adjusted the 'factum and then touched its input wand to the crystal in his forehead until the machine had a reading of it. Further input, in her dream state, she could now manage remotely. She put the wand down and ran the basic diagnostic suite. The crystal was attached correctly. Its signal might be a bit on the loud side, but it was within normal parameters. She pushed Taerlin's hair away from the crystal and traced the signal waves across and into his brain.

He watched her work, lacing tensed fingers together in his lap and keeping perfectly still.

Her own breathing was a little too shallow. She didn't want to meet his eyes, watching her, not while she was touching him. Instead, she ran two advanced diagnostic suites and carefully studied the results.

The device was in perfect working order.

She made the only adjustment indicated. "All right, I've reduced the gain," she told him. "You seem to be having these problems because it was too loud for you. The tolerances were within normal range, but perhaps you are unusually sensitive."

"I took a lot of the drug."

The drug. She hadn't thought of that. She nibbled at her lower lip and looked at him, considering, careful not to get lost in his gaze. Even his eyelashes were beautiful, dark on the ends but almost blond where they fringed his eyes.

"Yes, that might explain it." She turned back to the instruments, enabling the brain-scan function. She ran her hands over his head and studied the resultant holographic displays. The affected neurons were highlighted holographically. A display showed the out-of-parameter variables. She tried to ignore the tingling, light feel of his hair under her fingers, the warm touch of his skin.

Concentrate.

"The drug used is very powerful. It alters the brain both neurochemically and in other ways, to adapt it to the crystal. The changes are permanent. You've been oversensitized. This shouldn't affect your normal brain function, but you mustn't take any psychoactive drugs again, not ever. You might die or be . . . damaged. Do you understand?"

"Yes, I think so. Thanks for the warning." Even through his tan, she could see that his face had grown red. "I don't use drugs. I wouldn't have taken any this time either, but . . ." His words trailed off.

"It's part of the installation procedure."

"Yes, but . . ." He looked off into some memory, and he fell silent.

There had been something about the whynywir and his crystal, sketchy fragments retold by the early settlers. She would have to go through her records and see if she'd made any notes of it. But for now . . . he seemed visibly upset, and she wanted to soothe him. She smiled, and the corners of his mouth flicked in a subconscious response. Pain mingled with desire in his eyes, as if she had the power to fix whatever hurt him. She tried to put comfort into her voice. "I know, Taerlin. I know about you."

In an instant, he was angry. He stood suddenly, knocking his chair back. It clattered against the wall behind him and careened to the side. "You don't know anything! Not anything! I'm not like the others. I wasn't even born here. I murdered a whynywir. The crystal worked the way it did because that's how the whynywir wanted it, and that's what I deserved."

Her control of the situation was slipping away. What if he refused to see her again? The man had work to do, and she wanted to be by his side when he did it.

"No," she replied, keeping her voice calm. "The whynywir would not have wanted to cripple you. You are too important to Aran." And to Earth, too, but she couldn't say that, not yet. "I know who and what you are —maybe more than you do."

His scowl deepened. He drew a breath to blast her with a heated argument.

She took a step forward and cut him off before he could, marshaling the meager array of facts she had learned about him from the early settlers and those she had surmised from seeing him interact with his brother. "You were born on the world you call Earth, and Corodh-an-Aran is your half-brother. You'll be meeting a ship coming from Earth for you, right?"

Eyes wide, he stepped back and reached behind him for the chair. He groped for it but didn't find it, and looked around. It had rolled to a stop halfway across the room. He breathed in, out, in again. "How did you know that?"

"It stands to reason, doesn't it, since you'll be going back to Earth."

He folded his arms across his chest. "You've got that part wrong. I am *not* going back to Earth. I'm staying here."

Suddenly, she felt tired, a year of coming to this place, waiting for the man, a year of her life, and for what? This wasn't unfolding the way she had imagined. She rubbed a hand across her face and reminded herself that it would work out. Somehow. After all, it already had. She had seen the holo. "Are you sure?" she asked him. "Perhaps this is something you must consider more carefully. I think that you *will* go to Earth again. It is necessary."

"Why? Why would it be necessary? I'm a scientist, yes, but not an important one. I'll write up my research here and give it to them when they come. If they come. But I'm staying here."

She shook her head. "No, you will go. And it may be sooner than you think."

They stared at each other, stubbornness pitted against stubbornness, until he shook his head and looked away. "Maybe you're mistaken. Why do you keep calling me Taerlin? I'm not . . ." His words faded away, as if he weren't quite sure who he was or wasn't. He swallowed.

She felt embarrassed to see him so unsure of himself. "But you *are* Taerlin—to me."

He shook his head. His face was a map of bewilderment.

Explanations weren't her strong suit. What to say? What not? Why hadn't she discussed this with her committee? Why hadn't she made a plan? But of course, no one could have had any idea how ignorant the man would be of who he was. Of where he was going and what he would do. Of his destiny.

Aiana would be much better at this, the logical, practical side of herself, but if Aiana were awake, she would be on Earth, not here. Taera would have to do the best she could. The less she said, the better, but was there any reason not to show him? In an instant, she made her decision. She held out her hand. "I will show you. Come with me."

He took her hand. She felt an almost palpable jolt, as if he'd reached through her skin and touched her heart. She drew in an audible breath. Had he too felt that?

She couldn't meet his gaze. She gave his hand a light squeeze and then led him through a wall opposite where they had entered the 'port.

He looked around behind them, his mouth framing an O of surprise, and then he turned to the room they had entered. He stopped, eyes wide.

She couldn't show him the interior of the actual physical 'port; it was so full of equipment—and of course the bed—that there was hardly space for one person to stand. Instead she'd created a square room, maybe three and a half or four meters on a side and two and a half high, with walls of a dull metallic grey. There were no furnishings, no windows, no doors. No computer panels. The light grew more intense in the center of the room, highlighting an image of her own sleeping self captured from the cams that monitored her. The holo image of Aiana, different from her oneiromorphic image in that it realistically captured exactly the way she looked rather than the way she wished she looked, showed a young woman suspended horizontally, seemingly in mid-air, lying asleep on her back. Her arms rested peacefully at her sides. The curls of her red hair, glistening in the light, floated around her head. Her eyes were closed. Her chest rose and fell in light, slow breathing.

Taera's heart lurched. She'd never looked at herself sleeping, and the sight startled her.

Taerlin had his hand to his heart. His mouth was slightly open, as if he were having trouble drawing a breath of clear air. He met her eyes briefly, and then returned his gaze to the image of the sleeping woman. He looked at her the way he'd looked at Taera in that first holo. Like he wanted never to stop looking.

Was it possible for an oneiromorph to be jealous of her waking self?

Surely not. The conscious Aiana would be better than Taera was at keeping her emotions under control. Aiana would always remember who she was and what her project required. She would not feel such attraction to the man. "It is a hologram."

"Who is she? You?"

"She is Aiana."

For a fraction of a second, his face was filled with longing and aching and despair. But the expression vanished when he met her eyes. "But then . . . who are you?"

A bubble of loss, grief for a relationship she never had and never would, rose to her throat. She swallowed it down and breathed deeply to push it into a tiny corner of her heart where it was small enough to ignore. "I am Taera, her dream self. And you are Taerlin, the one . . ." Who is the most significant historical figure of the millennium. What a thing to blurt out! ". . . the one she dreams of. That's why I know about you. That's why I'm here. Do you see?"

For a moment it almost seemed that he did see, but then he shook his head like he was clearing it. He looked at the sleeping Aiana, then back at her, the puzzle of her two selves written on his features.

"I am an oneiromorph, Taerlin. A holomorphic, multidimensional, multisensory projection of her dream consciousness."

"Hers?" His head gestured towards the sleeping woman.

"Hers."

An expression that might almost have been pity softened his face. "You're not real?"

"Reality is not a meaningful concept. In the world of dreams, all things are real."

"In the world of her dreams?"

"Yes, her dreams."

"She sleeps and dreams of me? Why me?"

Taera realized with a shock that Aiana had never decided what to tell him concerning her interest in him. In all the months of searching, she'd been woefully unprepared for actually finding him—the real man, not the iconic figure. What should she reveal to this only-too-real man about his future and the reasons for her search? That was one thing that Aiana must decide, not Taera. Until Aiana reached that decision consciously, she mustn't say anything. Her lips pressed so tightly they were only a thin line, shutting in the answer. She'd had enough for one session. It was time to end this dream.

"Taera, I have to understand."

"Then say that it is because you are Taerlin."

He shook his head. "I am Taerlin because she dreams of me, but she dreams of me because I'm Taerlin? That doesn't make sense."

There wasn't one single thing about this encounter that was going well, but his preference for Aiana hurt. What had she been thinking? She had just made herself a shade less real to him. Tears welled in her eyes.

He lifted a hand as if to stroke her hair, but he stopped before he reached her, his face working with the effort to stay calm. "I didn't mean to upset you. I'm sorry."

"I too," she said. "But this is enough for today. I will come again for you later." She took his hand and led him from the room.

Chapter Ten

EARTH, YEAR 3223

Aiana raced up the last flight of stairs to Raj Smithjon's office. As her heart pounded and her breath came fast, she cursed his reclusive nature that preferred an isolated office under the eaves on the sixth floor, and her own sedentary lifestyle.

The door to his office was closed. She hoped she hadn't missed him. She took a deep breath and knocked firmly.

"Enter," came his voice from within.

Excellent. He was here. She opened the door.

"Oh. Aiana, it's you." Smithjon straightened the papers he'd been reading into a neat pile and stood. "I was just heading down to the meeting. I'm not late, am I? He consulted his chronometer, a quaint, gilded device of antique vintage that he carried in the pocket of his vest—another anachronism.

Aiana couldn't help smiling. The man was an archetypical history professor.

"No, don't worry; you're not. I was just hoping we might talk for a few minutes beforehand."

He motioned to a chair and reseated himself behind his desk. "What's on your mind? If it's about Taerlin, we should perhaps save that for the meeting; he's all anyone will want to discuss."

"No, not about him, exactly." She took the offered chair, and put her briefcase on the floor. "It's my oneiromorph."

He leaned back in his chair and raised an inquisitive eyebrow. "Oh?"

Aiana bit her lip. Where to begin? "I took the required courses in oneiroportation as an undergrad."

"Yes, of course."

"I also took an elective seminar on cultural evolution during the twenty-first century. We did several group excursions in that course. But . . . before this project I never 'ported independently. Given the initial nature of my thesis, there was no need. And for the last year while I was tracking him down, there was no problem."

She fell silent, pushing back a few stray strands of hair.

"But now that you've actually found Taerlin . . .?" he prompted.

Aiana dropped her hand to her lap and sat straighter. "Now that I've found him, the oneiromorph seems harder to control. I've planned out every session carefully before going into the dream state, exactly as the procedure indicates. But she . . . didn't follow the plan."

"For example?"

"Well, for one thing, she's taken a name of her own."

"You mentioned that the people on New Richmund called her, what was it, 'Taera'?"

"Yes. It didn't bother me before because it seemed like what *they* called me, and I was just going along. But somehow, I'm not sure when it happened, now she seems to call herself that, as differentiated from me. Have you heard of them doing that, Professor? Other oneiromorphs?"

Smithjon leaned back in his chair and ran his fingers through his unruly hair. "Yes, from time to time something like this happens. It's not terribly uncommon. The oneiromorph is your dream self, remember, and therefore a projection of your subconscious mind. And so perhaps you just think about yourself differently in your subconscious. What about when you're conscious, Aiana? Do you think of the oneiromorph as Taera now, awake?"

She nibbled on her lip, then spoke slowly. "Yes, I do, most of the time. Is that bad?"

Another long pause. "At least your conscious self and your dreaming self seem to be in some sort of agreement. But . . . it does suggest a troubling separation. Just the fact that you're talking about her as . . . well, 'her' and not you . . . Perhaps there are issues around this project that you haven't resolved consciously."

Issues! The oneiromorph was inordinately fond of the man. Aiana could feel her insides warming even now, when she thought of him. But of course, acting on those feelings was—*must* be—out of the question. Initiating any kind of relationship would cast doubt upon her objectivity and put the entire project at risk. And forget her thesis! No, her reputation in the department would be as a bad example to warn other students, and that would be the end of it.

Smithjon cleared his throat, bringing her back to the present. "And the name she's taken—Taera—it's an interesting name. Do you think she likes him?"

Aiana shifted uneasily in her chair. "Yes, I would say so."

"May I ask . . . Beyond the bounds of propriety?"

Her cheeks burned. She stood abruptly and picked up her briefcase. "It's time we started out for that meeting, Professor. We don't want to be late. The answer to your question is no. Of course not. I am a professional, and so is she. We are not a . . . a . . . tart."

Smithjon stood and took up his own briefcase. "I beg your pardon," he said, bowing slightly. "I meant no offense. But as your advisor, I had to ask."

He walked around the desk. As he passed by her, Aiana said, "She showed me to him, sleeping."

Smithjon turned, his hand hovering a few centimeters short of the door sensor. He stared at her. "She *what?*"

"You heard me."

"That's rather irregular."

"Yes. But she thought she needed to do it in order to explain to him what we are."

He peered at her closely, and she thought of her own image in the mirror this morning: the dark circles under her eyes, the hollows of her cheeks. "Why did you think you needed to explain yourself to him?"

She rubbed her nose thoughtfully but stayed silent.

"You have been using the machine too much."

Smithjon couldn't know that for a fact. Aiana was adept with computers; it would take a media forensics expert to uncover her carefully hidden usage record. She tried not to overdo her shrug. "Well, there was the one-year deadline, the short extension. I've been worried they might take the 'port away. Add to that the planning, research, documentation, and so forth, and I probably am working too hard."

He made a gesture, a mixture of a nod and a shake of the head, that suggested that he didn't quite believe her. "You do realize that the rules for use of the oneiroport are not arbitrary. The dangers of overuse are quite real. You could become seriously ill or suffer irreversible mental damage. You could die."

"I'll take a break," she lied. "Now, let's get to that meeting."

He put a warning hand on her arm. "This thesis of yours has become very important to the university. To our entire understanding of history. You have a bright career ahead of you, Aiana. Don't throw it away."

She looked down, brushing her fingers across her mouth. "Yes. I'll be careful."

"And if this topic comes up before the committee, be careful what you say."

She met his eyes and smiled. "Thanks."

⚜

When Aiana and Smithjon entered the conference room, everyone else on the committee was already there. The Guide hovered by the holo player as if waiting for it to turn to gold.

And for him, perhaps it would at that, though the segments she had queued up for today were short.

"So you have found our man," Zhou said, fingering a printout of the meeting agenda that Aiana had distributed. "And you're sure it's him?"

Aiana looked at Salvatore with concern, but he seemed distracted, more focused on the holo player than on her. "Yes, I'm sure. He looks exactly like . . . the holo we saw before. And there are other unique facts in his life. I've extracted a clipping from the 'port's records so that you can see for yourselves. Oh, we're speaking Arantu in the holo, so I've taken the liberty of overdubbing the conversation."

"Arantu?" Salvatore asked.

"Richmundian. Yes."

"I know what it is, Miss Kim, but why isn't he speaking Standard?"

"Old Standard, it would be. I'm sure he must speak that, too, but since we were both on Aran . . . um, New Richmund among other people we just naturally continued speaking Arantu."

The guide nodded curtly, his lips tight. He seemed ready to disapprove at the least additional provocation.

And additional provocation, there probably would be.

She inserted a media card into its slot, and the player came to life. Two people faced each other—Aiana, and the man known as Taerlin. They were looking at each other as if they had never seen another human being before, as if the 'port dimly visible in the background didn't exist. The holo was so sharp that the audience could see a blush fading from his cheeks.

"I know, Taerlin," said the Aiana in the holo. "I know about you."

This seemed to make him angry. He stood abruptly and spoke in a raised voice, the pitch high with agitation. "You don't know anything! Not anything!" He swallowed and unclenched his fists, continuing in a more normal tone. "I'm not like the others. I wasn't even born here."

The the segment came to an end, and the recording froze, holo images suspended motionless in the air.

"Fascinating," Zhou said. "He does indeed resemble the Taerlin we saw before. Does anyone think this is not the man in the original holo?" She polled the committee members with her eyes, daring any of them not to vote.

Silence folded over the group. All eyes turned toward Salvatore, who only reluctantly looked away from the frozen holo figure. He made a croaking noise, cleared his throat, and started over. "He is the one. Have you made other recordings?"

"Everything in the 'port is recorded," Aiana said. "It's standard protocol."

Given how much could occur outside the 'port, it was an evasive answer, but the guide didn't seem to notice. "Ah. Good."

And he would no doubt want a copy of every minute of them. Aiana didn't blame him. If she were religious . . . As it was, she was not religious, and she still savored every minute of these holos, though the guide would no doubt disapprove if he suspected how those encounters had made her—no, *Taera*—feel.

"Where is 'here'?" asked Hossen, sitting to Zhou's left.

"Professor?"

"He said he wasn't born here. Where are we talking about?"

"Oh. Aran. I mean, New Richmund. 'Aran' is what they call it in their language."

"And *when* is 'here'?"

"About seven hundred fifty years ago—contemporaneous with Taerlin on Earth."

"Where was he born, then?" asked Zhou.

"Earth." Aiana told them about Taerlin's mixed Arantu-Earthish parentage and how he'd arrived on Aran. "But that's not why he says he's different." She stood and walked over to the frozen holo tableau. "Did you notice the crystal—here—on his forehead?"

"Some of the early pictures show Taerlin with a third eye," Salvatore said. "Some show him with a beam of blue light emerging from his forehead or his eyes. It's hard to take these things literally. Perhaps the crystal explains them."

"Yes, perhaps. But the purpose of the crystal is to allow communication between the humans and the whynywir on Aran."

Salvatore nodded, but the others on the committee were looking around, one to another, searching for a clue. Aiana met the guide's eyes. She raised an eyebrow and lowered her chin, allowing him to explain.

"There was a mission on New Richmund for a few years, oh, a couple hundred years ago. We learned of the whynywir at that time. An elusive but reportedly intelligent alien species on the planet. The natives say that the crystals are the only way to communicate with them. Something similar to these crystals exists here on Earth, as well. Around the time of the mission, the temple entered into a joint venture with the One

World Foundation to initiate certain research projects, one of which was the development of a similar communication device. Perhaps the missionaries saw or heard of it on New Richmund and thought such a thing might one day have some kind of practical use here. I don't know of any, though."

"So you're saying that Taerlin was in communication with the whynywir?" Zhou asked.

"More than just 'in communication,'" Aiana said. "Apparently, the crystal was installed wrong, and at the time I found him, he was pretty much overwhelmed by the whynywir thought-stream. I adjusted the crystal, but he still seems to identify with them in some deep or mystical way. That's why he says he's not like other people."

"Half man, half whynywir, eh?" Smithjon waved his fingers outward, as if describing some mythological beast rather than a real person.

Yeah, you should see his wings. Aiana bit her lip, resisting the urge to utter the sarcastic comment. "Perhaps . . . but what it means for us is that going back to Earth is the last thing on his agenda."

Salvatore waved his hand dismissively. "Oh, but he will. He already has."

History has already been written. It was the guiding principle the entire History Department lived by. It was what made time travel possible.

"Yes, Reverend Guide. Of course he will go back to Earth. I will persuade him." She dearly hoped she would, at any rate. "What I wanted to discuss with this committee is how much I should tell him."

Smithjon saw the problem immediately. His face lit up with the enjoyment of its delicious irony. He combed the fingers of both hands through his hair and interlaced them behind his head, leaning back. He sighed deeply. "Just tell him the whole story, why don't you. Just tell him, and see how he reacts."

Aiana opened her mouth to respond, and then pictured how Taerlin would react. He wouldn't believe her. Who would? If he got angry when she suggested she already knew something about him, how would he take this unlikely story? She closed her mouth again. If Taerlin thought her odd now, just wait till she hit him with *that* one.

"No, no, no, no, no," said Salvatore, waving his arms as if trying to erase the idea from the air. "It would be utter gall to dare tell Taerlin his own future. No man knows the far-reaching consequences of his own actions. We should not deny him the same dignity."

"Miss Kim, how certain are you that you need to do anything?" Zhou asked.

This was the question Aiana had been expecting. "Completely. Watch."

She pressed the remote on the holographic projector, and the frozen image of Taerlin and Aiana skipped a few beats and came to life again. They were continuing a discussion edged in hostility.

"You were born on the world you call Earth, and Corodh-an-Aran is your half-brother. You'll be meeting a ship coming from Earth for you, right?" the holographic Aiana said. She leaned into Taerlin's personal space, hands on hips, her chin jutting forward aggressively.

Surprised, Taerlin took a step back, reaching for something that wasn't there. "How did you know that?"

"It stands to reason, doesn't it," answered the holographic Aiana, "since you'll be going back to Earth."

Taerlin folded his arms across his chest. His face darkened in a scowl. He shook his head. "You've got that part wrong. I am *not* going back to Earth. I'm staying here."

"Are you sure?" Aiana in the holo asked. "Perhaps this is something you must consider more carefully. I think that you *will* go to Earth. It is necessary."

"Why? Why would it be necessary? I'm a scientist, yes, but not an important one. I'll write up my research here and give it to them when they come. If they come. But I'm staying here."

The scene froze.

"What is this ship?" asked Srinivas Vikram, the fourth member of her committee. Vikram was so silent in these meetings that Aiana sometimes forgot he was there. But Vikram's specialty was the twenty-fifth century. It was entirely possible he knew the name and history of every starship of that era.

"I'm sorry," she said. "I don't know the name of it, only that there was to be one. Shall I find out?"

Vikram shrugged. "If you can. It might help us pin down more about him. What science?"

"Excuse me?"

"He said he was a scientist. What science?"

"Oh. Xenology. He was conducting some kind of field research. About the whynywir."

Vikram frowned and looked off for a moment, then said, "The whynywir were mentioned in Lennard Sirinin's book, of course." He saw no recognition from the other committee members and so continued. "It was an obscure publication of that era, a study of Richmundian culture that is not considered significant today. Nothing further was ever published on that topic."

"Could Taerlin be the same person as this Lennard Sirinin?" Hossen asked. "We know that the name 'Taerlin' simply means 'savior,' and there has always been some conjecture that this is not his actual given name."

"Conjecture is all it has ever been!" the guide said heatedly. "Conjecture that has been deemed heretical. The First Apostle, Holy Dheren, stated the meaning of the name but always referred to him only as 'Taerlin.' The Great Convocation of 2813, after much discussion and prayer, decreed that this was his actual name, not just a title. There is no historical record of any other name. The matter has been closed for centuries."

Hossen lowered his eyes. "Of course, Reverend Guide. I meant no disrespect. It just seemed an odd coincidence that this Sirinin fellow was also looking into the whynywir."

"No, I don't think that's him," Aiana said. "His brother calls him Mikel. Not Lennard."

"And so you're saying Taerlin never published this research he refers to?" Zhou asked.

Aiana shrugged. "Maybe he never got to it. Maybe he had other, more important things to do. Which brings us back to the issue of how to get him to return to Earth."

Zhou tapped her nails on the table in a slow rhythm, thinking. "I agree you will need to do something. I also agree that it seems unwise—perhaps even unethical—to tell Taerlin too much." She made brief eye contact with the other committee members, who nodded assent. "What do you think is the least intrusive action open to you?"

Least intrusive. She was already—though not in the sense that Zhou meant—beyond that. Aiana thought back to Taerlin's expression when he watched Aiana sleeping. Had the man been thinking what she thought he was thinking? And there was her own deep sense of loss. Taera's loss. She'd been unprepared for how much more than just research Taera wanted from him.

Taera. The oneiromorph. What to do about her?

And what to do about the response her body still felt when she thought about the man?

Aiana brought herself back to the present and addressed Zhou's question.

"I believe I have to tell him about the settlement of New Richmund," she said. "That much seems inevitable, and he will find it compelling. Once he returns to Earth, with any luck the rest will fall into place."

"Aiana, it appears that your report to this committee might possibly have a few holes in it," Smithjon said, opening into the leading question they had both agreed on. "What does any of this have to do with the settlement of New Richmund?"

"It astonishes me that no one has put this together before. Perhaps the religious explanation for the disappearance of all those people with Taerlin has blinded researchers to the connection." To Salvatore, she added, "Apologies, Reverend Guide, I mean no offense. No . . . heresy. This is just a hypothesis."

Salvatore nodded, his face a mask of neutrality, his posture rigid.

"To me the disappearances resemble oneiroportation." She glanced at the guide. "I suppose, of course, that the Blessed Ascension might well look like that, even though it's quite . . . different. We can review the original holo again if you'd like." Aiana paused to see if anyone would like to see the holo, but no one reacted. "And so naturally, when I went to New Richmund to search for Taerlin, the first place I went was the original settlement." Again she paused, meeting the eyes of each committee member in turn.

"That is, I tried to go there," she said, "but I couldn't. As you know, the earliest I could get there—a hundred years after the fact—they still remembered Taerlin. Most of what I know about him comes from those people, two or three generations removed from the original settlers."

Her eyes suddenly ached with tears wanting to be shed, and her voice came out thick through a throat tight from holding back the tears. "And they remembered me, too." The story of how she and Taerlin had loved and then lost one another still filled her with grief out of all proportion to the circumstances. That is, to the circumstances she knew about.

Hossen nodded as she spoke, over and over as if listening to some invisible music. "The settlement of New Richmund," he said. "It makes sense. See if you can get some genetic confirmation."

"All right. I can do that."

"You may tell Taerlin about this, if you think it will persuade him to do what he must," said Zhou. "Any settlement of New Richmund has no significance, historically speaking. Knowing about it will do him no harm. Unless anyone disagrees." She looked around the room with a frown so forbidding that it would have taken a committee much bolder than this one to dare to disagree.

"Yes, fine," said Salvatore, speaking for all of them. "But do not mention events on Earth under any circumstances. They must unfold as they are meant to."

Of course, with the complicated logic of the time loop, Aiana might have been meant to mention those events so that they would unfold as they did, but she wasn't inclined to argue with the guide, now that the committee had given her the permission she'd hoped for.

Chapter Eleven

ARAN, YEAR 2467

MIKEL'S RECORDING,
continued

After Taera adjusted the crystal, she led me through the strange liquid wall of her place and back to the meadow outside. All the voices of the whynywir flooded back into my mind, the beautiful voices, the community of the planet's consciousness.

I hadn't been inside for long, but everything had changed. The voices weren't as demanding. My head no longer hurt. I took a deep breath of the fragrant air, pungent and refreshing like rosemary or mint, and I laughed like a prisoner just released from his shackles.

Cort sat by a small campfire, cooking something. He looked up as we approached. Tension washed out of his features, and he stood to greet us.

Feeling better than I had in weeks, I let go of Taera's hand and took a few steps toward him, then turned to say good-bye to Taera.

She was gone.

When I turned back to Cort, he was looking over my shoulder at the spot where Taera had disappeared. I looked back—no Taera—and then again to Cort. He'd shifted his gaze to me. "How are you?" he asked. "How did that go?"

"Good. She . . . did something. She fixed it."

His gaze flicked over my shoulder, then back to me. "You're still pale. You sure you're okay?"

"Yes. Fine. I just . . ." How could I ever explain what I'd just seen? "That's a strange place she has in there, that's all." The vision of Aiana sleeping haunted me, and Taera watching, on the verge of tears. The two of them . . . like images from the right eye and the left eye almost but not quite identical, refusing to overlap.

"I like her," I said, putting as much meaning into it as I could. "I want to see her again." I didn't want him to get too interested.

"Mm-hmm. And—?"

I glanced over my shoulder once more. Still no Taera. "What do you mean, 'and'?"

"What do you think she is? Not human like us."

"Did she tell you that?"

I didn't want him to know anything about Taera I didn't know. But he was oblivious to my jealousy, and he had a way of turning questions around. "Do you think otherwise?"

I sighed. Taera and Aiana. Put them together when Aiana woke. If Aiana ever woke. Were they more than human, or less? Or other? "I don't know what to think."

"Well, she's not. So don't get too interested."

I could feel my jaw tighten, and my voice came out sullen as a child's. "Don't tell me what to do."

We glared at each other for a few awkward, silent moments. Then Cort shrugged and looked away, shaking his head. "Suit yourself."

Days passed. I told Cort how Taera had adjusted the crystal. Eventually I also told him about Aiana sleeping. I told him the strange things Taera had said about dreams. He didn't understand it any better than I did.

Neither did the whynywir memories offer any clue. The whynywir were never particularly interested in the affairs of humans and knew less about Taera than I did.

The more I thought about her, the more questions I had. Why was Aiana sleeping? How did Taera recognize me, when we had never met before? Was she even right that it was me she was waiting for, and not some . . . other . . . Taerlin? Why was she waiting for anyone?

What was this "Taerlin" business anyway? If indeed it was me she was waiting for, why didn't she call me "Mikel," like everyone else? And why me? All human beings have special and unique qualities, but it seemed unlikely that I, a twenty-year-old recent university graduate, would merit Taera's—or was it Aiana's?—long wait. What did she want of me?

What was the relationship between Aiana and Taera? If like Prince Charming I could have awakened my Sleeping Beauty with a kiss, what would have happened to Taera? Would she disappear when Aiana woke? And if that was true, could I bring myself to do the deed?

Most pressingly, I wondered why Taera had said I would go back to Earth. Was it because I didn't have an immortal spirit? Or something more . . . sinister?

Taera hadn't provided answers to any of these questions, and I found this lack of information disturbing. Despite that, I wanted to see Taera again. And if she was only the dream self of the sleeping Aiana, then I wanted to meet Aiana, too. Was that even possible?

When Cort and I returned to our camp one evening about a week later, Taera was there. The setting sun accented the red in her hair so that the curls that framed her face could have been a ruby halo.

My heart leaped. I dropped the birds I had been carrying and raced ahead. She smiled at me, and I reached out to—but I didn't know what I wanted to do. Take her hand? Hold her in my arms? I was sure Taera would be open to my touch, but my confused desire for her was complicated by the existence of Aiana. How could I settle for less than the real person? I brushed my fingers against Taera's arm. I could feel every pale hair, feel how the sunlight warmed her skin. Though she said otherwise, she seemed more real to me than Aiana. "I missed you," I said. And it was true.

She drew her arm back, no more than a centimeter or two, and gave me a serious, sad look. "You missed Aiana." Could an oneiromorph be jealous of her sleeping self?

I wasn't going to lie to her. "Her, too. Both of you."

Taera changed the subject. "You came searching for me for a reason."

"Yes, I . . ." Suddenly shy, I looked down and laughed nervously. "That is, I thought I would find a computer or something. From the original settlers."

She tilted her head at an endearing angle, amused. "You came here, in great personal pain, searching for an ancient computer?"

"No, I . . . Well, that is, yes. I had a question, and the whynywir couldn't answer it. So they told me to look for the . . . I thought it would be a computer, something from the original settlers."

"Me."

"I think so."

"Then ask your question, Taerlin, and I'll answer it if I can."

Something deep inside me clenched into a tight knot and then squeezed tighter. Now that the moment was at hand, I wasn't ready. I couldn't bear it if the answer were no. What if there was no answer? What if Taera wasn't who or what I was seeking? What if she didn't know, or was wrong? Worse: What if she thought the question was primitive—or stupid?

Sometimes ignorance is better than finding out what you don't want to know.

Cort had come up alongside us, and I suddenly hoped he might have a way to get me out of this. But he just raised an eyebrow and tilted his head, waiting.

I took a deep breath. I'd never learn the answer if I didn't ask the question. "I'm trying to find out whether I might, ah, have an immortal spirit on this world. You know . . ." I gestured toward Cort, "like him."

Taera's eyes widened slightly, and she studied me as if she had never seen me before. As if some blinding new idea had just occurred to her.

My heart pounded. I managed to meet her eyes. I straightened my posture, prayed that she wasn't going to laugh, and waited.

"I see," she said at last. "The original settlers. But of course the answer to your question is yes. You do, Taerlin, or you will. It makes no difference."

"How can that make no difference? And if not now, when?"

She held my gaze and lifted her chin, a defiant gesture. "It makes no difference because the time when you will have an immortal spirit like your brother's has already happened. And always will have."

Taera spoke Arantu very well—better than I did—but she'd gotten her verb tenses all wrong. I struggled to make sense of what she'd said, and failed. "Now?" I managed to ask, "or sometime in the future?"

Taera laughed. "Yes! Yes! And sometime in the past, too." Then she grew serious and added, "Will you come with me? I'd like to take a sample of your blood. Then we will know the answer to your question more precisely."

In itself, the idea of a blood sample didn't bother me. I had had blood drawn more times than I could remember between being accepted as crew on the *Falcon* and starting the mission to New Richmund. But coming from Taera now, it was a non sequitur, and shocking. It reawakened all my concerns about why she might have been waiting for me to begin with. "Why?"

"Because, Taerlin, you have just reminded me that I must prepare the . . . I don't know the word in this language . . . the substance that will change the genes of the ones who come to settle here, so that they will bond to Aran, and Aran to them. So that just like his"—she inclined her head toward Cort—"their spirits will be immortal."

I followed her gaze to see whether Cort was making any sense of this, but he shrugged, eyes wide, looking as confused as I felt. "I don't get it," I said. "Who's going to settle here? And what does my blood have to do with it?"

"People from your planet," she answered, calmly meeting my eyes. "From Earth. And your blood is necessary because your gene structure is mixed, one of each pair from Aran, and one from Earth."

This statement, at least, might go some distance to explaining why she was waiting for me in particular—me, the world's only interstellar hybrid.

Taera continued. "This will help me to identify the unique pattern that bonds humans to Aran, since one half of your genes will have it and the other won't. Whereas his"—she inclined her head toward my brother—"will have both matching. I will need both yours and his. And when I find the sequence, I will duplicate it and join it to a virus that will alter the genes of the settlers from Earth. Do you see?"

I didn't. The human genome—at least that of Earth—had been completely mapped and understood for a couple of centuries, and so I could see how Taera might hope to identify the differences between the Aran genome and Earth's by studying my blood and Cort's. But Taera had missed one crucial point. "No one from Earth is going to be settling here, Taera. It's forbidden."

"And a good thing," Cort said.

Taera ignored him. Her eyes gleamed with a laughter so infectious that I smiled despite my confusion. "No, Taerlin. It is only forbidden on your world, is it not, to settle on a planet that is already inhabited."

I felt like we were talking at cross purposes, using the same words but with entirely different meanings to entirely different ends. "And what do you call *him*," I asked, my voice rising as I gestured toward Cort, "if not an inhabitant?"

Taera's smile broadened. "Ah," she said. "But this is now. And that is then."

I had no idea what to make of this statement. After an uncomfortable silence, I could only muster, "When?"

"Four thousand five hundred and nine years ago, Taerlin. And a few months. For if you don't bring the first human settlers to this planet, how will anyone ever get here?"

"Me?" My voice hit a squeaky overtone, and I cleared my throat. "Are you suggesting that the original settlers on Aran came from Earth using . . . time travel?"

Taera shrugged. "How else?"

"There are a number of different theories."

She arched an eyebrow, tilted her head questioningly, and folded her arms across her chest.

"Most people think the people of Aran aren't at all related to the people of Earth."

"Better believe it," Cort muttered.

"And how would they explain you?"

I had the uncomfortable feeling in that moment that maybe she could see inside my skin. I broke eye contact. "They don't know about me."

"The doctors?"

"Never did any genetic testing. That would be 'profiling,' and it's illegal on Earth. Besides, the resemblance between people on Aran and on Earth could just be a coincidence."

"Highly unlikely."

I was unwilling to give up the point. "Unlikely coincidences happen."

"The odds against two races on two different planets arising completely independently that are so genetically similar they can interbreed are higher than the number of planets in the entire galaxy."

I had heard that somewhere myself. I gave up on it. "Perhaps there was a spacefaring civilization a long time ago on Earth that colonized here. Or the other way around."

She tilted her head again in that quizzical way. "Evidence?"

People had found no archaeological evidence on either planet, and it wasn't from lack of searching. Not that we knew Aran as well as we knew Earth, but we were motivated. We could have used evidence of a common ancestry to justify maintaining our control over Aran. I shrugged. "Maybe they came from somewhere else and settled both planets."

If that were the case, there would be archaeological evidence of that, too; and there was none.

"I have been there at the beginning, Taerlin. And so have you. Or you will. They came from Earth, and you brought them."

I gave up on it. "But time travel just isn't possible. The technology for it doesn't exist."

"But some of the foundations for it have already been invented. What is the light-bypass drive, if not a primitive form of time travel?"

Primitive. Here we were, traveling to the stars, twelve light-years in less than a month, and she found us primitive. "Where are you from, Taera? Or should I say, when?"

"I am not from any time," she said. "As I've already explained, I am an oneiromorph."

"Aiana, then. Is *she* from the future? So why don't her people settle Aran with their advanced time travel? Why me?"

"Because you are the one who settles Aran. Not her people. You."

I let that sink in for a moment. I knew that if I asked how she knew that, I'd get another one of her enigmatic statements that made no sense. So I changed my approach. "But time travel is impossible! It's been proven. The grandfather paradox, and so forth."

Taera laughed, silver bells in the clear air. "You are too much, Taerlin. As if anyone would travel back in time and kill their own grandfather." She held out her hand. "Now, come inside with me, will you?" She glanced back at Cort. "Don't go anywhere. You're next."

The thin needle that Taera used to draw blood was connected directly to the computer bank along the wall of the room. The needle was so fine that the blood must have passed through it only one molecule at a time, but Taera said that she didn't need much. The needle didn't bother me, but Taera's purpose did.

"How are you going to use anything that you create from my blood here and now to inoculate people that came here four thousand years ago?"

"Four thousand five hundred and nine," she said.

"And a few months. I got that. But how? It doesn't make sense, Taera."

Taera gently took the needle from my arm. A tiny drop of bright red blood welled up in the spot where it had been. She placed a light pink dot over it and said, "Disinfectant. Press here." She turned to the computer console. "You think of time as a linear thing that always moves forward carrying you along, quite out of your control. This is fundamentally inaccurate."

"What is it, then?"

She shrugged. "Like anything else. A mode of perception."

"But you can't stop time. It does go forward and never back."

"That's a matter of scale, Taerlin." Taera squinted at the holographic projection in front of her and gestured over her touchpad. The image enlarged, top and bottom portions cut off. Colors appeared, long sequences of them in random arrangements. "Like this image here. If you look at a small enough portion of a timeflow, of course it seems straight. But all of time swirls and eddies, and many of the flows are loops like giant whirlpools. If you could get above and outside it, you would see this clearly."

I could make no sense of the image she was studying, and I wasn't sure I followed what she was saying, either. "But if it worked that way, you'd think we'd see more unusual phenomena. People appearing or disappearing suddenly, that kind of thing. But we don't."

Taera looked at me. "You wouldn't see that if the loops were large enough. It's like relativity. Einstein's physics predicts that the faster someone travels, the slower they age compared to a person traveling more slowly. Yet you don't see people who travel all around the Earth all the time aging more slowly than those who stay at home."

"But that's because the difference between traveling all over Earth and staying at home is miniscule, compared with the speed that the Earth travels in space."

"So Newtonian physics is a close enough approximation for most things that people do on Earth." She enlarged the hologram further, then rotated the image. Markers and arrows appeared, blinking on and off as the image rotated. "But it's still only an approximation—accurate only when you are working at a small enough scale. Time is like that. At a small enough scale, linearity is a good approximation."

"But at the scale we're talking about—the scale of a human lifespan—we can only go forward in time and not back, and there's nothing anyone can do about it."

She arched an eyebrow. "Isn't there?"

"No!"

"Even in your dreams?"

I was suddenly on uncertain ground. "In your dreams . . . but that's different, Taera. That doesn't count."

Then that sad look was back in her eyes, and at that moment I wanted with all my heart to believe her. I wanted to go back in time and leave those thoughtless words unsaid. "I'm sorry," I said. "I didn't mean that *you* . . ."

"*I* can go back in time," she said angrily, "wherever and whenever and however I want, and you shall come with me because you already have. How do you think I already know you? And I'll tell you one other thing. Space is not as you imagine it either, so you'd better start thinking about going to Earth soon, perhaps today, and finding some settlers for this place, unless you want the explorers from Earth—the ones you already know about—to arrive here a hundred and fifty years ago and find Aran entirely uninhabited!"

I was shaken. I couldn't breathe. All I could say was "I need some air."

***

"What happened in there?" Cort asked. "You're pale. She take too much blood?"

I shook my head, still stumbling in the sunshine. Cort took my arm and offered me a drink of water from his bota.

"She says that if I don't lead a group of settlers from Earth to here—get this, four thousand some odd years ago—me! She says if I don't do that, there will be no inhabitants here ever, no you, no me, no one to chase away the explorers from Earth who came later to cut down the khena. Can you believe that?" I took a deep gulp of water as Cort looked over my shoulder.

I followed his eyes and saw Taera nod to him.

"Settlers from Earth to here? I was hoping you'd talk her out of that, with all your Starman science."

"Believe me, I tried, but her science trumps my science. She seems pretty sure of it."

He wrinkled his nose as if something smelled bad. "That's an unpleasant idea."

All at once, the idea didn't seem so bad to me. Cort had been making derogatory comments about starmen—*us* starmen, I now amended—for months. I smiled wickedly. "It would just serve you right if it turned out you're descended from us, too."

"I certainly hope it's not true," he said stiffly.

I relented. "Corodh-an-Aran, wake up! Don't worry. How can it be true?" I handed back the bota. "People don't zip back and forth to different places in time like . . . like bees in a meadow of flowers, do they?"

"No." He drew out the word. "Not normally."

Taera smiled at me with mock innocence.

"Even if what she says is true, I still have no intention of returning to Earth to recruit a bunch of people to travel back in time and settle here. First of all, it would be impossible to convince anyone on Earth of this . . . crazy . . . story. And anyway, I'm not going back to Earth. At all. Not now, and not on the *Falcon* when it gets here."

"Hmm." Cort ran his fingers up and down his jaw thoughtfully. Both he and Taera were looking at me, and I didn't like it.

"Hey! Cut that out!" I turned to Taera. "You've got the wrong man for the job. You'd need a salesman type." I glared at both of them, and then I had an idea. "Like Corodh-an-Aran here, for example. He's the one dedicated to saving the planet, and he's much more the kind of personality you'll need."

"What?" Cort said.

I realized that I was digging myself into a hole, but I couldn't stop. "He's outgoing. Personable. Nice smile. Hey, maybe you're mistaken and he's really your Taerlin fellow, not me. We look a lot alike."

Now I'd really done it. Not only had I given up a chance to do something truly worthy of my father—assuming, of course, that this wasn't all just Taera's dream nonsense—but I'd also handed a woman I really wanted over to my brother.

Tears ran down Taera's cheeks. "I know you, Taerlin, and you are not . . ." Her voice broke, and she gestured toward Cort. ". . . him."

She seemed way more upset than my suggestion should have made her. I was sorry to have hurt her, but I was also relieved. I *wanted* to be Taerlin—for her. "All right," I said, my voice just a fraction too husky. "Don't cry, Taera." I touched her arm, held my breath, and—wiped a tear from her cheek.

She let me.

"And," Cort added heatedly, "I am not going to Earth. That's *your* world, brother, not mine." He glared at me. "Besides, as you know, Taera is not an ordinary person." He paused meaningfully until I dropped my hand and turned toward him.

"Your point being . . .?"

"We need to consider her suggestion carefully before either of us does anything. But meanwhile, if she wants a sample of my blood, I think I'll oblige her. Just in case."

Cort walked over to Taera. She took his hand, and they both disappeared together.

"No," I said to no one in particular, "she's definitely not an ordinary person."

Chapter Twelve

ARAN, YEARS 2467 AND BC 2041

MIKEL'S RECORDING, continued

"I don't like this any better than you do, but we both ought to consider the possibility that Taera is telling the truth."

Cort and I had eaten in an uncomfortable silence. Long after the sun had set and the stars lit the sky, we sat at our campfire awkwardly without speaking. The freshness of the air was tinged with an edge of sharp smoke from our fire. Cort's words seemed unnaturally loud against the sound of insects chirping in the trees, against the harmonies of the khena.

"Listen. If anyone can travel around instantaneously in space and time, it would be Taera. I believe that. But she can just find someone else to do her recruiting on Earth. Why me? I don't want to go back to Earth, Cort! I can't, not now." My hand wandered toward the crystal that still brought me the whynywir's symphonic conversations. "I want to stay here."

"And I don't want to be descended from . . . starmen. But you would come back, with others. And I would still be me. Besides, I'll be busy recruiting here, on Aran."

"What?"

"Think about it, Mikel. If everyone in that early settlement speaks only Standard, how would Arantu originate? And who would teach the people how to hunt, how to weave, how to build houses the way we do? Which plants are edible, and which are poison?"

"Yes, I suppose that'll be necessary, if we do this at all. If what she's saying is true. But what if she takes me to Earth and then I can't get back? What then? I'd be stuck there! I'd die, like our father, alone on Earth."

A wolf howled in the distance and was answered by others even farther away.

Cort looked off into the distance, as if the wolves had been calling him. "I wouldn't like to run that risk either, but if I had to do it for the survival of Aran, I would. Our father did."

That was a low blow. I'd been thinking about our father all day. I slapped my palm hard on my leg. "That's just the point, Corodh-an-Aran! If I knew it was for the survival of Aran, I would do it, too. But we don't know that! We don't know any of it. All we have is what Taera said, and she might be . . ." I shrugged elaborately. ". . . dreaming. She *is* an oneiromorph. I'd have to know for certain that Taera really can travel in time and space the way she said before I would even consider starting out on this crazy venture."

The wolves were barely audible now, and Cort's eyes lost focus as he listened. The breeze carried a sweet smell. I thought of night-blooming jessamine, and suddenly Earth didn't seem such a bad place to go back to.

I had just about decided that the conversation was over when he said, "Maybe she could prove it."

We argued into the night about what would constitute such proof, coming from a person who could make dreams real. What kind of illusions could be created by the same combination of dreaming and technology that created the oneiromorph? Taera seemed more than real, but I knew that she wasn't, not in the same sense Cort and I were. I had her word—and I had seen Aiana. Asking to witness something—the arrival of the first settlers, for example—wasn't sufficient proof. How could we know that what we saw was real? It could be a dream—like Taera herself.

Then Cort slapped my shoulder, and I jumped. "Mikel! The whynywir!"

"What about them?"

"Your crystal! Think about it. We can both talk with the whynywir, you especially. So if she takes us back in time here on Aran and we can talk with the whynywir, wouldn't that prove that her time travel is real?"

"Maybe she can fake the whynywir conversation somehow."

"I don't see how. Remember, when we were talking with each other that way the first time in her place, when you fell, Taera didn't hear us."

"Maybe she was only pretending she didn't hear us. Or maybe she just wasn't listening."

Cort gave me a squinty, sideways look. "You sure can be a hard person to convince. But how about this? You can listen in and participate in the whynywir consciousness. Mikel, you can listen to the khena. I think that if we went back in time and you heard that, you would know if it was real or not."

I considered his argument. I considered it for so long that Cort must have given up on me. I allowed myself the luxury of listening in on the stream of Aran's consciousness, the richly textured tapestry of the whynywir's many interlinked conversations. In the end, I couldn't imagine any technology that would create a convincing illusion of the whynywir. "I think you're right," I said.

Cort startled. "You do?"

"I do. But before any of us goes back to the time before there were humans on Aran, I think we ought to ask the whynywir's permission."

"They might not answer. They don't like humans intruding on them."

"If they don't answer, I'm not going. I need to know what they think of this idea before I'm willing to take it any further."

He considered. "Yes, that seems right. Ask."

Never since leaving the valley had I dared to intrude my own considerations into the great conversation. My heart pounded at the idea of initiating a conversation topic. I took a deep breath to calm it, and I spoke up. *Whynywir, my brothers, we are agreed that the human settlement on Aran has been a great benefit.*

For all the Corodh-an-Arans alone, responded one of them, and dialog had begun,

> *(all the human protectors of Aran)*
> *the human presence here has been good.*
> *Where we understand*
> *(contemplate) humans act.*
> *(Impetuous creatures!)*
> *((Necessary, truly.))*

If it were possible . . . Here I hesitated. *If it were possible that the human settlement here came from the present into the past, what message should we send back to the whynywir of that time, with no experience of humans, to prepare them?*

A ripple of delight at the question spread through the collective consciousness, and I shared it with a smile.

> *Young friend, do you remember so little? (think*
> *. . .)*
> *Those who go back must explain the danger*
> *(don't you remember?) for only humans can*
> *save us*
> *((from humans))*

It would be easy to make up a story, I said. *Why would the whynywir believe a human?*

They had no comprehension of the fundamental concept of making up a story, but they took seriously the fact that I had a concern.

Then you must show them, they replied.

> *You, yourself*
> *(and Corodh-an-Aran with you)*

I didn't say that I was . . . I started to argue, but thought better of it. *Yes*, I said.

The conversation had already flowed to other topics, and I was withdrawing from it to return to the present, to the nighttime campfire I shared with my brother, when the voices spoke again.

Remember, said the whynywir.

> *that you have already succeeded*
> *(remember, young friend.)*

"All right." My voice broke the quiet of the night, and Cort jumped.

"What?" he asked.

"All right. I'll go back and talk with the whynywir. But you have to come too."

"Me?"

"That's what they said. If Taera can take us, we'll go ask the permission of the earlier whynywir. And as one of Aran's caretakers, you are the best reason why they should grant it."

"And if Taera can't take us there?"

"Cort, if she can't take you and me back in time to talk with the whynywir, then how will any of us ever get any settlers from Earth to here?"

Midwinter snow swirled in the passes across the mountains that bordered the whynywir valley, but Taera didn't take us through the passes. Holding Cort's hand and mine, Taera led us into her strange, austere home of grey metal where the silence of the whynywir voices stabbed my mind like needles. Without pausing, she led us out through another wall, and the three of us were there. The journey had taken no more than five seconds.

A high, thin layer of clouds softened the sunlight. The air was dry and smelled of fallen leaves. In my sleeveless vest, I shivered; we had brought nothing to warm us against the cool weather. There were goosebumps on Cort's arms, too, but Taera in her thin dress seemed completely comfortable, as if she couldn't feel the cold.

I bent down and touched the grassy undergrowth. It was soft and cool, and the dew on it left my fingertips moist. It seemed real enough.

Hearing the familiar, densely woven dialog of the whynywir, I relaxed. Whether we were in the past or not, I couldn't tell. But beyond a doubt, we were on Aran. Cort took a few steps down the hill, pointing toward the sky. "Look!" Far in the east, barely visible against the clouds, six dark spots moved. The whynywir had sensed us and were coming to investigate. "We didn't wear white," Cort said.

"If we're in the past, that custom will mean nothing to these whynywir," I said, "and they won't harm us for the same reason the whynywir didn't harm me when you and I came here. They won't know what kind of creatures we are or whether we belong here on Aran."

"But if we're not in the past . . ."

I sighed. "Then either they will acknowledge you and me and let us live, or Taera will rescue us, or we'll have another lifetime to learn not to be so foolish."

Cort flashed a broad you-really-are-one-of-us grin at me. "I can't imagine it will be as good as this one."

I tuned into the voices of the whynywir. They were as rich as I remembered with the textures and resonances of hundreds of conversations, all concerned in one way or another with the wellbeing of Aran. As always, I was drawn to and fascinated by all of them, and by the musical chords of the khenaran that underlay everything. There was no mistaking the experience. For a moment, I floated in the total consciousness of the whynywir, and then I remembered why I was here. I forced myself to focus, to find the single conversation of the whynywir that approached us.

Not food, my brothers, they were saying.

(No) None like them have we seen
In all our travels, none there have been
(but what then?) ((All that moves is food))

We will see
(Soon now)

So it seemed we were unknown here. An illusion? Could Taera construct such an illusion, so complicated and so perfect?

But underneath, below, beyond the conversation of the whynywir, there was the song of the great trees. This, I was sure, she could not fake. It was the proof I had asked for. I had to believe Taera.

I could have stayed in that moment forever. The physical life of a whynywir is so satisfyingly simple. Fly. Eat. Raise families. Not much to it. But the mental life; that is something!

Greetings, whynywir, I said. An ordinary beginning.

Greetings, strangers. A polite response.

What manner of creature are you?
(Breakfast, perhaps?)

This mistaken impression had to be cleared up right away. *No, no, no, not breakfast, not at all. But we are friends of Aran, as you are.*

How could any be otherwise?

Indeed. How could they? But I knew that there were a billion people like Efrim on Earth, who would follow their orders without a qualm, even if it meant destroying a planet like Aran. And another billion like Charl, who would despoil the planet without a qualm if they thought they could profit by it. I knew only too well the history of my people's presence on Aran. And on Earth, come to that, where we maintained only the most fragile ecological balance.

It will be otherwise one day, I said. *There are people who do not respect Aran as you do, and they will arrive here in the future. They will wreak horrible destruction. We want to make sure that Aran as we know it will survive. This is Taera, who makes this possible, and my brother Corodh-an-Aran, whose commitment to Aran life after life you will know well in time, and I am . . .* I paused. Which name had meaning in this context? *. . . Taerlin, the one she has dreamed of.*

The whynywir were now large against the sky, clearly avian, their great white wings flapping as they approached.

> *The names are nothing, stranger*
> *(but we will know your story)*

"Have a seat," I said to Cort and Taera. I settled onto the cool grass. "This could take a while." To Cort I added, "Listen in, if you can. I might need your help." And then I began to describe to the whynywir the world we had left, Aran as we knew her.

Taera sat next to me and put her hand on mine. I looked at her in surprise, and she smiled her support, slightly squeezing my hand.

Cort perched onto a rock that jutted knee-height from the grass, one of many boulders that were the beginning of a rocky shoulder that ran up to the peaks behind us. But as the whynywir came closer, he moved to the grass beside Taera and me. One of the great birds flapped down to occupy the boulder that he had abandoned. Others settled nearby.

I was not even halfway through my tale when the whynywir interrupted me.

> *You are a strange creature.*
> *Truly does your mind plod so slowly*
> *(And your friends) ((the one even slower))*
> *(the other silent)*
> *along such a narrow path?*
> *(They say nothing?)*

We are humans, I said. *We don't share your breadth of conversation. Still, we have our uses. We will love Aran in our way, as you do. And we will take action when it is necessary.*

You will allow us to see for ourselves?
(We would be here until summer with these
long, slow explanations)
Your mind has all its answers . . .
((Why do you not simply
(open your mind and) let us in?))

I . . .? Open my mind to the whynywir? They would find out how I got the blue crystal! What would they think of us humans? Of me? I swallowed and turned toward Cort. "Did you hear that? What do you think I should do?"

He shrugged. "I heard enough of it. Myself, I would do whatever the whynywir ask. But I am Corodh-an-Aran; obeying the whynywir is part of my commitment. But you . . . I can't advise you. I don't communicate with them the way you do, and I don't know the risks."

Taera shook her head and said nothing; she hadn't heard the comversation. The sun brightened behind a thin spot in the clouds. The world was silent, waiting, it seemed, for me.

Could I do less than Cort would? Less than my father would?

All right, I said.

In an instant, the world behind my eyes exploded. I might have screamed. I might have clutched at my head as if it, too, would explode with the sheer size and power of the force that had wedged its way into my mind. I know I collapsed to the ground, no longer able to hold my body upright, and that Taera held me. The whynywir pushed my own consciousness aside, a puny thing of no particular interest, as they sifted through my thoughts and memories. I was helpless, completely aware but unable to control or alter the merciless ravaging of the total experience of my life.

I couldn't even whisper a thought, the one thought that I might have wanted to say—*Stop!* The stream of my thoughts was no longer my own.

It is hard to describe the experience except by analogy. Imagine that you lived in a house that you loved, had lived there for a long time and collected many mementos of your experiences, some quite valuable, others worthless to anyone but yourself, that you had stored lovingly and carefully on your shelves and in your drawers and in the closets of your house. Now imagine that a gang of ruffians broke into your house and, finding you there, bound and gagged you, leaving you tied down, able only to watch helplessly and soundlessly. They tear open all your drawers, rummage through all your closets and shelves, throw the contents here and there on the floor as they examine everything that is yours. They leave every room in your house a shambles. They are not thieves. They take nothing, but they examine everything, touching, fingering, tasting all your private belongings, your special things, asking no permission, offering no thanks, commenting on the evidence of your life, judging you and finding you lacking.

Except, of course, that the whynywir had asked, and I had given my permission, little imagining what the experience would be like. I know that the whynywir never meant to harm me. I think they were totally unaware of their brutality. To them, it was a simple search for information that was unavailable by other means.

And they found the information they wanted.

Of course, they learned right at the beginning that I was a murderer of whynywir. The fact was in the forefront of my consciousness, the more so because I would have given anything to hide it. They learned of my deed and my remorse and the future whynywir's forgiveness, even acceptance. Unconcerned with either forgiving or blaming me, these earlier whynywir simply added the facts and memories to their understanding of what humans are.

Following the thread of my shame, as if it burned and beckoned them, the whynywir learned of the colonization of Aran by explorers from Earth. They learned how we murdered the spirits of the khena for wealth, blind and uninterested in the delicate web that bound the life of Aran together. And my own spirit writhed in the spotlight of that merciless examination. For I too was a member of this race of murderers of trees. I faced the truth of who I was in the cold assessment of the whynywir.

Inevitably, the facts of the colonization of New Richmund led to Corodh-an-Aran. My brother who had risked his life to help Aran rid herself of the humans who pillaged her.

My father, who sacrificed himself trying to help Aran. My father, whose spirit the whynywir assumed, from the circumstances of his death and my birth, to be the same as my own. The same . . .? No, my life was mine, not his! I struggled against the whynywir's conclusion, but my thoughts were not my own, and my feelings were beneath the whynywir's notice.

The whynywir poked and prodded deeply. They unburied memories that I carried from the future whynywir, memories I was not even conscious I retained. Memories of all the Corodh-an-Arans from the time of the first arrival of the humans.

The pain of holding onto consciousness against the merciless beating of my thoughts was too much. I slipped into insensibility, and I slept.

I dreamed dreams troubled at first with fragments of thoughts and memories from the whynywir's examination of my mind. But Taera still held me, and perhaps she was able to do something to adjust the crystal or to ease my mind so that I no longer perceived these fragments so strongly.

For I know that I dreamed I was walking, not in the whynywir valley but in the meadow where I had first seen Taera. Ahead of me was what I knew to be the outside wall of the place where Taera lived. Though in waking life, the inside of her place has always been rectilinear and the outside invisible, in my dream the outside wall was a shiny metal sphere, reflecting back the sun so brightly that I had to squint. At first, I was surprised to see it. I told myself that I shouldn't be surprised; this was a dream. And so, for the first time that I remember, I knew within a dream that I was dreaming. I walked around the sphere. There were no doors, but I didn't expect any. Taera had always walked through the wall. I put my hand against the wall. It felt solid, but I reminded myself that this was a dream, where anything was possible. I pushed. My arm went through the wall as if it weren't there, and I followed right behind.

I was in the room with Taera's computer consoles. No one else was there, but the room was as I remembered it. I laughed, giddy with the power of freedom from physical laws. My next thought was that I wanted to see Aiana. I remembered the spot where Taera had led me through the wall from her. I went over there and walked through the wall.

It was the same room. The same dimensions. The same bare walls on all sides. The same light illuminating the center of the room where Aiana ought to be. But Aiana wasn't there. I reached my hand into the light, half expecting, half hoping that the hologram might appear, but nothing happened. When the light hit my hand, a voice asked, "Are you looking for something?"

It was Taera's voice, but the person who spoke wasn't Taera. Her eyes were green, but there was brown and gold in them, too, a shade more hazel than Taera's brilliant emerald eyes. Her long red curls were tangled. When she brushed aside a strand that had fallen into her eyes, I could see freckles banding across her nose and scattering onto her cheeks. I drew in a sharp breath of disbelief. Then I remembered that I was dreaming, and I smiled. "You're awake."

"In your dream."

"I'm glad."

"Are you?"

I thought I was. But . . . "Where's Taera?"

"You're dreaming that I'm awake, and so she and I are one."

"Then I like it better when I'm the dreamer, dreaming of you." Because I knew it was just a dream I found the nerve to say, "Someday, I'm going to wake you. I want to be with you, together, my waking self and yours."

She shook her head and looked away. "There's too much to do," she said. "Let's not get distracted." Her eyes were bright with tears that didn't fall. It was a dream, but when Aiana caught my hand, her hand was warm and solid on mine. "Don't wake. Listen to me. We have to get through this. You must lead the settlers to Aran."

I nodded.

"Taera will help you. I am no use to you awake."

I nodded again. Dreaming, I understood this perfectly.

"And there are other things to do as well, before we can even think about being together. Do you understand?"

Dumbly, I nodded yet again.

Aiana looked at me in an affectionate way with an overtone of something I couldn't read. Kindness? Pity? "No, you don't. But you accept it. You'll understand when you wake up. Remember this dream. Remember me."

I was almost in a trance, almost ready to let the dream fade, but I thought of Taera helping me, and I cried, "Wait! I have to show you where to take me . . . on Earth . . . so that Taera will know." Not that I knew, myself.

Aiana laughed, a happy sound like a clear mountain stream rushing over the rocks. "She already knows. It is forever the same place. Your room in your mother's house."

My room! Of course my mother would welcome me, but the room was a place for a child—not for the man who would save a planet, the man I had to become. "I'm not sure . . ."

"Start there. Afterwards, you will know what you have to do."

Then Aiana reached out and touched my cheek, an electric tingle of a touch. I stroked her soft hair and cupped my hand around the back of her head. I leaned forward to kiss her.

Someone shook me. Cort. "Wake up, Mikel. Wake up! The whynywir are gone, and we have a lot to do."

"Go away."

But he persisted. "Wake up, Mikel."

"Go away! I said go away!" But I was awake, and near to tears. I hit his arm where he touched me and then punched wildly at him. He blocked my blows, which came to nothing in any case, a puzzled look in his eyes. The puzzlement was echoed on the face of Taera, who stood behind him.

I gave up. "Sorry," I said. "I was dreaming."

Chapter Thirteen

EARTH, YEAR 3223

"There has been a significant spike in your energy usage this month, Miss Kim." Zhou began the meeting without preamble, smalltalk, or the obligatory status update. She was leaning back in her seat, arms folded across her chest, ignoring the agenda Aiana had distributed.

Aiana swallowed nervously and pushed a strand of her hair back behind her ear. She glanced at Smithjon, who raised an eyebrow but said nothing. The entire committee seemed frozen in time, waiting for her to speak.

"Er . . . yes." Something tickled in her throat, and she cleared it. "Yes, I hadn't thought about it, but this is the first time I've done more than just create the oneiromorph. I transported a couple of people a few thousand years back in time."

The silence in the room was unsettling.

"But only for an hour or two," she added. "And then back again."

"Perhaps you are unaware, young lady, how close an eye Campus Operations keeps on the department's energy budget?"

"But the 'port has a built-in generator!"

"The 'port is equipped with only a low-output generator. It is barely adequate to the energy requirements of the oneiromorphic transformation itself. The cost is budgeted in your grant. We do not have enough budget for transporting matter. There was a momentary brown-out on campus. Certain delicate scientific equipment malfunctioned. Complicated experiments in the physics department will have to be started over. Where do you think the additional energy for all this is going to come from? The 'port will require a larger generator. And who do you think will pay for it?'

They were all watching her now, even Smithjon. Their expressions, though, she noted with surprise, were not hostile. They seemed to be waiting . . . for what?

All at once she knew. They wanted more money from the foundation. Quite a bit more, from the sound of it. Well, she was not going to take advantage of her relationship with Uncle Mark any more, not even for this. The project would have to stand on its own merits.

She folded her arms across her chest, matching Zhou's posture. "We discussed the need to bring Taerlin back to Earth, the unlikelihood that he would go on his own. We all agreed that we would engage him through a project involving the initial settlement of New Richmund. I have gone ahead and implemented that plan, and I have been successful. Taerlin is now committed to returning to Earth. However, it was necessary to take him and his brother back to an earlier time on New Richmund to . . . to check things out there for themselves. It was an approved part of the existing project."

"You have media of this?" Salvatore asked.

"No, Reverend Guide. I'm sorry. But we were outside of the 'port almost the whole time."

Salvatore tore his eyes from the holo player with difficulty. "Then perhaps you might tell us what he might have found there, that helped convince him to return to Earth, at such a tremendous price."

The lock of hair seemed to have escaped again, and Aiana pushed it back behind her ear. "He wanted to talk with the whynywir of that earlier time. To ask permission. I'm sure he didn't know about the energy usage because to be honest, I never thought about it myself."

"Well, you had better start thinking about it, Miss Kim." Zhou's voice was steel. She stood. "There is no energy budget on this project for moving people around from one place and time to another."

"Just a minute." Smithjon stood, facing Zhou. He towered over her. "We all agreed that allowing Taerlin to move settlers to Aran was part of the project. Acquiring the larger generator is a reasonable and necessary expense to that end. Therefore, it's up to the department to ensure that the budget is made available."

Zhou fisted her hands on her hips and jutted her jaw aggressively toward Smithjon, completely uncowed by his height. "If she is going to start moving numbers of people around, she will need a *much* larger generator. She will need a grant to pay for it."

"Wait," Salvatore said. "This is Taerlin we're talking about here. Perhaps he can move anyone he wants to move by himself, without our help."

Aiana blushed. "No, Reverend Guide. I'm sure he'll manage the Blessed Ascension by himself, but for the part about settling New Richmund, he'll need our help. At this point, he's . . . um, he's counting on it."

"In that case," Smithjon said, "the university will have to rethink its priorities. It seems to me we have a commitment that must be met."

Zhou planted her hands on the table and put her weight on her arms, leaning so close to Smithjon that he took an involuntary step back. "It seems to me," she said, "that the College of Arts and Sciences does not have enough energy in its entire budget to settle a whole planet. It seems to me that our candidate knows how to get a grant for the larger generator that will be required."

Aiana looked from one to the other, astonished at the strength of Smithjon's opposition to Zhou, glad for his support. If he could stand up to Zhou like that, then she could, too. It was time the committee approved her project on its own merits, and not just in order to take advantage of her financial connections. "I'm not going to ask my Uncle Mark for any more special favors," she said. "The foundation has already set me up with an oneiroport that will belong to the university when my research is done. I'm grateful to them, and you should be, too." She folded her arms across her chest. "I'll give up the research before I go back to them for more."

Her face felt too warm, and her voice came out a shade too high. She hoped they couldn't tell she was lying. Taerlin was counting on her, and she would do whatever was necessary not to let him down. But Zhou didn't have to know that.

Smithjon put a placating hand on Aiana's arm, but his eyes never left Zhou's. "Why don't we do it this way. The university will go to the foundation and request an extension of funding for this project. We—and not Miss Kim—will accept responsibility for the overrun. I believe the project has become significant enough that the foundation will support the added energy costs. And," he said, leaning back and pausing for effect, "of course they know whose project this is, and if that has some influence in our favor, so much the better."

"Very well," Zhou said, her jaw set tight. "I'll prepare the necessary forms." She gathered her papers and her comm and left the room without asking for the status update.

Aiana took a deep breath, let it out, and relaxed. "Thanks, Raj."

Vikram dallied until the other members of the committee departed, ostentatiously occupying himself with something on his comm, and then with gathering papers that up until today he had never allowed to become disorderly. "You believe this is the same man, don't you?" he asked. His dark eyes watched her from under a thatch of black hair so thick and unruly it might have hidden colonies of birds, an entire endangered species.

Aiana's breath caught in her throat. Of course it was Taerlin, the Taerlin from Earth. But Vikram was usually quiet in her committee meetings, and she'd never taken a class with him. She wasn't sure how to answer. She didn't know how religious he was. "Why?" she asked.

"I would, in your shoes," Vikram said. "Occam's Razor, as you've said. The simplest explanation is usually the correct one."

"Yes." Also, there were the stories the women of Aran had told her, stories of love and loss; and they seemed to fit with the way that she and Taerlin looked at each other that instant on the holo. The feelings, to be honest, she was already developing for him. But there was no sense in complicating an answer he'd already agreed with.

"The Reverend Guide has warned you to be careful, and if I were in your shoes, I would listen to him. Especially now that you are about to start working with Taerlin in transporting people."

"Unfortunately, the Reverend Guide's warning was so obscure I don't know what to make of it. Careful, how?"

"Young lady, I don't know how closely you have studied the history of the last century and the two before that, but the temple then was finding ways to . . . dispose of people who threatened its authority." He twisted the words 'dispose of' into something sinister.

"Nothing was ever substantiated," Smithjon said.

Vikram turned sharp eyes to his colleague. "Not then it wasn't, no. But recently, travelers have seen . . . things that they will never report openly, not even now."

"But why shouldn't they report it?" Aiana asked. "If it's true, that kind of revelation would make a stunning thesis."

Vikram looked at her, his dark eyes as penetrating as knives. "Come, Miss Kim. Surely you know that the temple even now has considerable control over what historical research may be published. You must start considering what you will say, and how you will say it." Vikram pocketed his comm. He gathered his papers, nodded at Smithjon, and left the room.

Aiana stared at where Vikram had been sitting, shaking her head. "If I can't publish this, then what do I have? Nothing!"

"Oh, it's not that bad. You could still return to your original research topic."

She shrugged, despondent. "No, I can't go back to that."

"Then you could do a thesis on the origins of human settlement on New Richmund."

"That's not my area."

"Come, Aiana. Let's go now. Nothing has happened yet. Just keep doing your research, and we'll deal with this one step at a time."

She stood and followed Smithjon from the room. One step at a time was good advice, of course, but she intended to complete this project. And publish it.

Chapter Fourteen

EARTH, YEAR 2467

MIKEL'S RECORDING, continued

"All my life I've wanted to do something that would be worthy of my father," I said to Taera. "Something that would have made him proud of me. I thought it might be some accomplishment in xenology that would advance our understanding of other peoples and help us to live as good citizens in the galaxy."

Taera inclined her head in acknowledgment, her green eyes sparkling as if with some great secret. "A worthy goal."

A few moments earlier, Taera and I had walked hand in hand through one of her liquid walls, and we now stood in my boyhood room in my mother's house on Earth. I hadn't lived here since before university, but the room was exactly the way I remembered it—small, with light blue walls and a single wide window, its blinds open. Below the window, my desk held my old tablet, several books, and a basket of pens, pencils, scissors, and a ruler, all ready for a few hours of homework. Opposite, the bed was neatly made, a few brightly colored pillows lying atop its dark blue bedspread.

Sunlight patterned the walls, floor, and bed, and captured a few dancing motes in the air. Except for the neatness of the room, I might never have grown up and left. The air smelled stale. I was uncomfortable here, as if I had taken a step back into childhood, as if this whole project were some kind of dream.

I shook my head to clear it. I studied my own face in the mirror, and my father's face studied me back, his golden eyes, his dark hair atangle with bits of feather and bone and tied with rawhide, the way he looked when he first came to Earth and made the news. The way I looked now.

"It was the most I could hope for," I said, "but it wasn't enough. In my heart of hearts, I always felt that no matter how well I did as a xenologist I would still fall far short of my father, the man who saved his planet. I felt I'd always be a midget in the giant's shadow."

Taera touched my arm, and our eyes met in the mirror. "That's not true, Taerlin. What you are about to do—"

I turned toward her and spoke with fervor. "Yes, that's different, what I'm about to do. If I can do it."

"But of course you can. And will." Her eyes glowed with that air of a special secret, and I realized that it was because she knew the future—or was it the past?—as I did not. She radiated such confidence that I had to smile, just a little, despite my doubts.

"*If* I can do this, it will truly be an accomplishment worthy of my father. A matching set, his and mine." My throat tightened. I ached to make a success of this, needed to—but could I? I was a scientist, not a demagogue or a prophet to persuade people to abandon their old lives and follow me. "That would mean a great deal to me."

Taera touched my hand. "Don't worry," she said. "This has already worked out fine."

I had the sudden idea that perhaps Taera liked touching me as much as I liked touching her. I took hold of her hand and held it.

And she held mine.

I wasn't at all sure that things would work out the way she thought. True, the whynywir had agreed to human colonization and had even volunteered—insisted, actually—to control the distribution of the crystals that Taera would provide. And Cort had begun the process of recruiting from what I thought of as the present time on Aran—a necessity, if the culture and language of Aran as we knew it were going to take hold from the beginning.

But could I succeed in recruiting on Earth? I had no idea what to do except that I might begin by contacting Lennard. I wasn't the kind of outgoing hail-fellow-well-met person that I thought of as a salesman. Other people schmoozed and partied; me, I hit the books or wandered the woods alone. I could so easily fail in my part of the enterprise.

The voices in my head were silent, the beautiful conversations of the whynywir that had become a part of me. While I was on Earth, those voices would provide me no consolation, no comfort. No back-up plan.

Well, they probably wouldn't have done that, even on Aran.

"Thanks." I met Taera's eyes in the mirror, and for some reason her eyes held an apology. I took a deep breath. "I guess we better get started. The first thing will be to comm my mother and let her know I'm here. She'll probably come home right away. Having me here so suddenly—and with you—will be enough of a shock, without my looking like . . . this." Like my father.

"You," Taera said. "*You* get started. I must go. I need to . . ." She paused. ". . . rest. I can't stay out in the world for long, like this." She gestured with her hand from her own head to her feet, my lovely oneiromorph. "It takes too much energy."

All my uncertainties got the better of me. I took her hand again. "Taera, don't go! The whynywir are silent here, and Cort's still back on Aran. I need you. I need your support."

She shook her head. "No, you don't need me now. But I will be here when you do. I promise." With the hand I was no longer holding tightly, she ran her fingers down the side of my cheek, waking nerve endings that seemed to run deep into my gut and out through my toes. She held my eyes with a look of such longing and sorrow that I wanted to hold her and protect her—against what, I couldn't imagine.

What I wanted was to kiss her.

And I did, very lightly on the lips.

She returned the kiss, lightly, gently, as sweetly as a whisper.

Then she drew back. "I shouldn't." But it was a half-hearted protest that lasted only a moment. Then she sighed, pulled me close, and kissed me hard. The shock of it, the joy, the wildness of it surged through my body. This was the kind of kiss I'd dreamed of, but never imagined actually happening. Oh, sweet heaven, thinking back on that moment, I still wish it had never ended.

But good as Taera felt in my arms, kissing me, something was not right. There was Aiana to consider.

Reluctantly, I pulled back and took a moment to calm my breathing. The desire I still felt was reflected in her large, dark pupils. It took all my strength to return to the business at hand. I asked, "How will you know when?"

"I'll come back in one week, just so that you don't worry." She gave me a slippery sideways look, her eyes not meeting mine. "Remember: I know when I will be here because all of it has already happened." What wasn't she saying?

"All of what, Taera?"

Still avoiding my eyes, she shook her head, a slight unconscious movement, and bit her lip. "I have to go now."

"No, wait! Suppose I'm successful and manage to recruit some people—"

"Of course you will."

"Then where do I take them? And when?"

"You tell me," she said.

I thought. "There's a park just down the street. In the center of it is a statue of Rodrigo Milan with his starship." Rodrigo Milan captained the first starship from Earth to land on another planet a century or two ago. "It's pretty distinctive. I can tell people to meet there, and they'll know where to go. Can we meet there in . . . say, two weeks?"

"Two weeks," she agreed. "In the park."

"I don't know if I'll have anyone yet, but maybe I'll at least have an idea how it's going."

Taera said nothing. She just smiled and touched my cheek. And then she turned, took a step, and disappeared.

The room suddenly felt cold, and I shivered.

I found some jeans and a denim shirt in my closet, right where I'd left them years ago, and set to combing the tangles out of my hair. I had to cut some of it, and I am not a skilled hairdresser. In the end, my hair was shaggy and uneven, but it was also clean and untangled—not a bad compromise.

To my mother's credit, she took my sudden appearance well. She was surprised, of course. Her eyes wide, a quaver in her voice, she asked, "Mikel?" as if she weren't quite sure whether the apparition in front of her would talk.

But talk, I did. "Mom!" I was suddenly overwhelmed with how much I'd missed her, and I caught her up in a hug that she returned strongly.

I told my mother why I had returned, the whole long story. I thought she might still know someone from the old days when we were demonstrating against settlement on New Richmund. It seemed a good place to begin.

But my mother had only one name for me. From her room, she took an old book and, pressed within its pages, found a yellowed calling card. "Aston Anisson," it announced. No profession was indicated.

The name was unfamiliar. "Who is this?"

"The man whose house your father lived in," she said. "I met him once. I think he's rich—at least, it's a fine house. He gave me this card and told me to call if I ever needed anything. I kept the card. I've never called him, but you might want to."

I did. I called within the hour, but Aston Anisson was not at home. I made an appointment to stop by the following afternoon. I called Lennard, too, but got his voicemail. I left a message but didn't want to say too much on his machine. I wasn't ready to alert the authorities of my return; I'd enlisted for a two-year stint in the merchant fleet, and they'd probably have some new assignment for me if they knew I was back. I left only my first name on the machine and said that I would stop by tomorrow morning early to explain everything.

Lennard was famous enough to have acquired a personal secretary. The man opened the door when I rang the bell the next morning. He looked me up and down with disdain and said, "We're not taking any solicitations."

I made a mental note to buy a new pair of jeans and maybe cut my hair a little shorter. Rudeness wasn't going to help, though I was sorely tempted. "It's a personal matter. I called yesterday and left a message."

"Yes. I receive all the professor's messages. Be sure I shall pass yours along to the professor. He is not at home. Good day."

"When will he be back?"

"Later," said the secretary.

"He'll want to see me."

The man gave me a look that indicated his disbelief of that statement.

Despite my resolve to be polite, I raised my voice. "Tell him that Mikel was here. Mikel Pelerin. Tell him that I have to see him."

"Indeed. Now, good day."

"I'll wait outside," I added on impulse.

A flicker of fright passed across the man's face. It was brief, but there was no mistaking it. I gave him my most wicked smile. "All day, if need be."

"He won't be home today at all," said the secretary. His eyes flicked rapidly from one side of me to the other, as if he were hoping for a rescuer. Or maybe an escape route.

I was by now certain he was lying. "Lennard!" I shouted.

"Who is it, Maris?" came a muffled voice from deep within Lennard's apartment.

"No one, sir!" the secretary replied in a loud voice, glaring at me. "He's a very busy man," he added for my benefit.

"It's me—Mikel!" I shouted. "Lennard, it's important!"

"I'll be right there," was the distant response.

"Please come in," hissed the secretary.

This was a great improvement. I walked into the foyer of the apartment, and he closed the door behind me. He did not, however, offer me a seat in the sitting room.

A moment later, the xenologist himself came into the foyer, still wiping his mouth with a napkin. His eyes widened when he saw me. "Mikel? What are you doing here? Why aren't you on Aran?" Then, with a "Thank you, Maris," and "Please bring some tea into the sitting room," Lennard dismissed the secretary, who glared at me over his shoulder as he left the room.

Lennard patted my shoulder twice, as if checking whether I was real. He shook his head. Then he looped his arm through mine, and led me into the apartment. The sitting room was decorated in shades of blue and green, with several ornately patterned silk sofas and chairs, as well as a number of small tables. A mirror behind the largest couch reflected our images back to us—the middle-aged professor still dressed in pajamas and a silk robe, and his young barbarian guest. Lennard steered me toward one of the sofas and took a chair nearby. "That's better," he said.

"Your secretary is not very friendly."

"He's doing his job. What with the book and everything, we receive a lot of visitors I don't have time for. I'd never get anything done if I entertained them all. But you! Mikel, how can you possibly be here? I know for a fact that the *Falcon* isn't leaving for another year to pick you up; I was going to be on it. Are you all right? Is Cort? You must tell me everything."

Given an eager audience and permission to talk, I didn't know where to begin. "It's complicated."

"Tell me how you got here," Lennard said. Then, "How's Cort? He was so reluctant to go to the whynywir. You did go there, didn't you? Is he all right?" He had more questions than I had places to begin.

I tried my best to radiate assurance in my smile. "Cort's fine," I told him. "He really was prepared to die at the hands—uh, the mouths, I guess—of the whynywir. And he almost did, too. He was right about so much."

"That's Cort." Lennard returned the smile. "Tell me about the whynywir, then. I'm terribly jealous, you know."

"Are you? You might still have a chance to meet the whynywir if you want. I wouldn't recommend it, though."

The corners of Lennard's eyes folded into a thousand wrinkles, and he rumbled with laughter so hearty he had to hold his sides. "Now you sound just like Cort. But you don't seem that much worse for the wear—and look! You have a crystal! Do those things really work? As for me—don't tempt me with the impossible. I have leave to be on the *Falcon*, but any kind of extended expedition to New Richmund is out of the picture for me, I'm afraid."

Which brought us very nicely to the heart of the reason I'd come. I leaned forward, intent on my point. "Perhaps not to New Richmund," I said, "but Aran is wide open for settlement, and I need your help."

Lennard sat back in his seat and stroked his chin, staring thoughtfully at me while Maris, still scowling, came into the room carrying a tea service. Lennard waited silently until his secretary left, then said quietly, "You know that it's illegal to establish a presence on New Richmund."

"On New Richmund, yes! But I'm talking about a world not yet inhabited by humans. A world—let us say, a world very much like Aran must have been before humans ever arrived. There's no law against that, is there?"

Lennard carefully poured tea into a cup for himself and one for me. Then he added sugar and milk to his own, shaking his head. "I don't know, Mikel. If I didn't know you, I would doubt your sanity. But as it is . . . Perhaps you'd better tell me the whole story slowly and from the beginning. It involves the whynywir, doesn't it?"

"Yes, in a way. But there's more to it." For the next hour and a half, I told Lennard everything that had happened to me on Aran, leaving nothing out. I hesitated when I came the murder I committed. My face heated with shame and my voice quavered with sorrow for the old one I'd killed. But what I had to tell him wouldn't have made sense without it. For a part of me is whynywir as truly as any fact of my life, and I needed Lennard to understand that my commitment to this enterprise was far more than academic.

I didn't tell him everything. I left out my feelings about Aiana and Taera. Those feelings were impossible to sort out, and I didn't see how they were relevant to the story at hand.

"I can't join you," he said after I was done. He shook his head, his lips pressed thinly together. "When I first met Lela

I wanted nothing more than to stay on Aran and live in her village." He sighed. "That volcano—the eruption and the departure of the last starship—ended that dream, and now, I'm afraid, it's too late."

"That's all right, Lennard," I said. "You don't have to join us. Do what's best for you."

"You said that Cort is recruiting on Aran. Do you think he might get to Lela's village?"

"He intends to. He has family there, too, you know."

"Yes. Yes, of course. I've been appointed ambassador to New Washington. I'll be going there at the end of this semester in a month or so. Except for my one last trip to pick you up—which I guess now I'm not going to make—that's where I'm going to be for quite some time."

"Lennard, that's great! It's a wonderful job!" This was probably an understatement. Appointment as ambassador from United Earth to any of the nine colonized worlds was as prestigious a position as a member of the cabinet or the president's personal staff. And, of the nine colonized worlds, only New Washington and New Bern were inhabited by alien civilizations. For a xenologist, appointment to one of these was particularly exciting since it was among the only positions left where actual ongoing contact with an alien civilization was possible.

"Do you think she'll come?"

"Who, Lela?"

He nodded.

"Cort thinks there's a good chance. He thinks the enterprise might appeal to her."

"Yes, I think it would." Lennard fell silent, thinking. Then he asked, "What kind of people are you looking for, Mikel?"

"Ideally, I think a background in xenology would be helpful. I'd like them to know Arantu and to know something about Aran. Maybe if they'd just read your book." I sighed. "The truth is, Lennard, I'll take whoever I can get. I just need people. The more, the better."

"I really can't come," he said. "I've already committed to the UE president and the legislature on this ambassadorship."

"I understand. I wouldn't ask you to. It's a great job."

"No," he said. "It's a lousy job. Of course, there are the Washingtonians to interact with, but the job itself is mostly going to be dinners and receptions and conveying messages between the United Earth and the Washingtonian governments. Terribly boring, really. But what's a xenologist to do these days, with all the inhabited planets off limits?"

I adjusted my response. "I'm sorry to hear that. But it seems to me that acting as an ambassador might be a good use of your skills."

Lennard sighed. "It's quite an honor, of course."

"Yes, of course it is."

He fidgeted with the empty teacup he still held. "Mikel, how would you like to lecture to my class tomorrow morning?"

"Your class at Harvard? Tomorrow?" I was developing a definite echo. "About what?"

"About Aran, of course." His eyes sparkled with mischief, and a smile tickled his lips. "About the whynywir. And who knows . . . You might find what you're looking for there."

Chapter Fifteen

EARTH, YEAR 2467

MIKEL'S RECORDING, continued

My mother was right: Aston Annison lived in a fine house. It was in an older neighborhood not far from the city's theatre district. The houses in that neighborhood were large and free-standing—a sign of wealth in the cities, where most of the people—even Lennard, who enjoyed a degree of fame and distinction—lived in townhouses or apartments. On Aston's block, the street curved around a lovely park whose green grass was covered with the red and gold early-autumn leaves from the stately old maples that shaded it.

The classical facade of Aston's house was made of white marble that had become blackened from the city's smog; repeated cleanings had left the black only in the corners and edges of the house's ornamentation, highlighting the beauty of its carved detailing.

This was where my father had lived.

An older man with wispy white hair answered the bell, and I introduced myself to him. "Come in," he said. He smiled, and his face etched into a hundred happy wrinkles.

"Aston has been looking forward to your visit." Thinking of Lennard's overprotective secretary, I returned this man's smile. But I didn't know whether the difference was due to the personalities of the various people, to Lennard's fame, or to the fact that I had an appointment here whereas I had just shown up on Lennard's doorstep.

I was led into a room that must have been a library. Shelves of books lined most of the walls from a waist-high wainscoting up to the tall ceiling. A large fireplace dominated the far wall, and, despite the afternoon sunshine that poured into the room's wide windows, a fire blazed in the fireplace. If I ever had a house of my own, I'd want it to have a room just like this one.

"Good day, young man."

I jumped. I hadn't noticed the man in the wheelchair in a far corner of the room. A blue blanket was wrapped over his legs. He held a brandy snifter in one hand; the other hand rested on an open book in his lap. He was an older man with receding, sandy hair. Smile lines traced a pattern from the corners of his sparkling deep blue eyes all the way to his hairline, and he was smiling as if it were the natural configuration of his features. "I'm Aston," he continued. "I'm most happy to have the chance to meet you in this lifetime, as your father might have said. Which, for me, is likely to be the only one."

"Perhaps not," I replied.

He laughed like he was born to laughter. "I guess I'll find out soon enough, now. But I'm sure you didn't stop by just to bring some chance pleasure into the life of an old man you've never met."

"No, I . . ." I flushed and looked down. "That is, I'd like to think I would have, if I'd known."

Again, Aston laughed. "But of course you didn't, and I'm not blaming you. Still, I've watched you growing up. I know a bit about you, though I confess that I thought you were still on New Richmund. Have a seat, will you? I can't rise to greet you, so you'll have to come down to my level. Now, tell me what you'd like to drink, and I'll have some brought in."

"Water, thanks." I sat in a chair near his. "It seems you know a lot more about me than I do about you."

"I've made a point of it, young man," Aston said. "Your father's company meant a lot to me while he was here, and I know he wouldn't have wanted you to have need of anything. Though of course, your mother seems to have done just fine without the interference of a meddling old man. So perhaps it was just my idle curiosity. You know, you're the exact image of him. I've seen holos of you, of course, but now that I see you in person . . . it might almost have been him walking in the door again."

The idea of looking like my father pleased me. "Really?"

"Yes, really. Do you have any idea what your father went through?"

"I've watched all the news holos."

"The news holos. Yes. 'The savage who came to save his world.' It was a joke, you know, because no one believed New Richmund was in any kind of danger. But few people had ever seen a real savage close up. The news holos made Cort-Naran famous, and so the famous sought him out. At first it was the avant-garde, the artists and musicians. But through them, he was introduced to others—scientists, the wealthy, politicians. No one took his message seriously back then. Well, a few of us did, but not many."

"No one wanted to give up harvesting the khena."

"Yes. The trees. I wish I could have seen them, those trees your father loved. I've seen the wood, of course, and read about its properties: stronger than steel, dulling even the diamond blades used to harvest it, as lightweight as it is strong. Growing shoots as flexible and strong as cables, yadda yadda. All of that, and beautiful too. You've seen it?"

I held up my hand, the khena ring flashing on my middle finger.

Aston sighed wistfully. "Like rainbows in amber. Living opals. It's beautiful. You know your father believed that the trees lodged the spirits of his ancestors, and to harvest the trees was to kill the spirits within. He was so earnest about it that people wanted to laugh, but so sad that they tried to be polite, at least in his presence. People loved the man but never seriously considered his cause. The idea of tree-spirits was, of course, preposterous."

"It's not preposterous in the least!"

"Ah. The father's son." Aston smiled, as if to take the sting out of his words, and then he added, "Good for you." His tone of voice was so warm that I knew he meant no offense. "It was different after he died. With his last breath, your father pleaded for his home world, and his death made him a hero and a martyr. While no one took his pleas seriously during his lifetime, after his death the non-intervention movement grew. You may be old enough to remember some of the rallies. I believe your mother took you."

"Yes. We went to a lot of rallies till I was around ten. Lennard Sirinin had returned by then, and everyone was reading his book."

"The volcano that destroyed the base forced everyone there to return to Earth. After that, New Richmund fell under the law that forbade colonization of already populated worlds. Or at least it became politically untenable to interpret that law any other way. The Legislature unanimously passed an amendment to the non-intervention law specifically removing New Richmund from the grandfathered list, and so your father's deepest wish was posthumously granted. And those of us who had been his friends during his brief sojourn here rejoiced."

"I'm glad he had you for a friend," I said. "Living here must have given him some happiness."

"You are kind to say so."

"Aston, could I see his room? Where he stayed when he lived here with you?"

"Yes, of course. Would you like to do that now?"

"If it's all right."

"Of course it's all right! I rather thought you might come here wanting to do that one of these days. I haven't had another guest; the room is pretty much the same as it was back then. You might even find some of your father's things still there. If you find something that appeals to you, I'd like you to have it. A memento. Go ahead! Look around. It's at the top of the stairs, last door on the right. You'll have to forgive me if I don't join you." He tapped the wheel of his wheelchair. "I've more or less abandoned the upper floors of the house. Come back here when you're done."

The last door on the right upstairs was closed. I stood facing it for a moment, afraid that after years of imagining my father's life, the reality might be a disappointment. But disappointment or no, the reality was what I wanted.

My heart in my throat, I opened the door.

My father's room was furnished simply—a bed, a desk, a chest of drawers, a single armchair, a wall of built-in shelves. The walls were painted a pale yellow, and diaphanous white curtains framed the room's two large windows. A beige rug with a knotted, geometric pattern covered the floor. The bed was neatly made, as if waiting for his return. I walked in and closed the door behind me, feeling in some vague way that *I* had returned.

For a few moments, I stood in the center of the room, arms folded around my chest, forcing myself to breathe regular, even breaths. Trying to imagine my father there.

A few knickknacks and some books stood on the shelves. I doubted that any of these belonged to him, though they might have decorated the room when he was there. Few people on Aran indulge themselves in collecting knickknacks, and my father wouldn't have known how to read Standard.

One of the windows of my father's room looked out over the small park in front of the house. From the other, a person could almost touch the branches of a large maple tree, whose red leaves screened the neighboring house. I imagined him spending many hours in this room, looking out, feeling, perhaps, frustrated and helpless. And ill. The trees weren't his trees, but they were something. I hope they soothed him.

I turned to the dresser. The top two drawers were empty. The middle drawer contained a spare blanket for the bed. There were some clothes in the next drawer. I looked through them, touched them, tried to imagine my father wearing them, but the mostly out-of-fashion Earth garments could have been anybody's.

I opened the bottom drawer, and what I saw took my breath away. Neatly folded on top of a number of items of Earth manufacture was a beaded and fringed suede vest that could only have come from Aran. I reached out to touch it, and my hand trembled, as if . . . as if I were about to touch *him*. I took the vest and put it on over my own light blue shirt and pants. In that moment, I wanted to be back home, on my world, Aran, so strongly that the longing was a physical pain in my heart.

Maybe the whynywir were right. Maybe something of my father was reborn in me. In that moment, I could have believed it.

This was the room I wanted to live in while I did the work I came here to do. I added this request to the list of things I needed to discuss with Aston. I wanted to share with him my experience on Aran and my mission. And I needed his help.

Someone here had to organize the transportation of animals and plants, those that had genetic origins on Earth.

I moved into my father's room in Aston's house the next day. The first night there, I woke instantly alert from a sound sleep. Moonlight streamed through the open window, and a warm breeze stirred the curtains, a breeze I somehow knew came from deep within the great forest of Aran. I breathed deeply the comforting scent of rosemary and mint and Aran's rich soil, the smell of home. I remembered closing the window before I'd gone to bed; here on Earth, the nights were cool.

I pushed back my covers and sat up. Taera stood by the side of the bed.

Not Taera, no. The silver moonlight picked out every freckle on Aiana's face. The breeze blew back her long, curly hair, which glistened reddish even in the pale light. If the scent of the khenaran hadn't told me that I was dreaming, I knew it now. "What is it?" I asked.

She said nothing, but slowly backed away from me. I stood and followed her. When Aiana reached the wall of my room, she reached back as if to make sure it was still there, and then she turned and walked through it.

"Where are you going?" I asked the empty room. Then I reminded myself that this was a dream, my dream, and I could follow. I touched the wall, and then I pushed through it.

I was in the silvery ship, if that's what it was, Aiana's place. She stood across the room by the opposite wall. A slight smile lifting the corners of her lips promised a secret soon to be revealed. She turned and walked through the wall behind her. Again I followed.

Aiana walked ahead of me on a narrow path that climbed along the face of a steep hill. The slope rose steeply to the left, all green with low grasses and flowering shrubs and windswept trees. To the right, the land fell away, and a blue sea stretched to the horizon. Sunlight glistened in bright sparkles on the water. Seabirds soared on the warm air currents that rose up the mountainside. "Aiana, wait!" The wind blew my words away, and I ran to catch up with her. I reached her just where the path turned to switch back, and the ocean spread before us as well as alongside. "What is it?" I asked.

Aiana turned and smiled at me and said, "This is the place. Remember."

I woke to find that I had somehow worked the window open, and I was shivering in the cold night air.

Chapter Sixteen

EARTH, YEAR 3223

"**W**alk with me," the guide said quietly to Aiana. The other committee members, straightening their papers and putting them away, appeared not to notice. The guide gestured toward the holo player. "May I . . .?"

May he just nonchalantly keep the holo. He'd kept every holo she'd played that had Taerlin in it. The man probably had a fine personal collection of holos of his Savior. No, that was unfair. The temple probably expected him to turn the holos over to them, and he probably did. In either case, she'd expected the guide to take this one. As always, she'd edited it carefully so that no one might see anything personal.

Personal. The oneiromorph had allowed Taerlin to kiss her. And what a kiss! A slight shiver raised the hairs on her arms. She was going to have to work harder at controlling Taera, or this might lead to . . . something it definitely shouldn't. Aiana reddened and turned away to straighten her own papers, so that the guide wouldn't see. "Yes, of course," she said. "Please."

She followed him down a corridor festooned with graphics of molecular composition, carefully sidestepping a holo of some long organic molecule, though they might easily have just walked right through it. What fluke of scheduling had landed them in the Chemistry building, of all things? They went out the door into warm air that smelled of newly mown grass, and they headed across the quadrangle.

"Are you religious?" the guide asked, looking at her.

Despite knowing there was nothing to be ashamed of, she could feel the blush on her cheeks. "No, not particularly. But I do have respect for—"

He waved the excuse away with a sweep of his hand. "Yes, yes, of course. No matter. I was just curious. Do you know what the Synod is?"

"Of course I do! I have the greatest respect for—"

"Then you know," he interrupted, "that if the Synod were to issue an Order of Desistation, as a religious person you would have to close down the project."

Aiana stopped and stared at him. Objections and questions crowded her mind. "But I already told you: I'm not religious."

He met her gaze. "But Professor Zhou is. And the dean of the College of Arts and Sciences is a member of my order."

She swallowed. "Oh. That would be trouble, then."

"Yes."

"Is the Synod . . . that is, are they considering such a thing?"

Salvatore continued walking toward the Liberal Studies building, and Aiana followed. "I am not generally in a position to know what they are or are not considering. I am a teacher of history, that's all."

"But . . .?"

"But they have asked for all my papers and notes on our meetings, and I have, of course, complied."

"Have they talked with you?"

"If they had, they probably would have sworn me to silence on this issue. As it is, I find your project most . . . interesting. Perhaps you will be able to conduct it in such a way as to divert such . . . unwelcome . . . attentions away from it."

Right. As if she had any say on where the Synod turned its unblinking eye. "What do you suggest?"

"The idea that the Blessed Ascension might not be . . . that it might be mere oneiroportation to another planet . . . Clearly, the Synod will find this unacceptable. You must make certain you keep a good distance from Taerlin. Don't intervene in anything unless it seems part of the pattern. From what I've seen, you've acted responsibly so far, but I can't stress how important this is."

"Yes, Reverend Guide. I intend to."

"Also, you must consider how information of your project will be received on Earth in our time. Do you understand?"

A strand of her hair had worked its way loose and blown into her face. Aiana pushed it back. "I'm not sure."

They arrived at the Liberal Studies building, and Salvatore stopped just short of the door's sensors. "The temple will not tolerate any threat to its established role. Information that undermines its authority in any way will not be permitted."

Her face must have reflected her concern, for he nodded in satisfaction. "Good afternoon, Aiana." He turned and went in the door.

Aiana stared at the place where he had stood, hoping her heart would stop pounding. Had he volunteered this information to help protect her? Or was he following instructions intended to rattle her? A couple of centuries ago, the temple had ordered the deaths of people whom it considered a threat. But surely it was more civilized now. Surely.

Chapter Seventeen

EARTH, YEAR 2467

MIKEL'S RECORDING, continued

I slipped into the back of Lennard's classroom just before the bell rang. Though I hadn't been gone long, being back in school again felt strange. Too much had happened in the interim. I felt older, and the students looked younger than I remembered.

I was half hoping that Lennard wouldn't notice me and would just go on with whatever lesson he had planned for the day. When I was in school, I'd never studied with him, though I would have given anything for the opportunity. But by the time I finally met the prerequisites for his course in my senior year, Lennard was on sabbatical.

The classroom itself was an anachronism, and I could imagine that Lennard had sought it out. It was in an old building, decorated in an even older style, complete with tan wainscoting that just possibly might be real wood underneath all the layers of paint. Some two dozen student desks had been arranged in three curved rows, facing forward; about two-thirds of them were occupied. Lennard's desk, covered with books and papers, was larger than those of his students and faced back toward them. At the back of the room, a state-of-the-art computer-controlled audiovisual center was the only thing that looked like it had changed in the room in the last several hundred years. The classroom was a cultural artifact; I felt like I was a xenologist studying my own species.

Of course, if I'd really wanted not to be noticed, I wouldn't have dressed as I did. I'd bound my washed and combed hair with the down-trimmed rawhide thong, and on top of my cleaned and ironed shirt, I wore my father's brightly beaded vest. Half Richmundian. The clothing suited me.

Lennard saw me at once and gave me a nod. After calling the class to order and dealing with the initial routines—collecting a paper that was due and answering questions on a reading assignment—Lennard smiled in the serious way I'd learned to interpret as mischief and announced, "Ladies and gentlemen, I know that some of you may have been counting on the opportunity to sleep through another dry lecture, but I'm afraid you'll have to postpone that nap until next period. We have the opportunity to hear from a colleague I greatly respect, who has just returned from several months among the whynywir of New Richmund. As you know, the opportunity to interact with other intelligent species is greatly limited these days, and so I'm sure you'll want to hear what he has to say. Allow me to introduce Mikel Pelerin."

Amid a smattering of applause from the fifteen or so students in the class, I walked to the front of the room and pushed aside a small pile of books to make room to sit on the edge of Lennard's desk. "Suppose you found yourself on an unexplored planet where there were no humans. No books about the culture. How would you know if there was any intelligent life?"

Silence stretched out long enough for me to wonder if I'd started the right way. The room felt unbearably hot. Finally, a young man who sat in the middle of the class said, "Artifacts? Cities or roads or monuments of some kind?"

And so we were launched on a discussion of the six signs of civilization and how they could not be applied to the whynywir. At the end of the list, a student in the second row called out in exasperation, "Maybe they're not intelligent!"

I stood and walked over to him. "Logical deduction," I said softly, remembering the one I killed. "There was a time when I also came to that conclusion. But I was wrong."

"How could you prove it one way or the other?" he asked.

"How could you prove it?" I echoed to the class at large.

"Do something to provoke them," suggested the blonde woman in the first row, "and study their reaction."

"Thank you." I settled back onto the edge of Lennard's desk. "It's good to know I'm not the only person to come to that conclusion. But in my case, I didn't think carefully enough about what kind of provocation to use. I almost didn't survive their reaction."

I pushed the hair back from the hairline above my right ear, revealing the crystal that, though silent now, had become another organ of my senses. "Do you know what this is?"

Gasps and murmurs among the class answered more clearly than words that they did. They were, after all, Lennard's students. They'd read the book.

"There's no evidence of communication among the whynywir because they're completely telepathic. Most people who receive a blue crystal can hear the whynywir only when the whynywir speak directly to them, which is not often. But among themselves the whynywir speak constantly, richly, deeply, in many hundreds of conversations at once. And all are intelligible to them at once. Their capacity for communication is like nothing we can imagine. It would be like entering a large, crowded room with hundreds of conversations going on and hearing and understanding everything. *Everything.* And being able to participate in several of those conversations at once."

"They told you that?" asked the round-faced woman at the back of the classroom.

"I experienced it myself. But humans aren't built with the same capacity as the whynywir. I can hear and understand everything, but I can't focus on it like the whynywir do."

The back of my throat threatened to knot up. I felt suddenly overwhelmed with homesickness for Aran. I missed the whynywir. "The whynywir love Aran with a passion and dedication that few humans can equal. Mostly, they talk about the wellbeing of the planet. Few of us could say that. And the khena . . . What the people of New Richmund believe about the trees is true. For the khena sing to the whynywir and dream Aran dreams. I have heard them."

I paused, remembering. And because I was remembering, I became aware of something that I hadn't noticed before: even on Earth, cut off from the community of the whynywir, with my crystal silent, I could still remember whynywir memories, or at least I could remember my memories of them, indistinct as they now were. The fact took my breath away. I had always thought of the collective memory of the whynywir as something that was 'out there,' something that I assumed I'd left behind along with the rich flow of conversations. But, whether I had the actual memories themselves, or just the remembrance of them, some small fraction of the whynywir memories was not 'out there.' It was 'in here.' I almost lost myself in that deep well of remembrance.

"Mikel? Are you all right?" Lennard's concerned question cut through my inner exploration. I focused back on the classroom, found Lennard standing by my side, his hand on my shoulder.

"Yes," I said, but I wasn't. I felt disoriented and a little dizzy. "Lennard, I can still remember!"

"Of course you can," he said. "Why shouldn't you? You were just there."

"I can't communicate with the whynywir from this far away, but I can remember their memories—all the way back to the beginning of the species. It's almost as if I were still there." For the first time, I understood that in some way I had, as the whynywir intended, replaced the one I had killed. Even far away from the whynywir community, I was no longer only human.

Returning to the classroom conversation at hand, I asked, "What makes one sentient life form 'higher' than another?"

"What do you mean?" a student in the middle of the room shot back at me.

"For example, we eat cattle and sheep, and we think that's all right because we're a higher life form than they are."

"No, it's because there's a symbiosis between the species. They have allowed us to domesticate and eat them in return for our breeding them and ensuring the survival of their gene pool."

"And deer?" I responded. "We don't breed them."

"Yes," came a voice from the back, "but we have better guns." There was some nervous laughter. Someone said, "Lucky for us," and someone else added, "Besides, we eat meat and deer don't."

"I don't eat meat," the blond woman in front said. "Does that make it right to kill me?"

I thought about the whynywir. They generally left humans alone, but they would kill humans who invaded their home territories. And eat them, come to that. I shifted nervously on my perch on the edge of Lennard's desk and said, "Let's say no one has guns and everyone eats meat. Could we still claim that one species was superior?"

The student who had objected about the cattle said, "In that case, it would be the ability to reason that makes us superior."

"And if two species can be shown to reason, could one still be higher than the other?"

The class was silent.

"Do you mean, would it be justifiable for one to eat the other?" asked the blond woman in the first row.

Of course, the whynywir thought so, but I wasn't going to bring that up. "Let's just say 'higher' without going into dietary habits. In your case, suppose they're both vegetarian."

"Maybe how consistently they resort to reason, as opposed to raw feelings?" asked a student in the back.

"Would it matter what they reasoned about?" I asked.

The class seized on the question. "It would have to be about important issues," said one young man, "not, you know, last night's holo shows or who's going to win tomorrow's game."

"That rules out humans!" quipped his neighbor.

"It would have to be which species kept in mind the greater good of them both. Of all of them," said the blond woman.

"Of the planet?" I asked.

"Yes, of course!"

The class seemed in general agreement on this.

"But Lennard says that the humans on New Richmund don't like the whynywir," said one of the students.

I thought of how Cort had struggled to avoid seeing the whynywir. "They don't," I said. "Humans avoid whynywir when they can. But the wisest among them recognize the wisdom of the whynywir, and, don't forget, the whynywir control the crystals."

"Why?" asked the woman in the front row. "Why do the whynywir control the crystals?"

"That's the way the first humans on the planet set it up." I realized as soon as the words were out that I'd spoken too quickly.

"But why?"

Cort and I had discussed the matter extensively. If the whynywir had not on their own insisted on control of the crystals, the first humans—meaning, it appeared, Cort and I—would have asked them to do it, and not just because historically it had been done that way. "Because no human on Aran could do it. Can you imagine the fighting there would be? But no one questions the wisdom of the whynywir."

"Are you guessing that that's the reason?" asked another student, "or do you know?"

"I remember. The whynywir remember." I could clearly remember the entire experience of evaluating and allowing the humans to colonize Aran, of insisting on controlling the crystals, just as if I hadn't been unconscious through the whole thing. I remembered the whynywir side of it. The odd perspective made me feel dizzy. I changed the topic. "The whynywir don't like the humans very much, either."

"Why?" asked the round-faced student in the back row.

I thought back to my own judgments, that is, the whynywir's judgments, of myself in that first meeting. "Humans are slow and single-minded," I said. "The whynywir believe them incapable of seeing the big picture and therefore all too likely to lose sight of what's important. I think that's not . . . an unfair assessment . . . from their perspective."

"Then why did they let humans settle on Aran at all?" asked a student in the middle of the classroom.

"Because humans are action-oriented, where the whynywir are more contemplative. Because the humans who settled there committed themselves to act for Aran's well-being no matter what, at least some of them did. And maybe most of all, because the humans promised to help protect Aran against later human invaders."

"Who?"

"Us. The people from Earth. Without the desire to protect a human culture we could relate to, do you think our government would have ever let go of New Richmund, given the planet's natural wealth?"

"But come now," said my interlocutor, "how could those humans have possibly known way back then that we would come?"

He had no idea how very well we knew. I felt like a child about to play a good prank. "Don't you think it was only a matter of time before someone found the planet and started trying to harvest its wealth? They must have anticipated that and, understanding what was at stake, committed to preventing it. Think about it. You're interested in xenology, in other cultures. If you had a chance to settle a world a lot like Aran, except no humans were there yet . . . a world with whynywir and khena just like Aran . . . If you thought you might have a chance to get a crystal for yourself, to know the world for yourself . . . If you thought that the government of Earth might discover this world and begin destroying it . . . would you go there to prevent that? Would you establish a human presence on the planet?"

The classroom buzzed with discussion. Almost everyone agreed that if they had a chance to be the first humans on a planet like Aran, they would do it.

Despite reminding myself at least a dozen times that the discussion was still hypothetical, I grew excited. "I do have that chance," I said. But I wanted to be careful of how much I revealed. It was still too soon, and some of the people in this room—perhaps most of them—would decide not to go. "It's a planet a lot like Aran, but with no human settlements as yet. And you can come with me."

With impeccable timing, the end-of-period bell rang. I had to raise my voice over the noise of people gathering their belongings. "Next week, after class. If anyone wants to talk more."

It was autumn, in my opinion the very best season, and this was a perfect autumn day. The sky was a deep, vibrant blue without a cloud, and the air was clear and fresh. The sun's warmth countered the cool temperature. Fiery red and orange and yellow leaves were everywhere. I had no plans for the afternoon. My dream of the previous night still clung to me; it seemed more real than waking life. I longed for some quiet time, and the ocean was on my mind. I was lucky to live in a city near the ocean, where a nature preserve protected the dunes, and the beach was miles long and open to the public. I decided to go for a walk on the beach.

My grandparents had lived in Baysby, and my mother and I had lived with them for a few years when I was young. After they died, their house had been reclaimed by the mortgage company—not an uncommon story—but I still had fond memories of the neighborhood.

I took the light rail to Baysby Station and walked from there rather than taking the shuttle that circled regularly along the five-kilometer route through the oceanfront community from the station to the beach. The houses were smaller than I remembered, and crowded closer together, but they were single houses, not apartments. Boats and lobster traps and sundry nautical gear cluttered the yards, but the houses were clean and well maintained, painted in bright and pastel colors that were absent in my own grey neighborhood.

As soon as the nights turn cold, people seem to forget how wonderful the ocean is. Despite the sapphire blue clarity of the water, and the warmth and soft resilience of the sand, the wide beach was almost deserted. I walked for a long time, enjoying the ebb and surge of the waves and the hissing of the sea pulling at the sand. Small birds ran looking for food at the shifting water's edge. The sun and sand were warm; the water and the breeze, cool with a fresh salt tang. I would miss living near the ocean; Aran's human settlements were far inland in forests and mountains. Then, with an insight so sudden I forgot to keep walking, I realized that Aran had wide oceans; I had seen them from space. The whole planet was open to me; I could live near the shore on Aran, just as I had on Earth!

I walked with renewed vigor, excited by the idea of starting an oceanside community, enjoying the water and the day and the life that awaited me. I was in high spirits as I noticed a small boat approaching the shore. Its lone occupant was angling toward me. The boat moved quickly, its single sail full with the wind. Then the sailor turned directly toward the shore, and the wind spilled from the sail, which flapped loudly. A wave carried the boat inward, and it beached in the shallow water. The sailor hopped out, grabbed hold of the boat's prow, and pulled it onto the land.

Noticing how I watched, the sailor nodded a greeting and said, "Nice day!" He was middle aged with reddish hair and a ruddy complexion; his round face looked boyish despite the wrinkles that spoke of sun and rain, smiles and tears, a lifetime of experience. He wore a visored hat, a T-shirt, and overalls. The legs of the overalls were rolled up, and his feet were bare. Without waiting for my reply, he untied a line to release the top of the sail, and then began folding the sail's material across the boom. As he folded, he tied the sail down.

"Beautiful," I answered. "Would you like a hand?"

The sailor laughed a polite refusal. "I can probably pack this thing up faster by myself." Indeed, he had already finished with the sail. He detached the boom from the mast and laid it in the small boat. Then he did something inside the boat and pulled out the mast, laying it flat from prow to stern. "You can give me a hand getting this to the road, though, if you're willing."

He picked up the front of the boat, and I lifted the rear. As we walked across the beach, I said, "I've been thinking of trying to live by the ocean."

"Long commute," said the sailor.

"Excuse me?"

"It's a long commute from here to anywhere you might find a job. Me, I work second shift over at the Longland factory. Takes an hour and a half to get there. Some of my friends go even farther. Lucky these days to have a job at all."

"Times are rough," I agreed sympathetically, not meaning much by it. "But I was thinking of trying to make my living from the sea and the land."

He stopped walking and turned to look at me, as if he were sizing me up. Holding the back of the boat, I had to stop when he did.

"Idealistic," he said. "You'll get over it. Can't make a living fishing. I tried it; you got to go too far out to find anything, need one of those million-dollar factory ships. Can't make a living building boats, either. Not when you're competing with those lightweight high-tech jobs with alloy and carbon fiber and all. I tried that, too. What do you think you're going to do?" He started walking again, and I followed. His pace was faster now, angry.

I decided to gamble on him. I had to start sometime, somewhere, and this man seemed as good as any. "I wasn't thinking about here. There's another place, a place where you can still live off the land and the sea. I could use the help of someone who knows something about fishing and boat-building—in case you know anyone like that."

The sailor stopped again and turned, sizing me up all over again. I returned his gaze and waited. "What's your name?" he asked finally.

"Taerlin."

I don't know why I said that instead of "Mikel." Perhaps because I was recruiting for Aran, and Taera was on my mind. It was the first time I'd used that name on Earth.

"You're not from here, are you, Taerlin?"

"No." The answer barely escaped my lips. I was breathing shallowly and rapidly.

"That's what I thought. Strange eyes you got, if you don't mind my saying. My name's Joe. What do you know about sailing?"

"I've been out, though not a lot. My grandparents used to live near here, and I sailed some as a child. I know port from starboard and jib from spinnaker. I know I like it."

Without a reply, Joe shouldered his side of the boat and started walking again. Bound to him by the boat I was helping to carry, I followed. We picked our way along a marked trail across the dunes and came in sight of the road. I had all but given up on the conversation, when Joe said, "You probably *do* need help; you're right about that. What do you want from me?"

Now I stopped, pulling him to a halt in front of me. He turned, and I said, "Teach me. Teach all of us that will be coming."

He laughed, enjoying the joke. "Two hours a day, ten to twelve in the morning. A hundred unis an hour."

But I didn't join in his laughter. "No, Joe. Not for money. Only for the love of it. Come with me and live the life you want to live."

I held his questioning gaze, and I saw desire in his eyes, and skepticism. Some communication passed between us, maybe only an agreement to be honest with one another.

Joe looked away. "I . . . couldn't. I have a family . . . friends . . ."

"Then bring them!" I smiled, serious and hopeful, when he looked at me again. "We need settlers. Where I'm heading, the place is beautiful, fresh, unpolluted, and free. We need people who know how to live off the sea and the land, like you do."

"Where is it?"

"Far. It's far from here. You won't have heard of the place, but it's real." That choked-up feeling started in the back of my throat again, as I remembered just how real the place was, how much I wanted to be back there.

Joe looked at me as if something in my face might reveal whether or not I was crazy, but what it showed must have been how much I wanted to return. His face softened. "You say your grandparents were from around here?"

"Yes." I told him their names.

"I knew the family a little. Their daughter was a year or two ahead of my wife in school."

"My mother," I said.

Now he looked at me with something like recognition. "So you're the kid," he said.

"I'm the kid."

"Seen you around occasionally, must be years ago."

"Yes, years. I still miss it, though."

"Gets under your skin, the ocean does. They say it's in the bloodstream."

"That's why I'm going where I'm going," I said. This was only a tiny fraction of the truth, but it would serve. "I could use some help from experienced seafolk like you."

"I don't know . . ." He turned and started walking again, crossing the road. Still bound by the boat, I followed. We walked silently alongside the road for a while; then we turned down a side road and into the yard of a small pink house. I helped Joe put the boat down and to cover it with a tarp. "I can see you're serious," he said, "but this isn't something to do on a whim. I'd have to know a lot more. But thanks for your offer."

"Just think about it."

"I *am* thinking about it," he replied roughly. "Can you come back Monday? About this time?" He left me standing in his yard, but at the door of his house he turned and said, "Oh . . . Maybe you could bring your mother? My wife would like that."

Chapter Eighteen

EARTH, YEAR 2467

MIKEL'S RECORDING, continued

"**I** want to go with you." The blond woman from Lennard's class was quite beautiful—in what I could almost hear Cort saying was "a Starman sort of way." She was tall and slender and so pale she was almost translucent. Her fair hair hung long and straight below her waist, and her eyes were a clear, light blue, set wide above high cheekbones and a generous mouth.

I must have looked at her a second or so too long, because she added, "I'm married. I have two children, a three-year-old and a one-year-old. I'm tired of people staring at me."

I felt flustered. "I'm sorry. I . . . I didn't mean anything by it, it's just . . ."

She sighed. "I know. No one means anything by it. But I'd like to live somewhere where the way I look doesn't matter so much. Where what matters is that I can make a difference."

"I can't promise that people won't look at you." She had cornered me immediately after the first class the following week, introduced herself as Ana, and offered to buy me a coffee. We were on our way to the coffee shop, fighting against a cold headwind that blew the fallen leaves in swirls that seemed to have a life of their own.

"No." She looked away. "Of course not. But I'd like to go wherever you've got in mind anyway. Lennard obviously thinks it's worthwhile, or he wouldn't have had you come and speak, and that's enough for me. There's not much of a future for xenologists here anymore."

I thought about that. There were fifteen or sixteen students in Lennard's class, perhaps an equal number every year. Given the advanced level of the class, they must have a serious interest in xenology, but at the moment, United Earth had diplomatic relations with only two other intelligent alien civilizations on other planets. Surely the field of xenology didn't require as many scientists as we were turning out. "What would you do, if not xenology?" I asked.

She shrugged. "Go with you."

"No, seriously."

"My husband and I have talked about that. I could be a receptionist somewhere, or work in sales." She pushed a strand of her long hair back behind her shoulder. "I'd probably be good in sales, but I don't like the idea of it. I could go for my doctorate and then teach xenology to poor sucker students who imagine there's any kind of career there."

I wanted her to come with me, but only if she was sure. "Maybe by then, there would be."

She laughed. "Maybe by then, the moon will turn to money and rain down on us. There just aren't enough jobs for all the graduates, and not just in xenology. Haven't you seen the unemployment statistics among younger people? Twenty percent! And the government says the unemployment fund is running out. Are you offering us a chance to settle a new planet, or not?"

"Well, yes, but . . . what about your husband?" I pictured a guy with thick lenses and lank hair, an accounting major.

"He just finished his degree in ecology and forestry. He's unemployed, of course. We talked about this a lot over the weekend, and he wants to come, too."

"But the children—"

She interrupted me. "There he is now. Dov! Dov!" She waved frantically until she caught her husband's attention.

If I had thought her beautiful before, that impression paled before the radiance of her face when her eyes met his. I couldn't help sighing. Why did I have to fall in love with a person I could only see when one of us was sleeping?

I turned to see the object of her affection. He was as handsome as she was lovely, and his smile was as warm and sincere. I decided that I was lucky to have two such radiant people coming with me. No more protesting.

Some of the other students from Lennard's class had caught up with us, and I was bombarded with offers. By the time we reached the coffee shop, there were almost a dozen of us. We occupied a large, round table that had been lacquered with so many coats of polyurethane that it barely remembered once having been made of wood. The eight chairs around the table were not enough. More chairs were brought, and more people kept coming. Not all were from the class. Like Dov, they were family or close friends as well.

"There is no infrastructure on this world, and no technology," I said. I found myself speaking to Dov. Lennard's students knew this already, of course, and I presumed they would have told the others, but I had to be sure. "No doctors; no drugs. No one to call when the children get sick."

"There are herbalists," Ana protested. "We read Lennard's book."

She was leaping to a conclusion I didn't want anyone to reach, not just yet. Not while some people in the meeting might still decide not to go. "There are, on New Richmund as we know it. On *this* world, though, there won't be any skills that we don't bring with us."

"Better do some recruiting at the medical school," said one of Lennard's students, and everyone laughed. It was becoming clear that I wasn't going to dissuade anyone.

"All right," I said. "Any leads?" It turned out that one person's sister was a doctor. Another person roomed with a med student, and a third knew a botanist who was currently unemployed. It seemed like a good beginning.

"Rules," I went on. "There are rules. Anyone coming with me is going to have to agree to them." Taera and Cort and I had discussed this subject at length. I held up my right index finger. "Rule number one. There will be no return trip. Get out now if you're not sure about this. There's no shame in leaving."

I waited, but no one left.

Two late-comers pulled up chairs at the already overcrowded table.

"Hey, people are leaving, not arriving," Dov told them, but no one got up from the table.

"Me, too," answered one of the newcomers, a thin young man with lank, flaxen hair. "When's the next starship? I'm on it, for sure."

"There's no coming back," I repeated. I'd never seen the man before, though there was something familiar about the combination of desire and fear in his eyes, almost a kind of desperation. He wasn't in the class. I wondered who had talked with him and what his story was.

"Don't want to come back," he said simply, looking away under my scrutiny. "Is this true confessions time? I heard it was a good place for a new beginning."

I couldn't argue with that. I decided to continue and held up the first two fingers of my right hand. "Rule number two. Put your affairs in order before you go. No distraught parents, lost spouses, angry creditors, paranoid government agencies. Pay last year's taxes. Write letters and make phone calls. Say good-bye to your loved ones. Whatever it takes. Clean it all up and close it all up. Understood?" There were murmurs of agreement around the table.

Three fingers now. "Rule number three. No modern weapons. You can bring knives, any kind of blades, but no stunners or lasers. It would be better if what you bring is useful as something other than a weapon, too. Knives are useful."

"Why no lasers?" protested the student on my right, a young man with a thin face, light blue eyes, and fine, wavy hair. "They're useful for hunting."

I flushed with guilt, thinking of the whynywir I had killed. "Yes, they could be. But they kill too much, too easily. They don't belong in this new world. The planet will give what's needed."

"Who says?" he insisted, his jaw jutting aggressively forward.

"I do. If you don't like the rules, you don't have to come."

Fear replaced the anger in his eyes. "No, it's all right," he said, shrugging as if it had never mattered. "We don't need lasers."

"Rule number four," inserted Ana, putting a hand on my arm to forestall me. "All clothing material should be biodegradable. No synthetics."

"Not just clothing!" added the slightly overweight young man two away from me on my left. "Everything! Especially packaging. We should watch what kind of food we bring."

This confused me. "Why would you want to bring food?"

A couple of the students looked at each other significantly and laughed. Soon the whole table joined in, calling out names of snack foods that they would all have to do without. The person who had brought up the topic blushed.

"Of course you can bring whatever you want," I said, "but when it's gone, it's gone. And you're right—any packaging should be biodegradable."

"Can I bring my dog?" asked a short-haired, elfin-faced young woman.

That was a question I hadn't anticipated. There were no dogs on Aran in modern time, although there were wolves as well as inthoi, carnivores that resembled foxes. But there was a simple solution to this question. "As long as it's neutered. Cats, too, if any of you want to bring any. Just make sure your pets are neutered."

"What about my elderly mother?"

"She has to be neutered, too!" someone said, and everyone laughed.

I nodded sympathetically to the man who had asked. I was hoping my own mother would come. "Bring whoever wants to make a new beginning."

The discussion went on a long time. Suddenly, I realized what time it was. I was late. I excused myself from the group, promising to come back the next day. I would have to be very lucky with the train schedule in order to pick up my mother and still get to Joe's house on time.

She and I were already in the station waiting for the Baysby train when the full import of the conversation in the coffee shop struck me. Eighteen people, along with several children and at least one elderly parent and one dog, would be coming back with me. "Yes!" I exulted aloud, earning a smile from my mother and averted gazes from several other passengers.

Joe's house was crowded when my mother and I arrived, still flushed with excitement. Despite having taken the shuttle from Baysby station, we were twenty minutes late.

Joe himself answered the door. "Where have you been? I was afraid you wouldn't come."

He *was* afraid. I saw it in his face. Afraid and needy. I had seen this look before. It was on the faces of the people in the coffee shop earlier this afternoon. It had been on the faces of all the people that climbed as pilgrims to the valley of the whynywir, who needed something so badly that they had risked their lives to seek out the alien and possibly hostile whynywir. "I'm sorry. I came as quickly as I could."

I thought that Joe would be coming with me, and I was not wrong. Of the close to thirty adults in Joe's house, I thought I recognized that need and that fear on all but three faces, and I was not wrong.

"We can't all commute to Longland, like Joe does," a young man said. He looked no older than me. A petite, very pregnant dark-skinned woman held his hand. "Some of us have a family to consider. Both parents need to work to make enough to live on, and then add to that the long commute, it's no life at all. There's got to be something better."

"Even if you're willing to make the commute," added a woman maybe ten years his elder, "what about the rumors that Longland's going to close, like Brannan did last year? What will we do then?"

"Form a knitting coop!" a woman sitting near the back called out. There was a scattering of bitter laughter, and the woman added, "We know how to make warm sweaters, much better than the junk from who-knows-where they're selling in the stores."

"True enough," replied the first woman, "but who can afford to buy them? Ain't no way to make a living with knitting, Cassy."

"Don't I know it," the other one muttered. "We can't fish, and we can't knit."

"And we can't work in the factories, neither," a man near the front added, "since they've all been closing. And the government ain't going to keep paying us unemployment forever, either."

Counting children, almost forty people from Baysby eventually came with me to settle on Aran, but Joe didn't come with the others from Baysby. He stayed for a while to recruit at the Longland factory. He said he knew dozens of people who would want to go, and I promised to join him and some of his colleagues after work one day the following week. Eventually, half a hundred people from Longland made the journey, too.

Chapter Nineteen

EARTH, YEAR 2467

MIKEL'S RECORDING, continued

The university was a good place to recruit. I probably could have recruited at a thousand universities around the world if I'd had the time to go to all of them. But I was busy enough right here. People I met told their friends. There were always people who wanted to meet me, always messages on my comm. Even those who decided not to go with me knew someone, often several someones, who might be interested. The people I met were idealistic; they wanted their lives to make a difference somewhere, somehow. They believed Earth no longer offered them this opportunity. Many, like the xenology students, faced a lack of job opportunities in their fields and so were interested in settling Aran because it also settled their concerns about what they would do with their lives. Some, such as botanists, nutritionists, and medical and nursing students, had skills that would be useful on Aran. But no matter what skills my recruits had, I accepted everyone who wanted to go.

Taera came each week, as we had arranged. We met in the park just down the street from my mother's house, and I brought with me five or twenty or twenty-five people, whoever was ready and certain they wanted to go—for there was no turning back—and could assure me they'd already put all their affairs in order. Taera brought each group into her 'port, where she administered her inoculum, and then she brought each group through to ancient Aran. The real oneiroport, I was given to understand, was a tiny chamber barely large enough to hold the sleeping Aiana, but Taera's 'port had no apparent limits. It had no trouble accommodating twenty people or more, the size and configuration of its interior changing according to Taera's dreams. Taera had also been working with Cort bringing Arantu from today's Aran, and these people helped the people I brought from Earth to learn the skills they needed: farming and firemaking, housebuilding and language.

I was deluged with calls, and I met people alone or in small groups from breakfast time until late at night. I probably didn't sleep enough, but I was filled with energy. It was a complex, wonderful, heady time, a time of everything and everyone coming together.

I began to recognize people on the street who would want what I offered. Strangers. Ah, but the need on their faces, the emptiness waiting to be filled . . . and when they looked at me, who was no longer quite of Earth, their eyes wondered whether I might have, or know about, or perhaps even just symbolize, what they needed. At times, it seemed that I could touch such people on the arm and meet their eyes, and they would know that I knew them, and their eyes would answer, *Yes,* even before I spoke the words, "Come with me."

The air was brisk and smelled of rain. Rain, and autumn leaves, and greasy sausages and overcooked coffee from the cheap restaurant down the street. It was half past five in the evening and already almost dark. The street glistened in the headlights of the cars that sped by. "Tropical Cafe," the voice in the comm message had said. The Tropical Cafe stood on the corner; the pink neon palm tree that decorated it reflected garishly on the wet sidewalk. Its facade was made of dirty red brick like those of all the other stores on the block. There were no windows. I pushed open the door and went in.

Inside, the Tropical Cafe was as warm as the evening was cool. Dim lights at each of the booths highlighted wood table tops and benches that were rounded and polished from much use. A large bar, surrounded by wooden stools, dominated the center of the room, its wooden countertop smooth and glistening with a warm patina. Behind the bar, shelves of glasses and bottles rose almost to the ceiling. Multicolored neon signs advertised a number of brands of brewed and distilled alcoholic drinks. A woman of middle years wiping glasses behind the bar looked up when I came in. She smiled a businesslike welcome.

It was a working-class neighborhood bar, where most of the customers would be neighbors and old friends. I liked it.

Later, the place would be busy, but it was still early. Not more than a dozen patrons occupied the café, mostly in pairs talking quietly. A few people looked at me and then returned to their conversations and their drinks. Not so the man sitting alone in a booth toward the rear. An untouched beer sat in front of him, and he studied me with cool appraisal that seemed to miss little.

His face was lean and angular, and his fair hair was cropped short. His light blue shirt was spotless and neatly pressed, as if he had either just taken it from the package or used a lot of starch in his laundry. Something in his relaxed, yet ready, posture indicated muscles and training. Lines at the corners of his mouth and between his eyebrows, etched strongly for a face otherwise young, suggested tension and judgment and disapproval. He didn't seem the type of person who normally called me. But then, I didn't know how reliable my sense of "normal" was.

I walked over to him, not sure whether I passed or failed his cool evaluation. "Jak?"

He nodded, indicating the seat across from him with his chin. "Buy you something?" he asked as I sat down.

"Mineral water. Thanks. I'm Taerlin."

"Yeah. I figured that out." He raised his arm slightly, signaling to the bartender.

She came over. "You going to drink that beer, Jak?"

He seemed surprised to see the drink on the table. "When'd you sneak that up on me?"

The bartender laughed like an old friend familiar with his jokes and clapped his shoulder. "As if anyone could sneak anything up on you! What'll it be now?"

"One mineral water. Add it to my tab." The bartender left, and Jak returned to scrutinizing me. "I expected someone a little older."

Given what I could remember, age seemed irrelevant. Was I twenty years old, or twenty thousand? I shrugged. "Does it matter?"

"I guess not." He fell silent when the bartender brought my water. Then he asked, "What do you do when you're not . . . recruiting? Student?"

"No. I finished school." I wasn't comfortable under his questions and decided it was my turn. "What about you? You're thinking about leaving Earth, right? Or you wouldn't have called me."

He shrugged, a slight rippling of the muscles under his light blue shirt. The blue matched his eyes. If the lines of his face weren't so set, he would have been handsome. "Maybe."

"Why? What do you do here?"

"That doesn't matter. Some people I . . . knew may have gone with you." The hesitation was so slight I wasn't sure I'd heard it. "My cousin, used to work up at the Longland factory. Then I heard a lot of people from there went with you. I grew up with some of them, so I wanted to know more about where you were taking them. Then to decide what I wanted to do."

I took a sip of my water. "I'm looking for people who want to settle a planet, start a new life. It's a primitive place. The people who go there are not going to be in contact with Earth ever again, and they won't bring much with them, either. They'll live by the work of their own hands. In a generation, they'll lose almost all of what we call 'civilization,' though of course they'll have whatever culture they create for themselves." I laughed a little self-consciously, wondering how I sounded to him. "I'm not much of a salesman, am I?"

"What do you offer, then? You must have offered those people something."

"It depends on what you want. Some of them are shipbuilders and fishermen, craftspeople, musicians. People who are interested in being part of starting a human society from scratch on an unpeopled planet." I hesitated. "It's nice there, if it's the kind of thing you're looking for. Truly beautiful. Temperate climate. Forests and mountains. Good hunting and fishing. No pollution. Lots of room. A chance to be part of the ecology of the place, if that matters to you. It's a simple life, but in its way an important one."

Jak narrowed his eyes and said, "Someone told me, 'paradise.'"

I laughed. "I think it's wonderful, but it's not for everybody. If there's something important to you that you'd feel you're giving up here, it's not for you."

An emotion rippled across his face too quickly for me to identify. Revulsion? Hatred? "Who *is* it for, Taerlin? People with nothing to lose? No one to miss them? Men, women, children, it doesn't matter?" He leaned forward slightly. There was a rough edge to his voice, like a serrated knife. "*Children*, Taerlin? How many have you taken over the last few months?"

I found myself on the defensive under that cold gaze. "I haven't counted the people. But no one goes with me unless they want to go. There's no crime in that, is there?"

Jak sat back and crossed his arms over his chest. "That depends on the exact nature of this 'paradise,' doesn't it? Some say that there's paradise after death, but that doesn't make it right to kill them."

The distaste on his face was evident now, twisting his mouth downward. I didn't like the direction the conversation was taking. "I hope you're not implying that I've killed anyone," I said stiffly.

He leaned forward. "Have you?"

My stomach muscles clenched, and I drew in a sharp breath, remembering the whynywir I'd murdered. But that wasn't where this conversation was going. "No!" I said, my voice coming out loud enough to make a couple of nearby people turn to look at me. Meeting with this man was a mistake. I stood. "This conversation is over. You know my number; give me a call if you decide you're interested in going to another planet. Other than that, I don't want to hear from you."

I started to leave, but Jak stood also. "Sit down, Taerlin," he said. His voice was cold and hard. He reached into the breast pocket of his shirt, and suddenly I knew what he was reaching for. Police ID. He was going to read me my rights and arrest me.

It was my worst nightmare. My heart rate surged, pouring heat into my body. I was afraid of being detained on Earth against my will. I was afraid I would die here, die forever, myself and maybe my father with me. I was afraid to face that.

I bolted for the back door.

Jak ran after me.

The back door opened onto a narrow alley, unlit and already dark in the twilight. To my right, garbage bins left barely enough room for a vehicle to pass. The solid wall of the buildings provided no way to hide or escape. To my left, the alley opened onto the street. I turned left and raced into the street, attracting a few startled looks from people I narrowly avoided bumping into. Ahead, the stairs from a subway stop spewed out a rush-hour crowd of people. I headed down the stairs and leaped over the barrier where people normally stopped to insert coins for the fare. I reached the platform just as a train was pulling away.

I banged futilely on the side of the train as it gathered speed and departed the station. In the holos, the hero would have made it onto the train, leaving his pursuers behind on the platform.

But this was no holo.

My heart still beat wildly. I looked for a way out other than the one Jak was about to come down. At the end of the platform, a narrow stairway led up, probably to an exit across the street. I raced for it, but was cut short by the clatter of footsteps running down the stairs.

An instant later, a woman in a police uniform, breathing hard, faced me. She leveled a laser at me and cried, "Halt!" Footsteps behind me announced that Jak had arrived.

The only thing that frightened me more than the prospect of detainment and possible death on Earth in the future was the prospect of certain death on Earth right now. I didn't know whether police lasers, like the ones allowed to civilians, were limited to only nonlethal force, or whether, like the military one I'd used to murder the whynywir, could be set to kill. But I didn't want to take the chance. I stopped and raised my hands in the air.

"You are coming with us," Jak said. He searched me for weapons and of course found none. "We'll handle the formalities at the station." A crowd started to gather. He clicked a pair of handcuffs on my wrists and then announced, "Show's over, folks. Go on about your business."

As each of the police officers put a hand firmly on one of my arms and led me from the train stop, I looked down, meeting no one's eyes. I said nothing. I was certain I was going to die.

Chapter Twenty

EARTH, YEAR 3224

"**S**omething's wrong." Aiana sank into the visitor chair by Raj Smithjon's desk.

Smithjon leaned forward, scrutinizing her. Aiana knew what he saw. There were dark circles under her eyes, and her face was pale. She was too thin. "Are you well?" he asked.

"Yes, yes, I'm fine. Never been better." That was patently untrue. She wished she hadn't said it. "It's Taerlin I'm worried about."

Smithjon studied his student. "I will not insult you by asking whether you're familiar with the story."

Her throat felt tight; she was on the verge of crying again. "The story. Yes. He dies in prison, and so on. Well, by all that's holy, not on my watch, he doesn't."

"Your watch."

"I was supposed to meet him in the park near his house, but I couldn't." She swallowed, close to tears. "I couldn't. The time was wrong. Decades off. I couldn't even get close."

Smithjon drew a deep breath and let it out slowly. "Aiana, there are documented events in his life. It's one thing to play the role you have already played and quite another to, ah, to try to rewrite history. You cannot."

Tears spilled over her eyes. She blinked rapidly, then ran her fingertips over her eyes. "I have to. He's so . . . vulnerable. He believes that he will be reborn if he dies on Aran, but not if he dies on Earth. On Earth, it's a final death."

"That's just a belief, Aiana."

"But it's *his* belief." *And mine.* "He must feel so frightened and alone! I brought him there. It's my fault. I have to save him. But . . ." She sniffled and ran her sleeve over her face. "I can't. You have to help me."

Smithjon reached across his desk and took her hand. For a long moment he said nothing, collecting his thoughts. Then he breathed in deeply and sighed. "I'm so sorry. I can see how hard this is for you. But you must look at this objectively. Remember, *history has already been written.*"

Aiana held his hand tightly. "I think I might love him," she said.

He squeezed her hand. He seemed at a loss as to what else he might do, and he shook his head. "That's probably not a very good idea."

She looked at him with bleak eyes.

"His life is pretty well documented, and you don't appear to be in it."

She stood. Of course there wasn't anything he could do. "Thanks, Professor. I know you're trying to protect me. But if he's in prison, he must get out of it somehow, still alive, or that holo I found in the vault couldn't have been made. And to get out, he's probably going to need my help. I have to keep trying."

Smithjon also stood. "What you have to do, young lady, is to log the requisite number of hours of rest between journeys, and to keep your traveling hours down within the established guidelines. Also, you'd better check your energy budget, or you'll find yourself lacking a 'port just when you need it the most."

She looked away from him. "Yes, Professor, of course."

He narrowed his eyes. "And if I ask to see your log, what will it show?"

That would depend on whether she showed him her real log, or the one she fabricated for the committee. "I have the log right here." She put her briefcase down on the edge of his desk and fumbled through its contents.

"Not *that* log, Aiana. I am not naïve. I'm talking about the auto-generated 'port log."

She blushed. "I might be a little over in my hours. Maybe my energy consumption, too."

He raised an eyebrow. "Mm-hmm?"

"All right, perhaps more than a little. But this is important."

"Get some rest, Aiana. That's an order. The right time will open up to you when it's supposed to—but not if you're sick or unconscious. Or dead. Do you understand me?"

She understood. He would not check the 'port log. Good. She kept her voice meek. "Yes, you're right. I will. Thank you."

Like hell was she going to rest while Taerlin was in prison.

Chapter Twenty-One

EARTH, YEAR 2467

MIKEL'S RECORDING, continued

J ak was silent as I was read my rights and then booked at the police station. He stood straight and still as a statue, arms folded over his chest, and watched me with unforgiving eyes. I was in trouble. Running from the police was a crime in itself. They could probably even hold me on fare-dodging at the subway stop.

"Name?" asked the officer behind the desk. The station was vintage half-a-century-ago, with faux-wood paneling everywhere and walls painted a shade of yellow that might have been cheerful ten years ago but now just looked dirty.

"Taerlin."

"Surname?"

I groaned; I'd given the wrong name. "You'd better write down Pelerin. Mikel Pelerin."

My trouble had just gotten worse. In addition to whatever crime they were going to accuse me of—not murder, surely?—that, and running from the police, no doubt some larger government database would now be triggered, and there would be charges related to evasion of my duty on Aran. That would be just the irony to top all the rest.

The booking officer looked up at me, sighed dramatically, and then reentered my name into her computer. "Birth date?"

The more I thought about that question, the more difficult it would be to answer. I didn't give myself time to think. I understood the response she wanted, and I told her. Then I asked, "What am I accused of?"

"Nothing yet," she said. Perhaps she had a little pity, for she added, "You'll be held at the facility since you've already tried once to escape, but you're not a technically a prisoner unless your guilt is established through questioning."

Questioning.

My heart sank. They weren't simply going to ask questions. This would be more of an interrogation by the police in a formal setting, using the powerful drug Emetol-9. When under its influence, the accused himself would reveal the actual deeds he had committed and any other facts he was aware of that pertained to the case. If asked, I would name the planet where I had taken the missing people. I'd rather die than do that—and if Taera was to be believed, the odds were pretty good that if I were administered the mind-altering drug, I *would* die.

"But then, what am I accused of?"

She looked at Jak, and he said, "Murder."

I had suspected as much—but when he said the word, my heart began pounding again. I couldn't breathe. The panicky feeling was worse than at the Tropical Cafe, but here, there was no chance of escape.

"Murder of over two hundred people, Taerlin," Jak said. He looked grimly satisfied, arms crossed, chin raised—the satisfaction of an officer of the law who had brought a criminal to justice.

"Wait, no! I haven't . . ." Haven't murdered anyone? Not the human beings he thought I had murdered, no, but what about the whynywir? I could feel the blood rising to my face. "I didn't . . ." I started again, but I couldn't complete the sentence.

I was going to die here. Forever.

And where was Taera? If I ever needed her, it was now.

"Questioning isn't so bad," the booking officer said, "assuming you're innocent. You have a right to a witness."

A witness. Someone of my choosing to observe the questioning process, to ensure that it proceeded fairly. A lawyer, if I could afford one. Desperation made me think clearly. "I'd like to make a call," I said.

I needed more than a witness. I needed someone who could get me out of this. My mind raced as I tried to think of who could possibly help me. Here, on Earth, now, there was only one person I could think of.

I called Aston.

Two hours later, I had a lawyer, and not just any lawyer. Pol Bitmon was a celebrity defense lawyer who had made his reputation and his fortune, and those of his clients, as a master of trial and media manipulation.

"I'm accused of murder," I told him. "They're saying I murdered two hundred people, but they don't have any evidence." I laid out what the police had said and, in general terms, what I had actually done, concluding with, "I'm not guilty." We sat in one of the police station's meeting rooms, a drab windowless place furnished only with a table and six mismatched chairs, and—as Pol had required—absolutely no recording capability.

Pol was a head taller than me and three or four times as wide, an intimidating person. His body shook when he laughed. "No one ever is, at first."

I could feel the heat in my face. "No, really. I'm not!"

"Well then, there's nothing to worry about. But you should be aware of the procedure. Are you?"

"I know there's questioning, but I—"

"It's a little more than just asking questions, young man."

"Yes, yes, I know. There's a room with a special chair, where they strap you in, and then administer that drug Emetol-9. But I don't want—"

"You needn't worry. The procedure is really quite safe. You'll probably be uncomfortable; most people are, but sensors will be attached, and a trained technician will carefully monitor the rate at which the drug is administered as well as all your vital signs. The police will also supervise the entire proceding to ensure the utmost legality."

The police! I thought of Jak. "No, Pol, I don't—"

He ignored the interruption. "The purpose of the questioning is to determine the facts as you know them. At your trial, the judge will interpret those facts according to the law. What will remain to us will be to paint the circumstances. If you are guilty, the extent of your punishment will then be determined through a statistical survey of the people following the trial in the media. And that's where I am worth my not inconsiderable weight in gold." He patted his paunch with satisfaction.

I leaned across the table, putting my weight on my palms to emphasize the point. "Look, I helped some people go . . . away, but I didn't kill any of them."

"Of course you didn't," he said.

"Then get them to set me free."

Pol laughed. "Look, Taerlin, you're my client. You pay me to believe you, and I do. And why not? The evidence is all completely circumstantial. There are no bodies." He narrowed his eyes. "Are there?"

"No! Of course not."

"So, then. No bodies, and from what I've been able to gather so far, there's no evidence of any violence or use of force."

I wanted to laugh at the idea that I had forced all those people to go to Aran, but there was little humor in it. "I told everyone to put their affairs in order. To say their goodbyes. To make sure there were no loose ends."

"And apparently, you did a good job of that. But of course, it wouldn't be the first time some cult figure spirited off a large number of people to some remote location, only to murder them or get them to commit some kind of ritual group suicide. Jonestown in the twentieth century and Red Harbor in the twenty-second, to name just two."

I was aghast. "No, surely no one thinks I—"

"Quite the opposite, young man. Your arrest is proof that they do. But fortunately, with questioning, the truth will be easy enough to determine."

"No, Pol. Please. You can't let them question me with the drug."

His eyes gleamed with the pleasure of the hunt. "Why on Earth not?" he asked. "If you're not guilty as you say, you will be able to sue the state for damages. A famous personage as you are, with public opinion on your side, as I can make sure you will have, that will be worth a great deal of money to us both."

"I'm not famous," I protested.

He sat back with a grin so wide that if he'd been a cat, there would have been feathers. "Ah, but you will be, young man, you will be. I shall see to it. Aston told me who your father is; I would never have taken this case otherwise. When I am finished with the media, if you are as innocent as you say, the police will wish they had closed down this station here and used all its personnel for fish bait. Even if you are the vilest mass murderer in the history of the planet, the police will be embarrassed by the time I am done, and I believe I can get the sentence lightened. But I do need to know which way it is, young man. The questioning will reveal it without a doubt in any case, and it will be critical for me to have advance knowledge." He leaned forward.

I began to despair of getting my point across. My stomach clenched so hard I could taste the bile. "Listen. I'm not guilty." My voice broke. "I haven't killed any of those people. They're all still alive; they're just not here. But I don't want to reveal where they are. There's too much at stake. I need your help."

Too much at stake. If I started shuttling people back and forth, their commitment to settling on Aran would vanish.

Worse. People on Earth would realize that the "natives" of New Richmund were none other than the descendants of their own neighbors and friends. That would inevitably lead to the conclusion among politicians and profiteers that Aran was Earth's colony. And that would destroy everything the settlement on Aran was intended to ensure. Everything my father died for.

If I had to, I would face death to prevent that.

"Fine," Pol said. He rubbed his hands together as if already eager to join this particular battle. "Everyone has secrets. We can draw some boundaries in the questioning. Happens all the time. But questioning is the only way to prove your innocence."

"Do you see this?" I leaned forward and pushed back my hair to show him the blue crystal embedded in my temple. "This crystal gives me telepathic communication with the whynywir, a species native to New Richmund. I'm not making this up. Contact Lennard Sirinin, the xenologist; he knows about these."

"*I* know about them," Pol said. "I read the book. As for how you got that one, if it's relevant to the trial, I'll need to hear the whole story."

"Yes, of course. But to the point of the drugs, you probably know that there's a drug used along with the crystal to open a person's mind to the communication. Too much was used with me. I almost died. I was lucky to find someone who could adjust the crystal, but still, even now, sometimes . . . I've been advised not to use any more mind-altering drugs. I don't think I'd survive questioning with Emetol-9."

Pol frowned. "I see. So this is just a conjecture on your part?" He tapped his fingers on the table.

"It's a conjecture, yes, but—"

"But you don't want to risk your life to find out whether it might be true."

"That's right, and it's more than my life; it's—"

"—Your immortal spirit. Of course. I read the xenologist's book, young man. I followed the news holos of your father. That does raise the stakes." He rubbed the thumb of his right hand across his fingers, dramatizing the point. "It's gold for me and you."

The man interrupted too much, but he was quick and focused. And he did seem to have good background knowledge. If there was a way out of my situation, Pol would find it. I took a deep breath and let it out along with the knot in my stomach.

"Don't relax too much," he said. "We'll play this whole thing as it must be played. First order of business, I'll look for any precedent in not administering the drugs for questioning. But off the top of my head, I don't know of any, so I'm not hoping for much from that angle. Of course you'll offer every other form of cooperation—" He raised an eyebrow and looked at me sharply until I nodded. "Good. The obvious one, of course, would be to bring some of those missing people back here."

I shook my head. "No, I can't do that. It's a one-way trip. Everyone who went there accepted that. I have to protect them and the place where they went. I'd rather die than—"

"And that place is—?" He sat back, looking as happy as a cat licking cream off its whiskers. Looking like he already knew the inevitable answer.

I couldn't let that idea stand. "You're thinking it must be New Richmund, but—"

"Aran," he said, pleased with himself, a man who had read the book.

"Yes, well . . ." I had to be careful here, treading the narrow border of a lie. "It's a lot like our Aran in some respects—climate, for example—but it's different. Those people are the first humans on the planet they went to. I'm not saying any more than that. And no one comes back."

Even if I wanted to bring anyone from Aran to Earth, I couldn't. I would need Taera—and where was she?

Pol leaned forward, acting the prosecutor. "Yet you yourself seem to come and go."

"I . . ." I was at a loss for words. "It's not under my control. Believe me, I'd be out of here right now if I could."

"So you come and go, but not at will?"

"That's right. There's an alien involved in this. A person not from here using a technology we don't have. I'm . . . allowed." Allowed! I was practically forced into it! "Maybe because I'm willing to be the recruiter. I'd like to see that planet settled by those who mean well toward it." Then I looked away, choking up. Swallowing didn't help. "Maybe because I'm willing to die if it comes to that." I looked back at him, afraid, near tears. "But I hope it won't come to that. Don't let them kill me, Pol."

"Relax, Mikel." He spoke gruffly, but put a gentle hand on my shoulder.

"Taerlin," I corrected him.

He squinted a bit at me, then shrugged. "Taerlin. I have to ask all these questions because you can be sure the court will. And the answers have to be good ones and ring true. You have been accused of the murders of two hundred fifty-five people, all missing, no bodies found. It's a serious charge. Headlines all by itself, even if you weren't your father's son. Being who you are, we could get you in the headlines even if the charge were just drunk and disorderly conduct. The combination of the two . . ." He shook his head. "Of course, if you were willing to undergo questioning, it would be easy for us." He moved his hand across the air above his face as if sweeping across a banner headline. "'Son of Alien Martyr Wrongfully Accused!' 'Pain and Anguish Beyond Reckoning!'" Here he paused to study me. "You get my drift?"

I nodded helplessly.

"But you aren't willing to undergo questioning. You're afraid for your life. Now we have to go for a court stay of the questioning, which of course will leave your guilt an open issue. And you have already run from the police once."

"But—"

He waved his arm to silence me. "No, the headlines will have to be different now: 'Son of Alien Martyr Threatened with Death!' 'Will We Kill Them Both?' We'll have to play the martyrdom angle hard and hope they don't focus on the fact that you might be guilty."

"But I'm not—"

"Of course you're not. But we'll never be able to prove that, now, will we? I assume you'd be willing to be questioned under a mechanical lie detector as long as no drugs are involved."

"Yes, of course."

"Good. Not that that would be conclusive, of course. The things are too easy to fool. But it would at least indicate a cooperative attitude on your part. Now, you'll just need a lot of media exposure and a little bit of luck. And a sympathetic judge won't hurt, either."

It turned out I was short on luck, and I didn't get a sympathetic judge, either. I did get media exposure, though. Pol saw to that. I met reporters who worked for more news-holos and other channels than I ever knew existed. It seemed I made the headlines even on days when nothing noteworthy happened in my case. I was in the running for "Eligible Bachelor of the Year"—if I survived the questioning and was proven innocent.

Messages poured in from around the world from people who wanted to settle this planet of mine, a planet played up by the press as an entirely unpopulated planet otherwise similar to New Richmund in its temperate climate and natural abundance, a paradise open to all. I could recruit more people than Taera could transport, if I managed to get out of prison alive.

If Taera ever showed up again.

Other messages sent money for my defense fund and wished me luck.

Pol fielded a visit from a government investigative agent wanting to know how I'd gotten back from New Richmund, and just where was this planet, exactly, that I was recruiting for? Fortunately, I was sheltered from this individual for the duration of my trial, but I began to understand that even if I were proven innocent of murder my troubles were just beginning.

Pol's research didn't turn up any legal precedent for bypassing the normal questioning procedure, nor any medical record of anyone being harmed by it. Of course, there was no record of anyone in my situation being questioned under the drugs, nor, as Pol was quick to point out, was there any record of the air on our planet, even unpolluted air, being poisonous to anyone until my father died of it. But the law was the law, and our judge was not swayed by analogies.

Nor were the police—Jak, with his cold eyes boring into me, certain of my guilt—going to accept questioning using only the mechanical lie detectors without drugs. Jak thought my effort to avoid the drugs was a ruse to get away with the greatest mass murder of our century. And he wasn't about to let me do that, even if it meant killing me.

The hearing was brief. The courtroom was packed with reporters. Pol sat at my side, and half a dozen police officers stayed no more than a few meters away, nervously eyeing the crowd and me to ensure that I didn't somehow just slip into the crowd and away.

But there wasn't a chance of that. Not without Taera.

The lawyer for the state was an elegant man with hair silvering at the temples and a suit that I would have thought no one on government salary could afford. He laid out the facts along with the state's presumptions: the number of people reported missing compared to recent years; my association with many of these people; my recruiting efforts as reported by people who had decided not to go; comments some of the missing people had made to friends they'd left behind.

Pol objected at every presumption, but since the state only needed to show that there was a reasonable enough possibility of guilt to justify the use of questioning, Pol was constantly overruled. In his turn, Pol argued the pointlessness of my insistence that people put their affairs in order, if I was just going to kill them. This, of course, was rebuffed by the prosecution, who noted what a perfect cover-up this was, adding to the appearance of going to another planet.

The one interesting fact emerging from this hearing was that no one from the police had actually witnessed Taera's transportation of anyone from Earth. No one would be able to testify that the people had just . . . disappeared. Perhaps their interest in me had been aroused only recently, and they'd been in a hurry to act, before they could plant an informant.

We then moved to my argument against questioning. Lennard was called to testify.

"Does the accused have on his forehead a crystal of the sort used on the planet New Richmund to communicate with the . . ." The state's lawyer squinted at his notes. ". . . the whynywir?"

"Yes, he does."

"You have examined it? You're certain?"

"Yes, I am."

"Tell us, then, what you know—as a xenologist, Dr. Sirinin—about how this crystal is attached."

Lennard told them, going into surprising detail, far more than was in his book.

"You say, a drug is used," replied the prosecuting attorney. "Can you tell us what it is?"

Lennard looked down, meeting neither his eyes nor mine. "I'm sorry. I can't say that any of the natives knew the name of it, and there's no reason why they should. It would mean nothing to them. As to the chemical nature of the compound, I collected a sample to bring back to Earth for molecular analysis, but unfortunately it was among the many artifacts that had to be left behind during the evacuation. The volcano, you may remember."

"Ah, yes. So you don't know what it is."

Lennard cleared his throat and answered, looking down at his hands. "I did some broad-brush preliminary analyses, enough to know that the drug comprises several compounds; several are organic, carbon-based, and quite complex. But . . . no, I don't know exactly what they are."

"Quite. How about the normal dosage? And the dosage Mr. Pelerin here received?"

When he looked up at me, Lennard's face was painted with an apology. "I'm sorry."

Blood samples and brain imaging were equally useless; there was no existing baseline for my half-alien biology. My attorney was quick to point out that the police must therefore proceed with extreme caution. The prosecuting attorney was equally quick to counter that there was no evidence, besides my personal opinion, that the drug administered with the crystal or the resulting changes in my brain structure and chemistry were any kind of counterindication.

Taera might have been able to answer these questions, but like the two hundred fifty or so people I was accused of murdering, she was missing.

The best that Pol was able, in the end, to wring from the judge was a gradual application of the drug, together with an independent medical observer.

It was a small victory in the midst of a large defeat. Pol began setting the stage with the media for the possibility of my incapacitation or death.

Chapter Twenty-Two

EARTH, YEAR 2467

MIKEL'S RECORDING, continued

The court upheld the prosecutor's motion to keep me locked up, though still presumed innocent. I understood this; I'd already tried to run from the police.

And I'd do it again in a heartbeat. I could see no good outcome in what lay ahead.

What they didn't know, of course, is that Taera could rescue me from this cell as easily as from a deserted beach somewhere.

Taera. Where was she? Why didn't she come?

I was incarcerated in a short-term detention facility located within a high-security prison. It was a federal facility intended to house serious offenders and those accused of such offenses who were considered security risks. For my protection, I was given a cell by myself; this was preferable to sharing a room with other inmates of the facility, though it didn't make for much conversation. I tried to talk with my guards, but they seemed to have been infected with Jak's cold hatred of the mass murderer they thought I was, minds made up even before my questioning.

I exercised as much as I could, but I was not allowed out in the yard or in the gym when the other detainees or the convicts were there. This left me only odd hours at dawn and mealtimes, which in turn made for rushed meals. Still, I used these facilities whenever possible, partly from frustration and boredom, and partly because I needed the physical activity. I trained with weights and ran endless circles in the prison yard and began working with the martial arts forms that I'd studied before I got too busy at the university. I'd been pretty good at karate back then, taught some classes, even won a few competitions. After a few days of simply trying to remember what I had once learned, I regained the ability to turn off my thinking and worrying, and simply to move with the flow of the forms.

I tried to read, but I couldn't concentrate. I brought my notes about the whynywir up to date and drafted a journal article. Of course, I was allowed visitors, but only for short periods at predefined hours. Pol came frequently, sometimes with members of the media in tow. Lennard came, and Aston. My mother visited every day.

There was no sign of Taera.

Finally, almost two months after I was arrested, the date of my questioning arrived. Pol came and brought with him an entirely new set of clothing and detailed instructions. I changed into these clothes—all in a pale blue, as it turned out—and then, Pol or no Pol, put on my father's vest. Pol accepted this with a nod of approval, but he made me undo the thong with which I'd bound back my still-damp hair. A hair stylist arrived, and the man set to work trimming and layering my hair.

I laughed nervously. "I feel like a holo star."

"You are," Pol said.

I looked up at him, bringing a sharp adjustment of my chin from the hair stylist.

Pol was perfectly serious.

"I'm not sure I want my death—my *possible* death, that is—to be so public." My voice echoed in the cell, and it was impossible to know who, just out of sight, might be listening.

"Then you shouldn't have hired me."

"I'm sorry. I didn't mean—"

"Look at it this way, Taerlin. If you live, and you're as innocent as you say, you'll be a very wealthy man. And if you don't live, your mother will never have to worry about money. In either case, it's important that you look your best."

At that moment, I doubted the wisdom of our system of justice, but it wasn't Pol's fault. He was a lawyer and good at his craft. "I appreciate your help," I said.

⸺ ⸗ ⸺

I was led to the questioning room, accompanied by Pol, Lennard, my mother, and two doctors. One of the doctors was assigned by the court and the other selected by Pol. Both were supposed to look after my health. Just in case. There were also three police officers, including Jak, whom I would rather have done without.

A medical technician stood ready to administer the drug that would compel me to tell all. Or kill me. Or both.

The room itself was cold and sterile, with metal walls that made me think of Taera's ship. The ceiling was at least three meters high. Near the ceiling on my right, the metal of the wall gave way to a mirror. Behind that mirror, Pol had told me, was another room that was packed with news reporters who wanted to witness my questioning. Allowing the reporters to witness and record the questioning had been the subject of an intense courtroom battle, though one in which my own presence had not been required. The press was not normally interested in questionings, but since I had gained some celebrity, my lawyer demanded their presence on my behalf. This demand was vigorously resisted by an increasingly worried state prosecutorial team. Given the publicity that had surrounded the other hearing, the court in the end had not dared to keep the media out. I would appear live tonight on holo channels all around the world.

Perhaps those would be live holos of my last moments.

Lennard Sirinin was also there as an expert witness, another concession Pol had won.

A large metal chair was attached to the floor of the room, almost in its center. Behind and to my left, a bank of computer displays sat idle, waiting to announce and record the level of the medication in my blood, and to display my heartbeat, brainwave patterns, and other evidence of my physical condition. It was not the least bit comforting.

And where was Taera? I hadn't seen or heard from her in weeks. I had already given up hope of a dramatic rescue, but I regretted that I had never told her even once that I loved her.

As I crossed the threshold into the room, I panicked. My heart pounded, and I felt faint. I might have run if I could have, if there was anywhere I might have gone. But the questioning room was in the center of the prison facility. There were three police in the room and probably three times that many just outside. And Jak looked like he'd welcome an excuse to use the laser holstered at his hip.

The knot in my stomach twisted so tight I could feel my gorge rising. The last thing I needed was to be sick in front of a hundred holo cameras. "Just a minute," I asked the policeman who led me by my left arm.

He stopped, and I took a deep breath to calm myself. I closed my eyes and prayed for life, if possible, but in any case, for strength and for dignity. Oddly, it helped; I felt calmer, though my breathing was still shaky. I opened my eyes and nodded my thanks to the policeman, and then I walked to the large metal chair that awaited me.

I sat in the chair feeling strangely detached while Jak and another officer fastened straps around my chest, upper arms, and wrists to keep me from struggling. How oddly things had turned out. How odd, when I'd always thought of myself as an Earthman, to be Arantu. How odd, when I'd always thought of myself as a scientist, to be a recruiter. And when I'd always thought I had my whole life ahead of me, how ironic to perhaps be about to die.

The medical technician attached electrodes to my head, chest, and arms. The gel he used to improve conductivity felt cold, but not as cold as Jak's eyes, which never left me. The technician inserted a thin needle into the vein on the inside of my left elbow, attached it to a bottle that hung suspended to the left of me, checked everything, nodded, and went over to read the output on his console. The needle felt like a huge and invasive insect, one I could barely tolerate but was powerless to swat away.

The room was quiet as everyone waited for the drug to take effect. The technician continued to study the displays on his equipment. "That's unusual," he said at last. "He's under, all right, but I've only administered about half the normal dose."

"Stop right there," said my doctor, and the one appointed by the court agreed. This was good. Maybe I stood a chance.

The medicologist did something at his instruments and then nodded a go-ahead to the police officer who had been assigned duty as the questioner. Not Jak, thank goodness, but a long-boned, angular woman who might have been his female clone. "What is your name?" she asked.

Name? The drug induced a kind of disorientation. My self-control weakened, I couldn't stop the whynywir memories from leaking into my consciousness. Name? "My name is . . . Mikel Pelerin." It was what I knew they wanted to hear, but the question wouldn't go away. It hammered inside my head.

Name? Name? Name?

I hadn't answered completely. The whynywir memories were asserting themselves more insistently. Many lives, one name. Many lives. Name? I spoke more loudly, more confidently. "My name is whynywir." Still not enough. "My name is Taerlin." There!

Where was Taera, anyway?

"When were you born?"

Born? When? How many times? How could I answer that? My mind raced, recalling a thousand births, a thousand thousand. Again and again. What was time? When? insisted the question burning in my mind. When?

"He's losing it," the medical technician announced from somewhere very far away.

Lennard leaned over and whispered something to the questioner. "When was Mikel Pelerin born?" she asked.

Mikel? I could answer that. I told her his birthdate. My birthdate. With so many memories swirling so vividly in my consciousness, it was hard to focus on which one I was. I was losing a sense of myself.

"Has Mikel Pelerin killed anyone?" asked my questioner. "Has Taerlin?"

Mikel? He was as guilty of murder as anyone. "Yes," I answered, and my lawyer groaned. But Lennard knelt beside me. He put a hand on my wrist and asked softly, "Who? Who did Taerlin kill?"

An easy question. I struggled to keep the memories clear and separate. My many murders . . . none of them Taerlin's. "No one," I answered. "I . . . killed no one."

"And Mikel? Who did Mikel kill?"

The memory was vivid, so vivid that it was hard to answer. I could see the poor great creature, its one wing hanging uselessly as it plummeted from the sky. Tears slid down my cheeks. "A whynywir. I killed . . . a whynywir. On purpose, Lennard. I didn't know . . ." I wept.

"Easy on the questions now," warned the medicologist from behind me. "There's a pattern here I don't recognize."

Lennard looked at my questioner for permission, and she gave it with a nod. "Did Mikel kill any humans?" Lennard asked, his voice sympathetic and calming.

Humans? Did he? "No," I answered hesitantly, then more certainly, "No, not directly. Not unless the whynywir I killed was human in a past life. He might have been."

"Never mind the whynywir, damn you!" Jak interrupted, anger blazing in his voice and eyes. "Did you kill any people?"

People? Did I kill people? I no longer knew which of the many selves in my memories I was answering for. Over the centuries, we had killed many. Intruding humans in our valley who came unwelcomed. Hostile humans who came for revenge of one sort or another. Unthinking humans who came in ignorance. Yes, of course we had killed humans. Killed and eaten them as was proper, as Aran required. I could remember clearly each death, each feasting.

Filtered through my human consciousness, the memories felt like cold-blooded murder, like cannibalism. I was aghast at the vividness of these memories. They tore me apart, yet I could also feel the appropriateness, even the pleasure in them. The events were too many, too difficult to recount. I swirled deeper and deeper, more and more helplessly into them. I couldn't bear it.

"I've lost him," said the medicologist. It was the last thing I remembered.

Chapter Twenty-Three

EARTH, YEAR 3224

"**H**ow many people have you and Taerlin transported to New Richmund?" Zhou asked. The vertical frown lines that were always present between her brows deepened.

Aiana was expecting trouble in this meeting. She'd been trying to reach Taerlin for a month now and hadn't managed to get within a century of him. Smithjon had begun suggesting that perhaps she'd been thrown out of the time loop entirely. But she knew this couldn't be true. Hadn't the first people she'd talked with on Aran said that she and Taerlin had parted there on bad terms? Hadn't she left them instructions? But these events had not yet occurred for her. In fact, the events on the initial holo she'd found hadn't yet occurred, either. Although she couldn't explain why she couldn't reach Taerlin, Aiana was confident she must still be in the loop.

But she wasn't prepared for this question. She looked up, trying to visualize her log. "It's all in the log, of course," she said, stalling while she added up the approximate numbers of people on eight separate trips.

"Of course," Zhou agreed in a flat voice, "but I'm asking *you*."

"I'd say it's over two hundred, maybe two hundred fifty. And probably the same number from New Richmund. They've all been through the 'port; there are holos of all of them."

"Yes, that seems about right. You have exceeded your energy budget by at least two hundred people. You have single-handedly exceeded the entire history department's energy budget for the year."

All Aiana could say was, "Oh." Her voice sounded small, a little girl in a room full of adults. "I didn't realize . . ."

"And how many people has Taerlin brought on the Blessed Ascension?"

Aiana glanced at Hossen and Vikram. They were both studying the papers in front of them, as if she weren't there. She turned toward Salvatore. He sat rigidly upright, arms crossed over his chest. He met her eyes, his face devoid of expression.

Smithjon shrugged in response to her questioning look. He didn't know any more than she did. They'd both been blindsided.

The room was silent, awaiting her answer.

"I . . . I don't know, Professor Zhou. I . . . wasn't present at any of those events."

Salvatore quirked an eyebrow and said, "But surely you must have gathered some evidence of their occurrence?"

Aiana rubbed her hands over her face, fingertips over eyes that were suddenly too tired for this, palms over blood-warmed cheeks. She wanted to give them the answer they wanted; she really did. It would work so much better for everybody. But what if there were no Blessed Ascension? What if the settlement of Aran was all there ever was?

She looked back at four pairs of eyes hungry for a truth she couldn't give them. "He's never—" Her voice rattled in her throat; she cleared it and started again. "He's never said anything about it to me." She waited for a blow to fall, but they were silent. "Perhaps as an oneiromorph I can't participate. Or perhaps he's found me unworthy."

"Or perhaps you have work that is still not complete—here, as an historian—before you can go," Smithjon offered, trying to be helpful.

She flashed him a wan thank-you smile.

No one else in the room was smiling.

Zhou began consolidating her papers into a neat pile, edges aligned. "There will be no more transporting people, do you understand? Not one. None."

"But what about Taerlin? He has to get back to New Richmund. At least him."

"No, Aiana. Taerlin will stay on Earth. That's where he belongs." Zhou spoke calmly with a little smile on her face that almost looked like pity.

"No!" Aiana half rose from her chair, her heart pounding adrenalin into her blood. "I can't abandon him! He needs—"

"Sit *down*, Miss Kim." It was a drill-sergeant order, not to be disobeyed. "You have overrun two time extensions and wreaked havoc with the department's energy budget. There is no further need for 'portation. You will wrap up this project at once."

Aiana's knees collapsed her back into her seat. "What?"

"Your research is done. You have enough material for a thesis. Further 'portation on your part would be a waste of your time and the university's valuable resources."

"But—"

"I said, 'Wrap it up.'" Zhou's voice softened. "You have excellent material. First-rate. Just interacting with Taerlin in person is worth . . . well, it will be enough to make your reputation. You've reached a wall, and there is no need to continue banging your head against it. No more oneiroportation, Aiana. Just write up what you have." She placed her papers into her briefcase, thumbed her comm on, and headed for the door.

Hossen followed without a glance back.

"You've done well," Vikram said on his way out the door. "Best to wrap it up now." He inclined his head meaningfully toward Salvatore, who paced up and down the front of the room by the door. From under folded eyebrows, Vikram gave Aiana a conspiratorial look. "No sense in letting things get any worse."

When only Smithjon and Aiana remained in the room with him, Salvatore ceased his pacing and turned toward Aiana. "Are you absolutely certain he's said nothing to you of the Blessed Ascension?"

"I'm sorry, Reverend Guide. Perhaps . . . if I manage to see him again . . . I could ask."

"No, no, no!" Salvatore waved his arms in front of him as if he were scrubbing the air between them clean of her suggestion. "If he wanted to mention it, he would. If he doesn't say, you mustn't ask. But perhaps he has given you some indication. Perhaps indirectly, such as being about to do something or go somewhere and telling you you're not wanted?"

Not wanted! It was always she who said she had to leave, and Taerlin who found one reason after another for her to stay a few moments longer. "Let me think about it," she said.

"Yes, good. Do that. And, Aiana . . ." He paused, as if he was deciding on the best way to express his thought. "I don't think it would be a good idea to mention the settlement of New Richmund in your thesis without some clear indication of the Blessed Ascension as well. We wouldn't want to be giving people the wrong idea, now, would we?"

"No, Reverend Guide, of course not. But if I have no direct evidence of the Blessed Ascension, and if I can't mention the settlement of New Richmond, what would I have left to put into my thesis?"

"Oh, I'm sure you'll have quite enough to work with. Good day, Aiana." He nodded to her and then to Smithjon. "Good day, Raj."

And he was gone.

Aiana fought back tears. She would not cry, she *would* not. She would *not*. She swallowed several times to clear the lump in her throat.

Smithjon put a comforting hand on her shoulder. "I know you're disappointed, but Professor Zhou is right. You can make a thesis from what you have, and a good one."

"Thanks, but . . . it's not that."

He raised a questioning eyebrow. "Oh?"

"I know . . . no one before me has seen Taerlin. And I've spent so much time with him, him and his brother. I've learned more about his background than we ever knew before, but . . ."

He waited.

"It's not finished," she blurted out. "The time loop isn't finished. I know about events in it that I haven't done yet. And . . . and . . . he needs me now."

"No," Smithjon said calmly, "if he needed you now, you would be there now. But since you can't get there now, this is not when he needs you."

"But then, when?"

"I don't know, Aiana. But if as you say, the time loop isn't complete, you will somehow manage to get back to wherever and whenever you need to get back to."

"But Professor Zhou doesn't want me to use the 'port any more."

A mischievous smile tugged at the corners of his mouth. "Oh. I see. Well, I guess there's nothing to be done about that, then, is there?" The smile broke free.

For a moment, Aiana didn't understand, and then she did. She gave him her best conspiratorial grin. "No," she said. "I guess not. Thanks, Raj."

Aiana left the conference room and went immediately to the 'port in the basement of the Arts and Sciences building, where the history department made its home. The door to the 'port led to an antechamber with a second door as strong and insulated as that of a vault. The 'port was like a vault in many ways, insulated on all sides against every possible type of interference, from minute electromagnetic waves to seismic disturbances.

She opened the second door, and stepped into a small chamber. It wasn't large enough to allow her to stand upright without hunching over; there was nowhere to go but into the zero G bed that occupied most of its volume. She ran through the pre-sleep checklist. All the equipment was powered up and functioning correctly. She lowered herself into the zero G, deepened her breathing, and slowed her heart rate.

Within ten minutes, Taera stepped into the far more spacious 'port of her dream world.

She checked the equipment. Over two hundred years past where she wanted to be!

A surge of anger and frustration sent her pulse soaring. She wanted to hit something, to smash every one of these pieces of miserable lying equipment that kept her from getting where she needed to go.

And of course, she could. Because it was all dream equipment and would all be perfectly fine the next time she wanted it to be. Taera sighed and let go of the anger. What was the point?

She doublechecked the equipment readings and then initiated the wakeup sequence.

That night Aiana couldn't sleep. She kept thinking about the time loop and how she seemed to be locked out of it. She had a persistent feeling that Taerlin needed her; it knotted her stomach and made the muscles in her forehead and jaw tense.

She didn't want to drug herself to sleep, so she resorted to the exercises she used in the 'port, though she knew that active dreaming would do her no good without the dream-enhancing technology.

Aiana dreamed.

She was walking in an unfamiliar part of the city. It was nighttime. The streets were narrow, barely more than alleys, and they were dark and poorly lit. Trash strewn on the pavement was blown around in the chill wind. Aiana pulled her jacket more tightly around herself, but it did little to keep her warm. The alleys kept turning against the direction she needed to go, and finally she reached a dead end.

A high chain-link fence barred the way.

On the other side, she could see Taerlin in the shadows of the buildings. He reached toward her, but he could not seem to get any closer. Aiana, determined, climbed the fence, but the more she climbed, the higher it grew. On the top she could see a roll of barbed wire.

"Taerlin!" she cried out. "I'm coming!"

The barbed wire tore her clothing and slashed long gashes in her skin. Warm blood ran down her arms and legs. Rats as large as her thighs with gleaming, sharp teeth gathered below her, drawn to the blood.

"You can't get through that way," he called. He sounded desperate. He needed her. "You have to go around."

But there were too many of the creatures, and they were already beginning to climb the fence.

"I can't!"

"You can. You must. Go around."

The rats were getting closer. One opened its mouth to bite her leg, its jagged teeth as sharp as knifes.

Aiana woke tangled in sheets wet with sweat. At first she thought it was blood.

Chapter Twenty-Four

EARTH, YEAR 2467

MIKEL'S RECORDING, continued

I woke to sunshine, the insides of my eyelids red in its brightness. Alive, then.

Alive, but my muscles ached with bruises that might be more emotional than real. I felt weak, damaged, raw. I couldn't remember what had happened.

I opened my eyes and was assaulted by white walls bright in sunlight. I groaned.

"Taerlin!" Lennard's face swam into the edge of my vision.

I turned my head toward him. The motion made me dizzy. I was lying in a bed, under a light cover.

Lennard bent over me. "How do you feel?"

"Awful." My voice scraped against my dry throat. The air was tinged with disinfectant and alcohol, insufficient against a permeating smell of decay. "Where—?"

"You're in a hospital. You passed out under questioning. You've been unconscious for three days. We didn't know if you would live, or if you would regain consciousness. The doctors have no medical explanation—"

I remembered the questioning then, and I groaned again.

"Are you all right? I'll get a doctor."

"No! Stay here, Lennard. Just tell me they aren't going to do that to me again. Please."

"Oh, I don't think you have to worry about that. You and your whynywir. You're something of a popular hero. The courts have declared you innocent of murder and issued an injunction against any further use of drugs in questioning, but I understand the police still want to talk with you." He pointed with his chin across the bed toward the other side of the room. I looked in that direction. An open door led to a hospital corridor. "Guards," Lennard said quietly.

"I see."

"They do keep out the crowds," Lennard added. "I doubt I could have done so myself. The media are full of you. I've never seen anything like it." He lowered his voice and spoke conspiratorially. "I would advise you to get your book out quickly, before they lose interest in you. You'll be a rich young man."

I laughed. It came out more like a choking cough. It brought bile to my mouth and made my head hurt. "Thanks, Lennard. You sound just like my lawyer."

"Smart man," he said.

"Has anyone seen Taera?"

"You're still under guard."

I didn't care. If the chance came to get back to Aran, I was going to take it. "I just asked if anyone had seen her."

"No," he said. Then he added, almost as an aside, "Aston has finished gathering the things you requested. He is prepared to travel with them. And your mother."

My mother! There would be nothing, then, to keep me here. I wanted to go back to Aran so much my heart ached. What could be keeping Taera away?

"And I will go with you as well," Lennard said, "that is, if you're still willing."

"Of course I'm willing! But what about your ambassadorship?"

"They can stuff my ambassadorship. It's a great honor, of course, but it has to be the most mind-deadening distinction that anyone could ever honor me with. If Lela is going to be on your world, then I shall go there, too."

"Your professorship? Your students?"

Lennard backed away as if seriously offended, but his eyes still twinkled with humor. "My students, young man, are all with you."

A man in medical whites entered the room, interrupting our conversation. Talk of going back with me was all theoretical in any case, without Taera. Behind the physician trailed Jak in police uniform. The cold distaste in his eyes made it clear that, in his opinion at least, I was as guilty as ever. He watched with clear antipathy as the physician took my temperature and pulse, examined my reflexes, and asked if I thought I could stand.

If the police ever were going to be allowed to question me again, Jak would be right there. It was personal. Might he become violent, seeing me getting away with what he believed to be murder? I wondered if my lawyer could somehow make him keep his distance.

Standing was difficult, but I did it. I probably stayed upright, the room swimming around me, for a good two seconds before my legs collapsed.

The next time I woke, I felt better. Lennard was still—or again—in the room with me, deeply involved in reading a book. The hospital room was light and airy; a large window behind Lennard gave a view of winter-bare treetops. Mine was the only bed in the room. A private room in a hospital, where most beds were in wards of six to eight! Usually only the rich could afford such luxury, and sometimes even then not enough rooms were available. I wondered if the government was paying for it. Knowing the media-savvy skills of my lawyer, I figured they probably were. There was an armoire in the room, and a holo projector was mounted on one wall. A narrow door led to what was probably a private or semi-private toilet. Maybe even a bath. Now that would be a pleasure! Another door led outside. A shadow thrown from the light in the hall against my open door suggested the presence of one or more police guards not visible to me directly.

"Lennard," I said softly.

He jumped slightly, snapping his book shut.

"Sorry; I didn't mean to startle you."

"You're awake! We've all been hoping—"

"'All'? Has Taera come?"

Lennard looked away. "No . . . Not Taera, but your mother and Pol and Aston and I, and the medical staff, and then there have been all the reporters, but I guess any change is good news for them, whether you woke up or d—or whatever." He recovered quickly, but I knew what he had almost said. "And of course, all the others," he added.

"Lennard, I have to get out of here."

"Wait a minute," he protested. "Two days ago, you couldn't even stand."

Had it been two days? Maybe I was weaker than I thought. Tentatively, I pulled back my covers and sat up, swinging my legs over the side of the bed. I felt all right. I stood, and Lennard raced around the bed so that he could be ready to catch me if I fell. But he needn't have worried. I felt weak, but not dizzy. I was also phenomenally hungry.

I also realized, embarrassed, that the hospital-issue dressing gown I wore hung open loosely down the back. "I'm hungry," I said. "I need clothes. I have to get out of here."

Lennard tried his best to look stern and shook his head, as at a difficult child. "In reverse order. You're not going anywhere; I'm sure the doctors will want to keep their eyes on you for a few days yet. They won't give you any other type of clothing while you're staying in the hospital. And I'll ask the nurse on call to order you a meal; I'm sure she can get it quickly."

"But I'm in a hurry!"

"You've been unconscious for nearly a week. Another couple of days won't hurt you."

"Maybe," I retorted, "but I want to discuss this with my lawyer." The truth was, it wasn't the days. It was Jak. He made me nervous. I wanted to get away from the man.

Lennard was right about all three things. The meal came quickly, the doctor wouldn't hear of my leaving, and although the bath was as great a pleasure as I had imagined, it was absolutely impossible to get any kind of decent clothes to wear, not while the doctors still worried about my recovery. And another thing: Jak's silent stare kept me under the covers in the hospital gown that otherwise would have left my entire rear in view.

Pol came the next day.

I was looking out the window of my room trying to figure out what the crowd below was up to. They filled the sidewalks on both sides of the street, as far as the eye could see. Only a police barricade kept the street itself clear. Yet there were no signs or placards, no indication that they were protesting or demonstrating about anything. The crowd seemed peaceful rather than angry, as if they had all just happened to gather for a family picnic at this one spot.

I couldn't make sense out of it. I turned on the holo to see if the news might shed any light. I found a program called "The Week in Review" and fast-forwarded past a lot of stuff on pending legislation and diplomatic activity. Guerilla activity in the mountains of South America continued; the people there lived in desperate poverty. They had no economic prospects and wanted independence from United Earth. Of course, it was unthinkable to the politicians.

I thought that many people in that area might come with me, if I could only go there and make the offer. It was an impractical thought.

Then I stumbled upon a holo of my own questioning. I watched, entranced, as the young man I barely recognized as myself entered the questioning room. I enlarged the holo. He looked good—short-cut sandy brown hair framing a frightened, innocent face. The policeman who had been leading him into the room dropped his hand from the young man's arm, and the young man closed his eyes for a moment, gathering his strength. Perhaps praying. Then he opened his eyes again, nodded his thanks, and walked calmly to the chair in the center of the room.

I would have watched the rest of it as well, but the holo image froze, and the news analyst announced, "The trial of Mikel Pelerin has dominated the news this week. In an unprecedented response rate, an astonishing ninety-seven percent of viewers believe him innocent, and the judge has agreed. A record-breaking damage settlement is expected. The son of the alien Cort-Naran, young Pelerin still lies unconscious as a crowd numbering in the thousands stands vigil outside the hospital. People everywhere are asking whether in our thoughtlessness we have now murdered two Richmundians, father and son, who came to us in peace."

I stopped the holo and zoomed in on the the young man in the chair who awaited his death. But the holo was like all the ones I had studied of my father: the man was present, immediate, yet at the same time unreadable. I turned off the projector.

Pol arrived with reporters from the *Times Chronicle* and *Channel 67 News on the Minute* in tow. Within minutes, he had both the police and the hospital staff in an uproar. He had brought me real clothes—a simple light blue shirt and clean, medium blue trousers, along with, miraculously, my headband trimmed in whynywir down and my father's vest, and I got myself dressed. He also had both the police guard and the doctor on duty sputtering protests, when he accused them of continuing my imprisonment.

Jak emerged from an elevator in a rush, still out of breath, scowling at everyone.

"Pol," I asked, "can we do something about . . ." I indicated Jak with a tilt of my head, trying to be subtle, unwilling to provoke the man.

"I assure you, he's not here on police business," Pol answered. "He's been reassigned."

"Then it's personal. That's worse!"

Pol nodded thoughtfully. "Harassment," he said. "I'll get a restraining order."

Not long after that, a telephone call from the police commissioner obtained my freedom and a promise of a restraining order first thing in the morning.

"Write your book now," Pol advised while we rode the elevator down to the lobby, "while you're still on everyone's mind. A year from now, you'll be history."

I felt a new confidence in my mission and its successful outcome. Live or die, my own fate didn't seem to matter so much anymore. I'd faced death. It was something I could do. "A year from now, I'll be gone," I said.

Jak, who for now still shadowed me, jerked stiffly upright, as if I'd said he'd be dead. "You can come with me," I added to Pol, grinning, knowing his answer. I ignored Jak's hostile stare.

"No thanks," my lawyer replied. "I have a book to write, myself. You've made me a small fortune, young man, and I intend to enjoy it. Speaking of which, if you need an investment advisor, I can recommend one."

"What investment?" I asked. "No book, remember?"

"No book," he said, "but the reparations will still come to a pretty sum. You would be surprised to find out how much the government will pay to make your case disappear. You're quite an embarrassment, innocent as you have proved to be"—a loud snort of disbelief reminded us of Jak's dogged presence—"and nearly murdered by insensitive treatment on the part of certain officials. After their murder of your father as well." Pol returned Jak's scornful look, forcing the policeman to look away.

"Thanks, Pol." I was as grateful for the relief from Jak's scrutiny as for the money. "Invest it for me, all right? I'll give you, what's the term? Power of attorney?"

"Power of attorney, yes. I can do that."

"Reinvest half the income, and give the rest to causes that work to advance our citizenship in this galaxy. Science and ethical responsibility, both. Would you do that for me?"

Pol shrugged, but he lightened the neutrality of this with a smile. "I'm a lawyer. Of course I'll do that for you—for a fee."

"Of course. Set it up the way it ought to be to pay you and your successors properly. I want only the best managers, but I also want the funds to grow and I want to have a fair percentage of it used to make Earth a good galactic citizen. We have to learn to interact with cultures not the least bit like ours. We have to have technology that will support us as our humanity improves."

"A good galactic citizen," Pol echoed. "I can set it up as a charitable trust. Call it, maybe, the One Galaxy Foundation. How does that sound?"

I grinned. "Sounds great."

Jak looked like he was going to throw up. I was beginning to enjoy this. I tried my best to give him a friendly smile.

We stepped through the front door of the hospital and out into sunlight so bright that I was almost blinded after so long indoors. I paused at the top of the broad marble stairs that led from the doors to the street and only then registered that the people from across the street now crowded the bottom of the stairs and the sidewalk, obstructed all traffic in the street, and almost filled the entire city block. Stonefaced police held them back, though reporters at the very front of the crowd, microphones held over their shoulders and holo recorders running, pushed against the police. A cheer went up from the crowd, and Pol gave a single, sharp, satisfied nod.

"Wave," he ordered, and I did.

The crowd went wild.

Sweating and red-faced, the police strained against the reporters. "Taerlin!" a reporter shouted as we came near. "Will you be taking anyone with you this time?"

I glanced at Pol, who made a noncommittal gesture. I could answer as I pleased. "If they want to come," I said. I had to shout. I searched the crowd, but there was no sign of Taera. Perhaps it was the mood of the crowd, but I was happy. I felt sure I would find her.

"When?" the reporter asked.

I stopped and looked at him, trying in that sea of faces to focus on his one, unique, singular human face. He looked, somehow, delicate and bruised, needy and determined, and maybe just a little afraid. "Tonight," I said. "You come, too."

Chapter Twenty-Five

EARTH, YEAR 3224

*G*o around.

    Well, how on Earth was she supposed to do that? What came next was the next scheduled meeting with Taerlin, but it looked like Aiana would never be able to get to the moment, or indeed to any more moments during Taerlin's entire remaining lifetime.

Which, as Raj Smithjon had pointed out, was likely to be short.

Obviously, it had just been a frustration dream, and not an uncommon one at that. Go around, indeed.

The coffee shop was beginning to fill up, as it always did when the residential dining hall stopped serving breakfast. The aroma of brewing coffee and bakery-fresh pastries filled the air. Aiana breathed deeply, enjoying the smells and the moment of freedom from the dream state, where it seemed she spent most of her life these days. What she needed was some good, strong black tea, and some cinnamon toast to go with it. She would sit in the coffee shop for a while and enjoy the smell and taste of both, and then she'd go back to the 'port and try again.

A couple behind her in line were laughing with the familiarity of close friends. The girl's sharp laughter cut across the crowded room, and Aiana couldn't help but overhear. "Cake?" the girl squealed, still giggling. "You haven't even eaten lunch yet, have you?"

"Noooo." The boy drew out the word as if he was considering the problem seriously. "But I want cake now."

The girl laughed again. "You have to eat something nutritious first." She made her voice serious, adopting a tone that might have been her mother's. "Clean your plate and then you can have dessert."

Aiana turned and glanced at the pair, trying to be discreet. The boy was rail-thin, with a scraggly beard. He could afford to eat dessert three times a day. "I'm not living at home anymore," he said. "I can have dessert whenever I want. And I want it now."

Aiana smiled to herself. Dessert before lunch. All right, then. Maybe she'd make that a cinnamon pastry instead of toast, and . . . Her mind froze.

Go around.

Who said that her timeline had to follow the same sequence as Taerlin's? Maybe she couldn't get to the meeting with him because it wasn't the next thing in *her* timeline.

But then, what else could be? There was only one thing that she knew well enough to attempt. She would go back to the first settlement on Aran, sometime after . . . after whatever had happened between her and Taerlin, and she would instruct them to wait with her. This had to be done sometime. Why not now? The sooner she got this out of the way, the sooner she could get back to him.

She couldn't bear to delay any longer. Ignoring the growling of her stomach, she slipped out of line and headed to the basement and the 'port.

Two guides sat on chairs in front of the door to the 'port. One was heavyset, with the dark skin and broad features of a person of African descent, and incongruously blond hair and pale gray eyes. The other was all bones and joints, with the sallow complexion of a person who never went outdoors. He fingered a string of beads without seeming to be aware he did it, an excess of nervous energy. The clack-clack-clack of his beads echoed in the basement hallway. Aiana had never seen either of the guides before. They both looked up when she entered the corridor, the stairway door swinging shut behind her.

"Hello," she said, hearing a slight waver in her voice. What were they doing here? She straightened her shoulders. "I'm sorry to disturb you, but I need to get into the 'port there."

They didn't move.

"The door just behind you," she said.

The thin guide stood. He was taller than she'd imagined. His robes billowed around him in the slight movement of air processed through the basement's purification system, blue and green and brown, with white at the collar and hem, symbolic of the Earth. The formal garb indicated a position in the temple hierarchy.

Suddenly the corridor seemed narrow and confined. Aiana drew in a breath. Her heart thumped so loudly she wondered if they could hear it. "Is . . . there a problem?"

"This 'port may not be used until further notice," he said.

"May . . . not be used?"

"Desistation Order of the Synod. Until further notice."

"May I see the order?"

"You are Aiana Kim?"

She swallowed. "Yes."

"Check your comm." He sat again, moving his chair slightly until it blocked the door a little more completely. The beads clacked in his fingers like insects.

Aiana ran the six flights of stairs from the basement to Smithjon's office under the eaves of the building. Her chest pounded with the exertion, but she pushed the pace. She didn't want any energy left for thinking.

If only he were there! What day of the week was it? Would he be at home, his day off? Teaching a class? Of course she should have commed. But she hadn't wanted to look at her comm for fear of what she'd find there. Besides, where else could she go? She ran harder, her lungs aching with the effort.

She knocked on his office door, the sound of it a little louder than she'd intended. She gasped for breath. "Raj?"

"Yes?" came his muffled voice.

She opened the door, and Smithjon looked up from what might have been a centuries-old book. Dust from it danced in the sunshine pouring through the window. He held a handkerchief over his nose. "Office hours are from ten till . . ." He paused, registering who his visitor was and noting her distress. He put down the book, very carefully, walked around his desk, and placed a gentle hand on her shoulder. "It's okay," he said. "Just catch your breath and then tell me what's the matter."

"There are . . . guides . . . in the basement." She drew a couple of deep breaths, trying to regain control of her complaining lungs while also trying not to dissolve into tears.

"Here, have a seat." With his hand still on her shoulder, he walked her to his guest chair and gave her a tissue. "What guides?"

"Guides from the Synod. Thanks, Raj." She twisted the tissue in her hands. "They won't let me use the 'port."

He frowned, as if he were working a difficult puzzle. "You're not *supposed* to be using the 'port, remember?"

"But . . ."

The corner of his mouth had that twitchy look it got when he was trying not to smile. Aiana tried not to return the smile that wasn't quite there. "Yes, Professor. I know that. I'm just saying that even if I were—hypothetically—interested in using it, they're not letting me. Doesn't that seem like, well, overkill to you? Given that I'm not using it anyway?"

He sighed. "Probably more of a case of the right hand and the left hand not coordinating their actions. I guess the bright side is that you weren't making any headway anyway, so maybe it doesn't matter too much. And you *do* have enough material for a good thesis."

She couldn't give up now. Taerlin would be expecting her, wanting her, needing her. Abandoning him was unthinkable. "But there's the time loop problem. It isn't complete. I think I found another approach worth trying. Isn't there anything we can do about the Synod? Some kind of emergency appeal or something?"

"An appeal. Yes, there's a procedure. Legal process, takes years. Expensive, too. While you're waiting for that to sort itself out, you might as well write your thesis and get on with your life."

"But if I write my thesis and get my degree, wouldn't that undermine my case against the Synod?"

He ran his fingers through already unkempt hair. "I'm not a lawyer, but I wouldn't be surprised if you're right."

"Maybe if the History Department initiates it?"

"That would be Professor Zhou."

They looked at each other, silent for a moment.

"That won't work, will it?"

"No. I imagine not."

Aiana grimaced. "I'll have to think of something else, then."

Smithjon looked at her, curious. "What?"

"I wish I knew."

The basement corridor was the same as two days ago. The sterilized, odorless air was the same, and yet the corridor looked completely different. Aiana still wasn't used to the wasp-eye goggles, but she'd been wearing them continuously since yesterday, and at least she wasn't bumping into things anymore.

The corridor seemed brighter than before, and cleaner. And much longer. The goggles gave her nearly total three hundred sixty-degree vision, and she'd begun to understand why techs and gamers favored them so much. But Aiana wasn't using them for the vision enhancement. She wanted the disguise that the vision band would provide.

Two guides still sat in front of the door to the 'port, but they weren't the same two. These two looked so alike they might have been twins, middle-aged, with short brown hair and neatly trimmed goatees showing a sprinkling of grey. They wore the formal robes, though, that marked them as representatives of the Synod, and they seemed to be playing some kind of game involving their comms and a number of jewel-like tokens that they passed back and forth.

Aiana ran her hands through her hair, surprised for a moment at how short it was. Then she remembered the mahogany-brown wig she was wearing, and the makeup that turned her skin olive. And the tech maintenance toolkit she carried, with its official IT logo stamped on the side. She touched her ID tag. It was fake. She never could have afforded to buy it, even if she'd had any idea how. But when she hinted to a friend in the IT department that an illicit time-travel romance was involved, the friend, a die-hard romantic, had insisted on helping.

She never could have worked out this plan without that help.

Without glancing at the guides, she used a passkey to enter the first 'port in the row. Leaving the door open, she set the toolkit down on the bed and made a show of clattering its contents from time to time, making just enough noise to give the illusion she was working.

After about ten minutes, she did the same in the second 'port.

That brought her to the door of her own 'port, where the two guides sat, barring the way. Her heart was pounding. "Excuse me?" she said, indicating the door. Her voice sounded a little too tentative. She'd need to be a lot firmer if this was going to work.

"Sorry," one of the Guides replied. "This 'port is not in use."

"I don't care if it's *in use* or not. I'm not *using* it. I don't *use* these things." She made her voice as scornful as she could. "This is routine maintenance."

The two looked at one another. "No one said anything about maintenance."

"Has to be done every month. You think these things maintain themselves?" She let out a breath of contempt. "People just expect that everything will always run perfectly by magic. Well, it doesn't. Now please move aside. I'm on a tight schedule here."

One of the guides looked into his comm, then at her, and then back at the comm. "Could you please remove the, uh, the visor?"

The toolkit was as heavy as her briefcase, but she managed to cross her arms impatiently. "What, you think I'm a holo star or something. I use the wasp-eyes to see."

"Yeah, you and all the other techs, but we have instructions regarding who can enter here."

"And they say no maintenance techs?"

The second Guide laid a hand on the arm of the first. "It's all right. Look at her. Dark, straight hair. She's not the one we're worried about."

"Leave the door open," the first Guide said, "like you did at the other places."

"Sure," Aiana said. "That's what I do."

They moved their chairs aside to let her in, and she opened the door with the passkey.

She stepped into the 'port and put down her toolkit.

Then she closed and locked the door.

Chapter Twenty-Six

EARTH, YEAR 2467

MIKEL'S RECORDING, continued

"Tonight. You come, too."

My face loomed larger than life in the evening news holos, and I was regretting those words. Although the park that I'd used in the past to transport people in groups of two or ten or twenty was a block down the street from my apartment, I could see that it was crowded. And every few minutes, more people emerged from the subway exit at the corner. How many of those came just for the spectacle, and how many wanted to leave with me? How many could Taera take?

More to the point, where was Taera? I could do nothing without her.

My mother put a hand on my shoulder. I stopped pacing, and she began kneading the muscles of my neck and shoulders. I hadn't realized how much they hurt. "Relax," she said. "She said that when you needed her, she would be there. I believe her."

"Where was she before the questioning?" I retorted. "I needed her then."

"Maybe not."

I pulled away angrily. "So by that standard, maybe not now, either."

"Maybe not," she said, still massaging the muscles at the base of my neck.

I sighed appreciatively. "You're right. She'll come. I think I'll go out."

She patted my shoulder again. "You'll never get past the police. They're here to protect you from that crowd. I can't even go to the grocery store without an escort."

"I'll get past them." I intended the words to sound lighthearted, but they came out with surprising grimness. I felt almost apologetic as I explained. "I'll bet the police don't know that the basements of the units on this block are interconnected. There are emergency doors in the firewalls. They'll probably sound an alarm, but I won't need much time to slip out."

Fifteen minutes later, cloaked in a dark grey cape with a hood, I walked out of the unguarded building on the corner, crossed the street, passed unrecognized by the police on the sidewalk on the far side, and merged with the crowd in the park.

It was getting dark, but like most areas of the city, the park was well lit. Although the day had been unseasonably warm, a cool breeze rose with the sunset, a reminder that it was still winter. I was one among many wearing cloaks or coats, scarves or hats, who stood in small groups or alone or wandered in the park.

On the edges of the crowd near the police, the media waited with their holo recorders and microphones. The crowd there was thick, anxiously peering up and down the street, waiting, no doubt, for me to arrive. But in the center of the park, the mood was different. People seemed to have settled in for the long evening. Some had even brought food, which they ate sitting on benches or on the grass, alone or with family or friends.

Taera was nowhere in sight.

But if she'd been cloaked and hooded as I was, would I have seen her in the crowd? For that matter, would she see me?

The cloak would have to go. I would hide from the police no longer.

A woman sat on a park bench nearby, her white hair haloed in lamplight. She wore only a thin dress with no coat. She hugged herself as she huddled to keep warm. There would be no problem about what to do with the cloak. I took it off and wrapped it over the woman's shoulders, aware now of the cold breeze on my own arms. She looked up in surprise. "Keep warm, mother," I said, and I gave her shoulder an extra pat.

"Eh?" She chuckled softly, as if she was unused to laughing. "For me? Thank you, son. I could use this." She pulled the cloak closer around her shoulders. She had not recognized me.

I turned to find a number of people approaching me. My father's red-and-white beaded vest and the whynywir down on my rawhide headband could have been a beacon. The sky burned an electric blue, and the air was sharp and unusually fresh.

Despite the cold, I felt elated. I nodded toward the nearest person, a young man of about twenty with wispy light brown hair and a thin face. "Good evening!"

"Good luck, Taerlin!" was his warm reply. I felt . . . connected to him somehow, connected to all these people who had come here to be near me. I touched him on the shoulder, and the contact seemed to satisfy. He moved away, but others approached: a young family, the husband carrying a baby of about a year, while a little girl held her mother's hand. "Good luck, Taerlin," the husband said.

"Thank you."

The baby watched me with wide eyes, innocent, alert, taking in everything around him. My breath caught for a moment. Whynywir eyes. I felt elatedly, unreasonably hopeful. Humanity was not beyond redemption, and I was going home to Aran. I was sure of it.

I walked in a daze through that park, touching everyone who greeted me, saying things I no longer remember, suspended between the pain of their short lives and the joy of loving them and their potential to change their world.

Of the many hundreds of people in the park, only a few were there because they wanted to come with me. I recognized the hunger in their eyes, and the fear.

The first of these was a man old enough to be my father. He was no taller than me, and stocky in a way that suggested muscle more than fat. And for reasons I couldn't fathom, he was angry at me. "You taking people back with you?" he challenged. The hunger was there, behind the anger. And the fear, too.

"Yes, but you should understand that there's no return." My standard answer.

He stiffened. "We will come." Only then did I notice the small woman who hovered behind his right elbow. If he was hungry for the journey, she was starving.

"Why?" I asked.

The man glared at me, but the woman answered in a quavering voice, "Please. Our son . . . our son went with you already." The man took his wife's hand and said, "Our only son."

"I usually ask people to wrap up their affairs. Pay bills, close out accounts, and say good-bye to family and friends. Don't leave any loose ends."

"We are ready," said the husband.

"All right. Then come with me."

Taera. Where was she?

Soon I had close to forty people ready to go with me. Some waited by the large statue that dominated the center of the park: Rodrigo Milan with his starship, the first Earthman to set foot on another star system's planet, nearly two centuries ago. Others followed me closely, unwilling to risk letting me out of their sight. Hundreds more simply wanted to say hello or to wish me luck, or to hear what I would say to them. In whatever way Pol and the media had crafted my story, I had become a kind of hero. My adrenaline was flowing. Despite the chill in the air, I was warm.

Each person was special. Each encounter was complete. Each touch seemed to truly reach another human being. For the moment at least, I forgot my whynywir side and reveled in my humanity.

One person never talked to me, though he followed me around the way a dog follows its master. He looked younger than me, though taller and almost painfully thin. He stared at me intently, hungrily, but when I returned his gaze, he turned away. Once, I started to walk toward him, and he almost frantically backed away, putting another group of people between me and him. Yet when I stopped trying to approach him, he came closer, and his eyes bored into me as if he were memorizing my every word and action. If he didn't want to actually talk with me, that was his affair. I tried to give him the space to come as close as he would like. He worked his way toward me hesitatingly, a few steps closer, a step or two in retreat, and then closer yet, looking as if he might flee the minute I looked directly at him. He reached out a shaking hand toward my sleeve, but then someone behind him called a name—"Dheren!"—and he turned away.

Inevitably, a few reporters found me. I ignored them. I was too involved with the people who had come just to see me, and, for their part, the reporters seemed content simply to record the events that unfolded.

"Taerlin." A boy tugged at my sleeve. He barely came to my shoulder. The hunger and fear in his eyes were unmistakable.

"You're too young," I protested. "You should be with your family." My strange shadow, Dheren, had returned, and he pressed closer to hear better.

"Don't have family," the boy said. I might have guessed as much from his shaggy hair and from the dirt and tatters on his clothing. "Don't have nothing," he said, lifting his chin, jaw set in determination. "You take people like me?"

"I take the people that need to go." I made up my mind. "Come." I held out my hand, and he took it.

I looked up, careful to avoid my shadow's eyes. I wanted to check how many people followed me now and how many waited by the statue. In the lamplight of the early winter night, Taera's red hair stood out among the hoods and capes of those waiting by the statue.

My heart leaped.

"Come," I repeated, then more loudly for all those who followed me, "Come with me," and I headed toward her.

A moment later, a commotion off to my left drew my attention. A man burst through a knot of people, running in my direction, pushing past people that were in the way. The intensity and energy, the haste, were out of keeping with the mood of the crowd. I could think of only one person that it could be. "Quickly!" I called to those behind me, and holding the boy's hand firmly, loped toward the statue.

I could see that Taera was organizing the group over there so that they all held hands, ready to go. As we reached the statue, I met Taera's eyes. She smiled at me, and the air got ten degrees warmer. I almost forgot why I was there.

Almost.

But Jak bearing down upon me was enough to keep me focused. I ran as quickly as I could with the boy in tow, but I wasn't fast enough. I was still half a dozen meters from Taera when Jak tackled me, knocking me to the ground. He fell on top of me.

"You aren't *going* anywhere, are you?" he said.

My strange shadow pressed closer.

I knew Jak didn't have the authority to stop me. I had been found innocent, after all. I gambled that he wouldn't overstep his legal bounds. "Yes, I *am* going, and these people with me."

"Then I'm going with you, too."

"Oh, no." I started to laugh, but his expression was grim and perfectly serious. "Jak, we're going to a new world. No one will die, but no one will return, either. There will be no police and no technology and no history or world events as you know them. It's not for you. Give it up. Go home. Let me be."

"You may have fooled these people, but you can't fool me, Taerlin. As far as I'm concerned, you've murdered all those other people, and you'll murder these, too. If I'm wrong, prove it to me. Take me there. Show me those people still alive."

I shook my head. "I could take you and I could show you, but don't you get it? No one comes back. There is no return."

"*You've* returned."

"That's different." It was a weak answer. "I'm not coming back anymore, either." Not much stronger.

"Yes, you will, Taerlin." His voice carried an undertone of menace. He shifted slightly to reveal that he held a laser pointed at my chest. "Now you listen to me. You will take me there, and then when I'm ready you will bring me back. Or I will kill you. Do you understand me?"

The weapon could have been the head of a cobra poised to strike. My heart raced. How ironic, to come so close to a safe return, only to be killed by a rogue policeman! I wanted more than anything to be back on Aran again. I didn't want to die here on Earth. And so, sadly, I said, "I'll take you." It came out strained, little more than a whisper.

"And you will bring me back," Jak said, "or I will kill you. Let there be no misunderstanding between us."

And so I gave up Aiana's and my hope for children, and my unfinished work shaping the human culture of Aran. Cort would have to pick that up; I knew he would succeed. As Taera would say, he already had. "I understand," I said.

"And you agree," Jak insisted, pushing me roughly.

I was shaking with anger, my fists clenched. "Yes."

"Good." Jak pulled away from me and stood, holstering his laser.

I, too, stood. I took the boy's hand in my right hand and held out my left hand to Jak.

He looked skeptically at me, and I raised an eyebrow and waited. There was nothing to say. He took my hand.

"Hold tight," I said. "No matter what."

I looked for Dheren, but the man seemed to know that I would look for him. He melted back into the front row of the onlookers, shrinking away from my question. For a moment his eyes once again met mine, and I was startled by their intensity. By the look of ecstasy, of . . . triumph in them. Then he looked away. He wouldn't be coming.

I took a step forward, and another. The group fell in with me, and Taera's familiar wall opened around us. It felt cool and liquid, quicksilver as I stepped through, pulling Jak and the boy firmly with me. The others followed. We were inside Taera's ship.

I took a deep breath of Taera's cool, pure, odorless air and let go Jak's hand and the boy's. Taera had prepared the inoculum, and now she began the inoculation process. She held in her hand something that looked almost like a laser, but smaller. She went around to each person and touched their hand or arm with its tip. They showed no reaction.

Jak looked at me, eyes narrowed, glowering. "What's she doing?"

"She's inoculating them."

His eyes narrowed further, and he almost snarled, "What? Why?"

"Jak, everyone needs to be inoculated." I spoke in my calmest voice, the one usually reserved for lost and frightened children. "We're going to another world with a slightly different biology than ours. This will change your body chemistry so that anything growing there won't kill you." All of this was completely true. What I didn't say was that it would also alter his genetic make-up so that he could breathe the air without being exhausted, adapt to the environment, and be born again, even as whynywir or khena. He wasn't ready to hear all that.

Jak drew himself stiffly upright as I spoke, and I recognized the tight set of his jaw.

Taera was approaching us, and I didn't want a scene. I did something I've never quite managed before or since. I lied wholeheartedly. "You don't want to contract an alien virus, do you?"

He relaxed slightly, considering.

"Worse—you don't want to bring some alien virus back to Earth, do you?"

But Jak had a different concern. "How do I know you're telling the truth?"

I was outraged. "What do you think, that I'm poisoning everybody?"

Jak shrugged elaborately. He looked at me with unconcealed hatred but said nothing.

I was tempted to let him pass on the inoculant, but I couldn't. He would be stuck on Aran like everyone else. Some day he might marry and have children. I couldn't allow his unaltered genes to be introduced into the gene pool of the planet. No one should be cut off from the eternal life that was offered, even Jak's children.

"You'll die here without this," I said. Which was true, in the long run. "The air has toxins in it." Which was not exactly true, though it did tire Earth people a great deal.

Taera came up to us and reached toward Jak with her inoculation gun.

He pulled away, indicating me with a gesture of his head. "Him first."

"Jak, look around. No one here has died, and I've already—"

His eyes were starting to narrow again, his spine stiffening.

"Never mind." I spoke in a rush. "Take it easy. I'll do it again, even though I don't need to. I'll go first. But you must be inoculated too, or I won't take you."

We stared at each other, deadlocked for a moment, and then Jak gave in.

"All right. But you first."

I breathed a sigh of relief and took Taera's touch gladly. The instrument she used felt like nothing, not even the tiniest prick of anything breaking the skin.

Jak stiffened, but he let her inoculate him, too. Some people just do not accept immortality gracefully.

Chapter Twenty-Seven

ARAN, YEAR BC 2043

MIKEL'S RECORDING, continued

We stepped through the cool metal wall of Taera's ship and onto Aran. A warm breeze of perfumed air rustled the leaves of the khenaran and caressed my face. The whynywir voices flooded again into my mind, harmonizing with a current of contentment among the khena. Morning sunlight angled through the trees, still low enough to paint long, golden stripes across the forest floor. If Jak hadn't been watching me with his predatory eyes, I might have wept in happiness.

As it was, I didn't have the luxury of joy. I had a job to do. I brought Jak and the other newcomers down the hill, through a khenaran that whispered of peace and eternity. It told me that all was well with the community long before I could see the people.

We came out of the forest in sight of the village still being built. Poles of wood from bushes and low trees that grew in the forest in spaces among the khena supported roofs of large thick leaves. People were building new houses, and others cooked or prepared food. Children ran, playing games with rules that only they understood. The village could have been anywhere on the Aran I had first visited. I stopped to watch, smiling like I'd never see anything so sweet again.

The newcomers stopped when I did, but I didn't want to be surrounded by a crowd. "Go on," I said to the person nearest to me, the father of the young man I had brought here earlier. "He'll be waiting for you." The man and his wife started down the hill toward the village, looking back over his shoulder at me, as if to be sure. A few people followed. "Go on," I told the rest more loudly. "They'll be used to receiving visitors by now." In ones and twos and small groups, the new arrivals started down the hill, until only Jak and Taera and I remained.

"Go on," I said to Jak. "You'll want to find the missing people. Some of them are down in that village. They'll be able to tell you where the others have headed. There are four or five villages here."

"I think," Jak said slowly, "you'll have to come with me."

"I'll be here," I said. He eyed me suspiciously, so I added, "I'm not going anywhere. I'll be waiting for you."

He folded his arms across his chest. "Not good enough."

"I'll *be* here, Jak."

For a moment, we just looked at each other. I think he was considering forcing me to go with him but couldn't find a way to avoid looking ridiculous in front of all those very-much-alive people. At last he grunted and walked down into the village, leaving me alone with Taera.

I reached out to touch the nearest khena. I could feel the warm aliveness of its sap flowing and hear the hum of its wellbeing. "I'm glad to be back," I said. "Thank you for finding me again."

"I came as soon as I could. I'm glad to be back here, too. With you." Her eyes pleaded for me to believe her.

And I did. "I know."

Standing in sunlight, Taera could have been made of light herself; red hair glistening with gold highlights haloed her face. I reached out to her, and she leaned toward me. I wrapped her in a hug that could have lasted forever. I knew she was an oneiromorph, but she felt real enough, warm and solid, and ever so wonderfully alive against my body. Her hair smelled freshly shampooed. I could feel her soft breathing. Her heartbeat.

What I said next took courage that I might not normally have had, but I couldn't leave it unsaid. "I love you."

She sighed and rested her head on my shoulder, but then pulled back. "You love Aiana."

"Yes. I do. You're two aspects of the same person, aren't you? I love you both."

Her eyes were moist with tears. "What's going to happen with that . . . what's his name?"

"Jak. Don't worry about it. It's between me and him."

"This isn't good, is it?"

Suddenly there was a lump in my throat about the size of a cantaloupe. I pulled her close and held her.

"Would you want me to take him back?" After a pause, she added, "If I could."

"No," I said. "It would be a great storybook thing to do. Jak would be gone, and I could ask you to marry me . . . you . . . Aiana . . . and we would live here happily ever after."

She made a low noise, almost a moan. I couldn't see her face, pressed against my chest. "To be with you . . ." she said. ". . . on Aran . . . That would be a fine happily ever after."

"There'd only be one problem. When Jak goes back to Earth, someone there would figure out who we are and where we are. Then they'd convince themselves that since people from Earth settled Aran initially, Earth still has a right to maintain a presence on Aran in our time. My time. They'd come back and destroy everything we've created here. I can't let that happen."

"It won't happen," she said. "I promise."

I swallowed and looked into the khenaran. "I'll be reborn," I said. "Maybe, with the whynywir in me, I'll remember something. Maybe you could find me again. And if not . . ."

When I looked up again, Taera's eyes were glistening. "You're a good person," she said, her face lifted toward mine, expectant. "You are everything she has dreamed of, and more."

Accepting praise is difficult for me. I know my shortcomings. But I'm not one to turn down an offer like that. I ran my fingers down her cheek, raised her chin, and kissed her. She returned that kiss, hard and warm and long.

I pulled away only with difficulty. Time was too short. "There are still some loose ends. Aston, and his animals and plants, whatever isn't here yet. My mother. Lennard."

"I know. I'll see to all that."

"Corodh-an-Aran. Is he here now?"

Taera shook her head. "He's back in his place. He also has, how did you call it? Loose ends."

I was sorry not to have a chance to tell my brother good-bye. "When you see Corodh-an-Aran, tell him I love him. Tell him I said that."

"I will."

"Thank you. For everything. Now, please; I want to be alone for a while."

Taera nodded. She kissed me on the cheek, but I turned her head and kissed her lips again, a lost lifetime of kisses to make up for. More than kisses, but this would have to do.

I heard when her soft footsteps on the moss disappeared. She was gone. I sat down under one of the khena and floated into the great conversation of the whynywir, knowing that I would never have another chance to do so. This, too, was important, and not just for the pleasure of it. I wanted to finalize as much as I could how the relationship between the two species would work.

I became conscious of Jak's boots in front of me, and reluctantly I pulled back from the great flow of whynywir consciousness. There wasn't much to the self that I thought of as 'me.' It wasn't going to be such a big thing to give up, after all.

I looked up, past Jak's crossed arms to his face. He wore a serious expression. "Did I keep you waiting?" I asked. The sun was high but slightly to the west, and bright enough to make me squint. Early afternoon—only a couple of hours.

"Not really. I owe you an apology." The man surprised me—pleasantly. He had seemed so fixated on the idea that I was a murderer, that I was expecting him still to find me guilty of something. Not that I am free of guilt, but never the way Jak thought.

"Accepted. No problem." I stood. "Are you ready?"

"Ready and eager to be back on Earth. I'll see that your name is cleared, Taerlin."

A decent man after all, I thought. Too bad, what I was about to do to him, but it couldn't be helped. If he hadn't been so stubborn to begin with, this could have been avoided. I headed back toward the spot where we'd left Taera's ship. I didn't want to be in sight of the village; this was between Jak and me alone. Jak followed, and I felt sorry for him, still thinking he would return to Earth.

When we reached the spot, I turned. Despite my resignation to my fate, my heart was beating wildly. I took a deep breath. "We're not going back to Earth."

He frowned and touched his holstered laser. "What?"

"You heard me."

Jak drew the laser. "You gave your word on this."

I opened my hands and held them palms out and away from my body to indicate that I would not resist him. "Yes, I know."

He arched an eyebrow. "So, then? What gives?"

"Jak, you said that I would take you back to Earth or you would kill me. And I agreed."

"Right. And?"

"And I am not taking you to Earth, so this is your chance to kill me. You're going to have to do it now, though, or forget about it. I'm not going to stand here waiting all night."

Jak carefully aimed the laser at my chest.

I faced him not more than five meters away. It would be a very large, very deadly hole he'd burn in me. Despite myself, I was shaking slightly. A scary business, death. But I'd given my word. I looked him in the eye.

I was an easy target, but Jak took his time. His hand shook. He narrowed his lips so tight they were invisible. He glared at me.

"You mud-sucking swine!" he shouted, throwing the weapon to the ground. Before I knew what had happened, he hit me, hard and square on my chin. My head snapped back, and I stumbled. I landed on my back, the air knocked out of me.

In a flash, Jak came at me again, but I rolled aside, narrowly missing another blow to the face. I had bought myself just enough time to get back on my feet. With a grateful gasp, I was able to breathe again. I could taste blood in my mouth, and in a moment of excruciating clarity I decided that granting the man permission to kill me did not extend to letting him beat me up.

I'd studied martial arts for years, even taught it, but I had never, until now, found myself in a real fight. This was different from sparring, different from practicing forms. This man was seriously trying to hurt me, and that first blow had already succeeded. To make matters worse, except for that short time in prison I was out of practice, whereas Jak was a strong, determined adversary with police training. The match would have been completely in his favor but for one thing: Jak was really angry, and I was not. He wasn't thinking clearly or reacting smoothly. That took away some of his advantage.

Feeling guilty, I settled for blocking his attacks, doing nothing to attack back. But after several minutes all that I had accomplished was to make him angrier, and his anger made him stronger. I wouldn't hold up much longer under the hailstorm of his attack, even if he wasn't thinking clearly. I began counterattacking when I could.

We settled into an oddly matched rhythm—block, attack, block, block, attack; sometimes punctuated by an unanticipated blow that sent me reeling, or knocked the wind out of Jak. There was no time for thought. Action was everything; the fight fought itself. Despite Jak's greater strength, I held my own. But I couldn't beat him.

Time lost meaning. The only sounds were the raggedness of our breathing and the slight rustling of the leaves in the breeze, an odd combination. Jak threw a vicious punch at my jaw, a target he favored since his first successful blow there. I swung my left arm up in a successful block that must have added another bruise to the mass of bruises already on that arm. For an instant, he'd left himself exposed, and I managed a strong right to his chest, followed by a kick to his stomach while he was staggering back. He landed against the trunk of a khena, the only thing that held him upright, and breathed heavily as he found his footing. I was too exhausted to pursue my opening. It was all I could do to catch my breath.

We stood, looking at one another. For a moment, neither of us had the energy to move. Then Jak attacked again. He struck out with a kick, which I dodged, then a left that I only narrowly managed to block, then a right that caught me squarely in the chest. I staggered back, tripped over a tree root, and hit my left shoulder hard against a khena, barely staying upright. Jak pressed his attack with a hard right to my jaw. I ducked, and his fist slammed into the tree. He cried out, and I slipped a solid punch under his arm to his chest, another to his face, and as he reeled back, a kick to his chest.

The kick knocked Jak off balance, and he fell heavily to the ground. He looked up at me, managing an expression of simultaneous surprise and hatred, but I was in no condition to press the attack. As soon as it was clear that Jak was not going to get up again, my own legs gave way.

For a moment, we sat, just out of each other's reach, breathing heavily. Then a voice to my left said, "It's about time." Cort emerged from the forest. Speaking in Standard, he added, "I was half expecting you two to kill each other." He stooped to pick up something from the ground. To Jak, he said, "You won't need this anymore." He tucked Jak's weapon into his own belt.

Taera appeared behind Cort. She came over to me and knelt by my side. She pressed a cool hand against my forehead and stated the obvious. "You're hurt."

"I'm alive."

"I want you to stop fighting now. It's finished."

I had no desire for more fighting. "Tell *him*." I moved my head to indicate Jak.

Taera stood and walked over to where Jak sat. "No more fighting. Make your peace with him, Jak."

"Have to get back home." His words came out slurred, through cut and swollen lips.

"It's not possible," Taera answered. "Not for you, and not for Taerlin any longer, either. Neither of you can go back to Earth again. No one here can, anymore."

"He did," Jak said. "Before."

"Yes. Before. But that path was sealed off the moment you pointed the laser at him and made him bring you here."

I wondered why she said it that way. Was it because we chose to protect Aran against the Earth, or was there some deeper reason?

Jak looked at her from under lowered brows. "Why?"

"Come with me," Taera said. "Let me tend to your wounds a little. Later, I will tell you the whole story. You have a right to know." She gave me a look so soft it could melt crystal. "You both do."

She helped Jak to his feet. Determined not to be left behind, I struggled to my own feet, grateful for Cort's helping hand. I was still leaning on his shoulder when Taera reached back to take his hand. We all crossed the invisible, liquid metal threshold of Taera's ship.

"I will heal you," Taera said to Jak, "but you must promise not to try to harm Taerlin again. It's finished now, between you. He has paid the price, and it's not his fault in any case."

"I'll listen to your story," Jak replied, casting a dark look my way. "Then I'll decide what I want to do about him."

"He's as stubborn as you are," I muttered to Cort.

Cort shook his head. "I'll take that as a compliment."

But if I was annoyed, Taera was unfazed by Jak's reply. "That's fine, Jak," she said. "Now lie back on this counter."

As Jak lay back, Taera touched his forehead, glancing at the instrument panel at her side. She moved her hands across his body, not quite touching him, and continued to check her instrumentation. As Taera swept her hand past his cheek, a large red spot that had been swelling up and darkening, disappeared. I could see Jak relax, and at one point he took in a deep breath and let out a long sigh. He closed his eyes. When she had finished, Jak continued to breathe easily and deeply. I was beginning to think that he had gone to sleep when he opened his eyes. "Thank you," he said.

"You're welcome." Taera gave him a beatific smile.

I was intensely jealous, both because he was now obviously feeling good, and I was not, and because she had given him such a gift, and not me. Also, I suspected he liked her.

But after Jak sat up, Taera turned to me, the smile still on her face. "You're next."

We get used to all the little aches and pains in our bodies. As with so many things that are integral parts of our environment, we often don't notice them until they're gone. Whatever Taera did, she melted away not only the pains and bruises that left me battered from the fight with Jak, but also all the aches and tensions that I had held in my body over the last few months. I have never felt more relaxed and open than when Taera finished her healing.

She offered the same service to Cort, but he declined on the grounds that he, at least, had had the good sense not to get involved in a fight and didn't need healing. But I think that, more than anything, he didn't want to be too relaxed while there was a chance that Jak or I might start something up again. "I will ask you to put this away someplace safe, though," he added, producing the laser from his belt.

"Toss it here," Taera said.

"Toss?"

"Yes. Don't worry."

With a shrug, Cort threw the weapon toward her as gently as he could manage. In the middle of its arching trajectory, the laser disappeared.

"There!" Taera said. "That should keep it away from all of you for a while."

"Is it gone?" Jak asked. "How did you do that?"

"No, not gone. But it is no longer exactly here. And how I did it is something that I will tell you, for it's part of my story. But let's go outside and find a comfortable place to sit and talk."

Cort found a place in the forest where the leaves were deep on top of the springy, cool humus, and we could sit together. Taera made sure that Jak had a comfortable place to sit, and then sat by his side. She turned and gestured to me to sit at her other side.

I did, scowling jealously, until she touched my hand and smiled warmly at me.

Cort, last, settled himself opposite Taera and between Jak and me, not taking any chances. He passed around a bota of cool water, which we all shared. I could hear at least five species of birds in the khena. I knew them all, could picture them exactly from the whynywir part of my memory, but I had no names for them. I was about to ask Cort, when Taera began.

"You asked how I made the weapon disappear," Taera said to Jak. "I use a technology that on my world is called focused dreaming. We have had it only for about the last hundred years. Your people have not invented it yet. But perhaps you will not be uncomfortable with the concept. You know the powers that you have in your dreams, where you can do almost anything. Perhaps, too, you know of lucid dreaming, in which the dreamer becomes aware that he is dreaming and learns to control the sequence of events in the dream."

"I've done that!" I exclaimed.

"Yes. You have." Taera smiled at me and then turned back to Jak. "Focused dreaming is predicated on the ability of the dreamer to dream lucidly. Not many people have the native talent or put in the effort to gain mastery of the technique. In that regard, it's an art form as well as a science. With those lucid dreamers, our technology can amplify the effects of the dream so that they are carried out in the waking world as well as the sleeping one. Obviously, this depends upon significant advances in low-voltage oneiromorphy and in EEG-phased computer input and output devices."

"Of course," I said. When she looked at me sharply, I gave her my blandest smile along with a small shrug.

"Joker," Cort muttered.

Aiana continued. "It wasn't until we invented focused dreaming that we were able, to some extent, to conquer the limitations of travel in space and in time. I say, 'to some extent' because both space and time travel are limited by the constraints of the actual, as predicted by Murdhen's equations that form the basis of subjective physics, but—" Here she gave me a warning look—"you wouldn't know about those."

"But what about all those time travel paradoxes?" Jak asked.

"Ah, yes, the paradoxes. They used to write entire novels premised on such puzzles, didn't they? A man travels back in time and kills his own father when the father is just a baby, and so on. These stories all assume that the time traveler in question can go anywhere or do anything. But in real life this is not the case. Events of significance in the history of a world or of an individual cannot be changed. We can travel anywhere in the wide river of spacetime, with or against the time current, but these significant events are like islands jutting up out of that river. They are inaccessible to us. The constraints of space-time itself are too strong for our technology to overcome. In some cases, we cannot travel to such events even in theory, for the resistance curve rises exponentially in proportion to the effect of the visit."

"So you're saying that time-travel paradoxes can't happen."

"Exactly. And this is why you two cannot return to Earth. There is no longer a way to take you there. Even in theory."

In the ensuing silence, I listened to the birds singing in the khena. Their song harmonized pleasantly with the contented chords of the khena itself.

"I don't get it," Jak said. "We can't be of such significance in the history of our world as all that. Maybe we made the news for a while, but these things pass."

"News passes, yes. But you have no notion of the significance of the events that you just initiated back on Earth." The look on Taera's face was of such glowing sadness that it might almost be rapture, making her look like some kind of secular Madonna. She touched my hand. "I've never told you about my world, Taerlin. I think that now is the time."

I held her hand in mine as she continued. "We were not always so technologically advanced. Several hundred years before I was born, my world was very similar to yours. We had the beginnings of space travel; we had met a few alien cultures and didn't really know how to deal with them. Xenology was an embryonic science. We almost killed the inhabitants of one of the worlds we visited in our ignorance and greed."

It did sound a lot like the Earth I knew.

"We might have evolved from there, but calamity struck. We were mining rare earths on one of the worlds, a place uninhabited by any species even remotely intelligent. We inadvertently imported a highly mutable virus from that world, and the virus evolved in response to human carriers into a toxic plague that our medical science of the time could not cope with. Half the world's population died. In some areas, it was more like nine people out of ten. The government was unable to deal with the crisis, and it collapsed. The world fell into a Dark Age deeper than any that it had seen in two thousand years."

Cort and Jak leaned forward, intent on Taera as she talked, spellbound like me.

"Only one thing saved us," Taera continued. "A new religion had sprung up a few hundred years prior to the plague. The religion stressed the highest ideals of understanding and cooperation among communities. It also taught personal immortality for those who lived worthy lives. It had, to that point, been only a fringe belief, one among hundreds, but with the spread of the plague and the government's collapse, its teachings met our need, and the religion found widespread acceptance."

Taera turned to me, her eyes luminous with sorrow. "You can imagine, Taerlin, that there was great comfort in that belief among those families in which good people, even innocent children, died. Had it not been for the consolation of that religion, wars would have finished what the plague began." Taera paused, and birdsong filled the silence.

"This is the hard part." Taera swallowed and then forced herself to continue, turning toward Jak. "The religion is centered on a savior with certain, I guess you might say, godlike powers. He was called Taerlin."

She ignored my indrawn breath.

"That he was an actual person, there is no doubt. We still have some old holos, a precious few, copies of copies, media only partially intact, most of them greatly retouched, in the vaults of the Great Temple Center. You probably wouldn't recognize any of the people; they've grown halos, and the retouching has made other changes as well. You probably wouldn't recognize most of the mythology, either, from the basic historical facts, but I suppose that's probably the way it is with many religions."

My heart pounded with increasing urgency. "Just a minute, Taera."

Taera ignored me, continuing to talk mainly to Jak. "The Sacred Teachings tell us that the savior took those worthy of redemption bodily into a better world, into Paradise. He went to prison for his convictions and was killed there, yet returned to life and once more took those he found worthy of redemption bodily into Paradise in a final Blessed Ascension. The holos show it. There is no doubt that the people disappeared."

The story was too familiar. "Wait a minute," I protested more urgently.

She wouldn't look at me. "Although it is not specifically written in the scriptures, many people believe that the savior came from here, from Aran. This belief is as old perhaps as the religion itself. You can see it in the way he is dressed in the ancient holos, although, of course, retouching might be responsible for that as well."

Her words seemed to mock the events I had just lived through. "No, Taera," I begged, "please say that this is just a story. A joke."

I touched her shoulder, and the face that Taera turned to me was not joking. Her eyes glistened with tears. "I'm sorry, Taerlin. But you must understand—you, and also Jak—why you cannot return to Earth now, not even in theory. For you see, the Sacred Teachings further tell us that the savior was betrayed by one who was sworn to protect him, and died at his hands. It is told that he died in his betrayer's arms, but before he died, he forgave him, and also took his adversary bodily into heaven. These miracles are all verified by the ancient holos."

It's hard to say whether the feeling choking my lungs was anger or frustration. Or maybe a fair amount of both. "Hold it, Taera. That's not fair to me or to Jak. I'm no savior, and I don't work miracles. That's your department."

Taera shook her head. "I never said that *you* . . . only that people believe—"

I ran over her words. "As for Jak, I guess he's been my adversary, but to say that he's a traitor is grossly wrong. He's as stubborn in sticking to what he believes as, as . . ." A thought intruded that I didn't have time for, and I brushed it aside before it could fully form. "He was acting in a good cause; it's just that his conclusions were mistaken. I've come to wrong conclusions too. Everyone has. The story is all wrong, and if we have to go back to set it right, that's just what we're going to have to do."

"Haven't you been listening?" Jak asked. He sounded tired. "I think the whole point of what Taera is getting at is that we can't go back, not even in theory. The survival of Earth as, uh, as it in fact survived is dependent on people's belief in that story."

Taera nodded. "The savior left no writings or dictations or holos, but there was a disciple." Taera sounded as tired as Jak. More, maybe. "His name was Dheren. He taught us that we must make ourselves worthy of Paradise. If we can live as worthy members of that community, then the savior will return and take us with him. Dheren taught us tolerance and self-respect. He was actually present at the Blessed Ascension to Paradise but was not at the time found worthy to ascend. He witnessed it, though, and was transformed by his vision of the Ascension."

"I saw him," I said. "A thin fellow, burning eyes. He followed me around everywhere, but he wouldn't look right at me."

"I saw him, too," Taera said softly, almost reverently.

"Taera, I would have taken this Dheren fellow, but he didn't want to come. And all of this savior business just isn't true. I was talking about the interstellar community, not one in Paradise. How can people believe this stuff?"

She smiled at me, a tender expression that at any other time I could have gotten lost in. "They believe it because it fills a need for them. This religion transformed our world. Perhaps not many people in modern times actually believe in bodily ascension to Paradise, but the values that the savior—that you—taught have played a major role in shaping a people that take responsibility in an interstellar community."

I wasn't happy with Taera's answer, or with the entire story, though I couldn't pin down the source of my uneasiness. Why should I care what happened on Earth after I left? I was finished with the place. But Jak wouldn't meet my eye, and, irrational as I knew it to be, I felt as if *I* was the one that had betrayed *him*, and Taera had betrayed both of us.

Chapter Twenty-Eight

ARAN, YEAR BC 2043

MIKEL'S RECORDING, continued

The next morning, I felt worse. I hadn't slept well, and finally awakened before dawn with the silver moon hanging gibbous among the treetops, and the smaller red moon a bright mark on its surface like a pinprick of blood.

I had to clear the air with Taera.

I found her later that morning working with a small group of women who were rending the roots of some plant into a red dye, and I pulled her roughly away from them. Seeing my scowl, no one objected. No one, in fact, said a word. I set a brisk pace away from the village.

"What?" Taera asked, freeing her arm from my angry grasp. But she followed me, half running to keep up.

"I want to talk with you."

"Then talk."

"Alone."

By now we were in the forest, out of sight of the village. I slowed down, picking my way down a gentle hill toward a stream that babbled below. Jaw set tight, Taera followed. I stopped at the edge of the stream and turned to her.

She was close enough to touch. Her hands were dark red to the wrists where the dye had dried, the color of old blood.

Her revelations of the previous day burned in my heart. I felt betrayed. "I want to understand why you did . . . what you did. Why did you come looking for me? You *were* looking for me, weren't you? You and all your 'Taerlin' business. I thought you wanted to send me back here to populate Aran, but that wasn't it at all, was it?"

Taera bit her lower lip, looking all around to either side of me but not at me. "That was part of it."

"A sort of accidental byproduct, was it?"

"No! It was a necessary part of the entire history, the part you'd most appreciate. I didn't know how you would take . . . the rest of it"

I grimaced. "Not too well."

Taera gave me a sad look so fleeting that had I blinked, I would have missed it. She lowered her gaze to the moss by her feet. "No. But it all had to be done. History demanded it."

"History? Or you?" Or . . . My heart skipped a beat. "Or Aiana?"

"She is an historian, and I am an aspect of her. It's all the same thing."

"Historians *study* history; they don't change it. Or is it different in your time? Are your people busy straightening out all the things that happened that you don't like?"

She glared at me, and her hand, her blood-red hand, twitched slightly as if it wanted to slap me. She crossed her arms, tucking her hands in tight. "That's not possible. But in this case I clearly had a role to play. We all talked it over. This approach seemed necessary."

Great—so she consulted a number of people, just not the one who would be most affected. Me. "'We all'? Who's that, Taera? I don't remember you talking it over with me. Or did you consider my opinion unimportant?"

Her face flushed almost as red as her hands, but she raised her chin, her mouth set in a hard line. "My thesis committee, especially my advisor. And a . . . a representative of the great temple." She pushed an errant lock away from her face and met my eyes defiantly. "I don't believe I'd had the pleasure of making your acquaintance at the time."

"And it wouldn't have made any difference if you had, would it."

"No." Her eyes wavered. "Everyone thought it best not to burden you with . . . such knowledge. It wasn't personal. My thesis committee said . . . insisted—"

I suddenly understood what she'd been saying. Taera had always appeared alone and with such powers that I'd never imagined who surrounded the waking Aiana. I gaped as she shifted into context. "You're . . . she's a student!"

"Yes, a student of history." She took a deep, jagged breath, then let it out slowly. She relaxed slightly, looking out into the forest and away into her memory. "I was studying the era before the Great Plague. It's a challenging period because the events around your appearance make time travel there impossible. Also, your presence makes the period a subject of interest for every student of history with any religious feeling. It's hard to find a new angle, but I had one."

Religious feeling! Could it be that what I thought might be love, or at least normal human attraction, was actually something like reverence? This raised bile to my throat. I swallowed to keep it down. "And you, are you religious? Is that it? Wanted to meet your savior in person?"

She wrapped her arms across her chest again. "No, not particularly. You are a significant figure in history. It wasn't religion, it was . . . oh, ambition, I suppose. I . . . that is, Aiana . . . had an idea that had never been explored. If I was successful, I would not only have a thesis from it, but considerable recognition. You see, it is not only the great temple that has historical links to you, but also the foundation."

"The foundation?"

"An institution that was set up in the same period. Some people say it was funded with money that you left behind—quite a bit of it—and chartered to advance scientific research in the cause of promoting intercultural harmony. Focused dreaming—the entire field of oneiroportation—would never have been possible without extensive funding from the foundation. Neither would the crystals that you use." She gestured toward my forehead.

"Pol Bitmon!" The name came out barely more than a whisper.

"Yes, the foundation's first director," Taera replied. "My research idea was that, even though the foundation was formed *after* your final disappearance, they might have source materials regarding your life that had never been examined. The foundation is privately held and very secretive—but my—Aiana's—Uncle Mark is its executive director. He gave me access to their historical records."

Taera paused, adjusting the hang of her dress. "I was in luck." She spoke so quietly that I took a step closer so that I could hear her over the sound of the water. "Way in the back of the executive vault, I found an old holo. It was in good shape, considering the age of the medium. I don't know if you'll appreciate this, but it was an original."

I shook my head.

"Most of the holos are copies of copies many times over, and old and much handled into the bargain. They show . . . what they show, there can be no doubt about that, but over the centuries they've gotten noisy. Much of the detail is chopped up beyond scientific reconstruction. And then there's the artistic rendering, of course, which allows a lot of artistic license. This holo, though . . ."

Taera looked right at me, an inviting softness in her eyes. "Reconstruction was not necessary; the images were as sharp as . . . as sharp and clear as you are now, standing right here. And it showed the moment of the Blessed Ascension, or what appeared to be that. That discovery alone, and a scholarly analysis of it, would have made my thesis and my reputation. But . . ."

Taera again adjusted her dress, though I could see nothing wrong with how it was. Then she looked right at me, eyes shining. "It was *you*, Taerlin. You. When you looked out at the camera, and your eyes were filled with wonder and knowledge and sympathy and suffering and faith and joy . . . I am not a religious person, but right then, for the first time, I understood that you were real. That you were in fact what they said you were."

I backed away, waving my hands in agitation. "No! Then that holo was a fraud!"

"It was *not* a fraud," Taera said calmly. "You were extraordinary. I was there that night, remember? We now know the Blessed Ascension was not a Blessed Ascension but your final trip to Aran. But *you* . . . You, Taerlin, are the real thing."

"This is sheer craziness!"

"Oh, I'm just getting to the crazy part."

Taera reached toward me, but I took another step away, almost losing my balance at the edge of the stream. "I'm not sure I want to hear this."

She dropped her hand, sighing. "I was on the holo too. Just for a second perhaps, but even that second should have been impossible. Do you have any idea what this meant?"

Taera echoed my blank look with a shake of her head. "No, of course not. How could you? But the laws of subjective physics are clear. Places and times of historical and personal significance are unreachable even in theory. And yet, there we were on that holo, you and I, and the only way that could have been possible is if I was meant to be there. With you. This was a career opportunity beyond measure, and so I took it. But also . . ." She lowered her voice, as if what she was about to say was a secret, even from the trees. Even, perhaps, from Aiana. ". . . though I'd never met you, the emotional connection between us was . . . unmistakable."

I wrapped my arms below my ribs and held on tight. Something pressed against my throat, making it hard to swallow. What had I been feeling that evening? What had I seen in her face? That moment had been so overshadowed by my need to deal with Jak that whatever had been between Taera and me was no longer clear in my mind. "What . . . emotion?"

"Love, perhaps," she said. She spoke as coolly as a news reporter, but her face was as full of pain as mine must have been. "Or perhaps just the flush of a shared victory. But it was definitely something much greater than a glance between two strangers. I had to raise the stakes on my thesis, to initiate the historical intervention that the evidence showed had occurred. My thesis committee was convened. Because of the . . . religious . . . nature of the events, we invited a representative of the Great Temple. In the end, we all agreed:

my discovery of the holo could mean only one thing. I myself had an active role to play in these events."

"Taera, you created them!"

She breathed out a small self-conscious laugh. "Not really. All this history had already happened. I just stepped into my role in it."

"And cast me in mine."

"Yes. Well. It didn't take too much intelligence to figure out from how you were dressed that you had either come from here or were going here. But if I was truly involved, you might have come from any time in the history of Aran. The question was—when? I started out as early as I could, a century or so after the first human settlements appeared. It turned out that the people there were descendents of . . ." She left the sentence unfinished, gesturing in the direction of the village we'd just left. "They said . . ."

She shook her head, then pushed back her unruly hair. "Well, that's unimportant. The point is that the first settlement was already too late in the time trajectory of your life. I came here often enough so that the villagers wouldn't forget me, but I focused on the era of your appearance on Earth, plus or minus a few decades. I was hoping that, in this entire wide world, whenever you were here you would learn of me and need me, and that you would find me."

"Which is just what happened."

"Yes."

"And you knew that I had to go back to Earth . . ."

". . . because I had already seen you there in the holo. And because I also knew the role you had played here. It all fit together."

It *did* all fit together, and I didn't like it, this little time loop I'd just played an unexpected and unwelcome role in. According to Taera's subjective physics, there was nothing any of us could have done to change it, but sometimes the rightness of a situation lies not in its facts but in its feelings. And this one felt rotten.

"The problem I'm having here is not about what you or I needed to do so that history would work out the way it did. It's about you and me. You *manipulated* me."

When Taera didn't respond, I turned to look at her. Tears ran down her cheeks. Her voice came out husky, like it didn't quite fit in her throat. "Everything I told you was true."

"Maybe so, but you chose carefully which parts of the truth you were going to tell me."

"My committee insisted that I say nothing about Earth's future. No one knows the long-term consequences of his own actions. Why should you be any different?"

"In other words, you chose to do what they wanted instead of what I would have wanted."

"Taerlin, I believe they were right. And, no matter what I'd told you, nothing would have changed what you did."

"Wasn't that for *me* to decide?"

Anger flared in her eyes so strongly that my heart stumbled. But she spoke in cool syllables. "I am an historian, not a palm reader. It's not my job to tell you more of your own future than people usually know. What do you want, an apology? I don't owe you one." She turned to walk back toward the village.

She'd almost disappeared among the khena when I thought of something even worse. Much worse.

"Wait! Taera!"

Taera stopped and turned. She folded her arms across her chest and raised an eyebrow as I walked over to her.

"What about that thesis of yours?"

"What about it?"

"You're going to go back to your own time and write it up? Everything, the way it happened?"

"Yes, of course. I'm an historian. That's what historians do."

"Are you going to mention Aran by name?"

She shrugged, a stiff gesture with taut shoulders. "That's how it happened."

"Taera, I went to prison on Earth in order to *prevent* people on Earth from knowing about Aran. I would have died if I had to, so that they wouldn't have an excuse for coming back here. But you . . . Are you saying your *thesis* is more important than the safety of"—I gestured back toward the village—"everyone here?"

She flinched and took a step back, as if I had struck her. Her cheeks flushed a vivid pink. "No. No, Taerlin. I love this place, too. These people." She reached a hand toward me. "But my

Earth is not yours. Maybe that's one good thing this religion of yours—"

"Not mine!"

She ignored the interruption. "—has accomplished. We don't ravage the planets the way we used to."

"And you're willing to promise me they won't do it again, ever, even if they believe Earth has a presence on Aran and a claim to it?"

Taera bit her lip and looked down, seeming to notice for the first time her blood-colored hands. Her voice wavered. "For what it's worth, people in my time have little interest in Aran. But obviously, I can't make you any promises. I'm an historian, not a politician. My duty is to the past, not the future. I report what happened. That's all." But she turned her hands over and back, looking at their dire color.

I pressed my point. "No, this is a problem you have to face. You more than anyone. And if you make the wrong decision, it's going to create a serious problem for everyone here, too."

"Well, but Taerlin, be reasonable. We already know that people from my time haven't come back here because we've been through this time loop together, and they haven't appeared anywhere in it."

"And can you historians guarantee that they won't appear the day after you publish your thesis? You historians don't see into the future, do you?" I frowned. "Or do you?"

Aiana shook her head. "No. I don't know. No one can see the future, not even historians. We make the best choices we can using the data we have available. Just like you."

That was rubbing salt into a wound. I grimaced. "Right. Just like me. But at least *you've* been warned. So you'd better start thinking seriously about how you want to make that choice."

"I'll think about it." She folded her arms back up and tucked her red hands in.

Thinking about it was better than refusing to think about it, but not as good as agreeing. "Doesn't all your work bringing humans to this world mean anything to you?"

"Taerlin, stop pushing. I said I'd think about it."

"Well, just in case your thinking goes the wrong way, I'm going to do what I can to keep your people away."

Her eyes widening, she let out a little surprised-sounding noise. "You? And just how do you propose to do that?"

"I'll leave something for the people from Earth to find, if they ever come back. Maybe the fact that I'm Taerlin will have some influence on them. We know where the planetary base will be. I have an audio recorder. Maybe I can get something to them there."

"It will do you no good, Taerlin. Listen to me. *History has already been written*. Nothing can undo it. Your starmen found no recordings. The missionaries that come here some seven hundred years later didn't either, though they traveled to every corner of what they referred to as 'this benighted planet.'"

I tried to keep my anger under control, but it was rising again. I had to push the words out through the tightness in my throat. "Missionaries! They converted the people here, too? This is unconscionable, Taera."

She sighed a great, long dramatic sigh. "No, they did not convert them, though they certainly tried. The mission was established here for thirteen years, but not a single conversion was made. Perhaps that's where you have made—or will make—a difference. But I can tell you that on Earth we are Taerliri, and nothing you can do will change that."

Taerliri! The word brought me beyond anger into a numbing, frozen calm. "Maybe it will not," I said icily, "but I will try, Taera, whether you help me or not. You've done me an injustice, and you're on the verge of doing the the same to the planet, too. I will do everything I can to set things right."

I turned away from her toward the woods. I could hear her take a few steps to follow. "Stop! Taerlin, wait!"

"Don't call me that!" I stormed into the woods, and I didn't care whether she followed me or not. I didn't want to talk with her anymore. Ever.

Chapter Twenty-Nine

ARAN, YEAR BC 2043

MIKEL'S RECORDING, continued

U nhappy with the lie I was living, I avoided everyone for the next few days. Except, of course, Cort. No one could avoid Cort if Cort didn't want to be avoided. I told him what I'd learned about Taera—I owed him that—but I didn't have much else to say, except to thank him halfheartedly for the food he brought.

I especially stayed away from Taera, though from a distance I saw her bring my mother and Aston and several other people who had been left behind in that sudden wild exit. So . . . Taera could go back to Earth but I could not. But of course: she was nobody important whereas I was . . . the great, overinflated savior figure she'd made of me.

Taera also brought cages full of sedated wolves and other animals into the new world, their genetic structure altered by a virus made in part from my blood. The arrival of the animals got Cort off my back, and then I was alone. This suited my mood perfectly.

I sat one afternoon on a warm, sunny rock as a cold-blooded creature might, a lizard or a snake. The place I had chosen was at the crest of a hill, and the treetops of the khenaran stretched down and out below me, then climbed again as another hill rose in the distance. I brooded over how neatly I had been tricked into falsely playing the savior for a planet, deluding perhaps millions of people, and allowing Jak's life to be ruined in the process. I was so lost in my own doleful thoughts that Jak was almost right next to me before I heard him.

I turned, half standing, but he waved me back down and asked, "May I join you?"

I wasn't in the mood for company, but given how events had played out, I felt I owed Jak something. I shrugged. "If you want."

With a grunt, Jak settled himself on the rock beside me.

I studied the view—the sunlit valley, with khena marching up the opposite hill, their lacy leaves waving gently in the breeze. A flock of birds rose from the trees and curved away beyond the hill. It was hard to be too absorbed in self-pity with another person sitting beside me. Reluctantly, I asked, "You settling in all right?"

"I guess. This is not exactly the direction I thought my life would take."

I turned to look at him. "I'm sorry. I didn't mean—"

"It's not your fault," he interrupted. "It's my own, and no one else's."

"Leave any family behind?"

"Family?" He laughed, without humor. "An ex-wife and a teenage son."

"Close?"

"No. Not really. I'm just a source of income for her, and as for the boy . . . He and I never did get along. He blamed me for the divorce, and I was so angry at her and at him, too, for taking her side, that I never tried to set things right. Haven't seen either of them in a couple of years. No, no emotional pain there, Taerlin, just an adjustment."

"At least that." One less thing to feel guilty about. "Look, Jak, about that whole religion thing, Taera's story, I want you to know that I don't blame you—"

His mouth twisted into something halfway between a wince and a smile. "Don't think I'm a traitor, eh?"

"No! I don't!"

"But I *did* betray you; the story was right about that. And, for what it's worth, I'm sorry." He shook his head. "I was so sure . . ."

"But that's just it!" I said. "You were pursuing what you believed was right. You weren't after personal gain or anything like that. You were after justice. Yes, you were wrong, but what motive could be better? Whatever it was you did, it wasn't treachery."

"But it was," Jak said. "Just like the story said. You had been judged innocent. As a policeman, I was sworn, like every officer there, to protect you. Despite my oath I did the very opposite. I have been a traitor to you, as much as traitors ever are."

"That's nonsense!"

"Then your feelings in the matter just show how perceptions can differ from the facts. And that makes *me* wonder whether you aren't maybe being a little too hard on Taera, too."

I said nothing. I couldn't speak. I already knew Jak was right. I'd been trying to imagine how this wild time loop of hers must feel to Taera. She probably never imagined that I—Taerlin—would cast *her* as the betrayer. Maybe she even cared for me a little and regretted what she'd done. Even if she didn't care at all for me personally, she wouldn't want to leave her Taerlin with a low opinion of her. And here was this time loop all bound tooth-to-tail like the worm Ouroborus, in which she would forever betray me and I would forever leave her, and there was no way out of it because *history has already been written.*

"I don't want to be some kind of religious figure," I said at last. "I had no idea it would be that way—for me or for you."

Jak shrugged. "I don't much care for it either, but . . . it could be worse. It sounds to me like that religion did a lot more good than harm, all in all. So what if we happened, by accident, to play the roles we did in its creation? We've both just seen how perceptions can be way off the mark. It has nothing to do with you and me as we really are."

I started thinking that if Jak was taking the whole thing so calmly, it was wrong of me to do anything less. "I guess," I said reluctantly.

"Don't brood about it," he said. "Your life is here and now. Do something with it."

"There's a group I promised to take to the ocean."

"There you go."

"What are *you* going to do, Jak?"

"I don't know," he said. "I don't miss Earth so much, but I really felt I was working for a good cause back there. You might think that sounds strange—"

"Not at all!"

"—whereas here, everything is so peaceful. Nothing ever happens." His shoulders slumped just a fraction, and his morose voice suggested the beginnings of chronic depression. "No one needs me."

The idea that had been nagging at the back of my mind came into my consciousness. In a rush of excitement I said, "But that's not true, Jak! Do you know my brother, Corodh-an-Aran? His name means something." I explained Cort's name as best I could, and concluded with, "This world needs people who are committed to justice the way he is—and you are—and who are as doggedly stubborn about it as you are, too. We need people who will be committed to that ideal, life after life, because there will be times when that will make all the difference."

He was silent. I couldn't tell how he was taking what I had said.

"Think about it," I concluded lamely. "Maybe your being here is no accident. Talk with Corodh-an-Aran if you want."

"I will," Jak said. "And if I can give you some advice too, talk with Taera."

After Jak left me, I walked alone in the forest. It was a healing of sorts. I decided to join the community again, and I didn't want what had happened to come between me and any person there—especially Taera.

It was sunset by the time I reached the village, the houses glowing in the warm, ruddy light. A few children played with a ball, dodging in and out among the houses. The smell of a meat stew hung in the air, making my stomach growl with hunger. Two women, talking quietly, stirred the stew, which cooked over a fire in the middle of the village. Not many other people were about.

"Good evening!" I said in what I hoped was a cheerful tone.

The women returned my greeting. "Dinner in about half an hour."

Just as if I hadn't been gone. I smiled. "Have you seen Taera?"

One of the women audibly caught her breath. She looked over her shoulder. "She just left," the other said and inclined her head in the direction the first woman had looked.

The direction of the clearing where Taera's ship invisibly waited.

I broke into a run, covering the distance to the clearing in what must have been a new personal speed record. I saw the flash of sunlight on her red hair at the far side of the clearing and called out to her. "Taera!"

But Taera took one more step and vanished.

Chapter Thirty

ARAN, YEAR BC 2043

She'd heard him. She couldn't pretend otherwise, though for an instant she was just angry enough to try.

But then she remembered the stomach-twisting grief she'd felt when she first learned—a year ago now and almost a hundred years in the future—how she and Taerlin had parted, angry at one another, trapped in a time loop of unending regret.

She couldn't let that happen.

She took a deep breath and stepped back out of the 'port.

He stood in the clearing, motionless. His mouth was open, his eyes wide in an expression of agony and longing, and her heart lurched to see his pain.

But in the instant he saw her he shifted from dismay through disbelief and into delight. "Taera!" He ran toward her. She opened her arms, and he swept her up in his, twirling her in three great loops of joy.

She laughed with the sheer, heady pleasure of it.

Then he put her down and kissed her; and after that, when she'd caught her breath, she said, "Everything I had to do is finished. I was just leaving." She thought of the two guides in the hallway of the Arts and Sciences building back on campus. They must be frantic by now. Maybe they had a passkey.

Maybe they would be able to force the door. Maybe even now they were initiating the emergency wake-up sequence. "I don't think I'll be able to come back. But I'm glad we don't have to part on bad terms."

He looked into her eyes and smoothed back her hair. He shook his head slowly, almost imperceptibly. "Don't leave. Stay here with me."

She moved his hand to her cheek, delighting in his touch. She listened to the birdsong, the breeze in the khenaran. She thought of the people in the village and the life they had chosen to live. The life she wanted to choose, too. Tears pressed behind her eyelids, and she willed them not to fall. "I wish I could. But I have to go. The project is finished."

He lightly touched her cheeks, traced the arch of her eyebrow, followed the rim of her ear, as if memorizing them with his fingertips. "Do what you must." His voice broke slightly, and he swallowed hard. "But just so you know: I love you. I'll always love you."

Oh, those beautiful gold-and-blue eyes. She couldn't look into them, suspended as she was in the pain of having-to-go-but-having-to-stay. "From the first moment I saw you on that holo," she said, looking at his feet, "I wanted to know you." Her voice was low, as if coming from somewhere far away. "When I saw how we looked at each other in the few frames of that frozen second . . ." She met his eyes. Tears ran down her cheeks. "I would have given anything . . . everything . . . just to be with you. But if I leave now, I won't come back. Aiana won't come back. I can't . . ." Her breathing was tangled in choking sobs, and he held her until they eased.

He brushed the tears from her wet cheeks, but they still flowed. Then he wrapped his hands into the tangles of her hair and kissed her. "I don't remember," he said. "In all the confusion, with Jak and everything, I don't remember how I might have looked at you then. But I know how I feel now."

She let him draw her close, his arms encircling her.

He smelled like some combination of sandalwood and sweat and something else entirely his own. He smelled like a place she wanted to call home.

She tucked her face close to his skin and breathed him in. She had never felt so . . . real. So independent. Oh, how she yearned to preserve this moment. Perhaps she would be able to break free of Aiana altogether. Perhaps she had already done it! The idea was heady. She and Aiana could go their separate ways, and she, Taera, would stay here with Taerlin forever.

What would happen to Aiana? She couldn't think about it. But Aiana was strong, Taera knew that. Stronger than Taera. Aiana would be all right.

She tilted her face up toward his, asking for a kiss. And he obliged.

Much later, she lay on the soft ground of the khenaran with Taerlin, the great old trees towering over them like a giant's wedding canopy. He propped himself up on an elbow and began picking the delicate khena leaves out of her hair. "They're on you, too," she said, and reached up to pick the leaves from his hair.

"I wish you didn't have to go," he said.

"I think . . . I don't." She laughed, giddily free.

"But you always—"

"That was Aiana, not me."

"What? She made you leave?"

"There was a plan for each appearance. Each had to be short and focused. But all that is over now. The project is finished."

"You can stay here with me?"

"Yes."

"All the time? Forever?"

"If you want."

"Of course I do!" He frowned, as if trying to think of something, but whatever it was, it hid somewhere out of his reach.

Taera put her arms around him and pulled him to her. They kissed, and the frown vanished.

The next morning when Taera woke, birdsong filled the khenaran, and the air was fragrant with the trees' sweet pungency. Taerlin sat by her side, watching her. He smiled when she opened her eyes. They could have been the first man and woman in a brand-new paradise. "Good morning," she said, feeling happy and free.

Taerlin sighed but answered, "Good morning." He watched her finger-comb the leaves from her hair. "What's happening with Aiana?" he asked.

The question hit her like a blow. She winced and put a protective hand over her chest, where it hurt. "Let's not talk about Aiana. Let's just be together, you and me."

He put his hand over hers. "I'm afraid we have to talk about her," he said.

Taera sat up, her brow wrinkled in thought. "When she sleeps and dreams, she projects me into the world. Since I'm still here, perhaps she's still sleeping."

"And when she wakes up?"

"Usually, she sleeps until I return. Remember, I am her subconscious self."

"So, while you remain here . . ."

Taera shrugged. "I don't know. It could be that we've already separated. I think that it's possible. I . . . I feel very real. So perhaps she is awake and living her normal life without me. Or . . . perhaps she remains asleep." She nibbled her lower lip. "That seems more likely. But remember that her time and our time are not the same. It may just be a few extra seconds of sleep for her but a lifetime for us."

"But you think she's still sleeping."

Taera nodded, watching him stumble toward the answer she already knew. Taera didn't want to think about Aiana, but Taerlin was right. They had to face the issue of her. "Probably."

"And she'll stay asleep as long as you're here with me?"

"I don't know, Taerlin. This is not a normal oneiromorphic event. Perhaps no time at all is passing in her world. Or perhaps, yes, perhaps she'll sleep. Or perhaps we've grown apart and separate."

"Or might she"—he choked on the word—"die?"

Taera looked away, her mouth twisting. Her answer was spoken so softly it was almost carried away on the breeze. "I don't think so. I can't imagine it, but . . . I don't know." She looked back at him, begged him with her eyes. "I don't want to leave you."

He turned away, looking all around as if somewhere nearby lay an escape route. He swallowed twice, struggled with his breathing. His voice, when he spoke, came out ragged with effort. "I don't want to leave you, either, but I think you have to go back to her."

"No, she'll be all right. She's always all right."

"But you're always there with her. She wouldn't be . . . herself . . . without you."

A great tsunami of sorrow swept over her. She didn't want to leave this man, not ever. How ironic, to lose him to her conscious self! Her eyes filled with tears. "You love her, not me."

"I love *you*, Taera. And her. Haven't you always said you're part of her?"

"But she doesn't want to live here on Aran with you, and I do. She wants to be a history professor, perhaps head of the department, and make a name for herself. She'd never be anybody here. I don't care about any of that. I love Aran. I love *you*. I want to stay with you here. Please." She swallowed hard. "Don't send me away."

Taerlin looked at her a long time, silent and sad. He took her in his arms and held her. Their bodies fit as if they were meant to be this close forever. "I want you to stay," he said. "You have no idea how much. But you mustn't. You have to go back and be part of her again."

He brushed tears from her cheeks even as they ran down his own. "Bring her back to me, Taera. Come back with her. I'll wait for you."

"No, she'll never—"

"Yes. She will. *You* will."

She wanted to believe it, but she couldn't. She sniffled and rubbed her nose with the back of her hand. "I can't. When she's awake, I'm so . . . buried in her."

A bird somewhere nearby trilled an alarm. The call was taken up and repeated in the nearby trees. Taerlin's features hardened with a new resolve. He lifted his chin, jaw set, as if facing an enemy twice his size. "All right," he said. "If you can't, then I will."

"Are you saying you want to go to Earth with me?"

"I don't want to, no, but I will."

"No, that's too much to ask. What about the danger of your dying . . . away from Aran . . . the final death?"

He met her eyes, resolve unshaken. "What about it?"

Chapter Thirty-One

EARTH, YEAR 3224

"You will not publish your thesis." The speaker, Reverend Guide Ord, was a slender man with pale, almost colorless eyes, and long, delicate fingers that played incessantly with the fringes of his stole. He had an incongruously deep, gravelly voice. He sat behind Zhou's desk, which was as clear of papers, equipment, and personal objects as if the office had always been vacant.

Though the room was heated, Aiana felt cold. Her fingertips were numb with it. She hugged herself tightly, tucking her fingers in her armpits. She looked at Salvatore, who stood behind Ord, ready to obey his superior's instruction.

Salvatore's expression was tight-lipped, every muscle in his face taut, as if to say, *Don't say I didn't warn you.* He didn't meet her eyes.

What was it Vikram had said? That the temple still killed people? No, it wasn't that. That they had killed people centuries ago, and they still had ways to keep this information from being published.

Were they threatening her?

The thought made her angry. How dare they! She was not going to let anything stand in the way of publishing her thesis, not if she could help it.

"You can't stop me," she said. "There is such a thing as academic freedom."

The tip of Ord's tongue licked his lips lightly. The image that sprang to Aiana's mind was of a boxer, a man far more powerfully built than the one who sat across from her. A man who enjoyed winning a good fight.

"Academic freedom, yes, but within the constraints of academic procedure. If you continue your work, your committee will not approve the thesis."

Her fingers just would not warm up, and there seemed to be a rock in the pit of her stomach. She would have liked to retort that the committee would never surrender its academic authority to pressure from the temple, but she remembered what Salvatore had said: Zhou was religious. Perhaps Zhou would indeed do as her guide instructed.

Aiana tried another tack. "Since when is the temple afraid of the truth? With all due respect, Holy Guide, I experienced what I experienced. I knew Taerlin personally." Oh, how she knew him! If he were here now, he'd be defending *her* position, not the temple's. "He was a great man, a worthy cornerstone of the temple. But he also loved nothing if not the truth. Can you do less?"

"We can do *more*." Ord smiled with cold eyes. "Taerlin showed us the way, but he didn't have to shepherd a flock. We do. Can you imagine the despair—the *chaos*—if the rumor were to get out that the Blessed Ascension is a hoax? A mistake?"

She took a deep breath. The rock in her stomach felt a bit smaller. This just might work. "It's the Blessed Ascension that you're worried about, then? Not the fact that I knew him? That I was there?"

"Yes," Ord said. "You were there. You're an historian. You travel in time. That's what you historians do. You had some extraordinarily good luck in your time traveling; who can question this? But for you to assert that the people who went with Taerlin did not go to Paradise but simply to some other planet . . . Worse, that it was not Taerlin but you who transported them . . . Miss Kim, that would be heresy. It cannot be permitted."

Aiana unfolded her arms and placed her hands on the desk between them. She leaned forward. "Reverend Guide.

Just between those of us here in this room," She glanced at Salvatore, who nodded almost imperceptibly. "We all know that the people were transported to another planet. And that my use of oneiroportation is what made that possible."

He matched her aggressive posture. "We all know that that's what you *believe* happened, Miss Kim. But word of this mistaken—and dangerous—belief will never be given any credence, academic or otherwise. Your thesis must be abandoned."

"Wait, hear me out. When Taerlin was in prison, he was willing to die to protect the planet where we brought those people. So, for *his* sake—not yours—I was already planning not to reveal the identity of the place. I have plenty of material for a fine thesis without it. A little editing of the holos . . ." She shrugged, turned her palms up, and relaxed. "I could easily go one step further and leave the Blessed Ascension alone."

Ord leaned back and stroked a finger along his cheek as he studied her. "Tell me then," he said, "how the story would go, the one that you propose to document in your thesis."

After that meeting, it took three months for her to receive formal approval of the thesis and to schedule its oral defense. Aiana bit her lower lip and looked around the hall. It was an old room in an even older building, meticulously maintained to enhance the image of time-honored tradition. Walls paneled in genuine wood gleamed in the warm glow of old-fashioned wall sconces, a mood not at all diminished by the modern lighting that banished shadows from every corner of the stage. Ampitheater seating allowed each observer an unobstructed view of the tables arranged on that stage: one for the three interlocutors on the left; one for Aiana, who would sit alone, in the middle; and a third table for her advisor and thesis committee on the right.

The room held two hundred fifty people. Between those already seated and those milling about either chatting or trying to find seats, it was going to be nearly full.

"I didn't expect I'd be so popular." She glanced at Smithjon, standing by her side in the dim lighting offstage where the audience couldn't see them.

He was smiling, his eyes crinkled in warm satisfaction. "You're a miracle of our times, you and that thesis of yours. The committee has already approved it; interlocution is just a formality. Relax. You don't have anything to worry about."

She wasn't worried about the thesis. Not now. But . . . "I don't see Uncle Mark and Aunt Jen."

Smithjon nodded toward the reserved seating in the first two rows, already filling with various dignitaries. "I believe those two seats next to the president are reserved for them."

Aiana drew in a breath. "You're joking! The president is coming?"

He laughed. "Anywhere your uncle goes on campus, you can be sure President Inoli is not far behind."

"Oh. Right." Just then she saw her uncle and aunt enter at the back of the hall and begin working their way down the crowded aisle. Her heart surged. As Smithjon had said, the president of the university was at their heels. And the dean of the College of Arts and Sciences was not far behind him.

She let out tension she hadn't realized she was holding. "They deserve this day."

"You do too."

Aiana had worked for this for the last two, almost three, years. She had persisted through times that seemed like every road was blocked. Yet now that she was within an hour or two of achieving her long-held goal, she felt empty of any feeling of accomplishment. The thesis no longer seemed important.

She looked down, tugging almost absentmindedly at her gown. As if it weren't already straight. She tucked a strand of hair behind her ear and didn't notice when it fell forward again.

She wished Taerlin were here. He was the one who deserved this moment, not her.

The interlocutors marched to their table, and the audience fell silent, the last few stragglers hurrying to find their seats. Aiana's committee filed solemnly to their table, and Smithjon escorted her to hers. He then joined the committee, but Aiana knew that if she ran into any difficulty, he would defend her.

The chief interlocutor stood. "All rise."

All rose.

"We are here today to test the thesis of doctoral candidate Aiana Kim. Does anyone see why this proceeding should not continue?"

Silence.

"Very well. Please be seated."

For the next hour, the interlocutors questioned every aspect of Aiana's thesis and picked at her answers. She had at hand the control of a holo projector to play the appropriate backup when the question called for more than a verbal answer.

"So you found Taerlin initially on New Richmund?"

"Yes. He had been conducting a study of the whynywir, the alien civilization that lives on New Richmund alongside the planet's humans."

"And you say that you were the one to convince Taerlin to return to Earth?"

A tittering rippled through the audience. That this slip of a girl would have been the one to convince the great Taerlin to come to Earth!

"No, professor. It was the whynywir who did that. He learned from them that eternal life could be the reward of anyone who lived well, and he wanted to spread the word. All I did was to bring him back a little more quickly than he otherwise would have gotten here."

"You barely mention the whynywir in this thesis, Miss Kim. Please tell us about them."

Aiana remembered how the creatures had invaded Taerlin's mind, how he'd shivered and huddled in her arms in the cold valley. The coldness of the great winged beings. "I never saw them personally," she lied. "I only heard about them from him. But you know that he had a crystal device that enabled him to communicate with them directly."

"Yes, you include the specifications as part of your thesis."

She paged through the index. "I can bring them up if you'd like."

"No, no; quite all right. Tell us instead of your search for New Richmund's initial humans."

Aiana cleared her throat and rubbed at a spot on the side of her nose. "I thought that he might have been involved in the initial settlement of that planet, but I was unable to find such a settlement. I did, however, find a place where they were waiting for Taerlin to arrive."

"How did they know about him?"

"That's a good question. All I know is that they'd heard it from their parents and grandparents. I never got back to the initial time, if indeed there was one. Perhaps the whynywir told them. But they were waiting for him, and they had some certainty about it. So I waited, too. And after a few millennia, he did in fact show up."

"Then can you at least tell us *why* they were waiting for him?"

Aiana looked the chief interlocutor in the eye, straightened her posture, and lied. "Why, for the same reason we all wait for his return today. The Earth has no monopoly on him. They were waiting to be redeemed."

A susurration rippled through the audience, and the interlocutors paused until it died down. "In general, Miss Kim, we find your thesis solid and your supporting documentation incontrovertible. We do, however, have one more question."

Here it comes. They'll ask about my relationship with him, and when I lie, I'll blush. Taera will give me away. She could feel her face growing hot just thinking about it.

"You were there at the Blessed Ascension."

"Yes." Good, quite a different direction. She looked down, thumbing through the index. "I can play it, if you'd like."

"That's all right. Just tell us. You had been accompanying Taerlin for some time at that point. Why didn't he take you? I see in the supporting evidence that you vanished along with the others, but here you are."

"I . . . I'm not sure why; I didn't have a chance to ask him. But my theory is that, unlike the others, I was not there in person. Only my oneiromorph was present. When he transported everyone, I was simply thrown back into my own body in my own time. I am . . . still hopeful that he might come for me some day."

Ironically, of everything she said that day, this at least was true.

Chapter Thirty-Two

EARTH, YEAR 3226

For the third semester in a row, Aiana was teaching "Intro to Third Millennium History," a survey course offered to lower-class students who had other majors, in fulfillment of their liberal arts requirement. It was a popular course despite Aiana's reputation as a tough grader, if only because the media presentations were extraordinary.

A late student slipped into the back of the darkened lecture hall after the lights were dimmed and the lecture was well under way, but she paid him no mind. In a class of over a hundred, there were always a few stragglers.

Her heart wasn't in this course, not really. True, she was the youngest professor in the university to be given tenure, but she hadn't been able to escape the dues that a new teacher must pay. And teaching the required survey courses was one of those unavoidable obligations.

She sighed and projected an interactive graph of world population growth over the millennium, highlighting the two crashes, the first as a result of the Religious Wars in the Middle East early in the millennium, and the second, a nasty business involving the deadly R-22 virus only a few hundred years ago. There was too little time to cover the material well. She was relieved when the buzzer sounded, signaling the end of the period.

"Remember that papers are due next Monday," she said, raising her voice over the shuffling as students packed up books, papers, readers, computers, comms, and the other necessaries of modern student life. She turned off the projector and raised the lights.

As students exited the lecture hall through front and rear exits, a few gathered around her with questions, or to angle for attention and a good grade.

"Aiana."

She looked up, surprised that any of the students would use her given name.

And the world went dizzy.

He wore a black jacket and under it, a white shirt. His hair was long, but neatly trimmed. He met her eyes and smiled and reached his hand toward her. Golden eyes with flecks of blue under arched eyebrows. Oh, by all that is holy, those beautiful eyes.

She braced herself with a hand on her table, closed her eyes, and wiped the back of the other hand over her forehead. She'd been working too hard, relaxing too little. But when she opened her eyes again, he was still there.

"Are you all right?" His expression had turned to concern. He spoke in Old Standard—but what had she expected? That he would suddenly be fluent in Modern Standard? The miracle was that he was here at all.

Most of the students, not understanding the archaic language, slipped from the room. Only a small knot of three, huddled over one of their comms, remained.

"Yes, I'm fine." She clasped his offered hand warmly but resisted the tug that would have ended in an embrace. With a small movement of her head she indicated the students still present. And then mischief took over. Damn this course, anyway. "Shall I introduce you?"

He melted her with a smile. Three years, and nothing had changed.

"Will it start a panic if you do?"

She turned to the three students studying the comm, who were now looking hard at her companion. "They look like they're about to figure it out in any case. I'd guess we have about twenty seconds to surprise them."

"Go ahead, then."

She wondered if any of the group spoke Old Standard. "Students, say hello to Taerlin."

"I knew it!" said one of the trio. Modern Standard. Aiana translated.

He thinned his lips into a smile and shook his head in resignation. But his eyes were kind. "Pleased to meet you," he said.

Her heart felt two sizes bigger as she translated. He was playing his role here on Earth very well. She was proud of him.

"Are you taking people back with you again?" asked one of the group in passable Old Standard, the owner of the comm. The boy fingered a necklace with a religious pendant—a gilded feather.

Aiana remembered how Taerlin used to wear whynywir down, but he didn't have any on him now.

Taerlin looked at Aiana as he answered. "Maybe your teacher."

No, not her. She couldn't. She looked at her hand, at the lecture notes underneath it, anywhere but at him.

The student objected. "Hey, that's not fair!"

Taerlin turned his gaze to the student, and something deep and serious seemed to pass between them. "Maybe later," he said, "but not this trip. You're not ready."

Aiana imagined hundreds of thousands of people all trying to crowd into the oneiroport for a one-way trip to a Paradise that was not going to live up to their expectations. How could he know which people were ready for that? And among the ready ones, how would he decide whom to take, when there were no doubt so many?

Wait.

How did he think he was going to take any at all? In fact . . . "How did you get here, Taerlin?"

"You don't know?"

She felt her skin prickling with goosebumps and shivered. "No. Should I?"

He sighed. A small smile moved his lips into an apology he didn't speak. "I'll tell you, but I think not here." He looked at the three students still gathered by them. "Friends, will you excuse us?"

Taerlin followed Aiana out of the classroom and down a long corridor. She didn't say a word to him. She marched briskly, upright, like a soldier.

"Are you angry?" he asked.

Aiana blew an audible breath of contempt out of her nose. Without answering, she trotted up five flights of stairs to the top floor of the Arts and Sciences building, a structure that could as easily have been built in his century as in hers.

He followed her without question.

She knocked loudly on a closed door. It sounded like real wood, a material that in his time was found mainly in ancient academic buildings and the homes of the very wealthy. His own school days seemed like a lifetime ago.

From within a man's muffled voice said something that sounded a lot like, "Enter."

Aiana opened the door, and Taerlin followed her inside. It was a professor's office. Books lined the walls, and from the looks of them, some were quite old. Dust had settled on some of the shelves, and the room smelled like antique paper.

The man who rose to greet them pushed back his disorderly hair, which had fallen into his eyes. He spoke a greeting to Aiana in their language.

She responded in Standard. "I need the oneiroport. Now."

The stranger noted the language shift with a raised eyebrow and turned his gaze to Taerlin. He frowned, for all the world as if he thought he should know him but couldn't quite place him. Then he turned back to Aiana. "What's the problem?"

Aiana gestured with her chin toward Taerlin. "I want to get him back where he came from."

The stranger looked at Taerlin again, still puzzled.

Taerlin decided that if Aiana wasn't going to make the introduction, he would. "Pleased to meet you. I'm Taerlin." He held out a hand.

"Raj Smithjon," the man said, shaking the offered hand. Then the name registered. He stopped shaking, but forgot to let go of Taerlin's hand. "Who?"

"He has to go back," Aiana said. "Now."

"Where did you come from?" Smithjon asked.

"Aran." Taerlin looked questioningly at Aiana. "What, four thousand years ago?"

"Five. And back you must go."

"Yes. And you, too." Taerlin freed his hand from Smithjon's grasp and clapped him on the shoulder instead. "Not you. Her. It appears we need your help."

Aiana looked down and turned slightly away from Taerlin. She bit her lip, wrapped her arms tightly around her chest, and said nothing.

"Why not me?" Smithjon asked. "I thought taking people there was what you did."

Taerlin studied him. He didn't seem the type. He looked too contented, too settled in. This was not a man who hungered for something missing in his life. "What, are you religious? You know it's Aran, not some kind of paradise?"

"No," Smithjon said. "And yes."

"Do you really want to go?"

"To tell you the truth, I never thought about it. It was never an option."

"Well, think about it, then. If you do want to go, ask me again. Later."

"Fair enough. So why do you need my help?"

Taerlin looked at Aiana, but she said nothing. "She can't take me," he said. "It's something to do with her last use of the 'port. You probably know more about that than I do. And she says she can't take her own self, even in theory."

"Ah. Pesky thing, that theory. The problem is that the oneiroportation chamber containing the physical body of the dreamer doesn't travel. Only the dream body travels. And of course, what she brings with her. To bring herself, she would have to bring the entire oneiroportation chamber with all of its equipment and herself inside. But she cannot bring any more than she can carry, or wear, or walk along with."

"But *you* could dream and bring her and me back to Aran."

Smithjon steepled his fingers loosely, then rubbed them back and forth as if they had grown cold. "Yes, I could. If she wants to go." They both turned their gaze to Aiana.

"I . . . No. My job is here. My aunt and uncle are here. My *life* is here. I can't leave." Aiana looked up sharply, chin raised. She held her chest tightly, as if her heart might otherwise leap out of it. As if she had to hold herself in this place and time with physical force. "But even if I did, I can't take Taerlin home. I can't . . . risk . . ."

"No," said Smithjon.

"Risk? What kind of risk?" Taerlin touched Aiana's shoulder gently. She was warm under his fingers and smelled slightly of something like cinnamon and roses. He ran his hand down her arm and took her hand, uncurling it from her other arm. She relaxed under his touch.

"I was in a coma," she said, "after the last trip, when I brought the last things. For three months."

"We didn't know if she would live, or if she would ever come out of it," Smithjon added.

"You and I had quarreled," Aiana said. "I didn't expect ever to see you again."

"But I found you just as you were leaving."

"Yes . . ." She sounded uncertain. "I hadn't made a plan for that, so Taera . . ." She bit her lip, and tears welled in her eyes. She blinked them back.

Taerlin finished the sentence, stroking her hand, which he still held. ". . . acted on her own."

Aiana nodded and put her other hand over his, lightly echoing his strokes.

"She wanted to stay with me. You know that, don't you?"

Aiana looked down at her hands, seeming to become conscious for the first time what they were doing. She pulled them away from his. "That's what I guessed. I don't remember it."

No one spoke for a moment. Taerlin walked to the office window and looked out at the treetops, which swayed in the March breeze. Leafbuds were beginning to turn green. When the leaves emerged, the view would be shady and closed in, but now he could see the roofs of academic buildings marching off into the distance, and the city beyond. The campus didn't look much different, at least from this height, than it had centuries ago.

"You sent her back, didn't you?" Aiana asked.

"Yes."

"Why? You had what you wanted, didn't you? Why bring me into it?"

Taerlin turned and walked back to her, touched her cheek, smoothed her hair.

Aiana shivered and closed her eyes for a moment, her face a perfect expression of longing. She leaned slightly into his touch.

"She couldn't say whether you would live or . . . or what would happen. How could I let her stay under those conditions? She knew she had to go back. She didn't argue. The only question was which one of us would talk with you."

"And you lost the coin toss?" Aiana opened her eyes and took his hand away from her hair. But she didn't let go of him.

Taerlin's eyes flicked down to where Aiana still held his hand and then back to her face. "I think we agreed we would both do it."

"Well, she hasn't." Aiana said, lifting her chin. "You've been duped."

She leaned toward him, their shoulders touching. Her body was warm against his. He breathed in her fragrance and let the breath out slowly. *You are so wrong*, he thought. *Your subconscious is screaming at you. Just listen.* "I don't think so."

Aiana seemed oblivious to her own behavior. Still holding Taerlin's hand she said, "Very brave of you to come here on the promise of a dream. Risking your immortal spirit, and all that."

Taerlin ignored the irony in her voice. "When that dream is Taera . . . is *you*, Aiana . . . it's worth the risk. Besides, soon we'll be back on Aran together."

"Soon *you'll* be on Aran. Taera may have decided about me, but I have not."

Smithjon cleared his throat. "If I may?" They both turned to look at him. "Let's postpone this discussion until we see when I might get onto the oneiroport schedule. It could be booked for . . ." He wiggled one hand in a line across the air and shrugged. ". . . weeks."

"Yes, of course," Aiana said, straightening her hair. "Can you check that now? It would be good to have a deadline to resolve this."

Smithjon shuffled the papers scattered on his desk until he found his comm, buried beneath them.

Aiana turned toward Taerlin and said, "I wish you had asked me before you just showed up here."

"I did," Taerlin said. "Who do you think brought me here?"

She flushed. "Taera is not me."

Taerlin studied her face seriously, looking for the slightest hint of irony. "In that case, who is she?"

"Damned if I know," she muttered. Then she frowned. "When did she do that?"

Taerlin looked confused. "Today."

"When was it on Aran when Taera brought you here today?" Aiana persisted.

"Oh. A day after she almost left the last time but didn't."

Aiana chewed on her lower lip. "So . . . she was on her own with you for a day?"

"Yes, about that."

"And then she brought you here, now?"

"Yes, that's right. I know it's two years later, but she couldn't get us any closer."

"I was unconscious for three months—but she was there for only a day?" She looked at Smithjon. "How can we account for that?"

"I don't know." He shrugged elaborately. "When it comes to elapsed time in the dream world, things get unreliable."

"Oh. Yes, of course." She glanced at Taerlin. "I guess it's a good thing she came back as soon as she did."

"Maybe for both of you," Taerlin said. "I don't believe you could have survived long with her gone."

"Nor I," Smithjon said. "But it's never been tested. Might have been an interesting experiment."

"Not with my life, it wouldn't," Aiana said. "Raj, when is the 'port available?"

"The 'port? Oh . . . right . . . let me check." He fingered his comm, scrolling up and down the schedule. He frowned and looked through it again. "Tomorrow," he said. "The 'port is available first thing tomorrow morning. There's been a cancellation. If we don't do it then, there's a two-month wait."

"Is tomorrow okay?" she asked Taerlin.

"Okay."

"Good," Aiana said. "Let's book it."

Smithjon thumbed the appointment into his comm.

"We can meet you tomorrow morning, right? I really appreciate your help with this, but we've kept you for long enough."

"My pleasure." Smithjon ran a hand through his hair, adding to its disarray. "Taerlin, if you need a place to stay tonight, I have a guest room."

Taerlin hadn't returned to Earth in order to stay in some stranger's guest room. But it was a kind offer. "Thanks. But I'm staying with Aiana."

Her eyes widened.

Taerlin put a hand on her shoulder, and she leaned toward him. She closed her eyes, breathed in and visibly relaxed, letting out a long, deep breath. "He's sleeping on my couch," she said.

❧

That night, Aiana put on her cotton kimono and slipped quietly into the living room. Taerlin had fallen asleep tangled in a comforter and stretched out on her long couch. She wanted to touch his cheeks, his lips, his eyelids, but she did not. Silently, she went to the kitchen and in the dim light of the ceiling's night glow made herself a mug of tea. Then she curled up on one of the living room's two armchairs.

She sipped her tea and watched Taerlin sleep. His chest rose and fell slightly, and his face was as peaceful as a child's. His hair was rumpled. She fought an urge to smooth it.

She wished he could live with her here, but of course he couldn't. It must have been hard for him to come here at all. To give up the community of the whynywir, which he valued so deeply. To risk a final death far from home. She admired his courage.

She wished she could go back to Aran with him, but this too was out of the question. She had only this year gotten tenure. How could she give it up—and for a man? What a disappointment that would be to Uncle Mark and Aunt Jen! That would be a difficult goodbye.

Aiana wished that she could enter Taerlin's dreams as she once had. Perhaps she could, and in their dreams they might be together in ways that were impossible in the waking world.

She smiled at the thought of such dreams. She placed the mug on the small table near her chair and closed her eyes.

The moon moved across the sky until it shone directly on Taerlin's face. The light woke him, moonlight that shone so brightly it cast shadows. Taerlin looked around the unfamiliar room.

He saw Aiana's sleeping form on the nearby chair, and he caught his breath.

His first thought was to touch her. He wanted to wake her, to kiss her, to hold her, to make love with her. His breath quickened. His body ached with the too-familiar desire.

But no. He refused to force his desires on her. Aiana must come to this in her own way, or not at all.

Taerlin sat up and watched the sleeping woman. Her red hair was pale in the moonlight and in total disarray. Her head was bent awkwardly to rest on her shoulder. She couldn't possibly be comfortable in that position. She was probably chilly, too. He stood and picked up his comforter to put around her, and then decided instead to carry her back to her own bed.

Carefully, gently, he scooped Aiana up in his arms, shifting her weight so that her head rested on his shoulder.

She made a low, sleepy sound and put her arm over his other shoulder. Still asleep, she snuggled closer to him.

He smiled and placed a kiss on her hair. And thought that he could carry her a thousand miles this way. But it was only a short walk across the threshold to her bedroom. He laid her carefully onto the bed and pulled the covers up over her.

And then he couldn't help himself. He sat on the side of the bed and kissed her cheek lightly.

She stirred and half-formed his name.

"It's all right. Sleep."

"Stay."

"Shhh."

She opened her eyes. "Stay with me. Here. Tonight. Please." She reached out to him, and he surrendered himself to her.

Smithjon commed Aiana in the morning, waking them both. "Just wanted to confirm that we're still on for this morning."

Aiana looked at Taerlin. He smiled at her, and her heartbeat quickened. It was a good thing the return was scheduled for today. Another couple of days, and she'd never be able to let him go. "Yes. This morning."

"I'm off to the lab, then," Smithjon said. "You won't be able to reach me for the next hour or so, while I get ready. I'm thinking that my office is an awfully cluttered place to try to do this. Why don't we meet at the quad behind the library instead. You know the one?"

It was a good location, quiet and surrounded by academic buildings that would almost certainly be empty early on Saturday morning. "Yes. Good. We'll be there at . . . let's say, ten?"

"Fine. Bring your comm. If for some reason I can't get there at that time, I'll try to get somewhere where I can comm you. My office, perhaps."

"Good. See you then. And, thanks, Raj."

Aiana disconnected. She forced her voice to be cheerful. "Ready to go?"

"Ready if you are," Taerlin said.

She swallowed, but it didn't ease the lump forming in her throat. She wrapped her arms around herself. Holding herself back. "I . . . appreciate the risks you took coming here. But I can't go with you."

"Taera said you don't want to live on Aran."

Her face grew hot, and she spoke a little louder than necessary. "That's not true!" She thought about her days, months, centuries waiting with that first village. How peaceful it had been, even from the beginning. She missed the beauty of Aran, the joy of its people. "But my life is here. My career."

"You can teach people there, Aiana. We need teachers, too."

She laughed, a small sound, hollow like his words. "Teach *what*?"

"I'm serious. We need history, too. It will be oral history, of course, but there are songs and stories that have come over with Cort's people that must be preserved. Myths, constellations. Even the language. People have dispersed, and we need to preserve our heritage. We need a historian."

Aiana caught her breath. It was true. It was worthwhile. It was work she would love to do. But it wasn't the teaching career she'd been working toward. She tightened her lips, looked down, shook her head.

He touched her arm. "Don't decide right now. Pack anything you'd want if you do go."

Was she really going to let this remarkable man out of her life? *Let* him out! She was practically forcing him out! She couldn't hold the intensity of his gaze and turned away.

"Okay?" he asked.

Her voice came out husky. "Okay."

The grassy quadrangle was framed in evergreens and azaleas just coming into bloom and protected from the wind by buildings on all sides. No one else was there.

"We're a little early," Aiana said. "So perhaps this is a good time to tell you that I'm sorry. I should have told you the whole story. It wouldn't have made any difference in the course of events, and it would have been the respectful thing to do. I treated you like a child, and I had no right—"

He put a finger on her lips to silence her. For a moment, there was nothing but that touch.

"No, what you did was a kindness. If you had told me what would happen on Earth, I still would have done everything I did, no differently, but I would have agonized over it. You spared me a lot of pain. It's I who should apologize to you."

Aiana laughed a little, grateful. "I guess we're even. At least this time we'll be parting on good terms."

He pulled her close, and she leaned into the warmth of him. "Not parting. Don't say that." He leaned down and kissed her, a gentle kiss, demanding nothing, promising everything.

They waited in the quadrangle for fifteen minutes. Smithjon didn't appear. Aiana checked her comm but there were no messages from him. "If he couldn't travel to this time, he'll go back, and then he'll come in person to get us. One way or the other, he'll be here." What would she do if Smithjon couldn't take Taerlin back? The 'port wouldn't be available for another two months! By then she'd be living with him for sure, and that would be the end of her career. Of everything. She fought tears.

Seeing that she was upset, Taerlin held her more tightly. She settled into his encircling comfort, and they waited. But not for long.

An apologetic cough broke the silence. "Er—excuse me."

Aiana turned, and there was Smithjon. But no, not him exactly; rather, it was a younger version of him, his hair fuller with less grey, his face almost clear of wrinkles. "Raj!" He must have been quite the ladykiller when he was younger. She thought, unexpectedly, about Taera, about her own inner and outer selves. Somewhere inside himself, Aiana realized, Raj still was such a man. To be honest, he was still attractive, but definitely not her type. She glanced sidelong at Taerlin. Her type. Would she ever find another like him? How many like him were there, in all of time and space?

"Sorry I'm late, but I couldn't get here until I was sufficiently into the future that there would be no overlap." Smithjon pulled his archaic chronometer from his equally archaic vest pocket and peered at it. "We don't have long. Only a few minutes. So, what is it to be, both of you, or just the one?"

"Both," Taerlin said.

Oh, it was tempting. To live on Aran, with its beautiful trees, its friendly people. To become its first historian. To live with Taerlin. But how could she go? What would her aunt and uncle think? How could she throw away everything they had given her?

"Just him," she said.

They looked at each other. His eyes were luminous with sorrow.

Aiana shook her head mutely and pulled free of his arms. "I can't. Not now. Not yet." She hefted the straps of her bag onto her shoulder. "Perhaps . . . later." She backed away from him.

His face was a map of concern and pain. He stretched out a hand to her.

She took another step backwards, away from him.

He dropped his hand. "I'm finished with Earth," he said. "I'm not going to come back here for you, or for anything, again. Come with me now."

"I . . . can't."

"Then I'll wait for you on Aran."

"I don't know . . . when."

"Aiana. Listen to me. I'll wait."

She nodded, then turned and walked away. Her throat closed up. She couldn't swallow. She willed herself not to cry.

He was watching her, she was sure of it. She didn't turn around, but she could picture the scene.

Right about now Smithjon would be putting a hand on Taerlin's shoulder. She heard him say, "There's not much time." Taerlin would turn, crushed, and he would allow the older man to lead him toward the invisible 'port.

Aiana reached the corner of the quad, the last spot where she might look back. She stopped, took a deep breath, and turned around.

The quad was empty.

Her heart stopped beating.

What could she have been thinking? She had just walked away from everything that ever mattered. The loss flooded into her, and it was too heavy to bear. Tears spilled from her eyes, and she called out in choked sobs, "No! Wait!" She ran across the quad and back again, calling, "Raj! Wait!" and "Taerlin!"—but the entrance to the 'port was gone.

Aiana sank to her knees in the cool grass, and wept.

Chapter Thirty-Three

ARAN, YEAR BC 2043

MIKEL'S RECORDING, conclusion

I refused to believe that Aiana wouldn't return. I kept busy in the village while I settled down to wait for her. But somewhere inside, I knew she wasn't coming. I worked at a frantic, restless pace. I couldn't stop, couldn't sit still. Couldn't give myself time to think.

I had no appetite and ate only when my mother sat me down and put a bowl of stew or roasted meat in my hands. Sometimes not even then. No one said it, but everyone knew what I had lost. Laughter was cut short when I approached. Conversations fell silent. Children were hushed.

The signs of her were all around: Aston, once confined to a wheelchair, now walked. His muscles were weak; he used them tentatively, but he used them. There was no sickness in the village, not even a sniffle. Taera had done her work well, she, the real miracle maker, not I.

I hung around like a third hand, extra and purposeless, waiting for Aiana, who was not coming back.

Finally, Cort took it upon himself to talk with me. "I think you should leave this place."

"But I'm—"

"Waiting for Aiana?"

I nodded, not trusting myself to speak it.

"This is the right place for that. This will be the village of those who wait," he said. "Where we first encountered Taera how many months ago?"

"Four thousand some-odd years in the future, as I remember."

"You won't live that long. For you, it's time to stop waiting. You have work to do. You're making everyone nervous the way you're looking over your shoulder all the time. You ought to get out of here."

I remembered Taera saying she couldn't reach this place until a hundred years after it was settled. I wouldn't live that long, either. I took in a deep breath and let it all out. "I promised to take a group to the ocean."

"Time to get started. The ocean—or come with me if you'd like." His eyes expressed an invitation that I couldn't deal with. I ignored it and focused instead on the problem of Aiana.

"What happens if she comes back, though?"

"Leave a message for her. The people who stay here will be waiting for her. They'll deliver your message, even if it takes generations until the first time she appears. Think about it, Mikel. She may already know where to find you."

I couldn't face the intensity of his eyes. "You're right," I said, looking away. He *was* right. "Even if the message doesn't reach her for generations, it'll be time enough, if she wants to find me."

I began getting the Baysby group ready for a long journey, and several of the Aran folk that Cort had brought volunteered to come along. The motives were quite different. The people from Earth longed for the ocean as a familiar home that they missed; the people from Aran desired it as a part of their world they had never experienced. But the groups were compatible. The Earth folk brought with them the lore of boats and sails and fish and the sea; the Aran folk, the skills of the journey and the plants, the language and culture.

Cort helped me, as he always had in so many ways. And yet there was a question in his eyes that he seemed unable to ask, and that I was not ready to face.

But time was growing short.

In the end, it was I who brought the question out into the open. "Do you remember saying that you thought I should leave this place?"

"Yes, I was hoping . . ." His eyes turned away from mine, and he fell silent.

"I've been thinking that I'll go with this Baysby group," I said. "I'd like to live near the ocean. I was hoping you might come with us."

He looked back at me, and his sad expression spoke his answer. "I can't. I'm planning to take a group south, far south of here. I want to start the village where our father will be born. There has always been a Corodh-an-Aran in that village. Sometimes more than one. I was hoping . . ." Again he fell silent.

I knew that the pain in his eyes was reflected in my own. It was only a year or so ago that I met Cort, but I felt that he had always been a brother to me. That, and more. He had saved my life when I might have died among the whynywir. He represented for me everything my father might have been, though I knew that if my father's spirit survived at all, it was within myself.

To leave him now could well be forever, at least in this lifetime. Could living by the sea be worth the price of such a parting? The ocean pulled at me, but it wasn't just that. I had made a promise to the people, never thinking what it might cost. Did I want to break it?

What swayed me the most, though, was my dream of Aiana. My lucid dream, one of only two. The place had seemed so real, the hillside overlooking the ocean. I wanted to find it if it existed, because I still dared to hope that she might be there. "I'm sorry. My life is richer just knowing that you're alive and on this world, however far apart the two of us may be." How the whole sentence made it past the lump in my throat was a mystery.

"I thought it might be this way," said my brother. His eyes were bright with tears, though none fell. "You'll do well in your journey; I feel it, and I hope you find what you're looking for when you get there."

"I, too." I thought of Taera. Of Aiana. "Maybe I'll come back and find you sometime." This seemed unlikely but not impossible. The world was full of surprises, nothing if not that.

I left within a week, I and Joe the sailor, and almost forty others from Baysby, my mother and Aston, and several of the people who had come back with Cort. I bid my brother good-bye, for he was heading south, and Lennard and Lela were going with him.

As for Jak, he was nowhere to be found, and so I didn't get a chance to say good-bye to him, my traitor and my accomplice in this great undertaking, and I regretted that omission more than the good-byes that I did say.

The going was slow. Children and others such as Aston could not walk either fast or far. Food was hard to find. Not that the forest lacked sustenance, but few in our group were sufficiently skilled to hunt or gather as much as a group of sixty people needed. To illustrate our plight, let it be said that I was one of our hunters, I who once was lucky enough to kill a rabbit with a knife when the creature was standing still, upwind, and unaware of me.

We had been on our way three weeks when Jak appeared, lean and strongly muscled, his vest and hair bloody. He carried the carcass of a fully antlered dhelo buck, a big one, over his shoulder. A red crystal gleamed at his temple alongside a smear of blood where he had wiped his forehead. Whatever the story there, I suspected that my brother played a role in it.

Jak found me among those who had stopped to stare at him. He spoke in his policeman's gruff voice, but his eyes were bright with joy. "Give me a hand with this. You think this doesn't weigh anything? What have you people been eating? You're all too thin. You're going to need someone knows how to catch enough food; this is a big group. Well, what are you staring at? Give me a hand, will you?"

I laughed in disbelief and delight. "Jak, I never, ever thought I would be so happy to see you again." Along with several others, I unloaded the dhelo from his shoulder. Someone began a song, and several people joined in. Somewhere, a flute piped a trilling harmony. There would be dinner tonight, and a long journey, months, perhaps a year or more, and then the ocean. We would form settlements of some kind, land-based or seaborne, I didn't know. There would be adventures. My heart would be wounded while Aiana was gone, a lifetime perhaps, though I hoped otherwise. But even without her, if it had to be that way, life would be good. I might not see Cort again, but I would not be without the company of a kindred spirit.

Jak returned my smile.

Chapter Thirty-Four

ARAN, YEAR 3113

His Most High Holiness
  The August Reverend Dheren Johon IV
Holy Guide,

I greet you and kiss the hem of your robe in love and humility.

As you have commanded the mission to preach to the savages of New Richmund, so it has been done. I write this report to you regarding our progress, which is as the Lord our Savior wills. These savages are a strange people, as you are no doubt well aware. Though they greet our missionaries warmly and make them most welcome, I cannot say that we have had much success in changing their behavior to acknowledge that our Savior is the Lord of all, who offers salvation in most blissful Paradise.

Indeed, the savages act as though their Paradise were here and now, on this tranquil though (I must say) benighted planet, and they remain set in their ways. They do not work harder than necessary to live comfortably, ignoring the inestimable wealth of the natural resources all around them, and they seem almost unable to comprehend the guilt of birth that has brought all humankind to the need for salvation. But I ramble, for you warned me of all this before I left to lead this mission. And I shall not fall short of your judgment in choosing me for this task.

Your Holiness, I enclose with this missive an audio recording that was given by the people of a small village near the seacoast to our missionary in that region. As you will see for yourself, this recording is, judging from the format, quite old, though amazingly well preserved, and obviously of Earth origin. How these villagers might have come across it is a mystery, since the previous settlement of this planet did not come within three thousand kilometers of the coast.

Though the missionary, Brin Selezar, whom you no doubt remember for his youthful enthusiasm and his dedication, is completely ignorant of the contents, I myself am a lover of antique media and so I have with me here the means to listen to the recording. It is thin through age, but still perfectly clear. What it seems to allege is nothing short of astonishing, but—No, forgive me, Your Holiness, for you must judge the contents for yourself. I am sending this missive marked for your eyes alone, and I trust that you will determine the wisest disposition of this artifact.

I await your further instructions and remain in all things
Your most devoted servant,
Jagom Tenevin,
Mission Commander to the planet of New Richmund

Chapter Thirty-Five

EARTH, YEAR 3113

"**I** might not see Cort again, but I would not be without the company of a kindred spirit. Jak returned my smile." The muffled voice on the audio recording fell silent, leaving only a barely audible static of background noise.

The old man took the recording out of the antique audio machine and put it on the table beside his chair. For a long time he sat in silence, his lips pursed thoughtfully, the long, delicate fingers of his right hand drumming quietly against the chair's padded arm.

"Kindred spirits!" he muttered. "Taerlin and Jak the Traitor! It's preposterous." But something in him was held by the story, as by an enchantment. "Ridiculous," he said, fighting its spell. "Absurd!"

A fire burned on the stone hearth. The lights in the room had been turned down so that the room was primarily lit by firelight. "Romanticist!" the man said angrily to himself, touching a knob on the table. The lights grew brighter. He touched another control, and the fire disappeared, leaving only an object that looked like a log, unburned, on the hearth.

"Worse than absurd. It is the very handiwork of the Trickster, who keeps us all in our chains and prevents us from reaching the Paradise that our Lord Savior promised." As he spoke to himself, the old man nervously fingered a ring of priceless Richmund-wood that he wore on the index finger of his right hand.

Something about the recording pulled at him. Though it turned the Holy Story on its head, still there was the ring of truth in it. This disturbed him, and he was one who knew well that the Trickster often wrapped his lies in truth.

The August Reverend Dheren Johon IV, leaning heavily on the brocaded arms of his chair, pushed himself up to stand. He paced the length of the room, a good eight meters, and looked vacantly out the window, a glass-paneled door almost three meters high that led to a balcony. Had it been daytime, or had the lights in the room not been so bright, he would have seen a sheltered courtyard where gardeners labored with some success to keep flowers blooming, despite the raw cold of midwinter. He was familiar with the scene, hardly noticing it even in daylight. He did not miss it now. He turned and paced back again.

The authenticity of the recording was beyond doubt. He had been obliged to have part of the casing destroyed in order to verify it. The technology was that of Earth from about seven hundred years ago, the time of Taerlin's life. There had been a brief period of attempted colonization of New Richmund. It was possible that a mission such as the narrator described to return a single native had occurred, but enough media had been destroyed during the Dark Age that no record of it remained now. Judging from the technology alone, either event might have been the source of the recording, except for one thing. Atomic particle-dating of the casing material placed its age at between forty-five hundred and five thousand years, long before the civilization on Earth had discovered space flight. There was no scientific way to explain the presence of this recording on New Richmund, no way to explain the recording at all.

The social implications were even more troubling than the technology. He reached the far end of the room and stared as unseeingly into the cold fireplace as he had a moment ago out the window. Though scholars argued the point, most believed that Taerlin came from New Richmund. Finding such an artifact on that planet would lend this belief a dangerous veracity. Taerlism had united Earth when Earth had fallen into chaos. This recording turned Taerlism upside-down and threatened the planet with chaos again.

"Why me?" he said, and instantly regretted his cowardice. He had become too comfortable over the years; often he had chastised himself on this very issue. This was reason enough, he thought, why it should be him. He would tolerate no more of his inner whining.

If any hint of the existence of this recording were to get out, if even the idea of such a thing were to reach the public, who could say how many souls would be in danger? The recording would be so attractive! It could do unthinkable damage. The mission to New Richmund had been sent to save souls, and now it seemed that far more was to be lost than gained.

The recording must be utterly and totally destroyed.

He could feel his own resistance to the idea. He considered keeping the recording in his personal vault. But then—Dheren Johon tried to keep himself physically fit, but at eighty-two years of age, how long could he hope to live? Another ten years? Twenty? Two?

He thought of his possible successors. Amos Inhedron, only forty-five, was the likely candidate. A financial genius, he had invested the temple's resources well, increasing its wealth, and therefore its influence, beyond anything they'd previously imagined. And his spiritual fervor was unquestioned. But the man had little backbone and didn't show the vision a leader should have. What would he do with the recording if he found it? Could Dheren Johon trust that he would maintain absolute secrecy? No. On reflection, he felt that he could not trust any of them. His personal resistance to the idea of destruction was the proof that it needed to be done.

Not allowing himself further time to think, he strode briskly back to his chair, picked up the recording from the table, and placed it in the fireplace. Then he set the knob that controlled the intensity of the fire to maximum. With a whoosh of air, the flames flared into a white glare, intensely hot, and a faint acrid smell of burning plastic filled the air. Dheren Johon sat down with a sigh, and watched the fire burn, feeling its heat on his skin.

"It's late, Your Holiness." The voice interrupted his reverie. How long had he been sitting here like this?

"Thank you, Owen," he told the man in the doorway, his personal secretary and faithful servant for more than three decades. Owen was ten years younger than Dheren Johon, but showed his age more. He was stooped, and he shuffled as he came into the room. "You should be in bed yourself."

"When I see you well and truly tucked in," the servant answered, as he did every night, "and not a moment before."

Dheren Johon reflected that he was lucky in his companions. "Do we start early tomorrow?"

"There are no appointments until your meeting with the chairman of the foundation at ten o'clock, but I have set aside the time from eight until ten for you to review the necessary financial documents. Amos has insisted upon it."

"Ah, yes. The foundation. Very well, Owen." The holy guide, spiritual head of the Great Temple, stood and turned off the fire. He walked over to the fireplace, picked up a poker from the set of tools at its side, and pushed at the pile of grey ashes that lay in front of the unburnt log, scattering it across the fireplace. He sighed. "I want to recall the mission from New Richmund."

The secretary's jaw dropped. "But, Your Holiness, you yourself initiated the effort to convert those poor heathen, when was it? Thirteen years ago already, and everyone agrees that the task has been a worthy one."

"Yes, of course it has. It's always a worthy effort to care for our neighbors. But I have had a new vision, and a compelling one. The temple must reinvigorate its efforts right here on Earth. Everywhere, we hear that the temple does not reach the poorer people. Our roots are among the people, Owen. There is missionary work to be done right here! We have been overlooking our own family in our efforts to care for our neighbors. This is not right, and I do not see that we can divide our efforts on two fronts. No, the mission to New Richmund must be recalled, I am sure of it. I would like for you to prepare for me a draft of a public statement on this subject at once. Make this a high priority. I'll want to review it tomorrow afternoon."

"As you wish, Your Holiness." The secretary bowed slightly, then frowned. "This doesn't have to do with that package young Jagom sent you from New Richmund, does it?"

"Not at all. In fact, Owen, we can forget that package completely. Do you understand?"

Owen had worked for the temple leader for thirty years. He understood exactly what his master meant. "Yes, Your Holiness. Of course."

Dheren Johon steepled his fingers together in front of pursed lips. Now came the worst of it, but undeniably necessary.

"And another thing," said the holy guide, almost as an afterthought. "About that young Jagom Tenevin . . . It would not displease me if some accident were to befall him on New Richmund. It would be most unfortunate, of course, given his youth and his great promise of achievement for the temple. But sometimes, certain unfortunate events have a way of serving the greater good, eh? And the completion of the mission on New Richmund will be a fine monument to him."

Owen bowed. He was a man of faith; Dheren Johon knew that Owen trusted him to act for the greatest good of the Temple. Owen had not known the man Jagom. And this was not the first time that such unfortunate events had been . . . arranged. "I understand, Your Holiness. It shall be as you wish."

Before going to bed that night, Dheren Johon IV, spiritual head of the Great Taerliri Temple, took a long shower. Of course the mission commander had to be disposed of. He had heard the recording; his letter left no doubt of it. Given what the recording contained, the man had been a fool to reveal any knowledge of those contents. Dheren Johon could not trust that Jagom would remain silent once he returned to Earth. For the good of the temple, such a return could not be permitted. He had taken the right action, but when he stepped out of the shower, Dheren Johon still felt dirty.

He didn't sleep well. He dreamt troubled dreams in which a red-haired child from the future came and dragged him out bed and pushed him into a primitive world of the distant past, a place from which there was no escape. He woke feeling tired and still troubled about the recording he had destroyed.

The financial statements he was supposed to review that morning seemed flat and uninteresting. He understood that the temple was doing well and that its joint investments with the foundation had paid off handsomely, but beyond that—what was the real issue? He couldn't focus. There was something else. The images of his dream crowded strongly into his consciousness, almost wiping away the numbers he had tried to memorize.

The red-haired child, Aiana. If the recording was true—preposterous thought, to be sure, but then there *was* the unexplained mystery of its age—if the recording was true, then a technology would exist in the not-terribly-distant future that enabled time travel. What was it called? Focused dreaming? Subjective physics, by all that was holy? He had never heard of such a thing, and he made it a point to keep well informed of the foundation's research efforts.

But if the recording was true—again his mind rebelled at the possibility, but he forced himself to consider it—if the recording *was* true, such a technology must be invented. Must be. If the technology of time travel were not in place for the girl Aiana to use, she would be unable to find the lad—what was his name? Mikel?—on New Richmund and recruit him, and there would never be a Taerlin. The world would not be redeemed.

It was a preposterous notion. Unthinkable.

And there was the issue of those colored crystals, wasn't there? The lad Mikel hadn't known where they came from, but of course one answer might be Earth. It wouldn't hurt to invest a small fraction of the temple's funds into a little scientific research. Indeed, there was much to gain and little to lose.

If the recording was false, a little money would be lost, that was all. Almost certainly, it would be lost, but it was no more than Amos could make in a half a year of careful investing. But on even the smallest chance that the recording might be true, the technology must be invented. The temple depended upon it. Earth depended upon it.

Owen coughed discreetly in the doorway. "Pyotr Noran, Chairman of the One Galaxy Foundation, is here to see you, Your Holiness."

"Good. Please show him in."

He stood as the chairman entered. "Come in, Pyotr, please do come in." He gestured him to a seat at the large table that dominated the room. "I have a proposal for some new basic research that I think you will find most interesting. Of course, the temple will make it financially worth your while. And if it's successful, who knows how it may change the future of the world."

Chapter Thirty-Six

ARAN, YEAR BC 2039

The sun glinting off the deep blue water was almost too bright for his eyes. The young man squinted as he scanned the shoreline, holding the tiller firm against the push of the wind and the tide. Noting that the boat had slowed, he checked his sail, and then tightened the sheet. The sail stiffened, and the boat heeled over to port. Its skipper shifted easily to the starboard rail, enjoying the sensation of racing against the sea, his eyes all the while studying the shoreline.

The land fell in undulating grassy hills to the sea, spotted in places with bushes or low trees. The prevailing winds came from the west, from landward, and a range of mountains many days' journey inland blocked most of the moisture. Though not barren, the seacoast was too dry to support the giant forest that covered most of the land west of the mountains. It was also entirely unpopulated, but that was as he expected. He had left the only human seaside settlement almost a month ago to the north, the beginning of a long journey. With ample supplies, fishing gear, and botas of fresh water stowed aboard, he didn't worry about food, though he decided that if he saw a stream, he would stop this afternoon to refill the botas he had drunk. But there was no hurry.

Approaching a headland that jutted into the sea, the arm of a hill taller than the others around it, the sailor eased off on the sheet and resettled his weight near the centerline of the small boat as he turned portward, away from the coast. Not knowing the area, he wanted to avoid any rocks that might be near the spit.

Running before the wind, the boat seemed to go slower, though he knew that the truth was otherwise. The air and sea seemed calm, and he relaxed, musing upon the events that had led to his departure on this journey.

The last four years had not been easy. With a group of some sixty people, he had traveled eastward through the great forest for half a year. The going had been slow; children and others in the group had trouble keeping up with a brisk pace for long. But, as if sensing its need for the humans, Aran had been kind. Food of all types was plentiful. Several of the people, himself among them, had developed at least adequate skills in hunting, while others had learned to recognize the berries and leaves and roots that enriched their diet.

More than once, some of the people had wanted to give up the journey, to settle down wherever they happened to be. Not all of them equally comprehended or appreciated the goal to which they were heading—the ocean. But somehow—through the influence of leaders or friends—they managed to stay together.

Crossing the mountains had been difficult. The group had camped for weeks in the foothills while several of the more capable individuals had scouted the terrain searching for a pass. Had he not been who he was—Taerlin, the one who had brought them here from the planet Earth, the leader who, despite his own discomfort in the role, was widely held in awe by the others—had he not been all this, he might never have held the group together then. In fact, Taerlin reflected gratefully, if Jak had not bounded into their camp the day he did, grinning and proclaiming the existence of a pass not more than a week's travel to the north, they might have lost a group of people from the Aran of the future, who never having seen the ocean, were vocally becoming more and more adamant about settling in the forest west of the mountains.

And that first day when the ocean had come into view! Barely a blue sliver seen between far-off hilltops, it inspired the entire group. People laughed and ran and shouted, frightening game for hundreds of meters in every direction. Though the pace had quickened considerably, still it was another week before they reached the ocean's edge. Then the real work began.

They lived in lean-tos while they built houses. Then they set to work building boats. A few of the settlers from Baysby knew something of the boat builder's craft, but there were problems to be solved.

Taerlin insisted that they work only with the materials that were available, since boats could be lost, but the skill of building them must be passed on to future generations. That meant, at least for now, no metal. They learned to work wood and reeds, sinew and stone. Then Jak, the hunter, reported that he had found a cache of ancient and very large bones, and an expedition set out. The bones appeared to have been petrified by a process of chemistry and pressure that the discoverers could not imagine. They came from animals that were impossibly huge compared to anything Taerlin knew of alive on the planet currently. And they were harder than steel.

It took three of them to carry one large rib bone back to the village, and they brought several smaller bones—toes, fingers—as well. With blade and grindstone, they learned to cut and shape the material and to fashion tools.

A year passed, two, then more, and Taerlin grew restless. Too many of the girls giggled shyly when he walked by, or blushed and wouldn't meet his eyes, though they stared when they thought he wasn't looking. When he began to notice that their mothers watched him too, sizing him up like a fish just brought back to be cooked, he decided it was time to visit his brother. Somewhere else.

Remembering, Taerlin smiled at how they had reacted when he announced his plans—as if that fish had jumped right out of the boat and swam away. And he knew that leaving was exactly what he needed.

Ahead of him and to his left, Taerlin could see a darker roughening of the water's surface. Knowing that it was caused by wind, he looked over his shoulder to see if he could identify the land formation that might have channeled it. A cleft between two of the hills, perhaps, where the wind would pick up speed. He thought he could imagine which one of many it might be, but the source didn't matter. Only the wind mattered. He angled the small boat portward, easing out on the sail. He picked up speed and was soon well past the jutting headland.

When he guessed that he had cleared any shallow areas off the point, he pushed the tiller to port, turning the boat to starboard; then he held the tiller steady with his knee while hauling in the sheet. The sail flattened and the boat heeled over, with the sensation of increasing wind as he headed up. The headland was now to his right and behind him, but he was too far from shore for his comfort and couldn't head any higher. He decided to come about.

Another adjustment on the tiller, and the sail flapped wildly as the boat headed directly into the wind, then past it. Taerlin pulled the sail over to starboard and hauled in tight and as high as the boat would point. Perched on the port rail, he raced southward along the coast.

He could see land ahead but was blind to his right, where the sail blocked his view. He sailed as close as he wanted to come, not knowing the coast, and then came about again, bringing the sail over to port. As he was adjusting his own weight on the starboard rail, a flash of color caught his attention on the shore—red and white. It didn't look like anything that would be growing on these hills. Surprised, he turned to face the shore directly, almost capsizing the small boat. Reflexively, he let out on the sheet. The boat righted itself, sail flapping wildly. It headed into the wind and came to a stop.

The spot of color had disappeared, but something about it held his attention. He searched the hills of the coast but could make out nothing unusual. At last he sighed and turned his attention back to the flapping sail. He was in no hurry. He decided to investigate. Using the tiller as an oar of sorts, he turned the small boat so that the wind came over the port bow. He pulled in on the starboard sheet, tightening the sail.

Carefully, Taerlin approached the beach, dropping the sail and pulling out the centerboard where the waves started breaking. He eased himself over the side and waded to shore, hauling the small craft up onto the beach. He made sure that the boat was in order—the boom released from the mast, the sail folded, supplies firmly stowed under the oilskin that protected them—and pulled it up well past the high tide mark on the sand. Then, finding a narrow track in the grass, a trail made by dhelo perhaps, he began climbing the hill.

When he reached its crest, Taerlin turned to survey the scene. Before him, to the east, the ocean stretched out clear and blue to the horizon, sparkling under a blue sky with only a few wisps of clouds. To either side, the hill rolled away into a valley, and there was another hill beyond. To the north, a second hill rose higher than the first. That, he decided, would be the backbone of the headland he had just come around. Whatever he had seen would be north of him, if anywhere.

Following the dhelo trail, he descended the north shoulder of the hill, looking around carefully. He enjoyed the play of wind across the long grass but saw nothing either red or white. Of course, he couldn't discount the possibility that something could be hiding behind a clump of bushes, but it seemed even more likely that it had simply gone. Or had never existed, except in his imagination.

Through the valley a clear, swift stream raced to the ocean. The water babbled and sang over the rounded rocks that formed its bottom, glistening in the sunlight. Taerlin knelt to swirl his hand in the water and found it surprisingly cold. He scooped a handful of its clear liquid and drank, savoring its freshness, wishing he had brought the empty botas to refill here. When he looked up again, he noticed for the first time in the shadow of low trees and rocks upstream a small, makeshift lean-to.

He frowned. He knew the entire human population of the seacoast, now numbering some seventy people, counting infants that had been born in the last four years, and he knew that none of them lived this far south. He wondered if any of the inland settlers might have made their way this far east.

Or if—

But no. He refused to allow himself to hope.

Taerlin stood and walked to the lean-to. It was made of sticks cut from branches of the local trees, draped with an oiled cloth that let in what light filtered down through the trees and looked like it might be waterproof.

"Hello!" he called, but there was no answer. No one seemed to be around. Inside the lean-to, there was little. A bedroll and an extra blanket, a pot, something wrapped in cloth and carefully tied, a small wooden box. When he noticed a knife hanging in its sheath from a fork in one of the branches that supported the lean-to, he reflexively touched the knife at his own belt and wondered who would go out, leaving his knife behind. Or what other weapons the person might carry that would make the knife unnecessary.

But there was nothing more to be gained by staying at the lean-to. Taerlin turned and headed northward, to the crest of the headland. As soon as he cleared the little valley, the wind picked up again, stronger now, out in the open. Taerlin smiled. It was a good wind for sailing.

The hill was steeper than it looked, and the narrow trail switched back and forth up its side. A memory teased him, but he couldn't place it.

Short of the crest, Taerlin paused. A movement tugged at the corner of his eye, downhill, seaward. He looked that way, but saw nothing that might have moved, just the grassy slopes with a few rocks and bushes, and the sparkling blue sea beyond. Nevertheless, he headed downhill. The sun, behind him now, cast his shadow long and rippling in the grass ahead, and Taerlin wondered whether the movement he had seen had simply been the rippling of the grass in the wind. Descending further, he came around a clump of leathery-leafed bushes and almost went right by her before he saw her.

She sat in the shade of the bush, still as a statue, looking out to sea. But she turned when he came by, as surprised by his movement as he was to find her there. She gasped and stood quickly, and now the sunlight glinted in countless golden highlights on her red hair, which, escaping the thong where it was tied at her neck, framed her face in a windblown ruby halo. Her white dress, too, was blown by the wind, outlining her legs and her body.

For a moment, neither of them spoke, and then he found enough voice to say, "Taera! Oh, how I've hoped—" It was half a whisper, but even so, she almost imperceptibly shook her head. He looked at her more closely. It had been too long. Her eyes—hazel, not emerald, for the sunlight highlighted flecks of gold and brown in them. Her skin—clear and ivory, but with a dusting of freckles across her nose and cheeks and a small birthmark beside her left eye. The nervous way she fingered a leaf of the nearby bush.

"Aiana." He breathed the name more than spoke it. And wanted to touch her very real body more than he wanted life itself.

Tears spilled from her eyes, glistening in the sunshine. "I was such a fool letting you go that day," she said. Her words came between sobs. He reached out to touch her. She took a step toward him, and then he caught her in his arms. She leaned into him.

"I . . . I knew it right away. I turned and came back, but you were already gone. All those things I thought mattered so much suddenly didn't matter at all without you." She wiped one eye with the back of her hand. "I came as soon as I could."

"It's been four years," he said, softly wiping the tears from her other eye.

"Yes, I know. I came here the first time Raj could get the 'port again; it was less than four weeks. But this was the closest we could come." She looked away, suddenly worried. "You said you'd wait. I hope . . ."

He turned her chin to face him again and kissed her softly. "Of course I waited. I'm glad you're here. But you took quite a risk." *Too much.* "I was living a long way north of here. I waited there . . . as long as I could, but there was an end to it. There had to be. Even if you made it there, I would have been gone. I almost didn't see you. If I hadn't come about just then . . ."

Her contented laughter made him smile. "If you weren't going to see me here," she said, "I would have waited somewhere else where you would."

"I was beginning to think I would never see you again."

"I got your message before I ever met you. The first time I visited that village, about a hundred years from now. 'Taerlin said he would meet you again by the ocean,' they told me. 'If you will come.' And then, almost apologetically, 'He told my grandfather that we must tell you this. It was a long time ago, but he said that you would know both the time and the place.' And I thanked them solemnly and waited until the message made sense, and now I'm here. Taerlin . . . Do you still go by that name, or would you prefer that I call you 'Mikel'?"

He thought for a moment. "I've been 'Taerlin' for so many years now, to everyone but Aston and my mother, and for a long time it felt right. But now . . . In a way I left the village because I wanted to leave Taerlin behind."

"Then it will be 'Mikel.'"

"Yes. I think so." He paused, allowing the wind and the waves to fill the silence, then said, "I dictated the story of what happened. My version. What really happened. I packaged the recording as best I could and left it with the people in my new village. If, as you say, there will be missionaries some day . . . The age of the recording will be indisputable. Maybe, some day, it will set the record straight, at least a little."

Aiana shook her head slightly. "If such a recording had been found some time in the past, someone in my time would know of it. *I* would know of it; I was a historian, remember. There is no such recording. There could not have been, or my journey, our very meeting would have been improbable. I hope you're not upset."

He sighed. "No. I'm resigned to it. I did what I could. That's all. Besides, maybe someone will still discover it sometime in the future. It's going to make a difference somehow, I'm sure of it."

"You did more—for two worlds—than most people dream of. And now, really, Mikel, let's not talk about it anymore."

And so he reached out and touched her wild, glistening ringlets and, still half unbelieving, drew her closer, noticing that her skin was warm and smelled ever so slightly of cinnamon and roses. And they spoke no more, but followed their hearts in the sunlight on the hillside by the sea, where nobody in the world was watching, and the record of what happened after is lost to history.

<<<>>>

Dear Reader,

Thank you for reading *Alien Son*. I know that your time is limited, and I'm honored that you chose to spend it with Mikel and Aiana in their struggle to escape the brutal net of a history that *has already been written*.

To be notified of upcoming releases and to receive special content that's for newsletter subscribers only, you can sign up for my more-or-less monthly newsletter at . Here too, you can follow my travels, still only on planet Earth.

If you enjoyed *Alien Son*, then don't miss *Saving Aran*, and find out how Cort got those two dazzling gems at his hairline, liberating planet Aran in the process. You might also enjoy the books in the *Ascent of Eden* series—*A Warrior of Eden*, *Freeing Eden*, and *The Last Lord of Eden*. Follow the lives of the people who would do anything to save their beloved home Eden from exploitation by an interplanetary drug cartel.

I greatly appreciate your help in spreading the word about *Alien Son*, including telling your friends and fellow readers. And remember, reviews also help readers find books they will enjoy. Please consider posting a review on Amazon, Goodreads, Bookbub, or your blog or website.

To follow me on Facebook:
https://www.facebook.com/gskenneyauthor
To follow me on Instagram:
https://www.instagram.com/gskenneyauthor

Now, turn the page for an excerpt from *Saving Aran . . .*

Saving Aran

by G. S. Kenney

C hapter One
Cort Earns His Knife

The cry of pain echoed in the alley and flowed out into the street like a liquid. Like blood. Cort drew in a sharp breath and touched the scar on his arm. "That's a child! He's in trouble!"

"None of our business," his friend Lor advised. His voice carried a warning.

Cort jogged a few steps to look into the alley, and his heart fell. It was Karl, the biggest bully in the school, with some of his gang. No friends of Cort, and a lot bigger than he was. Two of Karl's cronies were holding a struggling child while Karl was trying to cut the boy's arm. "No!" the child screamed. "No, stop!"

"Just cutting my initials." Karl said. There was a sneer in his voice. "Hold still."

Cort's friends had caught up with him at the mouth of the alley. "Four of them," Tark said. And three of us, he didn't have to say. "Leave it." Four fifteen-year-olds against three thirteen-year-olds were bad odds.

Cort touched the scar on his arm again, his breath coming more quickly. He'd been only eight when a gang of bigger bullies, teasing him about his father, had gotten nasty when he'd fought back. One of them had drawn a knife, and if a teacher hadn't intervened just then, he probably wouldn't have survived to help this child today. "Can't," he said.

He drew a deep breath, let it out in a whoosh, and stepped into the alley to rescue the child that Karl and his gang were tormenting. He waved his arms and trying to appear bigger than he was. "Hold off!" he shouted. "Soldiers coming!"

The gang members looked up, loosening their hold on the child, who ran off crying.

Of course, no soldiers came. It took Karl only a moment to grasp the situation. "You all alone, Street Scum," he said. "Now I cut you instead." He swept his knife in a broad, threatening gesture.

Cort drew back.

"Savage!" Karl's leering, singsong taunt cut the air like his knife.

"Not!" Cort retorted. His heart pounded so loud the sound seemed to fill the alley. He breathed shallowly and too fast, looking from right to left and back again. His friends were gone. No blame for that, but he sure wished that one or both of them had his back now. At least the poor kid had gotten away. Good.

But there was no escape for Cort. If he turned and ran, he was as good as dead. His back would provide too easy a target for four knife-wielding fifteen-year-olds.

Cort stood his ground.

"Where's your knife, Savage?" Karl passed his own knife from his right hand to his left, then back again. He made a mocking jab at Cort, who jumped back to avoid being cut.

Karl's three friends were moving around to block his escape.

"Yeah, where's your *bone* knife?" teased the boy at his left.

It had been a mistake last year when Cort had mentioned that knife—the only possession his father had left him. The school bullies never forgot. Cort clenched his fists, then forced them to unclench. If only he had a stunner or, even better, one of the starmen's lasers! He'd blast all of them, especially Karl.

By Earth, he just wanted to survive the next five minutes.

He didn't have much of a chance. The older boy was fast and mean, and, unlike Cort, he had a knife. But the odds were better against Karl alone than against Karl and his three friends. "So why does it take four of you to blast one person half your size?" he taunted back. "You afraid of me, Karl?" He tried to keep an eye on the three boys to his sides and rear. "You afraid I can beat you one-on-one?"

Karl snorted a contemptuous laugh. "I can take you, Savage," he sneered, his eyes narrowing. "I can blast you to Earth without a ship."

"Then get your friends off my tail."

Karl signaled with a jerk of his head, and the three other boys moved to the side of the dead-end alley where they had trapped Cort. Karl slashed at Cort, hard and vicious, not mocking this time.

Cort scraped against the wall as he ducked. "I'm going to cut you into little pieces and jettison them like garbage out the hatch. No one going to find the body." Again he jabbed forward.

Cort grabbed his arm and pulled. Off balance from the extended thrust, Karl fell to his knees. In an instant Cort was on the older boy's back, fighting for possession of the knife.

But Karl was bigger and stronger. He rolled over so that Cort was locked underneath him. Still, Cort refused to let go of his knife-wrist. Karl twisted so that he faced down toward Cort, now pinned to the street under the bigger boy's bulk. And he began driving the knife toward Cort's chest.

With every fiber of his strength, Cort fought to keep the knife away, but centimeter by centimeter Karl pushed the knife downward.

Cort's arms burned with the effort. When they started trembling, Karl's sneer turned to a grin.

Cort could hold Karl away no longer. Just before his arms gave way, he squirmed hard to his right. The knife meant for his heart plunged into his left arm. The cut seared like fire.

Cort forced himself to pull away, ripping muscle and skin.

Someone yelled, "Karl! Soldiers!"

In an instant, Karl jumped up, and he and his friends were gone.

Cort sat, pressing his right hand over the wound. Blood ran through his fingers and down his arm.

A squad of six soldiers ran down the deserted street toward him. Not aliens, of course. The starmen seldom visited the city, not even the few alien soldiers. Judging by the uniforms, these were in a private army, working for some rich kingpin who could afford to hire his own protection. Maybe even

Sleb's, the kingpin who owned the block Cort lived in. It was a job requiring little education, and Cort and his schoolmates usually scorned it—but right now he was thrilled to see them. Behind the soldiers were two boys—Cort's friends.

Breathing a sigh of relief, Cort tried to stand. He felt faint and stumbled.

"Bad wound you got, boy," said the first soldier to reach him. The soldier supported Cort as he stood.

"Babies playing with knives!" another soldier said. "It makes me want to puke."

"Easy, Osk," said the first, "we all played with knives when we were little. You aim to fly a ship, you need a practice run or three."

"Osk was probably one of the worst," added a third soldier.

Lor said, "He was trying to save a little kid."

"Were you, now?" the third soldier asked Cort, studying him as intently as if his face might reveal how to save, not just a little boy, but all the khena trees of Aran.

Cort drew a breath and straightened up. If the soldier laughed at him, he would have no regrets. He'd do it again if he had to. By Earth, he'd save all the khena trees of Aran, too, if it came to that.

But the soldier just nodded, then fumbled at his pouch and withdrew something. To Cort, he said, "Hold still, boy. This is a starman bandage. It'll stop the bleeding and prevent infection, too." He started to wrap the bandage around Cort's bleeding arm.

"What're you doing, Garn?" Osk said. "Sleb'll blast you to Earth if he finds out you wasted one of his expensive bandages on this street rat."

"Weren't you ever a child once, Osk? The boy did a good deed, so we'll do one for him, too. Sleb isn't going to find out, now, is he?"

Osk was silent.

Garn finished wrapping the bandage, then patted Cort on the shoulder. "Get out of here, boy, before those thugs come back."

"Thanks," Cort breathed. "You saved my life. I won't forget."

The soldier laughed and said, "Save someone else's life sometime."

"Hey, think big," Osk muttered. "Save the whole buggin' planet." He turned to leave, and the other soldiers followed.

Cort made a vow to himself that he wouldn't forget. He wouldn't forget the kind soldier, and he'd save other lives, too, if he ever had the chance. More immediately, he wouldn't forget Karl, either. He intended to repay both.

The house was small, only one room, with one door, one window, one worktable, and one shelf for storing cooking utensils, but Dilia was grateful to have any kind of home at all. In the lawless nighttime people died out on the street, or went missing, which amounted to the same thing.

She was kneading dough for the bread that would be their dinner when she heard the door open. Preparing dinner was her responsibility, since Cort went to school, and his mother Mara had to work. Dilia turned to see Cort silhouetted against the glare of daylight. He was thirteen, the same age as her, but taller. Someday soon, if he kept growing, his head might almost reach the top of the doorway. She put a hand up to shield her eyes while he, uncharacteristically awkward, took off his pack and closed the door.

Dilia caught sight of a fresh white bandage on Cort's arm, and her heart leapt in fear. Had he been in a fight? How badly was he wounded? Might he... Dilia had trouble even thinking this...die? An injury could easily mean death in the city, where infections were not unusual, and the medications the aliens used were hard for the city people to come by, even on the black market.

She covered the dough with a damp cloth and came over to look at his arm more closely. The bandage was shiny and unusually white. "Is that an alien bandage?"

He nodded and looked at his arm, as if he too was still marveling over the exotic dressing. And maybe he was.

Dilia felt a wave of relief. With one of the aliens' bandages, whatever wound was underneath it would heal quickly, and it wouldn't get infected.

She turned his arm one way and another, examining the shining white bandage as if she might by sheer intensity see the cut underneath. "Is it bad? Does it hurt?" she asked in a shaky voice. Dilia loved Cort as something like a brother and a best friend, rolled into one. His death would be devastating, as bad as losing her father, as bad as then losing her mother. Cort was a bright flashing danger sign that said, "Don't dare love him too much. You could lose him, too."

Cort shrugged. "No, it's nothing. I'm fine—really." But he winced when she turned his arm a certain way, and Dilia now understood that he'd been awkward with the door because he was favoring that arm.

"What happened?" she asked. "Are you in a gang?"

"No," Cort said, looking away.

Maybe he wasn't, yet. But in another year or so, he and his school friends would all be in gangs, making trouble and getting hurt. There must be a hundred gangs ranging from school children to adults, city-born to newcomers newly arrived from the forest. Everyone was out to get what he could, however he could. Anyone not out making trouble was bound, sooner or later, to be a victim. Someday, Cort would be seriously hurt. And there was nothing she could do to prevent it.

Dilia had to stop thinking about this. She took Cort's school tablet out of his pack and sat against the wall with it, using her bedroll as a cushion. "We're really getting your money's worth out of your tuition—two for the price of one."

Cort flopped down to sit next to her, rearranging the bedroll so that it would pillow both of them. He smiled at her. "I learn more, too, when we go over it together."

Instead of attending school, Dilia worked in a shop near the gate to the base. Her meager earnings barely paid for her food; anything left over was added to Cort's mother's earnings and to whatever Cort managed to steal so that they could pay the tuition to keep sending Cort to school. But Dilia had no complaints. She was grateful to Mara for taking her in, and she loved being part of this family. Besides, she was learning so much just by sharing Cort's homework.

Turning to today's Mechanics lesson, she hunched over the tablet as if it contained all the riches they owned, her long auburn braid falling over her shoulder. But the lesson might have been written in a code for which she had no key. She couldn't concentrate. All she could think was that Cort was going to get himself killed.

"And then, when I get out of school, I'll be able to support you and Mama by myself," Cort said. "I'll make sure you have everything you ever wanted."

Dilia patted his hand affectionately and gave him a wan smile. "Not if you keep getting hurt in fights."

"I don't plan to," Cort said, a defensive tone edging into his voice. He turned back to the lesson on the tablet.

Maybe he was already in a gang. Dilia shivered. "Oh! And you think this will be under your control, do you? So tell me how you got that wound."

He looked away. "They were bigger boys. Bullies, picking on a little kid. Couldn't have been more than ten or eleven. I gave the kid time to get away, that's all."

Dilia stood up. She could just picture some gang of sixteen-year-olds turning on Cort when the child ran away. Their long knives would already be out, flashing in the sun. Adults' knives. Sharp. How many of them would there be? Four? Five? She walked the five steps to the far wall where the door was, then back, upset all over again. She tried to shake off the image, but she couldn't. She pictured Cort facing the bigger boys alone, without a knife. "Maybe it's time for you to start using your father's knife," she said.

Cort drew in a breath. He had coveted that bone knife ever since Dilia could remember. Maybe he would take it this time. It was the only thing besides his name—Cort-anaran, a savage name—that Cort's father had left him, his father who had come, already a grown man, out of the primeval forest into the city, fathered Cort, and then disappeared.

Cort stood and gave the tablet back to Dilia. He reached up and touched the high shelf where they kept the knife. Then he paused and lowered his hand. "I'd like to, but I'm not ready for it. I'm not going to take that knife until I know I can win with it."

"And how are you going to know that?" Dilia asked, suddenly angry. "By fighting some more? You'll get yourself killed!"

"I'm not that stupid!" Cort returned anger for anger. "I'm going to find a way to learn, that's all." Then he softened, smiling at her. "Don't worry. I wouldn't want anything to happen before I'm ready to take his knife, now, would I?" He touched her cheek, and she couldn't help but return the smile.

"You're lucky you have that knife," she said. "I wish I had something of my father's to remember him by."

"Come on, Dilia; don't be jealous. You actually remember your father. That's more than I do." Cort's mother said that his father had gone to Earth, but Dilia thought it was improbable that a barbarian from the forest would go to the starmen's home planet. Going to Earth was simply the slang phrase people used to say someone had died. Died, like Dilia's own parents.

"Yes," she said, "I remember my father, but so faintly and long ago, almost like a fairy tale, kind of shining in sunlight and unreal. I remember him smiling at me, and then putting his arm around my mother."

Dilia sighed, a feeling of sadness stealing over her. Her parents used to always hug each other, but all of Dilia's memories were of looking up at them touching while she remained on the ground below. It was like, in some deep way, she was defective. Unlovable. Not like them.

Regardless of whether anyone would ever love her, at least she had one true friend, Cort. And now he seemed to be heading toward an early death. She wanted to scream at him. *Take the damned knife! Protect yourself!* But it would do no good. She gave up on studying and turned back to the bread she'd been working on for dinner.

Read more of *Saving Aran* at
https://www.amazon.com/dp/B0B46X6RJ7/

Acknowledgments

J ohn Donne famously said that no man is an island. This is certainly true of writers. I would like to acknowledge the other people who contributed to this book.

My husband Daniel Kenney, above all others in my life, has supported my writing career even when, sometimes, it meant sacrificing his own time with me. Sweetie, I hope this book, and my others, make it feel worthwhile.

My children Adam and Margot, now grown, were my first beta readers way back when. They encouraged me to publish my stories long before I felt ready, and they encourage me still.

James Frenkel, my agent and meticulous editor, has also become a good friend. I greatly appreciate how he's always gone "above and beyond." He's a great editor and even better sounding board.

Thanks, too, to Deranged Doctor Design, who created this wonderful cover, and to Laurie Cooper of Pub-Craft, my marketing guru and mentor, and now also a friend.

Other writers are crucial to any writer for support and feedback. I'm fortunate to belong to two critique groups. Not only have these conscientious readers helped make my books better, but they've also kept me writing to a schedule when sometimes it was the hardest thing in the world to do. And Jeanne Estridge, my writing partner and friend, helps me remember to show up at the computer, even when I can do no more than staring at the screen.

And you, gentle reader, thank you for opening your heart and mind to these books. I hope to see you again in this journey.

With warmth and gratitude,
G. S. Kenney